ONE
MISTAKE

RONA HALSALL

ONE MISTAKE

bookouture

Published by Bookouture in 2020

An imprint of Storyfire Ltd.
Carmelite House
50 Victoria Embankment
London EC4Y 0DZ

www.bookouture.com

ISBN: 978-1-83888-6202
eBook ISBN: 978-1-83888-619-6

This one is for my writing buddies, Freddie and Molly, who take me out for walks and keep me company.

PROLOGUE

Her head felt thick, stuffed to overflowing with all the worries that kept her awake. She couldn't tell Matt, couldn't tell anyone.

It was the only thing I could have done, she told herself. And was it really *that* wrong?

The answer to that was yes. However she might dress up the situation to try and disguise her actions, the answer was always going to be the same.

She'd thought she was solving a problem, but she had in fact created a monster. One that followed her round every minute of the day, scaring her, making her break out in a cold sweat and keeping her awake at night.

Nobody knows, she reminded herself as she wrapped her arms around her chest, hugging herself tight. There's still time. Time to put it right.

ONE

The day started like any other. Ezra crept into their bed at his usual 5.30 in the morning, his little hands sneaking round Sara's neck, his head nuzzled into her shoulder as he mumbled a sleepy 'Are you awake, Mummy?'

She pretended she wasn't, hoping he might settle and drift off to sleep for another couple of hours.

He gave her a sloppy kiss on the cheek. 'I love you, Mummy,' he said in a stage whisper. She opened her eyes and looked into his four-year-old face, his skin lit by the chink of light that slid across the room from the open doorway into the hall.

'Love you too, little smudge.' She kissed him on the nose and cuddled him to her for a moment before whispering, 'Come on, let's go downstairs, shall we?'

She knew from experience if she didn't move now, Ezra's voice would grow louder, the questions would start, and Matt would get cranky about being woken up so early. Matt was a night owl, rarely coming to bed before midnight, whereas Ezra was an early bird, and the two things added a new dimension to Sara's marriage as she tried to juggle both of their needs.

At least Sophia and Amelia – or Milly, as she preferred to be called – were old enough at fourteen to look after themselves in the mornings and help a bit around the house. As identical twins, they reflected a mirror image of each other, inheriting their father's angular face, light brown hair and wide-set grey eyes. They'd always been a tight unit, two halves of a whole, making Sara feel a bit redundant as a mother at times because they relied on each other so much. Ezra, though, took after her in looks, with his wavy black hair and almond-shaped brown eyes.

Unlike his sisters, Ezra was a cuddly child, a sensitive little soul, who loved spending time with her. He'd been a surprise baby, born when the girls were ten and they'd had no plans to expand their family. Not a mistake, more of a bonus, a joyful addition to the clan. It had meant putting her own plans on hold for a while longer, but Matt had been ecstatic to finally have a son. 'A boy to play football with, do all the rough-and-tumble stuff,' he'd said. Which was ironic, given that the girls were both mad keen on football and played in the local team while Ezra, so far, seemed to hate anything physical. He liked to think and question and do crafty things and bake cakes and draw. Not exactly the son Matt had hoped for, whereas he possessed many of the qualities Sara had expected but not found in her daughters.

She got out of bed and clasped Ezra's hand in hers, putting her finger to her lips to make sure their exit was as quiet as possible. Funny how life turns out, she thought, a warm glow spreading through her at the thought of her family and their little peculiarities.

They padded down the stairs and into the lounge, where Sara flicked on the lights and Ezra ran to the art box and opened the lid. 'I'm going to draw you an elephant,' he declared, while she stretched and yawned and wandered through the dining area into the open-plan kitchen.

The new layout downstairs was still a source of joy to her, inspired by a TV makeover series, and although it had cost an alarming amount of money and meant they'd had to extend their mortgage, it had made life so much easier. Three rooms had become one big L shape, where she could cook and keep an eye on Ezra and help the girls with their homework all at the same time. They'd even gone for bifold doors opening into the back garden, a luxury that Matt had persuaded her would add value to their Victorian end-of-terrace property should they ever decide to sell. After years of struggling with ill-fitting cupboard doors and drawers that kept coming off their sliders, even the simple act of watching the cutlery drawer close on its own made her smile. Simple pleasures, she thought, grinning to herself as she opened the new dishwasher to retrieve her favourite mug.

Matt had bought her a coffee machine for her birthday, which had become her prized possession and something of a lifesaver with these early starts and the lack of sleep. She put in a pod, topped up the water and switched it on, breathing in the scent of freshly brewed coffee as it spluttered and gurgled into her mug. She was hoping Ezra would sleep a little later once he started school in September, but that was still months away, and in the meantime, she wondered if she should go and ask the doctor for something to help with her insomnia. Then she remembered her sister Hailey's experience with sleeping pills, how she'd become addicted and struggled to get herself right again, and decided that the new yoga class at the community centre might be a better alternative.

'Mummy, look!' Ezra called as he came running up to her with a piece of paper flapping in his hand. She took the drawing and gazed at the grey squiggles.

'That's lovely,' she said, unable to remember what he'd said he was going to draw. It could be any number of things and he got offended if she didn't know what his pictures were supposed to be. 'Let's put it on the fridge with the others, shall we?'

He jumped up and down, clapping his hands, excited to see his artistic efforts displayed.

'Are you ready for breakfast?' Sara asked, pulling a carton from the fridge and pouring milk into his Thomas the Tank Engine mug, the only one he'd drink from. He guzzled it down, licking the white moustache from his upper lip.

'Not yet. I've got more drawing to do.' And off he went, back to the art box. She watched him for a moment as he carefully chose the right colours for his next picture.

She picked up her coffee mug and cradled it to her chest, a to-do list for the day writing itself in her mind. So many things to remember with three kids, a husband and a house to manage. Especially now she'd started working part-time as well, something she'd been desperate to do, if only for a bit of adult interaction. But meeting everyone's needs, including her own, was like herding cats, and she inevitably forgot things. She sipped her coffee, relishing the taste, the warmth of it in her throat. The best cup of the day.

She watched Ezra, his tongue poking out as he worked away, and knew she wouldn't change a thing; even if it was a bit chaotic and hard work, it was worth every minute. Matt and the kids were the centre of her world, and keeping them all happy was her job, her reason for being. After the shambles of her own upbringing, it was the focus of every decision she made, and she was determined that her children would have the stability she'd craved when she was growing up.

I'm never going to turn into my mother, she promised herself. However hard things get, we'll make it work.

Her childhood memories were something she refused to visit voluntarily. Instead they wormed their way into her brain at night, waking her in the form of nightmares, chilling her heart. She and her sister had a tacit agreement to never discuss it. It was the past; they'd got through it and it was best forgotten. That was the theory. But how did you forget being taken into care from the age of six?

The first time, it was eight months before she was allowed to go back and live with her mum again and was reunited with Hailey. After that, it was a cycle that was repeated with a dreadful regularity until she was eighteen and was spat out of the care system.

Life changed when she went to university, funded from a bursary for underprivileged children. A label she'd felt was tattooed on her forehead, making her a silent teenager, a wisp of a girl who slid in and out of rooms unnoticed, just keeping herself to herself and studying with a grim determination to make a better life.

She shuddered, shaking the thoughts from her mind, letting them fall away as she gazed around the beautiful room they had created, the wonderful home she and Matt had worked hard to afford. She had everything she'd ever wished for and never expected to achieve. Don't ever take it for granted, she cautioned herself, aware that her tiredness had made her snappy recently. Her gaze settled on the studio portrait that hung on the dining-room wall. *My family.* Her heart swelled with love as her eyes moved from face to face. They were all that mattered, and she knew she'd do anything, anything at all, to keep them happy.

TWO

Three weeks later

'I'll be late tonight,' Matt said, as he grabbed his bag and took his car keys from the hook next to the back door. He was a snappy dresser when it came to work, one of those men who actually looked good in a suit, his brown hair kept short at the sides, combed back on top, his face clean-shaven, bucking the facial-hair trend.

'What? Again?' Sara couldn't hide her desperation. 'I'm supposed to be going to see that tribute band tonight with Hailey.'

Matt stopped and turned. 'Christ, is that tonight?' He looked surprised, even though she'd been talking about it only the night before, reading out the rave reviews, her excitement mounting.

'Yes.' She closed the door of the dishwasher more forcefully than usual and dried her hands on a tea towel. 'It is tonight. I've been looking forward to it for weeks. You know I have.'

It wasn't often she went out, and managing to coordinate a date with her sister, free from the distraction of children, had become as rare as hen's teeth. Hailey worked for a charity that supported young people in crisis; they were short-staffed and her work hours were variable, as she had to be on call. Recently, every time they'd tried to go out for an evening together, just the two of them, an emergency had flared up and Hailey had cancelled. But this time, she'd promised Sara she'd move heaven and earth to make sure they got to the gig. Now it was Sara who would have to cancel.

Matt pulled an apologetic face. 'It's work, I'm afraid. I told you we lost that big contract and it's all hands on deck to try and pull more work in.' He glanced towards the door, keys jingling in his hand. 'I know I'm working stupid hours, but I've got no choice.'

'Oh Matt, we've had this organised for months.' Her words clogged in her throat and she looked at the floor while she tried to wrestle a surge of emotion under control. 'You know that. And I told you—'

The door slammed shut.

She looked up and hurled the balled-up tea towel at the space where her husband had been standing, snarling with frustration. Yet again, her plans had to make way for his. For the last few months he'd been working late most weekdays, except for Thursdays, when he went to football training with the girls after work, an activity he magically managed to make time for. Then there was the obligatory Saturday out with the lads, going to the match and then on somewhere after. No question. No interruptions to *his* plans.

She took a deep breath, reminded herself they relied on his income to pay the bills and it wasn't his fault if he had to work long hours. But still… She'd been really looking forward to a few hours of proper relaxation, a time to kick back, be herself and forget for just a little while that she was a mother and a wife, not to mention administrator at the busy community centre.

With an exasperated sigh, she slipped her phone out of her back pocket and dialled her sister to tell her there'd been a change of plan, leaning on the worktop while it rang.

'Hiya!' Hailey sounded cheery and upbeat this morning, which made Sara cringe. She hated cancelling plans. 'How's things?'

'Oh… you know.' It wasn't possible to explain in a sentence how things really were. That would take a few hours and probably a bottle of wine for Dutch courage if she was going to be completely honest. 'Fine, everything's fine.' From the despondent tone of her voice, this was obviously a long way from the truth.

'Well, you don't sound fine. You sound like someone's stolen your secret chocolate stash.' Hailey laughed. Sara burst into tears. 'Hey, what's wrong?' Hailey said, suddenly concerned.

Sara sniffed, unable to speak for a moment, and when she finally found her voice, it sounded thin and weedy, not like her at all. 'I'm going to have to cancel tonight.'

'Oh no! I've been looking forward to seeing Fake That for ages!'

'Matt's got to work late.'

Hailey cursed under her breath, then said, 'It's your day off, isn't it? Are you at home? I'm in town, not far away, and I'm kicking my heels for half an hour or so, waiting for social services to get their shit together. Shall I come round?' Sara tried to swallow the lump in her throat, but couldn't seem to manage it, her silence enough of an answer for her sister. 'I'll be there in ten,' Hailey said, before she rang off.

Sara put her phone back in her pocket, grabbed a piece of kitchen roll and wiped her wet cheeks, slightly panicked. *What have I done?* She generally kept her problems to herself, reluctant to open up to Hailey, who could be like a Rottweiler when it came to protecting her from upset. She didn't want her sister having a go at Matt. *It's not his fault there are problems at work.* The poor man was slogging away day after day to keep them comfortable, and Sara's minimum-wage job was little real help where their finances were concerned. In fact, once you took out childcare costs, there wasn't much left.

It's not about money, though, is it? She gave herself a mental shake, pushing her negative thoughts to the back of her mind where they belonged. She sniffed and took a couple of deep breaths to chase away the tears. It's just tiredness, she told herself. Stop feeling sorry for yourself, you silly woman.

She scanned the room, her heart giving a little skip when she registered the mess, the detritus of family life littering every flat surface. She leapt into action, scurrying round shoving things out of sight as best she could. No time to do anything about the dust, or the dirty windows, or the crumbs on the floor, she decided as she bundled an armful of children's clothes behind the sofa.

As much as she loved her sister, they weren't in and out of each other's houses, and in Sara's eyes this was a bit of a godsend. Hailey was a complete neat freak, thanks to the training she'd received from one of her foster parents. She'd become worse now that her daughter, Cassie, had gone off to uni and she was on her own. She liked everything lined up just so, every surface clean, floors spotless, windows gleaming, making Sara feel completely hopeless in the home-making department.

Hailey lived in Skipton, ten miles or so from Sara's home town of Ilkley, and her work took her all over the local area. The fact that she happened to be nearby at the very time Sara called was a coincidence; the last thing she'd expected was for her sister to turn up for coffee and a chat. 'I'm fine. Everything's fine,' she muttered under her breath as she finished her flurry of tidying. Hailey had her own struggles and didn't need Sara whining about problems that would seem pathetic in comparison. Not to mention all those youngsters she worked with and their mountains of troubles. No, she didn't need anything more to worry about.

Sara dashed upstairs and changed out of her joggers and the T-shirt that had Ezra's milk splattered down the front. Thank goodness he was at nursery in the mornings now and the intense parenting of those first few years was behind her. She found a pair of jeans and a clean top that didn't cling to the stubborn roll round her stomach, which had arrived during pregnancy and refused to go away. She ran a brush through her shoulder-length black hair, smeared a bit of foundation on her blotchy face, patted a bit of powder over the top and immediately felt better.

She studied herself in the mirror. Turned this way and that. Yes, she was a bit heavier than when she'd met Matt, but she'd only been twenty then, and after three children, it wasn't surprising that her stomach muscles weren't what they used to be – especially after bearing twins. Her hair still shone, her complexion was good, and although her eyes were a bit pink round the edges from her earlier tears, she knew that would quickly fade. 'Not bad for thirty-eight,' she reassured her reflection with a satisfied nod.

The ringing of the doorbell sent her running downstairs to find Hailey on the doorstep, looking anxious, frown lines creasing her forehead.

'Come in.' Sara stepped to one side to let her sister pass. 'You didn't have to dash over. I know you're working, and I was just having a moment, you know…'

'Get the coffee on,' Hailey said as she headed for the kitchen. 'And stop trying to cover things up.' She dumped her bag on the floor and pulled out a chair at the table, looked at her watch. 'I've got a meeting in… about half an hour.'

Sara busied herself getting mugs from the cupboard, milk from the fridge. 'I'm not covering things up,' she said with a little laugh, as if the idea was ridiculous.

Hailey snorted, then her expression softened. She brushed a hand over her short, spiky hair, which was naturally ginger but currently dyed magenta – a striking contrast with her pale complexion. 'Come on, get your fancy machine going and tell me what's up.' She tilted her head, slate-grey eyes assessing her little sister. 'I can tell when something's bothering you.'

Sara leant a hip against the worktop while the coffee machine gurgled and hissed its way through its cycle, wondering what to say, whether Hailey would think she was being stupid. She turned and gave her a sheepish smile. 'I think you're here under false pretences. Just me being tired, you know, with all these early starts, and now that I'm working…'

Hailey's job took her to the heart of troubled families and she was a keen observer of human behaviour. She could tell when people were lying, but would never judge. Not when she'd had such a difficult childhood herself. She knew things went wrong, that people made mistakes then had to live with them. She knew that just because a child might be neglected it didn't mean they weren't loved. She of all people understood complexity and was absolutely the best person to talk to about problems. But Sara felt awkward laying her marriage bare for somebody else to inspect, even if that somebody was her sister.

She took the first full mug from the machine and set it going to make a second one. How much should I tell her? she wondered, then caught her sister's eye as she placed her coffee on the table and made a decision.

'He's never home, Hailey. Always working late.' She hesitated, eyes firmly on the floor. 'It's not just that, though. When he is home, he's always on his computer. Very secretive, like he's chatting to someone, you know?' She swallowed, a swell of emotion taking her by surprise, and when she spoke again, her voice was little more than a whisper. 'He doesn't see me any more. It's like I'm invisible. The housekeeper, here to look after him and the kids. I don't feel like we're a partnership. That closeness we had – it's gone.'

Hailey stared at her, mouth gaping in astonishment. 'Are you kidding? That man thinks the sun shines out of your arse.'

Sara huffed and went to get the second mug of coffee from the machine. 'No, he doesn't.'

'In all the years I've known him, and that would be… what?' She scrunched up her nose while she did the calculation. 'Eighteen years now? I've never heard him say a bad word about you. Not one. How many wives can say that?'

Sara came and sat at the table, her mug cradled in her hands, determined now to lay out all the facts.

'You only think that because he hasn't said anything in front of you.' Her mouth twisted from side to side. 'We have our moments. Disagreements, just like any other couple.' Hailey raised an eyebrow, clearly unconvinced. Sara continued. 'He's been really snappy and short with me recently, like there's something on his mind. A secret.' She leant forward. 'There's something he's not telling me. I know it. And it's making me wonder…'

Hailey frowned. 'Wonder what?'

'Well…' Sara bit her lip, hardly daring to speak her thoughts out loud because that would make them real. 'Do you think he might be having an affair?'

Hailey sat back in her chair, mouth opening to speak before she closed it again. She picked up her mug and sipped at her coffee while she thought. 'How long's he been like this?'

'I'd say it must be three months now.'

'And have you spoken to him about it?'

Sara gave an exasperated sigh. 'It's never the right time. I just seem to annoy him, and I don't want an argument. Don't want the kids getting upset. Poor Ezra hates raised voices, you know that. Gets himself all worked up.'

Hailey frowned. 'So who do you think he's having an affair with? Have you any clues? Or is this just a wild guess to rationalise his behaviour?'

Sara shrugged. 'I don't know. But I can't get the idea out of my head. It seems the only explanation.'

Hailey put her mug down and leant forward. 'Is it, though?' She raised an eyebrow.

Sara scowled. 'What's your theory then?'

'Maybe he's telling you the truth. Maybe he *is* just working late. I mean, he's a bit alpha male, isn't he? Thinks his job is to bring home the money and yours is to look after the house and the kids. Perhaps his boss is putting pressure on him and he can't say no.'

Sara considered this for a moment. Hailey was right about Matt's black-and-white view of marriage, instilled in him by an armed-forces upbringing, his father coming from a family with a long tradition of men who'd gone off to fight in wars and women who'd stayed at home.

'Look what a fuss he made a few weeks ago when you started work and Ezra went to nursery. He didn't like that, did he?'

Sara pursed her lips. Her sister was right; it had been quite a tussle of wills. Done in the most civilised of ways, of course. Not all-out war, but sniper fire over the cornflakes. No obvious upset of any kind, apart from the clenching of her teeth as his barbed comments found their mark, wounding her. Eventually she'd compromised and set her sights much lower than she would have liked. Instead of looking for a job that would use her business studies degree, she'd decided to seriously consider the offer of part-time work at the community centre.

She remembered the night well, having shipped the kids off to Hailey and made a special dinner for her and Matt so they could have a proper chat without the children listening in.

She'd said her piece, the one she'd rehearsed a dozen times that day, and he'd sat very still, gazing at her across the table as she laid it all out, making the point that she'd put her career on hold, spent fourteen years at home, and now felt a bit claustrophobic. Also, she'd argued, it would be good for Ezra to start at nursery part-time because he needed to get used to being away from her before he started school in September.

Matt had reached for her hand across the table. 'I suppose it makes sense, and I want you to be happy, love. So if you need to work...' He smiled. 'A local part-time job seems the best idea. As long as it doesn't get in the way of looking after the kids, and it doesn't make you too stressed, well, I'm fine with it.'

Hailey's voice broke into her thoughts. 'For what it's worth, I really haven't got Matt down as a cheater. I mean, the way he was brought up, it's just not something he'd even think about, is it?'

Sara chewed her lip as she considered her sister's words. Although Matt had a strong bond with his parents, she didn't know them very well. Their home was in Cyprus now, a place where they'd lived for a time during his father's armed service. Both of them suffered from arthritis, and the climate was a blessing for their health, but it meant she and Matt didn't see much of them, and most of their interactions were by Skype rather than face to face.

'Hmm. You're right that his parents really drummed it into him that marriage was for life. In fact, when he proposed, he said he'd always be true to me, and told me that I shouldn't accept unless I would totally commit to our relationship.' Sara picked up the teaspoon and stabbed it into the sugar bowl, at a loss to know why things had suddenly changed between them. 'But right now, it's not working. Even when he's here, it's like his mind's somewhere else.'

'You can't go jumping to conclusions, though.' Hailey reached out and took the spoon from Sara's hand, moving the sugar bowl out of her reach, much as one might do with a child. 'Communication, Sara. That's where most marriages go wrong. People not talking to each other. If you want to find out what's going on, you'll have to ask him. Just be straight. What harm can it do?'

Sara looked at her sister and gave a rueful laugh. 'What harm? You haven't seen him when…' She stopped herself, sucked in a breath and chose her words carefully. 'You know what I'm like about confrontation. After everything with Mum…' She stopped herself, lips pressed together. 'I'm not like you. I can't let it bounce off me. It stresses me out. So I'm not going to pick a fight until I know the facts.'

Hailey leant across the table and gave her hand a comforting squeeze. 'I know. It's okay, don't get yourself upset.' She smiled. 'If it's facts you need, then let's do a bit of sleuthing. If he's supposed to be working late tonight, I'll drive by his office and see if there's anyone still there. How about that? Now Cassie's off at uni, I've nobody to go home to.' A flash of sadness crossed her face and she looked away, gulped down the rest of her coffee.

Sara knew Hailey was struggling a bit without her daughter around. They were very close, and Cassie's absence had left a big hole in her life. A hole that she filled with work and exercise and obsessive house-cleaning. She was an exemplary mother, and even though her husband had left when Cassie was eight, she'd made sure that her daughter had the sort of upbringing she and Sara would have wished for themselves.

'No, you don't have to do that,' Sara said, appalled at the idea of her sister snooping on her husband. But Hailey was undeterred.

'I'll wait outside his office this evening. I can be there about four to make sure I don't miss him. Then when he leaves, I'll follow him, and if he doesn't come home, at least we'll know where he's going and who he's meeting.' Her eyes met Sara's. 'The only way to sort out problems like this is to confront them, and if you're not ready to ask him… Well, this is the only way to find out the truth, isn't it?'

Sara thought about it for a moment. What harm could it do? Hailey was right: knowing would be better than not knowing. Then her mind could stop racing around looking for solutions to problems that maybe didn't exist.

'Okay, you're on.' She almost managed a smile. 'Thank you, I really do appreciate your support, you know.'

Hailey shrugged off her thanks. 'What are big sisters for, eh?'

'I'm going to see if I can find anything in the house that might give me a clue as to what he's up to. Because I honestly don't think it's work.' She frowned as she tried to put her thoughts into words. 'When he says he's going to be late, he always looks away. Seems a little antsy.' She sighed. 'It's hard to explain, but when you've been with someone for as long as we've been together, you just know that something's not right.'

Hailey checked her watch and pushed back her chair. 'Gotta go. Look, I'll keep in touch and I'll see you later.'

Sara stood and went to the door with her, gave her a quick hug. Will Matt recognise her car? she wondered as she watched her sister drive away. It was a silver hatchback, very common, nothing standout about it, she reassured herself, and Matt wasn't the most observant of people.

She crossed her arms and leant against the door frame, letting her eyes take in the scenery, the view over the jumble of slate roofs and gritstone buildings of the town to the moors above. Their terrace would have housed quarry workers back in the day, and stood proud on the lower slopes of the valley. If she looked to her right, the road was elevated enough to give a panoramic view over Wharfedale. This was her world, where she'd felt safe bringing up a family, but she had a horrible feeling the past was about to repeat itself, rupturing the life she'd crafted, and there wasn't a thing she could do to stop it.

THREE

A comprehensive search of drawers and cupboards uncovered nothing obvious to explain Matt's recent change in behaviour. Sara had been so absorbed in her task that she'd lost track of time and now, she realised with a start, it was time to pick up Ezra from nursery.

Her phone rang as she was walking to the car. It was Fiona, a school mum, whose daughter Chelsea was best friends with the twins.

'I just wanted to check… are your girls supposed to be coming back to mine after school today?' Fiona had a very distinctive voice, the sort that carried and could quieten a room. She sounded flustered, which was unusual, and Sara stopped walking to listen. 'It's just I've gone and double-booked myself. I'm supposed to be at a PTA meeting. The secretary just rang to go through the agenda, and I'd forgotten all about it!'

'Wow, Fiona, you are human after all,' Sara laughed. 'I bet that's a first, isn't it?'

She waited for a reply, but none came, and she hoped her joke hadn't caused offence. They'd known each other since their girls had made friends when they'd started secondary school, but Fiona was also sort of her boss now that Sara worked at the community centre, and it had altered the dynamic between them.

'Well, I've had to change my plans,' she said quickly, to fill the awkward silence. 'Matt's working, so I've had to cancel my night out. I can pick them up now.'

'Oh, thank goodness.' Sara heard a quick intake of breath. 'No, sorry, that sounds wrong. I'm sad you're missing your fun. You've been looking forward to it, haven't you?'

'Yeah, I was.' Sara could hear the disappointment in her own voice and didn't want Fiona feeling sorry for her. It's only a night out, she told herself. There'll be others. 'Anyway, it's not a problem,' she said, making herself sound brighter than she felt. 'Not a problem at all. In fact, why doesn't Chelsea come to ours, then at least the girls get their evening together?'

'That would be perfect.' Fiona sounded delighted. 'You sure you don't mind?'

'Of course not. I owe you a favour anyway, don't I? After giving me a job, it's the least I can do.'

'Honestly, I'd cancel the bloody thing, but I've got to be there, you know, as chairwoman. Wouldn't look good if I didn't turn up.'

'Look, don't worry about it. You go and do your chairwomanly thing. You're doing a brilliant job, by the way. Everything seems to be running much better since you've been on the board. At least we parents know what's going on these days.'

Fiona had moved into the area three years ago, and had already made quite an impact, finding herself positions on the management boards of several organisations, including the school and the community centre where Sara now worked. She'd explained to Sara that she'd made some money when she'd sold her previous business, and wanted to take a bit of time out to give back to the community while she decided what to do next. Not that she needed to work.

She and her family lived in one of the big gritstone villas that would have belonged to the quarry owners in times gone by. The house had been rundown when they'd moved in, and they'd done a complete renovation, adding a huge orangery across the back with the most stunning views over the Wharfedale valley. Sara had only met Fiona's husband Maurice a handful of times, when she'd gone to collect the girls from sleepovers, and he seemed pleasant enough, if a little distant. He was fifteen years older than Fiona and ran a clothing business, with factories in India that he visited on a regular basis. It seemed to suit Fiona that he was away a lot – absence makes the heart grow fonder, she'd commented – and it gave her space to be queen bee in her own world of charities and public sector bodies, which were always on the lookout for board members with business acumen. Sara wouldn't be surprised to see her standing as an MP in the future. Or finding some other influential position. She was definitely a mover and shaker, and Sara had to admit to being slightly in awe of her. At the same time, though, Fiona was easy to get along with, which was probably the secret of her success.

She laughed now, an earthy sound at odds with her perfect diction. 'Oh, stop it. I don't think it's all me. There are a few new faces and we do seem to be pulling in the same direction, unlike the last set of board members. Anyway...' She strung out the word, clearly looking for a way to end the conversation. 'I'll see you later. Is nine okay for me to pick up Chelsea?'

'Yeah, that's fine. Hope you have a good meeting.' Sara ended the call, pushing the phone into her pocket before running down the path to her car. She was cutting it fine now, and Ezra got upset if she was late.

She made it just in time. Ezra was already in his coat, standing by the door, his backpack in his hand. It would be fair to say that he'd learnt to tolerate nursery, but he definitely didn't love it, and as for making friends, he hadn't managed to develop strong connections with any of the other children as yet. He didn't seem to be interested, happier in his own little world, surrounded by his familiar things, with Sara in the background if he wanted company. Self-contained, that was how the nursery teacher had described him, and Sara didn't know if that was a good or a bad thing. If she tried to organise play dates, he resisted, so she'd given up, hoping he'd get the hang of social interaction when he started school.

It was a lovely sunny day, quite warm for the end of April, and Sara had made them a picnic to take up onto the moors, which stretched for miles above the town. She felt the need for fresh air and exercise and knew that Ezra would sleep better for a good stomp around the boulders, where he liked to play hide-and-seek and look for little creatures. She'd sleep better too, she hoped, the planned outing as much for her benefit as his.

'We're nearly there, aren't we, Mummy?' Ezra said as they drove out of town and up the hill towards the moors. He wasn't a good traveller, but as long as he knew where they were going, and looked out of the window, he seemed able to cope.

'A few more minutes,' Sara said as the hill steepened and the valley was laid out in her rear-view mirror. She felt her heart quicken as she turned a corner and the land fell away to her left, while the boulder-strewn moors rose up to her right, wild and rugged and inviting.

Although some people found the vast open space unnerving, the moors were one of her favourite places. She remembered coming up here as a child on the bus with her mum and Hailey. She'd been quite a tomboy when she was young, and had loved to run and explore and climb on the boulders. She'd enjoyed picking bilberries when they were in season, little explosions of flavour straight from the bush. Just thinking about them now, she could taste the sourness on her tongue.

The smell of peat and heather created an earthy mix that awakened so many happy memories, not just of her own early childhood, but also of coming up here with Matt when the children were little. The moors were a part of her, their wildness an expression of how she felt inside, even if her life was a bit more contained these days.

It made her heart sing that Ezra enjoyed being up here as much as she did. Unfortunately, the girls were no longer so enthusiastic. At fourteen, they would be starting their GCSE courses in September and had morphed from girls to young women in the space of a couple of months. These days they didn't want to scramble over the boulders, or pick bilberries to make into a pie, or have a picnic. Instead, their time was spent deliberating about hair and eyebrows, nails and spots and clothes. So much stress! Sara thought it had been much easier when she'd been young, with no social media or filtered photos setting impossible standards and instilling a fear of not being quite good enough.

At least the girls had each other; but did they spend too much time together behind their closed bedroom door? Recently it seemed they only came out of there to eat and go out with friends or to football practice with Matt, and she hardly had a proper conversation with them. It saddened her that their relationship was becoming more distant than she would like.

'Mummy! Mummy, what are you staring at?'

Startled by Ezra's voice, Sara realised she'd arrived at the car park on autopilot, lost in her thoughts, and now she was sitting staring out of the windscreen, not even registering the landscape in front of her.

'Nothing, little smudge.' She turned and grinned at him as he wriggled in his seat, desperate to be freed.

She got out and unfastened his seat belt, waiting for him to clamber out of the car before leaning over to grab the rucksack containing their lunch. He reached for her hand. 'Let's say hello to the cow and then the calf, shall we, Mummy?'

Sara laughed. The Cow and Calf was a rock formation at the top of the hill and a favourite picnic spot with the most wonderful views. The rocks also gave shelter from the wind, whatever direction it might be coming from.

'Okay. Let's go.' She swung her arms, doing an exaggerated walk, and they laughed their way up the path, making up silly marching songs as they went.

Once they'd found a good spot for their lunch, and Ezra had made sure their blanket was in exactly the right place, he went insect-hunting with his magnifying glass, while Sara gazed across the valley, thinking about Matt and how their relationship had cooled over recent years. Ever since Ezra was born, if she was honest. That was when the problems had started.

It had been hard having a baby again, when the twins were ten and wanting to be active. Especially when Ezra had been the sort of baby who didn't sleep more than a couple of hours at a time. The result had been Matt taking the girls under his wing while Sara looked after Ezra. That was the point when the family had fractured into two units, and they hadn't yet managed to bring everyone back together again.

She wondered if it was too late now. If they could ever be the cohesive family she'd dreamed of, that she'd yearned for when she was a child. *Not if Matt's having an affair.* The thought made her shiver. Hailey was right, she reminded herself. Cheating was not part of his make-up. He was as committed to his family as Sara.

People change. Look at Mum. She'd gone from being a doting mother to a reckless idiot after their father had died. He'd obviously been the stabilising influence in the partnership, and without him, her mum had gone completely haywire, in a way Sara couldn't begin to comprehend. She was too young to remember a lot about it, only six years old when disaster had struck, an accident at work that meant her dad never came home again. Hailey, four years older, had a clearer view of it all.

She shook the thoughts from her mind, telling herself it did no good to dwell on the past. Her mum had gone, and all the trouble with her. But the scars remained, both physical and mental.

Nothing intentional, but inflicted by neglect, by a woman who'd stopped caring about anything for long periods of time.

Sara shivered in the sudden breeze. Had Matt stopped caring too? She watched Ezra following a butterfly as it fluttered among the bilberry bushes, trying to remember when her husband had last focused all his attention on her and her alone. Nothing came to mind.

I'm losing him.

She swallowed, the very thought making her eyes sting. Don't be so stupid, she told herself firmly. Hailey's right. Matt wouldn't cheat on me. He isn't like that. Or at least he hadn't been. But something in him had changed, and now her assurances lacked conviction.

She jumped up and went to join Ezra, marvelling with him at the patterns on the wings of the butterfly, wanting to fill her mind with anything but her niggling suspicions. Matt wouldn't do anything to destroy the innocent life of his little boy. Or those of his beloved girls. *He wouldn't.*

FOUR

'Pizza for tea,' Sara called up the stairs at the girls' disappearing backs. 'About an hour, okay?' She watched the three of them hurtle round the corner and out of sight. Heard the bedroom door slam, excited chatter on the other side. What happened to teenagers? It was the weirdest thing. One minute they were all cuddly children wanting attention, the next it was like you had just stepped out of the grave and they couldn't get away from you fast enough.

'Mummy, come and watch with me,' Ezra called from the lounge, where she could hear the familiar theme tune of a particularly annoying children's programme. 'It's your favourite.' She cringed. If she never heard that song again, she would count it as a major blessing.

'Five minutes. I'm just going to make a cup of tea.' She popped her head round the door, smiling when she saw her son already snuggled up with his cuddly Pikachu toy, which was his constant companion at home. 'Do you want a drink?' She could see his eyelids already at half-mast and knew it was going to be a struggle to keep him awake until bedtime. 'How about a milkshake?' Sugar and milk, the best of both worlds and her go-to solution at this time of day to give him enough of a boost to keep him conscious until after they'd eaten.

'Thanks, Mummy,' he said, voice drowsy, and she hurried to get him a drink before he nodded off.

Ten minutes later, his empty cup in hand, she drifted back into the kitchen to make her own cup of tea. She had just sat down at the table when her phone pinged. A text message. She checked and found it was from Hailey.

Matt left early, so following now.

Her pulse quickened. It doesn't mean anything, she told herself. She checked her watch: just after 4 p.m. Bit late for a meeting. But he'd said he was working late, so perhaps it was an evening meeting – dinner with clients or something. It had happened quite a lot lately. If it *was* actually clients he was having dinner with. She busied herself with the laundry, putting another load on, hands shaking as she stuffed clothes into the machine.

Finally she heard another ping from her phone.

He's gone to the pub. The Flying Duck.

Sara's heart skipped. She called her sister, could hardly ask the question. 'Is he on his own? Did he meet anyone?'

'I'm not sure. It's pretty quiet, but you know I can't go in. I'm still banned after… well, you know…'

Sara's heart sank. Hailey dealt with young people who were the victims of abuse and neglect and helped them find a more positive future, but she was fiercely protective of her service users and that sometimes got her into trouble. She tugged at her hair. So close to finding out what was going on, and yet… 'Can't you just peek through the door? Nobody will notice.'

Hailey sighed. 'Okay. He wasn't looking excited, though, I can tell you that. In fact, he looked like he had the weight of the world on his shoulders.'

Guilt would do that to a person, Sara thought. 'Go on then,' she urged. 'Please.'

Hailey's breath crackled down the phone. 'Right, back in a sec.'

Sara paced up and down the kitchen as she waited. Turned on the oven. Got the pizzas ready. Set the table. At last her phone rang. She picked it up. 'That was a long bloody sec.'

'Yeah, well, I couldn't see him from the front door, so I walked round the back and sneaked in. But he wasn't at the bar. I had a quick scoot round before anyone saw me, but I couldn't spot him anywhere. Must have been in the loos, because his car's still out front.'

'Any women sitting on their own, like they were waiting for someone?'

'There were all sorts of people in there.' Hailey sounded a bit cagey and Sara wondered if she was telling her everything, worried perhaps that she would jump to the wrong conclusion. 'Look, I'll wait outside and keep checking on what's happening if you like.'

'Are you sure?' Sara stopped pacing. 'I don't want you hanging around.'

'No problem.' The line went dead.

Nerves tugged at Sara's belly. It wasn't like Matt to drink during the day. In fact, he had a rule that he didn't drink during the week, saving his alcohol quota for Saturdays. It was what he'd always done. Or at least she thought he had. Now she was wondering if she knew his habits as well as she'd thought she did.

She busied herself with getting the pizzas in the oven, checked that Ezra was still awake and spent ten minutes folding clothes into piles, one for each family member. Just as she was about to call the girls down for their food, the door opened and in walked Matt.

She gaped at him in stunned silence as he threw his briefcase on the floor, slung his jacket after it and headed straight for the fridge, where he pulled out one of his weekend beers and cracked it open, taking a big slug.

'Matt, what's going on?'

He glugged his beer, not stopping until the bottle was empty. Then he wiped the back of his hand across his mouth before he finally looked at her. 'We need to talk.'

He had a strange look in his eyes, a sadness about him, a heaviness in his stance. *Oh my God. He's going to tell me he's leaving.* She clung to the worktop, and for a moment, time seemed to stand still, the two of them looking at each other in the sort of silence that never has a happy ending.

The girls must have smelt the food because they came thundering down the stairs before she had a chance to call them, chatting and giggling, phones in their hands as if they'd grown there and were part of their anatomy. The noise shattered Sara's fearful thoughts, bringing her back to the moment and the smell of burning. She dashed to the oven, relieved to see it was just the edge of the top pizza that had caught. The other one looked fine, and she quickly cut it into slices, jiggled the pieces onto plates and put them on the table, where she'd already placed the bowl of salad.

'Thanks, Mrs Whitlock,' Chelsea said with a broad smile. 'Smells lovely.'

Despite her concerns about Matt, Sara smiled back. Chelsea had such beautiful manners and she wondered where she'd gone wrong with her two girls, who were helping themselves to salad without even acknowledging her existence.

'You're welcome,' she said as she went to get Ezra from the lounge. She tried to make sure the whole family had their evening meal together, so there was one point in the day when they could chat and have a catch-up, but it was tricky keeping Ezra awake long enough for him to join in.

When she got back to the kitchen, Ezra clutching her hand, Pikachu dragging along the floor in his wake, she was surprised to find that Matt had gone.

She frowned. 'Where's your dad?' she asked Amelia.

'He went outside. With a couple of beers.' Amelia pulled a face. 'What's up with him? Looks like he's in a stinker of a mood.'

Sara shrugged and gave a fleeting smile, not wanting Chelsea to get the impression there was a problem. 'I've no idea, love. Will you sort out Ezra while I go and see if he's eating with us?'

She left without waiting for an answer, knowing exactly where she'd find Matt. He was in the garage, which sat on the other side of a covered walkway next to the house. His man cave, as he liked to call it. Not long after they'd moved in to the house, when the twins were still infants, he'd divided the garage in two, making a room for himself in one half and a storeroom in the other. Gradually, as finances allowed, he'd installed electricity, then heating and a bit of furniture, and now this was where he came with his mates to watch football and play on the Xbox. It meant they could be as rowdy as they liked and not disturb the kids.

He was sitting on the sofa, staring at the blank TV screen, his face wet with tears.

Sara's heart stuttered and she stopped in the doorway. Matt never, ever cried and a horrible uneasiness settled in her stomach. She was in uncharted territory with a storm brewing and no shelter in sight. The sound of her pulse filled her ears.

She hesitated, just for a moment, before she rushed over and sat beside him. 'Bloody hell, Matt, what's wrong?' She put an arm round his shoulders and gently wiped his tears away, but he didn't look at her. His empty beer bottle hung from his fingers, swinging backwards and forwards, like the pendulum of a clock, as he stared straight ahead.

He can't tell me. Oh my God, this is it. This is where he says he's leaving. She couldn't bear it, couldn't stand the not knowing. Her hand tightened on his shoulder and she held him close, breathed in the spicy scent of him as if it was the last time. 'Tell me, Matt. You've got to tell me.'

Seconds turned into minutes, his body shaking with the force of his heartbeat. He heaved in a deep breath and let out the longest sigh before he finally spoke.

'I've been laid off. Made redundant.'

His words hit her hard, like she'd just run into a wall. Her jaw dropped as she processed what he'd said. *Oh God, I got it wrong, so wrong.* The relief slackened the muscles that had been holding her rigid, but after a few moments, she realised this news was just as bad, but in a different way.

She gulped, hoping she might have misheard. Misunderstood. 'What? They can't have. They were taking on staff not long ago. Talking to you about promotion.'

He nodded, still staring at the wall as if he was in a trance. 'We lost that big contract. A major bit of work for a government department.' His voice was thick and weary. 'They just pulled it without warning. A change in policy, would you believe? They've spent millions building this system, but there's a new project team, and when they looked at all their budgets, they decided to mothball it.'

The bottle slipped from his fingers and clattered to the floor, spinning off under the sofa. She flinched, startled by the noise. He didn't seem to notice, though, his eyes still fixed on the blank screen in front of him.

'The company has overstretched itself, apparently. Didn't read the warning signs. Everyone's been laid off.' He turned to her and she could see that his eyes were brimming, chin quivering, his emotions barely under control. 'They've gone bust. There's no redundancy pay. Probably no salary this month.' He leant forwards, elbows on his knees, head hanging between his shoulders. 'That's it,' he mumbled to the floor. 'I'm unemployed.'

Sara laid her head on his shoulder and rubbed his back, trying to think of something soothing to say while her mind started doing mental arithmetic, adding up their monthly outgoings. They had a mortgage. An overdraft. Credit cards. Two car loans. Three kids. None of that was cheap. A surge of panic flowed through her, bringing her out in a cold sweat. *How are we ever going to manage? What if we can't?*

Images from her childhood flooded into her mind, her and her sister being picked up by the ladies from social services. 'Just for a couple of weeks. Think of it as a holiday,' her mum had said. 'Until I get everything sorted.' But things never did get sorted and they boomeranged between being at home with their mother and living with foster parents. It happened three times, until the new caseworker decided that their mother shouldn't ever be given responsibility for her children. Sara was ten at the time, and the next eight years were spent with four different families, always an outsider and always resented by the foster parents' natural children. She was alone, separated from her sister, because very few foster placements could take siblings, and anyway, Hailey was out of the care system four years before her. They did what they could to stay in touch, but geography and finances didn't make it easy.

She pulled herself straight, a determined set to her jaw. *That's not going to happen to my family. It's not.*

Matt drew in a deep breath, his voice shuddering. 'I've let you down, love. I promised to look after you and now… now, I can't. I'm a failure.'

He picked up the second bottle of beer, looked at it for a second, then hurled it against the wall with such force that it exploded into smithereens, beer and glass flying through the air. His scream of anger filled her ears, the room, the air she breathed. She jumped away from him, shocked not only by the sickening crash and the splatter of beer, but by the violence of the action, the primeval sound of his despair.

Her body shook as she desperately searched for ways to calm him down. He'd never been this upset before, never shown her this side of himself. This raw fury. And if she was scared, then imagine how it would affect the children. Maybe the girls would understand but Ezra would be petrified.

Empty words wouldn't help; she needed to think of something definite, something tangible that they could do. It was impossible to imagine that her life could shatter just like her mum's had all those years ago. Debts had started that whole downwards spiral, and she couldn't let the same thing happen to her children, couldn't bear to think of them going through that pain and confusion. Her hands clenched. *I've got to sort this out.*

FIVE

Sara gazed at her husband as he sat on the edge of the sofa, his face turned away from her, shoulders shaking as he wept, and her heart broke for him. Being the family provider was central to his view of himself, a source of pride, and if that was taken away, it was like removing the foundations of a building. Without a job, she was sure he'd crumble.

She shuffled closer, no longer scared now his anger had faded.

'Hey, don't go thinking like that. It's not your fault, is it? These things happen.' She ran her tongue round dry lips, her mind scrabbling for solutions. 'Look, it's not that bad. I can work more hours. If you're at home to look after Ezra, I can probably go full-time for a bit, until you find something else.'

He turned to her with an impatient shake of the head, eyes red from crying, frown lines etched across his forehead. 'It's not enough, though, is it? Even if you work full-time, with you being on minimum wage, it's not going to cover the bills.'

She bristled for a moment, a flash of annoyance that her efforts could be dismissed as irrelevant, before reminding herself it wasn't far from the truth. 'But it'll help. And we can go and see the bank, ask if we can extend the overdraft for a bit.' Finally, the adrenaline kicked in and her mind began to feed her solutions. She started to gabble, desperate to make things better. 'We can talk to the mortgage company about missing a repayment or two, can't we? This must happen to people all the time. And I'm sure you'll get another job in no time. I mean, your IT skills are—'

'Specialist.' He spat out the word as if he'd eaten something disgusting. 'There's not another company in Yorkshire that does what we do. It's all London-based, and we don't want to move down there, do we?'

Sara blinked, her positivity stalled for a moment. That couldn't be right, could it? 'Oh, come on, there must be companies round here that could employ you. Even if it's more general...'

She tailed off, because in reality, she hadn't got a clue exactly what Matt's skill set was. Something to do with websites, but the back end, not the front end. Writing code. Problem-solving. Something along those lines. In all honesty, he told her very little about his work these days, and she'd stopped asking, because when he did try to explain, his words flew right over the top of her head, making no impact on her brain whatsoever. She was more of a people person; he was the abstract techie, his mind working in a different way to hers. She'd always thought their skills complemented each other, something that made them perfect together.

The urge to sink her head into her hands and give in to despair was strong, but one of them had to be up for the fight. One of them had to look for the positives, find a way out of this crisis.

Her hands clutched at her scalp as if she was trying to press inspiration into her panicked brain. When she had first become a mum, she'd considered herself lucky that Matt earned enough for her to stay at home and look after the kids. Over time, she'd managed to hide her frustration, her ever-increasing need to use her mind and learn new things, interact with people on a different level to the mummy world she'd inhabited for so long. Maybe now was the point when she could flip things round, give Matt a break while she went out to work and got her career going again.

Suddenly, a new idea burst into her head and she gasped with relief.

The money! I've got the money.

She'd almost forgotten about her little nest egg, the inheritance from her Auntie Wyn, carefully tucked away and growing nicely last time she'd looked. She opened her mouth to remind Matt about their safety net. Then closed it again.

He thinks it's still in the deposit account.

She remembered the conversation when they'd first discussed what to do with the money. It had been the perfect opportunity to tell him about her ambitions and her idea to enrol on a course she'd fancied. It would make her degree more relevant to today's business world, and as soon as Ezra was at primary school, she'd thought she'd have some time to invest in herself.

They'd been out for a rare meal, Hailey on babysitting duty. Matt had reached across the table and poured the last of the wine into their glasses. 'Look, I'm all for continual improvement,' he'd said. 'Honestly I am. But those tuition fees for an MBA are ridiculous, don't you think? And I'm really not sure what you'd get from it.' He'd scrunched up his nose. 'Seems like a bit of a rip-off to me.'

'I see it as an investment, though.' She wondered if the tinge of resentment in her voice would register with him. His speech was a little slurred, she'd noticed, but then he'd drunk most of the first bottle of wine and half of the second one.

'Yes, but we need that money as a contingency fund, don't we?' He wiped his mouth with his napkin. 'In today's financial climate, who knows what's going to happen? Best to leave it in the deposit account, where it's safe.'

And that was that. As usual, she'd let him talk her out of her plans because he made a lot of sense and at the end of the day, the security of her family was the most important thing of all. Her dreams could wait another few years, couldn't they?

What Matt didn't know was that ten months ago, she'd transferred the money to a high-interest fund. She'd done her research, and the promised returns were substantial. Every time she'd opened her quarterly statement – and she'd had three now – she'd been delighted. One day the interest would give her the extra money she needed to improve her qualifications and secure the career of her dreams.

Now, her mind was screaming at her to go and open the letter she'd received the other day. Another statement, she'd assumed, and had put it away to look at later, then forgotten about it.

She stood, wanting to go and check. *Can I take the money out? Are there penalty clauses, time delays?* She couldn't remember the details, but needed to find out.

'I'd better go and see how the kids are doing,' she said, giving Matt's shoulder a reassuring rub. At least he'd stopped sobbing now and seemed calm enough for her to feel comfortable leaving him on his own for a few minutes. 'I've left the girls keeping an eye on Ezra, and you know how that can work out.' She checked her watch. 'I need to get him into bed, anyway.'

Matt didn't respond, lost in his woes, his gaze fixed on the floor.

Sara hurried out of the garage and into the house, stopping when she saw the deserted kitchen. She checked the plates, and was relieved to see that Ezra seemed to have eaten most of his food. She found him curled up on the settee, watching a cartoon that one of the girls must have put on for him. *I must remember to thank them. Maybe I don't do that enough?* However distant she might feel her daughters had become, they always helped with Ezra when she asked, and she wanted them to know she appreciated their efforts.

A ping on her phone alerted her to a text message. Hailey again. *Saw he came home. Assuming all okay? Had to dash off to an emergency.*

What could she say? Far too much to fit into a text message, and there was no point trying to explain when Hailey was distracted by a crisis with one of her service users. She sent a quick reply.

Talk tomorrow. Thanks for your help x

She was too shell-shocked to speak to her sister tonight, and by tomorrow she would have had time to think about things. Her head was spinning with the enormity of it. How easy it had been to assume that life would go on as it always had. That they would have Matt's steady stream of income. *What if he doesn't get a job?* A little shiver ran through her, the ghosts of her past flashing through her mind. It didn't bear thinking about, because he'd been right – even if she did go full-time, her wages would only scratch the surface of their living costs.

With her mind on money, she ran upstairs to their bedroom, where she kept all the household paperwork in an old desk. It doubled as a dressing table, a large mirror hanging on the wall above, with a shelf for make-up so she had the desktop clear to work on. She was the administrator of the household, and Matt didn't know where anything was kept, leaving all that side of things to her. Hurrying to the desk, she found the envelope and ripped it open, scanning the piece of paper inside.

It wasn't a statement; it was a letter.

She blinked and read it again. *No, no, that can't be right.* She slowed herself down, read the whole thing word for word a couple more times. There was no mistaking what it said. She swallowed, her heart galloping in her chest. The letter was from a firm of accountants. The investment company had gone into administration, and the nature of her investment meant it was outside the Financial Services Compensation Scheme. She could appeal, the letter said, but it was unlikely she would be getting any of her money back.

It's gone. All of it.

She sank onto the chair, legs weak, and closed her eyes. She hadn't understood that the investment was unprotected; had just seen the high interest rate and official-seeming website and had assumed it would be covered. *Matt will be furious.* Not only had she gone against his wishes, but she'd ignored all the warnings about investments. About risks and returns. Had thought she knew better, so desperate for some extra money to follow her own dreams that she'd taken a chance with their nest egg.

She heard the muffled sound of the back door opening and closing, Matt calling her name. Quickly, she fumbled the letter back into its envelope and stuffed it under a pile of documents where it wouldn't be easily found. Her pulse raced, her head squeezed tight by the grip of dread. *What am I going to do? I can't tell him.*

'Sara?' he called again.

'Coming,' she replied, her legs wobbly, as if they had a mind of their own, reluctant to take her downstairs, where trouble lay. They hadn't a penny in savings and it was all her fault.

What if he asks about the money?

A bead of sweat worked its way down her back, panic tightening its grip. She'd seen how angry he was, how upset. Devastated by the loss of his job. Now this. She stood at the top of the stairs, unable to descend, her hand clasped to her forehead as she tried to work out what to do. She'd betrayed Matt's trust, let him and her family down by putting herself first.

'Sara?' His voice had an edge of impatience now, and she stirred herself into action, her decision made. He couldn't know. She wouldn't tell him. Would stall if he asked. As she made her way slowly downstairs, she vowed to keep it to herself until she'd worked out how to put it right.

SIX

The knock at the door was a welcome intrusion. Tension buzzed in the air; the atmosphere so charged that Sara had developed a splitting headache, which pounded at the base of her skull. Ezra was in bed, the girls still shut in their room, muffled chatter drifting down the stairs. Matt and Sara were in the lounge, sitting next to each other on the settee but lost in their own worlds. The late-evening news flickered on the screen, the words unheard as Sara's mind searched for ideas to try and put right her terrible mistake.

She jumped up and opened the door, glad to see Fiona on the doorstep, immaculate as ever in a red puffa jacket, black trousers and leather ankle boots. She wore her blonde hair cropped close to her head, in a style only people with her elfin features could pull off, emphasising her large blue eyes. Her look was effortlessly chic but down to earth at the same time, and probably cost a fortune to achieve.

'Hiya.' She gave an apologetic smile. 'Sorry I'm so late. We had quite a few thorny issues on the agenda and I was determined nobody was going home until we'd got everything sorted.'

Sara opened the door wider, gave a tight smile. 'No problem,' she lied, knowing that she'd have a tussle on her hands getting the twins up and ready for school in the morning. Nine o'clock was their cut-off point for friends during the week, something Fiona was well aware of, but she didn't feel she could say anything. Not when she wanted Fiona to do her a favour. She tried to inject some warmth into her voice. 'Come in, come in. To be honest, I'd lost track of what time it was. I'll go up and get Chelsea.'

Fiona tutted, frowning. 'You're upset with me, aren't you?'

Sara realised how uptight she'd sounded, and quietly closed the lounge door. Just tell her, she counselled herself. It's better than her thinking you're mad about her being late. 'Bit of a crisis, actually,' she murmured, not wanting anyone else to hear. 'Matt's just lost his job, so we're reeling from that bombshell.'

'Oh my God, you are joking!' Fiona's eyes widened, her hands covering her mouth for a moment, before she lowered her voice to a conspiratorial whisper. 'But the company have been expanding. In fact, I had them down for some sponsorship funding for the community centre. I thought…' She shook her head slowly and blew out a long breath, clearly shocked by the news. 'That's terrible.' She put a hand on Sara's arm, a reassuring touch. 'Look, if there's anything I can do to help, just let me know.'

Be brave, seize the moment.

'Well actually, there might be.'

Fiona's mouth gave a little twitch before she let her hand drop, her eyes searching Sara's face, waiting.

Sara cleared her throat, forced herself to speak. 'We're just trying to sort through our contingency plan, and I wondered if I could work more hours at the community centre. Just for a little while, until Matt gets back on his feet.'

Fiona was silent for a moment, her steady gaze making Sara uneasy, part of her wishing she hadn't asked. It was a horrible feeling, being needy.

'Look, I can't think now,' she said after what felt like an entire week. 'My brain's fuddled with all the school stuff I've been through at the meeting tonight. I need to switch gears, go into community centre mode.' She put her hand back on Sara's arm, reassurance that she wasn't dismissing her request. 'Why don't we have a good chat about it tomorrow, when we're fresh? You're in early, aren't you?'

Sara nodded. 'Yeah. I should be there at half eight.'

'And James is in tomorrow as well, isn't he?'

'He said he would be, just to sort out priorities for the next few days.'

James was the manager of the community centre, but after his father had suddenly been taken ill, he'd had to drastically cut his hours in order to keep an eye on the family sportswear business. Sara was covering for him while he was away, doing three half-days a week, but she was aware that some aspects of the work weren't being kept up to date and felt sure she could persuade Fiona to give her more hours, if only for a short while.

Fiona smiled. 'Perfect. I need to have a word with him anyway, just to see if he knows what his long-term plans are now that his dad's obviously not well enough to carry on running the family firm. Let's kill two birds with one stone and have a proper planning meeting. We can have a look at the finances and identify all the jobs we've had to drop since James has been on reduced hours. See exactly what needs doing and what we can afford.'

Sara leant against the wall, her body sagging with relief. 'It would be such a help. I honestly don't know how we're going to manage.'

Fiona pulled out her phone and swiped and tapped. 'There we are. It's in the schedule and I've sent that to James, just so he knows.' She gave Sara a quick smile. 'We'll sort something out, don't you worry.' She glanced at the stairs, car keys rattling in her hand. 'Right, um… Shall I go and get Chelsea?'

Sara pushed herself off the wall. 'No, it's okay, I'll get her. Have to be quiet so we don't wake Ezra. He's such a light sleeper, and once he's awake, he's a devil to get settled again.'

The following morning, Sara made sure she was as smart as possible, wanting to look the part. She'd been temping at the community centre for almost two months now and was still getting used to being back in the workplace, but with James's guidance, she was starting to feel comfortable with the routines and how the place worked. He'd been the manager there since it had opened seven years previously, so he was the one who'd set everything up originally. It involved more work than people imagined, managing a building with several rooms for hire, all different sizes and used by a variety of groups for a surprising array of activities. Then there were the accounts to do, on a computer system Sara was unfamiliar with, as well as the admin for board meetings and preparing figures and documents for a number of grant applications that were in the pipeline.

After completing her business studies degree, Sara had only worked for two years before she fell pregnant with the twins. She'd been a junior in a hectic office, and her job had consisted of endless filing, running errands and making tea. She'd been bored to tears. Now, she found she loved the work at the community centre, being part of something that was at the heart of the town, making sure everyone's needs were catered for and sorting out problems as they arose. It was surprisingly satisfying work and she'd started to make new friends in the process.

The job felt like a second skin, a perfect fit, and the prospect of being in charge, if James was going to take over the family business full-time, brought a glow to her heart. A proper salaried job after all these years. She had so many ideas for raising funds, using the space more effectively and reaching out to new groups, she was excited to go to work. Fiona had been impressed with her suggestions and had even mentioned that she might like to consider an Open University degree in community development, which had really got Sara thinking about her future.

The focus of her dreams had changed, and she'd decided she'd like to do a course that was more about people and less about making money. Also, if she studied with the Open University, it would be more affordable and less intense; a better fit with family life. She'd checked the cost and it wasn't too expensive. With the interest on her investment accumulating, she'd thought she'd have enough to cover the first instalment and had quietly started planning a January start. Now, though, with their household finances tipped into the danger zone, she would have to shelve the dreams and concentrate on the fight for survival.

She hurried to the car, still thoroughly annoyed with herself. *How could I have been so stupid? Why didn't I just leave the damned money in the deposit account?* She got in and slammed the door, started the engine. The truth was, she'd never been good at doing what she was told; 'naturally contrary', Hailey had always called her. At least living with Matt had tempered that impulse, made her a bit more sensible. Until this. She chewed at her bottom lip as she drove, thinking through the things she wanted to say at the meeting. Her sales pitch.

She arrived to find the centre unlocked, which was unusual as she was always first to arrive, opening the place up being part of her job. She went into the kitchen to put on the water heater for drinks, but it had already been done and was up to full steam. Whoever had got there first had been there a little while. She did a quick tour round and found Fiona and James in a meeting room on the upper floor. They were sitting at the far end of the long rectangular table, deep in conversation. Fiona was in full flow, animated, James frowning as he listened.

James was a bit older than Sara. Probably mid forties, his hair already silver, contrasting nicely with his tanned skin. He was a tidy man, always well turned out in chinos and a shirt, nothing too casual, his hair kept short and combed back from his long face, his beard neatly trimmed. The most remarkable thing about him was his voice, a deep bass that seemed to make the air vibrate, and would be perfect for doing voice-overs for movie trailers.

She stopped outside the door, reluctant to disturb them, watching for a moment through the glass panel. Are they talking about me? she wondered, desperate to know what was being said but unable to hear anything through the thick fire door. As she studied their faces, trying to work out what was going on, Fiona glanced at the door and her expression froze. She put a hand on James's arm just as he'd started talking and he turned and looked at the door too.

I hope they don't think I was eavesdropping.

She pushed open the door and went in, cheeks burning. 'You two are early,' she said, forcing a cheeriness into her voice, while her stomach churned, her nerves starting to get the better of her. She needed this to work out, needed them to trust her to take on more responsibility. 'Can I get you a drink?'

Fiona flashed her a quick smile. 'That would be lovely. Coffee for me. And you, James?'

He nodded, his face pinched and Sara had the feeling he was annoyed. She grabbed their mugs and headed back to the kitchen, willing the universe to come to her aid and give her a break. She'd just finished reading a book by Deepak Chopra about sending out positive vibes if you wanted positive things to happen, and although she couldn't wholeheartedly commit to his philosophy, or understand the quantum physics of his explanation, she felt she had to give everything a try. She stopped for a moment and took a deep breath, told herself not to second-guess other people's conversations, and by the time she returned to the meeting room, her resolve had returned.

Fiona and James were sitting next to each other now, the paperwork cleared into a neat pile, and Fiona motioned for Sara to sit on the opposite side of the table. She carefully put the mugs down, and smoothed her skirt before settling in her seat, feeling like she was at an interview. This was so much more formal than she'd anticipated, and she could feel damp patches appearing under her arms.

'Now, Sara,' Fiona began. 'We've been having a look through the finances, something we should have done weeks ago, if I'm honest.'

She gave James a sideways glance and he scowled. It was a dig at him, a suggestion he wasn't on top of things. *Maybe that was what they were talking about? Not me at all.* Sara tried to make herself look more relaxed, forcing her shoulders back and unclasping her hands. 'And we've had a chat about James's situation, which he assures me will be clarified in the next couple of months.'

James's jaw hardened and he folded his arms across his chest, angling his body away from Fiona. 'It's not easy getting my father to accept this change in his health. Have a heart, will you? I can't push him to step down. It's going to take a doctor's advice to make him finally bow out. In the meantime, I'm doing what I can to juggle the two jobs.'

Fiona put a hand on his shoulder. 'I'm not having a go, James. Honestly I'm not. But we do need to make sure we're not letting important tasks slip. And it's my responsibility as chair of the board to oversee the staffing. So I would like to suggest that we change the contracts of employment to make you both part-time. A job share, if you like.' She winked at Sara, who felt the warmth of relief flow through her body. 'Realistically, James, you are going to need to take a more active role in your family's business. That time commitment isn't going to diminish, is it?'

James pursed his lips, his frown deepening. 'I think Sara needs a bit more experience before we can consider a job share.' He flashed Fiona a tight smile. 'Can I suggest an alternative?'

Sara wondered when anyone was going to ask her opinion, but without an invitation to speak, she could only observe the back-and-forth of the conversation. Fiona was in charge and knew what Sara needed. If there was a way to engineer a positive outcome, she would persist until she achieved it, of that Sara was certain. She'd seen her in action at a couple of board meetings and she was quite awesome when she got going. A definite role model.

Fiona cocked her head. 'Fire away.'

'I agree we should give Sara more hours and I'm pleased with the way she's learning the job. But she does still need supervision for a while longer. A job share suggests equality, doesn't it? And I don't think she's ready.'

Sara glanced at Fiona, who raised an eyebrow.

'Maybe you could elaborate? Because from what I've seen, she's more than capable of taking on a management role. Not only that, but she's come to me with so many great ideas that I'd like us to consider. I think her fresh thinking is exactly what we need.'

'I'm not trying to push you out, James.' Sara's words burst out in a hurry. 'Please don't think that. But I believe I've got lots to offer. And it doesn't need to be formalised. I'd just like to help more while you've got family issues to sort out.' She smiled at him. 'It can be temporary, if that would make you feel better.'

Fiona's mouth twitched and Sara wondered if she'd done the right thing, speaking up. But James rewarded her with a warm smile. 'If we're talking about temporary – to get us over this glitch and pick up the strands of work I've not been able to pursue as effectively as I'd like – then I'm happy for you to do more hours.' He turned to Fiona. 'We've established that our income stream is strong for the next two months, so if we transfer the hours I'm not doing to Sara, then we can make sure the wages bill is kept within budget.'

Fiona glanced at them both. 'To be honest, I'd be happy to sanction a temporary increase in the budget if it means we can bring everything up to date. I've spoken to the treasurer this morning and he agreed with this as a suggested way forward. So if you're both happy, I suggest Sara has full-time hours on a temporary contract for the next month, and James, you carry on with the two days a week you're doing now. Then we'll review at the next board meeting.'

Sara beamed. James pursed his lips, then nodded.

'Excellent.' Fiona gathered her papers together. 'Sara, can you write that up for me, please? Then I'll circulate it to the rest of the board, just to keep them up to speed.'

James got up, the meeting over. 'I'll be in on Friday, Sara. We can sort out a list of things you still need training up on, okay? By then, I'll know which days I'll be in each week, and we can try and get things into more of a routine instead of me flitting in and out when I have a moment.' He ran a hand through his hair, gave her a tired smile. 'I'm sure it'll be better for all of us, won't it?' There was something in his voice that made Sara think he wasn't as happy with the arrangement as she was, and he hurried out of the room before she could respond.

Generally, she got on well with James, and he'd been more than patient when he was showing her how to work the accounting software and the booking system for the rooms. But he was a hard act to follow, as he was one of those people who appeared to know everyone – their families, their backgrounds – and made them all feel so welcome, while Sara still forgot people's names and wasn't close to being the consummate host that he was. He's right, she thought as she stood to collect the empty mugs. I'm not quite ready to run the place. But she was more determined than ever to learn and improve. In fact, she saw it as a challenge, something to work towards. *I'll show him.*

Fiona's voice broke into her thoughts. 'That went well, didn't it?' She grinned as she packed a pile of paperwork into her bag.

Sara grimaced. 'I'm not sure James was so happy.'

Fiona laughed. 'Oh, that's nothing to do with you. Well, not directly. I had to give him a bit of a bollocking, you see, for not keeping everything up to date. That's why I made sure I got him in early, prepared the ground for making changes, so it would be easier to get him to agree to you having extra hours.'

The tension in Sara's shoulders relaxed a little when she understood that his mood was not her fault. She followed Fiona downstairs, glad that at least she had some good news for Matt and there would be some extra money coming into the house. *It's not enough. Nowhere near enough,* said a little voice in her head and a chill trickled down her spine when she thought of what might lie ahead.

▲

SEVEN

Fiona had asked Sara to work the full day, instead of just the morning, as there were papers that needed preparing for a meeting. It seemed her full-time hours had started with immediate effect and she'd felt she couldn't say no. She got home to find that Matt had tidied up, done some shopping and had a pasta bake in the oven. Ezra was asleep on the settee, and Sara bit back a comment about keeping him awake because it would be a hell of a struggle to get him to sleep later. It was going to take a bit of time to adjust, she counselled herself, and Matt wasn't great at taking criticism. Too tired and anxious to be able to dance around any aggravation, she let it drop and wandered into the kitchen.

'Smells delicious,' she said, wondering what sort of mood he was in. He'd been silent and thoughtful before she'd left that morning, and snappy when she'd phoned to ask him to pick Ezra up from nursery because she was working the afternoon. But now he turned towards her with a big grin on his face. He opened his arms for a hug and held her tight, his cheek resting on top of her head as she relished the familiar warmth of him.

'Sorry I was a bit grumpy,' he murmured into her hair. 'Losing my job was such a shock, and I'm still worried about how we'll manage. But I spoke to the mortgage people and they've agreed we can have a repayment holiday for three months.'

Sara pulled away, looked into his smiling eyes. *When did he last look at me like this?* So long she couldn't remember. Maybe the problems at work had been going on for longer than she'd thought.

'That's great news,' she said, wanting to savour the loving mood, wondering if this was the silver lining to their crisis. Maybe it would bring them close again. She leant back against the worktop and caught hold of his hand, lacing her finger with his. 'I've got good news as well. They've said I can have full-time hours at the community centre for a month. We need to catch up on everything that's fallen behind with James being off.'

The smile fell from Matt's face, replaced by a look of horror. He dropped her hand, took a step away from her. 'But who's going to look after Ezra? Childcare is way too expensive. Even the mornings he does now at the nursery cost a packet. It won't be worth it.' He shook his head. 'No, I'm sorry, love, that's not going to work.'

Sara tensed, annoyed that he was slapping down her efforts to help, to take a lead role for a change. And she'd been looking forward to being out at work a bit more, getting stuck in to some of the meatier projects they were developing at the community centre, instead of her head being filled with nursery rhymes and SpongeBob bloody SquarePants. She wasn't ready to give that up. 'You're at home, though. You can pick him up from nursery, can't you? Realistically, it could take a couple of months before you get another job.'

She went to the sink, ran herself a glass of water and gulped it down, just for something to do, to make her pause and consider her words, take the edge off her annoyance. It was all organised now and she'd feel stupid going back to Fiona and saying she couldn't do the extra hours after all. Not when Fiona had bent over backwards to help her.

'Actually, no, I can't,' he said, as if she was being awkward. She turned to look at him, the empty glass clasped tightly in her hand. He was animated, his eyes lit with excitement. 'I've got a plan. It's something I've been wanting to do for a while, and I've been doing some research and I'm pretty convinced I can give it a real go.'

She scrunched up her nose, thoroughly confused. 'I'm not sure I know what you mean.' She scanned his face for clues but could only see the delight shining in his eyes. 'You've been headhunted? Is that it?' Relief bubbled inside her. A seamless transition from one job to another would be the ideal solution. Maybe she could work flexitime at the community centre, do a few hours in the evenings if she had to be home at lunchtime to pick up Ezra. Her mind sped along, reshaping her life around this new scenario.

'No, that's not it.' His delight morphed into frustration, his hand slapping the worktop. 'Christ, Sara, why do you always have to jump in and second-guess what I'm about to say? Just let me speak, will you?'

She shrank back against the sink, hurt by the sharpness of his words. He could be so snappy these days, when all she was doing was trying to keep everything nice and smooth, no upsets to spook the kids.

He sighed and put a hand on her shoulder, apology in his eyes. 'Sorry, love. I didn't mean to have a go, it's just that sometimes you…' He shrugged, and his hand fell away. 'Anyway, what I was trying to say is I've got a business idea. I want to set up as an IT consultant and… you're not going to believe this, but I already have my first customer. They heard I'd been laid off.' He laughed. 'News travels fast and it's such a small world, isn't it? You know, the way this opportunity has landed at my feet, it just makes me think it's the right thing to do. It's a really specialised project, not many people around with the skills to do the work, and it's perfect to get me started.' Her eyes widened in surprise, her mind scrambling to keep up with this sudden turn into unexpected territory. He nodded, a wide grin on his face. 'Big bucks, love. We're talking proper money once I'm up and running.'

'Wow. But you never said anything. How come you didn't…' She stopped, the narrowing of his eyes a warning that her response wasn't the one he wanted, and having witnessed his devastation the previous day, she didn't want to break his upbeat mood. She smiled instead, genuinely delighted that he'd found a new direction. 'Your own business, eh?' She reached for his hand again, desperately trying to smooth things over. 'And big bucks, you say? Tell me more.'

His hand squeezed hers. 'There's a bit of a risk with it – a puzzle to solve – but I'm pretty sure I can do it. It's exactly the sort of challenge I've been wanting.' He looked so happy, so full of excitement, like a little boy who'd been given the toy he'd been hankering after but hadn't been able to afford. 'And if this contract works out, then who knows where it'll take me? I just need to get set up with the right bits of kits and I'll be off.'

Sara tried to take in what he was saying; the idea of him setting up his own business so unexpected, the implications hadn't really registered. His excitement was infectious, though, and a glimmer of hope ignited in her heart. Surely they could manage for a couple of months until the money came in. A conversation with the bank, maybe a temporary extension to their overdraft… Her administrative mind carried on working through the list, identifying what they'd have to do to make ends meet, and at the end of it, she allowed herself to consider the possibility that, actually, they were going to be okay.

Matt was still talking, bursting with enthusiasm for his new project. 'It's our future, love. I've wanted to be my own boss for ages. After I'd got over the shock of being laid off, and I got this email enquiry, I realised this is my opportunity to follow my dreams. Just get on and do it.'

'Wow,' she said again, unable to form a more coherent response, but Matt didn't seem to notice.

'I'm going to turn the garage room into a proper home office. I've already got electricity, broadband and heating in there, so that'll be easy. A few more sockets maybe. Better lighting. Security system. Then I'll need…' He stopped talking and laughed, reaching out to stroke her cheek with the back of his hand. 'There's actually no point telling you the details, is there? You haven't got a clue about this stuff.'

She put the glass down before she threw it at him. Why did he assume that because she didn't understand IT-speak, she was clueless about everything? She was the one with the business studies degree, so she did understand about running a business – probably more so than he did. She kept her thoughts to herself, though, letting him ride the crest of his wave.

He took her other hand, making her look at him. 'I've been costing it out. I've even been talking to suppliers today and sweet-talked some excellent discounts. I'm thinking it should take a month or so to get it all set up and ready. And the best news is that it's only going to cost nine grand or thereabouts.'

She gasped, panic filling her head, making her pulse race. 'But we haven't got that sort of money, have we?'

He looked a bit taken aback, as though she was missing something obvious and he couldn't quite believe she was being so dense. 'I thought we could use the contingency fund. You know, the money your aunt left you. In fact, I was going to look for the account information today, then I remembered it's in your name, so I can't access it anyway. Ten grand, wasn't it?' Sara tried to hide her dismay, but he caught the change in her expression and his voice had a harder edge to it. 'I know I said we shouldn't take risks. Keep it in the bank for a crisis. But this *is* a crisis, love. And an opportunity at the same time. It would be an investment in our future. The kids' future too.'

She chewed at her lip, unable to find a single thing to say. How could she tell him the money was no longer there?

He misread her silence and dropped her hand, his disappointment bringing a sudden coolness to the air and a snap to his voice. 'Don't you want me to be happy? Don't you want me to follow my dreams?'

She cleared her throat. 'Of course I do, love. It's just a lot to take in, and I think... I think... Is that the pasta burning?' She grabbed the oven gloves and pulled the dish out of the oven, putting it on the hob, where it bubbled and spat. 'Just in time.' She gave him a quick smile. 'Let's talk about it later, when the kids are in bed and I've got a clear head, okay?'

He nodded, mouth twisting from side to side. 'Sorry I went off on one. I'm just so pumped about the whole thing. I truly believe I'm on to a winner.'

'It sounds exciting. Honestly it does.' She tried to force some enthusiasm into her voice. 'But you're going to have to explain it a bit more, so I understand exactly what we're investing in. Because once that money's gone... well, there's no getting it back.'

She loathed her own hypocrisy, telling him this when she had been lured by the promise of high returns and put everything in that one investment.

What's Matt going to say when he finds out?

Her heart clenched at the thought of smashing his dreams. Seeing him so full of optimism and ideas reminded her of the young man she'd first met at university. He'd just started his first job on the help desk there and had come to sort out an IT problem for her. He was funny and kind and didn't make her feel stupid, and the ideas he had, his take on the world, were so refreshing and different, she'd quickly become besotted with him. Somehow, in the intervening years, that spark had been extinguished, the pressures of life robbing him of the joy she'd seen on his face just moments ago. She couldn't take that away from him. Not when he'd clearly been slogging away in a job he wasn't really enjoying for her sake. For the family's sake.

I can't let him down like that, can't jeopardise our future. But she was going to have to think of something pretty damned quick to make sure that didn't happen.

EIGHT

By the time the kids were all settled in bed, Matt was pacing the floor in his eagerness to discuss his plans further. Sara felt the contents of her stomach lurch as soon as she entered the lounge and realised that she couldn't avoid the conversation any longer. *I'm going to have to confess.* Bile shot up her throat and she dashed back upstairs, just making it to their en-suite bathroom before she was sick.

She knelt on the floor in front of the toilet as her stomach heaved until there was nothing left. Exhausted and shaken, she leant against the bath, her heart hammering in her chest, nausea swirling around her belly, making her reluctant to move. Footsteps thumped up the stairs and Matt appeared in the doorway.

'You okay, love?' His face was etched with concern.

She shook her head, her voice feeble. 'Just feeling a bit sick. Must have picked up a bug or something.'

'It wasn't my cooking, was it?' he joked, but she could see the worry on his face. He always struggled to know what to do when she was ill.

'I had a prawn sandwich for lunch and forgot to put it in the fridge at work. I think it must be that.' She couldn't look at him in case he could see the lie in her eyes. Her sickness was nerves, pure and simple, with a side helping of fear. *When did I get scared of telling him the truth?* she wondered, then told herself not to be so ridiculous. There was nothing scary about her husband. Nothing.

'Let's get you into bed,' he said, helping her up from the floor. 'Can I get you anything? Hot water maybe, to settle your stomach?'

She shook her head. 'No thanks, I think I just need to lie down.'

'Don't worry about the business stuff,' he said as he helped her to the bed. 'We can talk about that tomorrow.' She changed into her pyjamas before slipping under the covers and he sat beside her, stroking her hair away from her face, fingers caressing her cheek. His tenderness made her feel even worse. A sudden sob caught in her throat and she turned away from him, burying her face in the duvet so he wouldn't see how upset she was.

He left her alone, saying he was going to start work on setting up his office, and as soon as she heard the back door close, she hopped out of bed and retrieved her phone from the pocket of her jeans.

'Hiya,' Hailey said when she answered the call. 'So what's going on? Have you had a chance to talk to Matt?'

'He's been made redundant. That's what's been going on.' Once she'd started, Sara couldn't stop the whole story coming out, telling her sister how distraught Matt had been when he'd got home the night before.

'Fiona's wangled full-time hours for me for a month, maybe more, so we'll have a bit extra coming in. Not enough to cover all the bills, but it's a help. Matt's got the mortgage repayments put on hold, so that's good. But...' She stopped, closing her eyes for a moment before making herself go on. 'Oh Hailey, I've done something really stupid.'

Hailey was quiet for a minute. 'Come on then, spill the beans.'

Sara took a deep breath and told her about the failed investment and Matt's sudden plans to launch a new business. 'Look, I hate to ask,' she said. 'But I don't suppose you could lend me the money, could you? Just temporarily, until I get a chance—'

'No, absolutely not.' Hailey cut her off, anger thundering through her words. 'I can't believe you even asked me that, after everything we went through with Mum. And you know...' She stopped, her breath crackling down the phone, her voice more measured when she spoke again. 'No. The answer's no. You'll just have to come clean. Or… could you get an overdraft extension or a short-term loan from the bank? Get a new credit card and put it on that?'

'There's no way I can borrow any more money. We're maxed out on all our cards. The bank will want income details for a loan.' Desperate tears welled in Sara's eyes. 'I can't tell him I've lost it all, he'll go mad. Please, Hailey.'

'No, Sara, I can't. It would be just about all the money I have, and I can't risk it. It's never a good idea to lend to family members. What if his business idea doesn't work and then I lose my safety net as well?' She sighed. 'I'm sorry, I really am. But I've got to make sure me and Cassie have a bit of security.'

'Right,' Sara whispered and ended the call without even saying goodbye, because she knew it would set off the tears.

She lay in the dark, her mind going round and round the same circular route until she had to accept there was no way out of the mess she'd got herself in. She was just going to have to tell him.

With a sigh, she got out of bed, wrapped herself in her dressing gown and padded downstairs to the kitchen, where she filled the kettle and got out two mugs ready to make tea. It'll be fine, she told herself, a shiver of unease running through her. She pulled her robe tighter, arms tucked round her body. *It was a mistake. We all make mistakes. Not the end of the world.* But it felt like it. For her, anyway, because her upbringing had made her wary of mistakes. Mistakes meant punishment, and that could be anything from a punch or a slap to going without food or being locked in her room. There was no consistency. Not when her parenting had involved a stream of her mother's boyfriends and seven foster homes, each with its own set of rules.

Her hands were shaking as she dropped the tea bags in the cups, her mind trying to rationalise the situation. *You're not a child any more. Nothing bad is going to happen.* Apart from her feeling foolish and guilty and ashamed. Matt wasn't going to give her a slap that would send her spinning across the room, or tip scalding tea on her hand. After the experiences of her childhood, she'd consciously chosen a partner who she was confident would never resort to physical violence. His only weapons were words, and she could cope with that. He would be angry, justifiably so, and she would have to suck it up while they worked out what to do next.

She looked up as the back door opened and Matt walked in, whistling.

'Hey, love. Let me do that. You go and sit down.' He shooed her into the living room, following her in and grabbing a fleece blanket to tuck over her legs as she sat on the settee. He came back a couple of minutes later with the tea, put the mugs on the coffee table and sat down next to her, pulling her into a hug.

'Aw, you're shaking. Still feeling wobbly?'

She nodded, fear robbing her of words.

He kissed the top of her head. 'I'm making progress, shifting everything around.' His upbeat mood rang in his voice, and Sara's queasiness returned. 'I think it'll make the perfect workspace for me. I'm going to get security glass for the window, you know, with bars in, so I'll have a bit of natural light. A good, solid door.'

His hand stroked the top of her arm as he spoke, tender and loving, his excitement fizzing in the air. She hated herself for what she'd done, couldn't force her mouth to form the words she needed to say. Instead, she let him chatter on about his plans. 'I've rung Ash – you know, from footie – and he's going to come and put a couple of extra electric points in, see what we can do with the lighting.'

He was desperate to do this. It was his dream, and she knew what moving towards a dream felt like, even if hers hadn't quite materialised yet. She couldn't take this anticipation from him, she just couldn't. Nausea stirred in her stomach again and she jumped up, ran back upstairs. She couldn't tell him. Not tonight.

NINE

The following day, she was up early and out of the house while the chaos of the morning routine was in full swing, making sure there was no time for Matt to ask her about money. She'd decided, as a last-ditch attempt to pull this back, that she'd have a word with Fiona, see if she knew anywhere that might be able to give her a quick loan at a good rate. It seemed like a long shot – mission impossible – but she was running out of options. A headache already thumped at the base of her skull.

As soon as she was settled at her desk, the centre still quiet at this early hour, she started researching loan companies, appalled at the interest rates. The more she thought about it, and how much the repayments might be, the more she understood it was a non-starter.

The arrival of the yoga teacher, quickly followed by her students, made her focus on her job, and the morning became too busy for her to think about her own problems. It was only the appearance of Matt and Ezra at lunchtime that brought her back to reality.

'I thought we could go out for lunch,' Matt said, as Ezra clambered onto her knee, desperate for a cuddle.

Her skin prickled, her mind desperately searching for an excuse not to go.

'I'm really sorry,' she said, pointing to a pile of receipts on the desk. 'We're way behind with the accounts and James asked me to prioritise inputting all these today, but this morning's been mad and I haven't even started yet.' She forced an apologetic smile. 'It's a lovely idea, but I don't think I can. Not today.'

Matt's face fell. 'I've got to make decisions, love. If I'm going to get this business up and running, I've got to order equipment.'

She couldn't hold his gaze, concentrating instead on Ezra, who clung to her like a limpet. She stroked his hair, his head resting on her chest. 'I missed you, Mummy,' he murmured. 'Are you coming home now?'

'I've just got a bit more work to do, little smudge.'

She couldn't tell Matt the truth with Ezra there, knowing the conversation would get heated. There was no escape from the consequences of her actions, but she could try and delay the inevitable a little longer.

'Can we talk tonight?' She glanced up at Matt, cringed when she saw the disappointment in his eyes. He was about to reply when Molly, who ran the mums and tots group, popped her head round the door.

'Is it all right for me to set up a bit earlier than usual? There's nobody in the room, but I just wanted to check.'

Matt gave her a full-wattage smile. 'I don't suppose you'd like a little helper, would you?' He nodded towards Ezra. 'We've just got a bit of a crisis to sort out.'

Sara tensed. Molly stepped into the office and held out her hand. She and Ezra knew each other well, as Sara had attended the mums and tots group with him before he'd started going to nursery. 'My favourite helper,' Molly said. 'And there's always a treat for helpers, isn't there?'

Ezra scrambled down off Sara's knee and grasped Molly's hand. Sara watched him leave, her heart racing as her excuse for avoiding the conversation walked out of the room. Matt closed the door, his eyes locked on hers. She swallowed, unable to look away.

'What's going on, Sara? I get the feeling you're avoiding talking to me about my business.'

She chewed her lip, unsure where to start.

He pulled up a chair and sat down, leant forward with his elbows on the desk, a determined glint in his eye. 'We don't really need to discuss this, do we? All I need is for you to transfer the money to our joint account. I've been into the bank this morning and set up a business account, but it's going to take a few days before it's up and running.'

'I'm not…' She bit her lip. 'I can't…'

He frowned, throwing himself back in his chair in frustration. 'I get it. You're not behind me on this.' He folded his arms across his chest, anger flashing in his eyes. 'You don't think I can do it, do you? Think it's too risky, is that it?'

She shook her head. 'No, no, that's not—'

'I've been a wage slave for bloody years so that you could be at home with the kids, enjoy being a mum while I took all the pressure. Years of my life on the treadmill. All yes, sir, no, sir, three bags full, sir. Dealing with bloody idiots. Years of my life, Sara. And now I've got the chance to actually do what I want, you're blocking me.' He glared at her, but his chin was trembling and she could swear that his eyes were brimming with tears. Her heart pounded and she looked at her hands, fiddled with a paper clip as she searched for an easy way to tell him.

'You know what I think, Sara? I think you don't actually believe in *us* any more. That's what I think.'

Her mouth fell open, her eyes meeting his angry glare, appalled at the turn the conversation had taken. 'No, you've got that wrong! Of course I believe in you.'

His eyes narrowed. 'But do you believe in *us*? That's the question here.' His voice cracked and he ran his hands over his face, looking at the ceiling for a moment while he gathered his emotions. This was the second time she'd seen him in tears in a matter of days, and his hurt hung in the air, in the sound of his ragged breathing. 'I thought we were a team, you and me.' His voice was thick and unrecognisable. 'But now that I'm asking for your full backing, you're wavering, and that makes me think…' He dropped his head, red-rimmed eyes searching her face. 'It makes me wonder about the state of our relationship.'

Sara gasped, her chest so tight she could hardly breathe. The idea of her relationship – her family being destroyed by her stupidity – was more than she could bear.

'Oh Matt, don't be like that. I just needed a little bit of time to get my head round it all. Of course you can have the money,' she said before she could stop herself. 'Of course you can.'

His body wilted with relief as hers became rigid with panic, her mind shrieking that she was a weak, stupid woman, telling her to just be honest with him. *But it'll break us if I do that. I can't tell him, I can't.*

Her eyes stung and she couldn't speak, couldn't even say goodbye when Matt got up to leave. She just gave him a watery smile and watched him shut the door as he went in search of Ezra. Her fingers had been clasped so tightly in her lap that they ached, and as she stretched them out, she knocked against the mouse on the desk. The computer screen came to life, and with a lurch of her heart, she realised that the answer to her problem was staring right back at her.

She'd been familiarising herself with the online banking system when Matt had come in – checking through the various accounts – and had come across a deposit account that hadn't been used for years. She'd checked back and found out it was contingency money from a building project completed ages ago. Nobody looked at the statements, not until the year-end accounts were prepared, a process that had been completed only last month. She stared at the figures, the sound of her blood whooshing in her ears as her heart raced.

Nobody will know.

And before she could think about what she was doing, she had transferred nine thousand pounds to her personal deposit account, her details already on the list of payees because she was on the payroll. Easy. Way too easy.

She stared at the screen, heart skipping, hands flying to her mouth and she almost made the decision to reverse the transaction, appalled that she'd done it in the first place. Stealing wasn't the answer. It's just borrowing, she told herself, her mind full of Matt's words, the depth of his hurt. Her hand was shaking, her finger on the mouse undecided. Reverse the transaction or live with her decision? There was a choice to be made.

She logged off the banking site.

I've got to choose Matt, got to choose keeping the family together.

TEN

Sara had been living on her nerves for the last two weeks, ever since she'd transferred the money. She'd lost weight, wasn't sleeping, had nightmares that she'd be found out and dragged off to jail, leaving her children motherless. Every morning she woke up with the intention of confessing her sins to Matt and seeing if they could work out a solution together. But every day, something happened to stop that conversation. It was never the right moment: there were children to deal with, she had to get to work, Matt was off out to meetings or locked in his office where she wasn't allowed to interrupt. Life, it seemed, was unwilling to give her the opportunity to address her mistake.

But her biggest barrier to confession was the change in her husband. He was happier than she'd seen him in recent years, whistling, laughing, playing with Ezra, helping the girls with their homework, being affectionate towards her. Family life was a hundred times better than it had been before, and telling Matt the truth would ruin everything. Not just for him, but for the kids. They were loving having him at home, and so was she. He'd even agreed to pick up Ezra from nursery and look after him in the afternoons, on condition he had some time in the evenings to work. On the surface, it looked like everyone had got exactly what they wanted.

Hailey commented on it when she called in at the community centre one lunchtime, the first time Sara had seen her since she'd come round for coffee a couple of weeks ago.

'Sorry I haven't been in touch, but work's been mad,' she said, handing Sara a ham salad baguette she'd picked up for her on the way over. 'And then I was at football practice with one of my service users last night, and I saw Matt with the girls and realised how long it's been.'

'Well, I know you've got a lot on.' Sara put her baguette on the desk, aware of the elephant in the room, the real reason why her sister hadn't been in touch. 'Look, I just wanted to apologise for asking you for money.' Her cheeks burned with the shame of it. 'I shouldn't have done it. Honestly, I don't know what I was thinking.'

Hailey wafted her concerns away with a flap of her hand. 'Doesn't matter. As long as it's all cool between us now.' She grinned. 'Let's just forget about it.'

Sara took a bite of her lunch, thankful that the awkwardness between them had been dealt with. She'd been avoiding Hailey, too embarrassed to call, not sure what sort of response she'd get.

'Matt was telling me he's really getting stuck into setting up his business. Honestly, he's puffed up like the cock of the rock, isn't he? I've never seen him looking so pleased with himself.'

Sara laughed and almost choked on her food. Her sister came out with some weird sayings, and she had a habit of chucking them into conversations like little grenades, guaranteed to get people laughing.

Hailey licked mayo off her fingers, her baguette leaking drips of it onto her lap, which was thankfully covered with the paper bag she'd brought them in. 'You managed to rustle up the money from somewhere, then, without Matt finding out?'

Sara bit into her sandwich and nodded while she chewed, giving herself a chance to come up with something feasible. She swallowed, eyes on her food. 'Yeah. We've got it sorted. His dad...' She took another big bite, no intention of elaborating any further. Hailey could come to her own conclusions, and really, it was none of her business. Anyway, Sara couldn't tell her the truth. That she was a thief. A chill ran through her at the very thought.

Not a thief, she corrected herself. I didn't steal. It's a loan and I'm going to pay it back. Matt had said he'd return the money to the savings account when he got paid from this big contract he'd been talking about, so it wouldn't be long before she could put everything right.

Hailey changed the subject then, talking about Cassie and what she was up to on her art course in Lancaster, but Sara's thoughts were stuck on her predicament. Even when Hailey had left, and she was alone in the office, it remained glued at the front of her mind.

Nobody knows, she told herself, as she wiped crumbs from the desk, hoping it was true.

'Morning!' James called to her when she arrived at work on Monday after a hectic weekend of football for the girls and play dates for Ezra as she tried to improve his social connections. She was surprised to see him, as he didn't usually arrive until after ten, going into the family business first to sort out the work for the day with his staff there. He was sitting at their shared desk, papers spread out in front of him, looking every inch the boss, which Sara supposed he was, although she rather liked to think of it as her job when she was in the office on her own.

He gave her a warm smile and the tension in her shoulders eased a little.

Sara would be the first to admit that her working relationship with James had got off to a rocky start, mainly because Fiona had parachuted her into the role when he was away sorting out his family's affairs. There had always been a slight air of resentment about him, she'd thought, a coolness, and even though he'd agreed to the new arrangement, she suspected he still wasn't completely happy with it.

A week ago, it had all come to a head, brought on by a casual comment that felt like a dig at her.

'I see you're settling in,' he'd said when he'd come into the office early that morning and found her already there, sitting at the desk. 'Feet well and truly under the table.' He'd said it with a smile, but his voice had a crispness to it that left her in no doubt about his meaning.

She went and made them both a cup of coffee, pulled the packet of biscuits she'd brought out of her bag and sat down on the other side of the desk, determined to clear the air. She had enough tension at home and didn't need it at work too.

'I'm only temping, James,' she began. 'I'm not after your job. I'm just helping out full-time for a month while your dad's not well.' She broadened her smile, seeing that he was going to take a bit of convincing. 'By which time, it'll be half-term holidays and I'll be at home with the kids.'

He gazed at her over the top of his mug, blue eyes assessing. 'That's not what Fiona told me.'

Sara sighed, wondering if Fiona had misunderstood. 'Well, she has her own ideas, doesn't she? Realistically, I can only work part-time until we see what happens with this new venture of Matt's. If that takes off, well, maybe we can afford childcare for Ezra.' She shrugged. 'That's how it is.'

'And I thought the two of you were trying to oust me.' He gave a brittle laugh. 'A coup.'

'I wouldn't ever try and take someone's job from them,' she said firmly. 'If you wanted to leave, that would be different. But as far as I'm concerned, you're my boss and that's how it's going to stay.'

He'd put his mug down, looking thoughtful. 'To be honest, I have no idea what I want at the moment.' He sighed. 'That's my problem, you see. And Dad's not sure either. He doesn't want to let go of running his business – believes he's the only person in the world who understands sportswear – but he knows he's not really up to it. At the same time, though, I don't want to stop working here just yet. I know I don't make a fortune, but that's not the point.' She noticed his eyes then, how they lit up when he talked about the community centre, how his voice brightened. 'It's such a vibrant place, so many different things going on and so many opportunities to help develop and support the local area.' He shrugged. 'It's my baby.'

She understood then how much the community centre and the work he did there meant to him. As far as she was aware – having had little opportunity for chats about their personal lives – he was single with no children, and she could see how it could become the focus of his world, his *raison d'être*.

'Working here is quite addictive, isn't it?' she said as she offered him the packet of biscuits. 'Such a happy place. Lots of positive vibes.'

James smiled at her. He was attractive when he smiled, she thought; when his eyes crinkled at the corners and the frown lines were wiped clean.

'You fit in very well. And all these new ideas of yours have got the board very excited.' He pulled a face as he took a biscuit, waving it in the air as he spoke. 'Mind you, I'm not so keen on Fiona using them to demonstrate how lazy I've become. Do you know, I overheard her telling the secretary exactly that before the last meeting? Cheek of the woman.' He took a bite of his biscuit, looked her straight in the eye. 'I feel I can trust you to manage when I'm not here, though. You're a quick learner and the clients clearly like you.'

After that, their relationship had grown warmer and she'd found he had a dry wit that she rather liked.

Trust. If only he knew, she thought now as she went to put her coat and bag in the cupboard behind the desk. She turned back to see that James had the bank statements up on the computer screen. Her heart leapt up her throat, her body frozen in place like it had short-circuited.

Oh my God, no!

She had taken on responsibility for the bank reconciliations now that he was confident she knew what she was doing, and she did all the online banking as well as posting everything to the accounting system. She'd been sure he wouldn't bother with the detail, didn't think he had the time. In fact, he'd told her as much. Maybe he hasn't seen, she reassured herself, recognising the cheque account on the screen. He had no reason to look at any of the other statements. No reason at all.

'You know we've got a new treasurer starting?' he said, still staring at the screen. 'I'm not sure I mentioned it, did I?'

Sara coughed, too shocked to speak for a moment. 'No, I don't think you did.'

'Eddie decided he was getting too old for the job and resigned on Monday. Fiona's delighted. She's been trying to winkle him out ever since he fell asleep in the last board meeting, and to be honest, he hasn't been on top of things for a while now. Anyway, she asked the rest of the board for nominations and they've come up with Julia Prentice. I think her daughter is friendly with Fiona's.' He looked over his shoulder at Sara. 'You might know her too?'

She nodded, a flush of heat travelling round her body. Panic gripped her by the throat, making a reply impossible. Julia moved in Fiona's professional circle – one of the great and good of the town, another superwoman who seemed to have it all and the energy of three normal humans. Sara found her cool and intimidating and they rarely spoke, even though their daughters were friends and played together on the same football team. She'd heard Julia was an auditor, a detail person, who worked for one of the large accountancy firms in Leeds.

The blood drained from her face and she busied herself in the cupboard, tidying the lost property shelf, not wanting James to notice her dismay. *She'll be on to what I've done in an instant!* Her chest tightened with fear.

She heard James's fingers tapping on the keyboard.

'The thing is, she's asked to see bank statements so she knows where we're up to.' Sara stopped what she was doing, but couldn't turn to look at him, dreading to think where the conversation was heading. 'I noticed in one of the deposit accounts – the one we haven't used since the new kitchen was done – there's a transfer – nine thousand pounds…'

She could imagine the accusation in his eyes, felt his stare searing the back of her neck. She straightened up, sweating profusely now, her shirt sticking to her back.

Silence.

Her heart beat even faster, so fast it felt like her chest would explode. She could hardly breathe. He was waiting for her to say something, give an explanation.

He knows.

Slowly, she turned, aware that she was cornered. There was no escape. 'Don't tell anyone, please, James. I just needed a loan. I was desperate and…' This was what she'd been dreading, and her body reacted like a deflating balloon, making her fold in on herself, shoulders hunched, her head hung low. She covered her face with her hands, ashamed and embarrassed and devoid of hope, wanting to crawl into the cupboard and curl up in a ball. An unexpected sob burst from her mouth and tears sprang from nowhere.

She felt a hand on her shoulder, slowly guiding her backwards, round the desk until she was gently pushed into a chair. He sat on the desk in front of her, and when he spoke, his voice was soft and soothing, quite the opposite of what she was expecting. 'When you're ready, you can tell me all about it.'

Although she knew she couldn't hope for a happy outcome, she needed to explain herself, and when her sobs had finally hiccuped to a stop, she wiped her face and told him everything. Her lost investment, Matt being made redundant, their financial difficulties and then Matt's business idea, an opportunity to get them back on their feet again if they just had that initial lump sum.

'I am going to pay it back.' Her eyes stayed on her hands, which were knotted together in her lap. 'Honestly I am. As soon as Matt's new business is up and running.'

'And he doesn't know anything about it?'

She sighed and shook her head, her voice no more than a whisper. 'I couldn't tell him. Didn't dare confess to what I'd done. He'd told me, you see. Very specifically told me not to take risks with the money, and we'd agreed to leave it in the deposit account. But then I had this moment of madness.'

She clasped a hand to her forehead, her mind taking her back to the moment when she'd made the rash decision, reliving the feelings of frustration that had led her to a choice she now regretted with all her heart.

'It was my money, you see – a legacy from my aunt – and I thought I should be able to use it how I wanted. And what I wanted was to have a career, and for that I felt I needed to upgrade my qualifications.' He handed her a tissue from the box on the desk and she dabbed at her eyes, finally plucking up the courage to look at him. 'I know there's no excuse for what I've done, but...' She gulped back her explanation, resigned to her fate. 'Anyway... at least you know why I did it.'

He adjusted his position on the desk, one arm across his chest, the other hand tugging at his beard. His expression was pensive as he looked over her head at the wall, obviously thinking about her sorry tale and what he should do now.

She scrunched the damp tissue in her hand. 'I know you'll have to tell Fiona and the board. I know you'll have to sack me. And I know I've committed a crime. But I promise I will pay it back. I will.' She pressed her hands together, as if in prayer. 'Please don't tell the police. Please?'

He looked down at her, sympathy in his eyes rather than the judgement she'd expected. 'Look, I understand.' He raised his hands, palms up. 'We've all made mistakes. And I know this is totally out of character.'

He gazed at her, his eyes fixed on hers, his hand tugging at his beard again as the seconds ticked by. The silence smothered her, and she could hear herself taking shallow gasping breaths as she waited for him to carry on, her mouth opening and closing like a fish out of water.

'Hmm,' he said, at last. 'I think I might have an idea.' He smiled at her. 'How about I repay this money for you, then nobody needs to know. I can tell this new treasurer the transfer was an error, done while you were still learning. She won't have a clue which account the money was transferred into.' He nodded to himself as his idea gathered steam. 'She won't have time to double-check every transaction, will she? And if it's gone back into the account, then there's nothing to worry about. The status quo has been restored. The books are balanced. No harm done.'

She frowned, unable to believe what he was proposing. 'What? No. I can't let you do that. You don't even know me that well. Honestly, I would pay you back, but…' She shook her head. 'No, I can't let you do it.'

He looked at her, eyebrows raised, clearly surprised by her response and she found herself caught in a surreal landscape that her brain was struggling to register. She'd surrendered herself completely, put herself at his mercy, and now that he'd given her a way out, it appeared her mind wouldn't accept it. *Could it possibly be this easy?*

'It's a genuine offer, Sara. I honestly just want to help, and tell me… what's the alternative?'

He got off the desk and walked back to his chair, letting his question hang in the air while he settled himself, waiting for her to say something. But words wouldn't come, because now she thought about it, there really was no alternative.

Her throat tightened. She couldn't imagine the consequences if the police were involved. She'd go to prison, as sure as night followed day. And what would happen to her family then?

'Thank you,' she said, before she could think about it any more, a tacit acceptance of his offer.

He gave her a smile. 'Here's the deal. I'll pay back what you stole.' The word 'stole' loomed large in her mind, and she understood then that whatever the deal was, she'd readily accept. 'You can pay me back as and when you have the money.'

She chewed at her lip, unable to believe she'd got away with her misdemeanour quite so easily.

'And in the meantime, while you're in my debt, you can do me a little favour.'

ELEVEN

Sara couldn't think, couldn't speak, couldn't do anything but stare at James, who still had that gentle smile on his face. Then he laughed. 'Don't look so worried. It won't be anything horrible. It gets you out of trouble and it helps me out too.'

A favour?

She swallowed, her voice wavering. 'I've no idea what you're suggesting.' *It doesn't matter. Do anything, whatever it takes,* a voice in her head was shouting at her. It sounded like her mother. *He's letting you off! You've escaped.*

She remembered whispered conversations in the kitchen at home, when she'd been back there with her mum: 'Sometimes you've got to do unsavoury things. Just grin and bear it if it helps you get through another day or week.' Her mother was pragmatic, a woman whose dreams had come to nothing and had learnt that life had a seedy underbelly when you ran out of money and had two kids to look after. She'd drifted from man to man, becoming a hollow shell of the cheerful mum Sara liked to remember, the essence of her more faded every time her daughters were allowed to see her. Until the day she overdosed. Accidental or intentional, it was never clear, but Sara hoped she was finally at peace.

Now Sara was older, with her own family, she understood what a struggle life had been for her mum. Yes, she'd made bad choices, but at the time she'd made them, she'd been doing her best.

I've got to do what's right for my family, and going to prison isn't an option.

She looked at James and steeled herself. His eyes were very blue, she noticed, with a navy ring round the edge, the first time it had really registered with her. Kind eyes, she thought.

He's doing me a favour, she reassured herself. Getting me out of trouble. Being nice. But then a more unsettling thought wormed its way into her head. *Does he want sex? Is that what he means?* She could feel herself squirming inside, a nest of snakes in the pit of her belly. *I can't. I can't do that.* Apart from the fact the idea of it appalled her, it would be the end of her marriage if Matt found out.

James laughed, his eyes sparkling with amusement. 'You look like you think I'm going to eat you alive. I'm not proposing anything illegal or immoral. I just need an occasional companion.' He folded his arms across his chest. 'Nothing romantic, I promise. It's just embarrassing turning up to business events on my own, and to be honest, it would be nice to have some company. Dad can't do these things any more, so I need someone who can help me sweet-talk people into giving me good deals. Suppliers, buyers, clubs. That sort of thing.'

Her body sagged with relief and she leant back in her chair, head spinning. She tried to smooth her panic into some semblance of calm. It didn't sound onerous, what he was suggesting. Her hands gripped each other more tightly as she thought it through. *I can wangle the odd night out without Matt knowing. Doesn't sound too bad, does it?* The voice in her head made it sound like the logical thing to do.

She nodded, glanced up at him. 'Okay.'

He put out his hand and they shook on the deal, his clasp firm, his palm dry against her sweaty skin.

There, I've done it. Whatever happens, it'll be worth it.

And the truth was, she believed it.

Her giving Matt the money had energised him, and he'd set about organising his new business with a focus and commitment she hadn't known he possessed. In fact, in the last couple of weeks, she'd hardly seen him. As soon as she came home, they'd eat and then he'd head off into his office and work all evening, having had to pick up Ezra from nursery and look after him for the afternoon. The pattern of their life was like a game of tag, but he was happy and that was the important thing, their argument a thing of the past while he was focused on their future.

He won't even notice if I go out for the evening, she thought, as she scurried out of the office on the pretext of making coffee while she let the ramifications percolate through her mind. Hailey would be happy to come and keep an eye on the kids for a few hours, and she made a mental note to ring her, prime her for babysitting duties. Shall I tell her? she wondered as she spooned coffee into cups and filled them from the water heater. No, she decided, shocked that she'd even considered it. No way could she tell her sister what she'd done. She could hear her now, shouting at her, disgust in her voice. *Have you learned nothing from our childhood? From what Mum went through?'*

It appeared that in some ways she hadn't. In fact, she could understand why her mum had made some of the decisions that had led her into 'trouble, always trying to do what was best for her children, even if it was illegal, or had horrible consequences. She'd done it for them, and although it had backfired on more than one occasion, she'd always felt the risk was worth taking. Or maybe she'd found herself backed into a corner and her choices had narrowed down to one? Her mum used to say she was the unluckiest person on earth. Hailey thought she was reckless, lacking something in her make-up that alerted her to unacceptable risk. She and Sara had talked about it many a time, promising each other they wouldn't make the same mistakes.

It's *not* the same, Sara told herself as she stirred milk into the steaming coffee. I'm just doing a lonely guy a favour, that's all. She replayed James's words in her mind and nodded to herself. A couple of nights out at business dos. No harm in that, and it was certainly better than the alternative. It's only temporary, she reminded herself, until I can pay him back.

By the time she returned to the office, James's offer didn't sound too bad. The occasional night out might even be quite nice, mixing with movers and shakers. It would lift her out of her humdrum existence, and James could be quite funny, so spending a bit of time with him might not be such a terrible thing. It wasn't like a blind date or anything; wouldn't be awkward in that way. And if she'd read it wrong and he started making moves on her, then she'd tell him the deal was off and accept the consequences.

She pushed the office door open with her bottom and swung into the room. *That's it. Set boundaries and make sure he knows what they are.*

He glanced up when she put his mug on the desk, and she drew herself up to her full height. 'Right, I've been thinking about your deal. I can manage the odd night out, and I'm fine about helping you with your family business, but I need plenty of notice so I can arrange babysitting.'

He pursed his lips, looked puzzled. 'Aren't the girls old enough to babysit?'

She gave a wry smile. 'Oh yes. Technically they are. But Ezra won't let them put him to bed. He makes a right fuss. We've had to come home from nights out a few times, and in the end we stopped trying. Then we discovered that he doesn't object to my sister, Hailey, because apparently she smells like me and she sounds like me and she reads stories just like me. And that,' she said with a smile in her voice, as she thought about her little boy, 'makes it all okay.'

James laughed. 'Kids. They're all so different, aren't they?'

'They are that. You've never said, but… have you got children?' There was so much she didn't know about James; their conversations were generally about work-related things.

He looked down at the desk. 'I do. I have a daughter. But I don't see her because her mother...' He stopped and picked up his mug, took a sip and put it back down.

Sara blushed, embarrassed that she'd asked, making a mental note to avoid talking about families when they went out. Boundaries, she reminded herself. Tell him about boundaries.

She cleared her throat. His eyes met hers. 'I just... I need to make it clear that nothing romantic is involved in this agreement. I love my husband, we're very happy together and I'm not going to do anything to put our relationship in danger.'

He looked slightly horrified. 'Of course, of course,' he spluttered. 'Please, don't worry about that. This really is all above board, although I understand that your husband might not be too happy about you spending evenings with another man. I can assure you, though, that any events I invite you to will be out of town, not local.'

Events, she registered. Plural. More than one. And she wondered just how many times she would have to accompany him before she could find the money to repay the debt. Realistically, it could take a while for her to get nine thousand pounds together, and in the meantime...

'Right,' she said, in an over-bright voice as she headed for the door. 'Things to do. The U3A group will be here for armchair aerobics any minute, and I haven't sorted out the room yet.'

TWELVE

Sara arrived home to find Hailey building a Lego fortress with Ezra, and Matt nowhere to be seen. She frowned. 'I didn't know you were coming round. Something wrong?'

Hailey looked at her for a moment before continuing the crenellations she was putting together for the top of the walls. 'Lovely welcome,' she said sarcastically. '"Thanks for entertaining my son while my husband works" might have been more appropriate.'

Sara cringed. 'Christ, I'm sorry. Is that what happened? Did he call you?'

Hailey pressed the Lego into place, then got to her feet and stretched, her spine clicking. She wriggled and massaged her lower back. 'You get out of practice with this stuff, don't you? Not that Cassie was ever into Lego; more of a dolls and unicorns sort of girl.' She looked fondly at Ezra as he started putting his Power Rangers into their places in the fort. 'I feel like I missed out.' Finally she met Sara's eye. 'A cuppa would be nice if you're putting the kettle on.'

They went through into the kitchen, where Amelia and Sophia were doing their homework on the kitchen table. They looked up, said, 'Hey, Mum,' in disconcerting unison, and went back to their work.

'How's it going?' Sara said, walking over to them and giving them each a hug and a kiss.

The girls looked at each other. Sophia shrugged. Amelia rolled her eyes and said, 'Maths. Jeez, it's horrible.'

Sophia gave a rueful smile. 'Calculus, Mum. It's the work of the devil.'

Sara and Hailey laughed, neither of them having excelled in the subject.

'Know what you mean.' Sara filled the kettle. 'I'm sorry, but I won't be much help with that. If you're stuck, you'll have to ask your dad. He's the maths expert in this house.'

Amelia scowled. 'Yeah, well, he's never here to help now, is he? Too much work to do. I wish he'd never started that stupid business.'

Sophia nodded. 'Can't you tell him to have a break, Mum? He just told us he won't have time to come to football on Thursdays for a few weeks.'

Sara's heart went out to her girls. They had such a strong bond with their father, so strong she'd felt pangs of jealousy at times, when they got all the attention and she felt forgotten, taken for granted. Until she reminded herself that he was everything she'd ever wanted in a father; she should should be happy that her girls would grow up with a stronger sense of self-worth than she'd ever had and be in a position to make good decisions when it came to relationships.

'It won't be forever,' she said as she made the tea. 'It's just temporary. Anyway, I can come and watch if you'd like.'

The girls looked at each other, an unspoken message passing between them. 'But you don't even like football, Mum, so what would be the point?' Sophia said. 'You don't understand it, do you?'

Sara reeled, stung by the way her suggestion had been so quickly dismissed.

'I can come if you like,' Hailey said with a grin. 'One of my service users goes every week now, so I usually go to support her.'

Sara turned to look at her sister, blindsided by this turn of events. It was unusual for Hailey to volunteer her time for anything, due to her unpredictable hours.

The twins looked at each other, eyes wide. 'Would you?' Sophia said, clearly delighted by the idea.

Hailey knew all about football. She'd been captain of the Ilkley women's team until she'd ruined a ligament in her knee and couldn't play any more. 'Me and your mum can come together,' Hailey said, glancing at the girls, then back at Sara, giving her a wink. 'And we'll train her up – educate her on the ins and outs of football – how about that?'

The girls grinned, gave each other a fist bump. 'That would be so cool.' Amelia pointed at Hailey, then Sara. 'We're going to hold you to that, aren't we, Soph?'

'Oh yeah.' Her sister nodded. 'And we'll have to teach you about post-practice rituals too, won't we?' Sara caught the sneaky look she flashed at Amelia. 'Like milkshakes. That's right, isn't it, Milly? We always have milkshakes afterwards.'

Amelia's eyes widened. 'That's right, we do. And a McDonald's. Have to replace all those calories we've used up.'

Sara shook her head, laughing, playing along with them. 'Seems I have a lot to learn. I'll have to ask your dad for the details.'

The girls glanced at each other in sudden alarm. 'Oh, you don't want to bother him,' Sophia said with a dismissive wave of her hand. 'He's too busy doing important stuff.'

'Yes, he is,' Sara said, a note of weariness in her voice.

The girls started packing up their books. 'We'll go upstairs,' Amelia said. 'Let you two have a gossip.'

Hailey pretended to be appalled. 'Gossip? We don't gossip.'

The girls gave her a knowing look, and Sara saw Amelia whisper something in Hailey's ear as she walked past. 'Thanks, Auntie Hailey,' Sophia said. 'And for the chat—'

Amelia cut her off with a sharp dig in the ribs before pulling her into the hall. Sara listened to them thundering up the stairs, heard the bedroom door bang.

She turned to Hailey, puzzled. 'What chat would that be?'

Hailey gave a quick shake of the head, picked up her mug of tea and went over to sit at the table. She's stalling, Sara thought, aware that her sister was avoiding eye contact.

'Oh, it was just about some kids at school playing up in class. You know, coping with a bit of bad behaviour, that sort of thing.'

Sara wasn't sure she believed her and made a mental note to talk to Sophia later, see if she could get to the truth. If there was anything bothering her girls, she'd sort it out herself. Her jaw clenched. She didn't need Hailey butting in and taking over, however experienced she was with difficult kids.

Calm down, she told herself, taking a deep breath. You're overreacting. A bit wound-up. She blew on her tea and took a sip before going over to join her sister. It was good the girls felt comfortable talking to Hailey about things that mattered, she decided as she pulled out a chair. *It doesn't mean they think any less of me, does it? She was here, I wasn't.*

Hailey had always been part of the family's lives and Sara counted herself lucky to have her support – an older sister to guide her through the tribulations of parenting. She was glad that Hailey's relationship with her nieces was so close because if anything happened to Sara, she knew her children would be in good hands. Not that Matt wasn't a good father; it was just he didn't see what needed to be done around the house, didn't understand how much organising she did to make things run smoothly, and if she wasn't there, Sara knew the household would descend into chaos in the space of a few days.

I'm not planning on going anywhere, she thought, nerves swirling in her belly as the events of the day flooded back into her mind. The discovery and cover-up of her crime. The transfer of debt from money to the currency of favours.

James had been true to his word and done the bank transfer straight away, showing her the internet bank account so she could be sure the money was back where it should be.

'Nothing to worry about,' he'd said with a reassuring smile that had made her palms greasy, because now she was committed to his deal. Committed to attending more than one event with him. Committed to lying to Matt at least twice.

He hadn't elaborated any further on how many events constituted interest on nine thousand pounds, and she hadn't wanted to ask, because then she might have to agree to a specific number. A large number, one that would stoke her anxiety to even higher levels. Better to wait and see how it goes, she decided. There was still a chance that eagle-eyed Julia would spot the two transfers and then it would be game over for both of them. Straight to prison. She shuddered at the thought, but at least if that happened, she'd have Hailey to step in to look after the children. One less thing to worry about – her contingency plan already in place.

Would the kids even miss me? she wondered. Or Matt? She remembered the mug of tea she'd made for her husband, still sitting on the worktop and put her own mug down, pushed her chair back. 'I'll just take Matt his tea,' she said to Hailey as she stood. 'Then he'll know I'm home and I've not forgotten him.'

She opened the back door and walked the few steps to the garage, knocked on the door and waited. No answer, but she could hear voices and wasn't sure if he was on the phone, doing a video chat, or if there was someone in there with him. She knocked again. 'I made you a cup of tea,' she called, her ear to the door. The voices didn't stop. One of them sounded like a woman.

She listened, heard a tinkling laugh. Definitely a woman. Her scalp prickled and she knocked again, harder this time, a proper rapetty-rap-rap-rap! The voices went quiet and she tensed, remembering how annoyed he'd been the last time she'd interrupted with a drink a couple of days ago.

'I'm running a bloody business,' he'd snapped. 'Trying to be professional. And it doesn't look great if there's someone in the background shouting through the door. I've got video meetings going on.' She'd thought she was being supportive, but the force of his stare had made her feel two inches tall. 'You're making me look like an amateur.'

She'd winced, completely understanding his point. Her cheeks felt like they were on fire and she'd hung her head, not wanting him to see the tears welling up. He'd relented then, put a hand on her shoulder and given it a rub. 'Sorry, love. I didn't mean to have a go at you. I know you're trying to help, but the best thing is to just leave me to it. This is a sensitive business I'm dealing with and it's taken me a while to persuade the client that I have the correct safeguards in place to ensure their data will be secure. You shouting that you've got a cup of tea for me sort of undermines everything I'm trying to do here.'

She'd pressed her lips together, clenching her teeth as her emotions built to a crescendo. She took little breaths through her nose, counting backwards in her head, a technique she had for fighting off tears. It was a trick her mother had taught her after one of her boyfriends had given Sara a whack for having a meltdown about something.

Matt's voice had droned on, a background noise, while she counted. 'I've got Josh coming to put a sink in next week, then I can make my own brews. In the meantime, I'll sort myself out. Okay?'

When she noticed that he'd stopped talking she'd nodded, still too choked-up to speak. It was so hard to do the right thing at the moment. If she left him to his own devices, he was all cheery and chirpy, but as soon as she tried to help in any way, she was either fussing or interfering. He definitely didn't want her involved in his business, and that hurt, given her qualifications.

She understood that he was a control freak about his work and consoled herself that it was just his nature, nothing to do with her. He wanted to get it right. Wanted to secure this first contract, then their money worries would be a thing of the past and he could be the breadwinner again, the figurehead of his family. She wanted to do her utmost to make sure he succeeded, in the hope that family life might return to a semblance of normality. So on the whole she did as he asked and left him to it, even if it did go against the nurturing side of her nature.

Now, with his mug of tea in her hand, she remembered the conversation and did a U-turn back to the kitchen, hoping he hadn't heard her, ready to deny she'd even been there. *Who was the woman he was talking to, though?* She tipped his tea down the sink and rinsed the cup, so he wouldn't know of her mistake.

Shaking the question from her mind, she sat back down at the table and remembered that her earlier question had gone unanswered. Why was Hailey here in the first place?

'Did Matt ring you? Ask you to come round?' She frowned. 'Because that's not fair if he did.'

Hailey took a big glug of her tea, put her mug down. 'No. I've been having a bit of a clear-out now Cassie's away. I was sorting through her clothes and there's loads of stuff she's grown out of that I thought might fit the girls.'

'Oh, right. Good. Thank you.' It wasn't what Sara was expecting to hear and it put her on the back foot for a moment. She looked around for bags of clothes. 'Go on then, let's have a look at what you've got.'

Hailey gave an embarrassed laugh, a flush of pink colouring her cheeks. 'That's the stupid thing. I packed it all up in bags and managed to leave them at home. Honestly, I'd forget my head if it wasn't screwed on.'

Sara stared at her sister, who was picking at a bit of egg that was stuck to the table, left over from breakfast. She had the definite feeling there was something Hailey wasn't telling her, the clothes an excuse to cover up the real reason why she was in her house. *But then I'm not being up-front either, am I?*

She chewed at her lip – on the brink of telling Hailey what she'd done – then stopped herself. Hailey worked in a position of trust and had a close relationship with the police, several of the young people she worked with being ex-offenders or deemed to be at risk of offending. *What if she tells me to confess or go to the police?* She gave an involuntary shiver, knew she couldn't risk it. She couldn't quiz Hailey about the real reason she was in her house either, because getting secrets out of her sister was a tricky challenge at the best of times – she had a tendency to go on the attack, winning arguments between them by shouting the loudest, which would upset Ezra. Ruin the whole evening trying to settle him down again.

They drank their tea in silence, Sara thinking that her life was veering out of control, the people around her dancing to a tune she couldn't hear, moving to a rhythm she couldn't grasp. She rubbed the muscles at the back of her neck, where the tension tended to knot them together, staring at the table, eyes unfocused as her thoughts whirled on a continuous loop.

'I'm not sure this full-time working is doing you any good,' Hailey said, apropos of nothing. Sara glanced across at her, saw concern in her eyes. 'You're looking stressed. What you need is a spa day. A bit of pampering and relaxation.'

Sara huffed. 'Chance would be a fine thing. It's not something we can afford at the moment. And I'm fine, thanks.' She gave her sister a watery smile. 'Honestly. It's just a new routine, that's all. With all the changes, It's taking time to settle into the swing of things.'

Hailey finished her tea and stood up. 'Well, I'll get out of your hair.' She slung her bag over her shoulder and grinned. 'See you at football practice on Thursday.'

Sara watched her go, so many concerns filling her head, all the unanswered questions building up to create an almighty headache.

She got up and found some paracetamol in the cupboard, swallowed them down and massaged her temples.

As a mother, she'd always been at the heart of her family, but since Matt had started his business and she'd been working full-time, she felt on the edge of everything, out of touch with her family's lives.

Something's going to change, she promised herself.

THIRTEEN

Once the paracetamol had begun to take effect and her headache had subsided, Sara was clearer about how to put her world to rights. She was not going to do anything too confrontational, nothing up-front and accusatory, even though a voice in her head was shouting at her to ask her family over their evening meal what the bloody hell was going on and why none of them were talking to her about it.

She would bide her time, wait for the right moment.

Typically, the girls and Matt disappeared as soon as they'd eaten, while she was still struggling to get Ezra to finish off the last of his vegetables. Once he was settled in bed, though, she popped her head round the door of the girls' room, where they were lying on the floor watching something on the laptop.

She noticed their wide eyes, the shocked expressions when they saw her in the doorway, before Amelia tapped a few keys and slammed the laptop shut. Sara frowned. What were they watching? They had parental controls on the internet, but she was never sure how effective they were. The girls seemed to be addicted to YouTube, people playing practical jokes and doing weird tricks. Or they watched football training. That was what they told her anyway.

'Mum, you can't just walk in,' Sophia snapped. 'You've got to knock!'

Amelia's face was blotchy – red round the eyes like she'd been crying – and she turned away, got up and started tidying the clothes that lay strewn all over her bed. She was the messy one. Sophia was the opposite. Two halves of a whole.

'Since when?' Sara asked, hands on her hips. This was the first she'd heard of it, and she objected to Sophia's tone of voice.

'Since we stopped being little girls,' Sophia said, sitting back on her heels.

'You all right, Milly?' Sara advanced into the room, concerned that Amelia was upset, but she turned round with a big grin on her face.

''Course I am. We were just watching these funny videos and it made me laugh so much I was crying. Didn't you hear us? Soph told me off for being too loud in case I woke Ezra.'

Sara studied her face, knew there was more to it. She sat on Amelia's bed, next to the pile of clothes. 'I just wanted to thank you both for all the extra jobs you've being doing round the house since I've been working more. It's been a big help.'

The girls shared a look. Sophia leant against her bed. Amelia went to sit next to her. 'That's okay,' Amelia said with a sniff, bowing her head as she swiped her hands across her face. Sara wasn't buying the crying-with-laughter story. She knew her daughter, and Amelia was definitely upset.

'Look, you two. I know there's something going on. And I just wish…' She stopped herself, the tone all wrong. Tried again, her voice softer, the accusation gone. 'I want you to know that I'm here for you both. If you've got a problem…' she gave what she hoped was a reassuring smile, 'well, I can help you.'

The girls stared at her, nodded in unison, their faces blank. She waited. The silence filled her ears, tension crackling through the air like static.

'I heard you say to Auntie Hailey that you'd been having a chat. It's nice that you can do that, isn't it?'

The girls nodded again.

'But I'd really like it if you'd chat to me too.' Emotion swelled in Sara's chest, her voice cracking. 'I just feel that recently I've been closed out of your lives, and I... well, I miss you.'

The girls looked uneasy now, shuffling closer together on the bed, Amelia's arm snaking round Sophia's waist. Solidarity.

'You don't have time to chat, Mum. That's the problem,' Sophia said eventually. 'Auntie Hailey is used to talking to people our age. She knows what goes on.'

Sara frowned, hurt stabbing at her heart, making her voice waver. 'We live together, I've known you all your lives. I'm used to talking to kids your age too, aren't I?'

The girls glanced at each other.

'And what does go on?'

'It's nothing,' Amelia said, sounding a bit annoyed. 'Just some lad playing jokes, that's all. Auntie Hailey knows him – he's one of the lads she looks after in her job – so that's why it was good to talk to her. You wouldn't...'

Sara swallowed her frustration, her voice shaking. 'I wouldn't what?'

Amelia looked away, picked at her peeling nail varnish. 'Nothing.'

'But it is something, isn't it?'

'Don't go on, Mum,' Sophia said, glaring at her. She put an arm round her sister's shoulders. 'We've done nothing wrong. All we did was chat to Auntie Hailey. She was here, we talked to her. It would be bad manners to ignore her, wouldn't it?'

Sara couldn't argue with the logic and recognised that she wasn't going to get any further. 'Sorry.' She smiled and backtracked – aware of how delicate a mother's relationship with teenage daughters could be – and tiptoed back across the eggshells to firmer ground. 'I'm not getting at anyone. Not at all. I just feel a bit left out these days.'

Sophia locked eyes with her before she spoke. 'Well maybe if you were here, like you used to be, we'd be able to talk to you more.'

Sara closed her eyes for a moment, unable to meet the challenge of her daughter's stare. Because it was true. 'I have to work since Dad lost his job. I really don't have a choice. And there'd be plenty of time to talk in the evenings if you weren't stuck in here or over at Chelsea's or…' She was going to say 'playing football', but that was their passion, and she didn't want them to feel bad about it. She forced a smile. In the past she would have suggested a shopping trip to Leeds, something they'd always enjoyed, but now money was tight, that was no longer an option. She'd have to have a think, see if she could come up with something that didn't cost a lot but would feel like a treat and help them to bond again.

Maybe football's the answer, she thought, as she stood up. The way we can reconnect. She'd left that side of things to Matt – it was his passion as well – and it was tricky keeping Ezra happy through a whole match so it was easier for her to go and do something different with him. She'd always thought it was nice for the girls and Matt to have a shared interest, but she realised now that she should have made more of an effort to be involved.

'Well, I'll definitely come to footie practice on Thursday,' she said, with an enthusiastic grin. 'I'm looking forward to it.'

Sophia snorted. 'Bet you only do it once, Mum.'

Amelia wouldn't look at her, and she could feel the weight of her daughters' disappointment sitting on her shoulders. I've let them down, she thought as she said goodnight and left their room, closing the door behind her. She waited for a moment, but they were both silent, no doubt waiting to hear her footsteps walk down the hall before they said anything.

Still a mystery, then. But something's bothering them.

She went back downstairs, made herself another cup of tea and rang Hailey. Best to do it while she was all fired up, otherwise it would get put off and she'd never get to the bottom of whatever was bothering the girls. It seemed to be Amelia's problem, and Sophia was trying to help her sort it out. Or was she making assumptions? The two girls were so different, it was hard to know. Sophia had a hard exterior and a soft centre, and Amelia was more sensitive, wore her heart on her sleeve.

After a few rings, Hailey's voicemail answered. Sara was about to leave a message, then decided that she probably wasn't in the right frame of mind. It would come out all wrong. Like an accusation. Better to wait until Thursday. They'd have plenty of time to chat at football practice, and Hailey was less likely to get in a tizzy if there were other parents around. She nodded to herself. It was only two days away. Not long, and in the meantime, she'd keep a closer eye on the girls, see if she could find out what the problem really was.

She went into the lounge to watch TV while she waited for Matt to come in, but when the ten o'clock news began, her eyes started to close, tiredness engulfing her. She'd never imagined that working full-time would be so hard. In her mind it was a mental challenge, something she was desperate for, but she'd overlooked the sheer physical effort of getting three kids up and ready for school, feeding them, doing all the laundry and the shopping, keeping the house in some semblance of order and sorting out childcare when Matt couldn't do it.

Thank goodness it's only for a month, she thought as she turned off the TV and dragged herself up to bed. There was still no sign of Matt.

As she lay staring at the ceiling – the house still and quiet – she heard the murmur of conversation drift in through the open window. It sounded like it was coming from right underneath it, although it couldn't be, because their house stood back from the road. A tinkling laugh. Just like the one she'd heard coming from the garage earlier.

Sound travels at night, she told herself, but she was wide awake now, ears straining to hear every sound. The click of heels, the

clink of a gate opening and closing. *That's our gate.* She was sure
of it – the weird clang it made – and she clambered out of bed,
rushed to the window and peeked out, but there was nobody to
be seen in the darkness of the night.

The back door thumped shut. That couldn't be a coincidence,
Matt coming in just after someone had gone out of their gate.

Fired up, she hurried downstairs to the kitchen, where Matt
was standing looking in the fridge, his hair sticking up all over the
place. He turned when he saw her, gave a sheepish grin. 'Just going
to make some supper. I completely lost track of time out there.'

'Who was that woman?' She hadn't meant to go on the attack,
but she couldn't help herself.

He frowned, looked confused. 'What woman?'

'The one who was in your office just now. I heard her leave.'
Sara's voice was getting louder, higher, her finger jabbing the air.

He laughed, looked back in the fridge. 'I think you must have
been dreaming, love. Nobody in the office except me.' He pulled
out a packet of ham and the tub of margarine, opened the bread
bin and slapped a couple of slices of bread onto the worktop. He
turned. 'Shall I make you one as well?' The kettle came to the
boil. 'Cuppa?'

His nonchalance whipped her anger away. She shook her head
and made her way back to bed, thoroughly puzzled. *Was I dreaming?*

FOURTEEN

Sara woke the next day to the sound of Matt singing in the shower. She felt groggy and unsettled as she fumbled her way out of sleep. Working full-time was exhausting, and poor Matt had been doing it without a murmur of complaint for all these years. She hadn't appreciated his efforts, she realised; had focused instead on her own niggles of discontent, always wanting a bit of what he had. Now she wasn't sure why she'd felt like that. She wanted things to go back to how they were. Was that possible?

Be careful what you wish for. Who'd said that to her? It might have been Fiona. She had a saying for every occasion and liked her daily motivational posts, which popped up on her phone. Or maybe it was Hailey. She couldn't remember, but it had struck her as an odd saying at the time. Now she understood. Thank goodness half-term was only two weeks away, at which point her full-time stint would have finished and she could take some time off. Then she'd take a step back and decide what she really wanted.

In her heart, she already knew. Family had to come first, and working full-time while Matt got his business going was part of keeping their home life stable. It was disruptive as well, though, because while she was out all day, the housework wasn't being done, they kept running out of things, which meant a dash to the shops, the kitchen floor was... She stopped her mental list, knowing that she'd feel more despondent if she laid it all out.

Something's got to change, she decided. And it meant a proper conversation with Matt. Although that might be a struggle, given the shift system they seemed to be working at the moment, never in the house at the same time without the kids around. No opportunity for a proper heart-to-heart.

Thoroughly distracted, she stumbled out of bed when she heard Matt come out of the shower and passed him in the doorway, hardly awake enough to acknowledge his presence. A routine done on autopilot. She leant against the tiles, letting the hot water run over her body, shampooed her hair and thought about the corner she'd boxed herself into.

Her wage was the only money coming in to the house until Matt's contract paid out, but they hadn't spoken recently about where he was up to, and she wondered how much longer it would be. The mortgage payments would start again in a couple of months, and by that time, it would be the summer holidays. Maybe she'd have to continue her part-time hours through the break to keep some money coming in. But would Matt be happy with that when the kids were at home?

Already her head was throbbing as she tried to work out what was best for everyone.

When she got down to the kitchen, Matt was tucking into scrambled eggs on toast.

'You're up early,' he said before stuffing another forkful of food in his mouth, eating like he had a train to catch and was running late.

She'd assumed that it was their regular getting-up time, but when she glanced at the kitchen clock, she saw it was an hour earlier than she'd thought. She groaned and flopped into a chair at the kitchen table. 'What the...' She checked the clock again to make sure. 'You mean, on the one morning that Ezra has actually stayed asleep and not woken me up, I could have had another hour in bed?' She dropped her elbows onto the table and cradled her head in her hands.

Matt got up and made her a coffee, slid it in front of her. 'There you go, that'll help.'

She sat back in her chair, hugging the mug to her chest, breathing in the welcome aroma, while she waited for it to cool. It was a moment before her brain cleared a little and she understood what was puzzling her. 'Why are you up so early?'

Matt chewed his mouthful, swallowed. 'I'd hit a bit of a roadblock. It's a puzzle I needed to solve, but I think I just worked it out.' He grinned at her. 'Woke up at five, and *ping*, there it was, the answer. I just want to get on with it before I forget.'

She nodded, sipped her coffee and realised this was the moment she'd been waiting for. Just her and Matt, no kids. A chance to have a proper conversation. She cleared her throat. 'You know, Matt, I hate to say this, but you were right about me going full-time. It's not really working, is it? I never see you, and when I get time with the kids, I'm too tired to enjoy it. I don't think it's good for any of us.'

Matt stopped chewing and stared at her. She carried on, glad to have his full attention. 'My full-time contract finishes in a couple of weeks, though, so it should get easier when I go back to part-time, but I was just wondering if—'

'What do you mean, it finishes in a couple of weeks?' He looked horrified.

She frowned, not sure why this came as a surprise to him. 'I told you it was only temporary.'

He dropped his knife and fork onto his plate, pushed the remains of his breakfast away. 'I'm nowhere near finishing this piece of work.' He shook his head. 'I need another month at least, and even that's...' He grimaced, ran a hand through his hair. 'No, it's going to take longer than that probably.'

Sara's stomach swirled as the implications started to register. 'Well, it's half-term in a couple of weeks, and I've got to be home when the kids are off school.'

'But we need the money, Sara, can't you see that?' He banged the table in frustration, making her jump, spilling hot coffee onto her lap. 'We've got the delay on the mortgage, and the bank are happy with the extension to our overdraft, but all that was agreed on the basis of you working full-time. If money suddenly stops going into our account, we'll be in real trouble.' He wiped his hands over his face. 'I'm so close to cracking this thing. So close. But I can't do it if I'm under pressure.'

He stared at her. She stared back, icy fingers clawing at the nape of her neck.

'So I've got to see if the community centre will keep me on full-time, is that what you're saying?'

'Yes. That's exactly what I'm saying. I'm sure the girls will help out with Ezra in the holidays, and I can work evenings like I do now. But honestly, Sara, I need to keep going with it. We're talking a couple of months at the most, then it'll be done.'

She bit her lip, the idea of missing half-term with the children almost too much to bear.

'I thought you'd support me in this.' His stare hardened, his voice sharpening. 'I've done everything I could to support our family, and now I'm asking you to do for two months what I've done for years and you're making a fuss.'

Sara shook her head, a tinge of desperation in her voice. 'I'm not making a fuss. I'm just exhausted.'

He gave a frustrated sigh. 'You wanted to work full-time. It's what you've wanted ever since you started that job.'

'I know, but I've got all the other jobs to do as well. Me working full-time is not the same as you working full-time.'

His eyes widened and he reeled back in his chair, mouth gaping. 'Are you saying I'm not pulling my weight?'

Sara looked at her mug, regretting her words. She wasn't up to a fight, didn't have the energy to go through all the things he took for granted. Things he didn't even notice she did around the home.

He got up, pushed his chair back under the table. 'I'm doing this for us.' He leant forwards, hands on the back of the chair.

'I'm doing my best. But it's never bloody good enough for you, is it? You always want more. Well, I don't have any more to give. This is me doing the best I can, and if it's not good enough, then maybe we need to think about a different future. One that better suits all of us.'

His words landed like a weight on her chest, sudden and shocking, taking her breath away.

He turned and stormed out of the back door, slamming it behind him. She heard the office door open and close. He didn't mean it, she told herself with a shake of her head, as if that would put all her thoughts back to where they'd been before their conversation. *But what if he did?*

She arrived at work feeling flustered and definitely not equal to the myriad tasks she had lined up for the day, her mind fixated on her row with Matt and his final words. A couple of groups were booked in to the centre, and one was using the kitchen for a course about healthy eating for families. There was a lot to organise. And the board meeting was coming up, so she had reports to prepare for that, as well as a list of information Fiona wanted to have a look at for a new project that was under development.

By the time James arrived at noon to go through the board meeting papers, she was teetering on the edge of losing control. He gave her a warm smile and shrugged off his coat, hung it on the hook behind the office door.

'Are you okay, Sara?' He frowned. 'You look a little... out of sorts.'

She shuffled a bundle of papers together for him, unable to meet his eye. 'Fine. I'm fine,' she said, her voice cracking. She handed him the documents and sat opposite, ready to go through them. 'It's going to be a bit of a struggle to get everything ready this afternoon, though.' She straightened the pages in front of her, vision blurry as sudden tears filled her eyes. 'Do you think it will matter if the reports don't go out until tomorrow?'

'Hmm, Fiona's a bit of a stickler for making sure people have time to read everything, isn't she?' Although he hadn't directly said it, the answer was yes, it did matter. She would have to stay late now if she was going to get everything done.

A tear escaped and ran down her cheek. She gritted her teeth and wiped it away. *Get a grip, will you?* But none of her techniques for calming herself down were working. Another tear escaped. Thankfully, James didn't notice as he scanned the agenda and flicked through the supporting papers. He asked her a question, and she fidgeted in her seat as she counted backwards again, willing the tears to stop, not hearing a word he said.

'Hey, you're not okay, are you?' James's concern broke her concentration, and her emotions took control. She couldn't look at him – mortified that she'd got herself so upset – and now the first tears had escaped, more soon followed, her body shaking with the effort of stopping the sobs that wanted to erupt from her throat.

His hand stretched across the desk and rubbed her arm. 'Is there anything I can do? Can I get you a drink or something?' He handed her the box of tissues and she took one, wiping her face, her cheeks burning with shame. *Why am I being such an idiot? You can't do this at work. Come on, shape up!*

She heard him get up and leave the room, and she took a few deep breaths, pinching the bridge of her nose as she tried to stem the flow of tears. By the time he came back, carrying a tray with drinks and cookies that the group of mums in the kitchen had been baking, she'd managed to calm herself enough to stop crying and at least felt able to speak.

James put the tray on the desk. 'Look, you can tell me to mind my own business if you like, but if there's anything you want to talk about, I'm happy to listen.' He shrugged. 'It helps to share, doesn't it?'

She let out a long breath, felt that she owed him an explanation if they were going to put this behind them and get on with the meeting. 'Oh, I had a row with Matt before work this morning and it's thrown me. He's completely focused on setting up his business and... well, my full-time month comes to an end in a couple of weeks but he says we can't afford for me to stop and I need to be more supportive. I'm so worried about money, but then there's the kids...' She halted, embarrassed, her mind in knots. 'I feel so torn.' Her voice clogged with tears. 'I don't know what to do for the best.'

He took a cookie, then held out the plate to her. 'Special recipe. Low sugar, high fibre, apparently.' She watched him take a bite and nod appreciatively. 'Not bad.' He gave her a reassuring smile and she noticed, for the first time, that he had dimples.

'Okay, well... I've been meaning to talk to you about hours. Other than Christmas, this is the busiest time of year for Dad's business, so I really have to be there more over the summer months. I've already spoken to Fiona and said that I can only do a day a week for the foreseeable future, and she's agreed to continue your full-time hours until September.' He raised an eyebrow. 'I was going to talk to you about it when we'd gone through these papers, but you beat me to it. Does that help?'

Sara sighed, threw up her hands. 'But the point is, I can't do it. I've got the kids. I can't do everything.'

'Well, I don't think you're in a position to refuse, are you?'

She looked at him, startled. 'What do you mean?' *Is he going to force me to do it? Can he do that?*

'If you're the breadwinner at the moment, the show must go on, mustn't it? It's just how life works, unfortunately. If you and Matt have switched roles, then childcare is surely his concern, not yours.' He finished his cookie, wiped crumbs from his lips with a tissue. 'Looking at things in the round, if the two of you are a team, then I'd say, however much you don't want to hear this, you need to work full-time.' He held up his hands. 'Your call, although Fiona was insistent that you wanted full-time hours, and if you decide that you will do the job over the summer… well, you'd be doing me a favour.'

She blinked. A favour? She'd thought the favours he'd previously alluded to were like interest payments on the debt she owed him – something she had to do before she found the cash to pay him back – but now she wondered if there was another possibility, a way to get rid of the debt faster. Was it going to sound cheeky? She cleared her throat, urged herself on. 'Can I ask if you'd consider this favour as part repayment for the debt?'

She held her breath, waiting for his answer.

He took a sip of his tea. Considered for a moment before he spoke. 'Well, if you want it to be, I suppose we could take it into account. But I'd still need you to come to events with me.'

He was being obtuse. She frowned. 'But you'd take a favour instead of money? I mean, by doing this, I'd reduce my debt to you?'

He pursed his lips, nodded. 'Yes, why not. If it makes you feel better and it gives us both what we need, then yes.'

They sat in silence for a moment while she thought it through, relieved by his answer but slightly annoyed with Fiona for making assumptions without speaking to her first. Still, she had asked Fiona for the extra hours and hadn't really spoken to her since, assuming that she'd know she would want to stop for school holidays, same as she'd done at Easter.

Christ, life's got complicated!

She sighed. James was right, she didn't have a choice.

'It's okay, I'll work over half-term. And keep doing full-time over the summer.' She wondered how she'd tell the kids. But at least Matt would be happy now, and as James had said, if they'd swapped roles, then sorting out childcare was as much Matt's responsibility as hers.

'Excellent.' James smiled at her and picked up another cookie, but hesitated before taking a bite. 'Talking about our deal… I have a networking meeting next week. In Harrogate. There's a dinner on the Thursday night if you're free? It's a new thing, organised by a local business group I've just been introduced to, where suppliers and buyers get together. Apparently, there's a lot of potential to strike good deals, so I really could do with your help. Getting the right price on stock can save us thousands.'

Thursday. Why did that ring a bell? *Football practice.* The girls would be livid if she missed it after promising she'd go and support them.

She shook her head. 'I can't make next Thursday.'

'Oh, I think you can,' he said.

FIFTEEN

Sara blinked, a shimmer of dread running through her. James gave an exasperated sigh, fingers tugging at his beard. 'I'm sorry, that came out wrong. I'm just panicking, you see. I really must be there, and everyone's taking a plus-one. If I don't have a partner, I'll look like Billy-no-mates – which is close to the truth, if I'm honest, but it makes me seem… I don't know, vulnerable, I suppose, and that's never a good negotiating position, is it?' He gave her a sheepish grin. 'I thought with it being over a week away, there'd be plenty of time for you to sort out babysitting. So I bought two tickets and, well… I need you there.' His eyes met hers, and in that moment, she felt sorry for him. 'It's what we agreed, isn't it?'

She put her cookie down, the smell of it making her feel nauseous now. She thought about the stolen money, how James had put himself in danger of reprisals to conceal her crime. She felt ungrateful. Unprofessional. They'd made a deal and she had to stick to it, and to be honest, he wasn't asking a lot, was he? Going to a sales dinner with him didn't sound that onerous. *What choice do I have?*

'Okay.' She forced a smile. 'I'm sorry, James. I know we have a deal, and of course I'll stick to it. Thursday night is football practice for the girls, you see, but my sister said she could take them, so maybe there isn't a problem. I'll talk to her tomorrow, see if I can arrange it.'

A relieved grin lit up his face, eyes sparkling. 'Excellent. I'll look forward to it, and I think you might quite enjoy yourself.

It'll take you out of your normal environment – and you know they say a change is as good as a rest.'

She nodded, hoping it was true, even as her mind presented her with the real problem. *What am I going to tell Matt?*

The next day, the fine weather had been replaced by a drizzly rain and Sara wasn't enjoying the hour and a half she had to spend on the touchline while her daughters did their football practice. But she'd promised, and it was especially important to keep her word now that she knew she'd miss the following week. They seemed excited she was there, but she wondered if it might have more to do with the promise of treats afterwards. I wish Hailey could have come, she thought as she stomped her damp feet, trying to keep them warm. There'd been a change in plans because Hailey's service user was ill, and with no obligation to be at football, she'd ended up staying at the house with Ezra so Matt could work and Sara could have a bit of time alone with the girls.

Sara moved from foot to foot, her trainers squelching, socks soaked through, glad to see her girls enjoying themselves but unsure exactly what the appeal of football might be. When the final whistle blew, she could have wept with relief.

The girls came running over, red-cheeked and mud-splattered, while the rest of the squad headed to the dressing rooms.

'Let's go, Mum,' Sophia said, slinging her bag over her shoulder, Amelia doing the same.

Sara frowned. 'What? Aren't you going for a shower? Don't you want to get changed?'

'Nah,' Sophia said. 'The showers are grotty here. I'd rather wait till we get home.'

'I was going to take you for a McDonald's, remember?' Sara looked at her mucky daughters and shooed them away. 'Go on. It'll only take ten minutes. Then we can have a nice chat while we eat. I feel like I haven't had a chance to catch up with what you're doing for ages.'

Amelia shook her head. 'Not happening, Mum. We decided we're not using the showers here, didn't we, Soph?'

Sophia nodded, and the two of them started walking towards the car park.

'I suppose we can get a takeaway instead,' Sara said as she followed. She wondered if there was trouble with other members of the team and that was why they didn't want a shower. She decided she wouldn't push it. Girls that age were always falling out with each other, and it would probably blow over and be back to normal by the following week.

It was after eight by the time they got home, and Hailey was watching TV, Ezra asleep upstairs. Sara heard the back door close and frowned. 'Was Matt just here?'

'Matt? Yes, he came in for a break, and he bathed Ezra. They had a right old time up there. Took me a while to clear up, but I've never heard Ezra laugh so much.' Hailey gave an indulgent smile. 'He's such a good dad, isn't he? Don't you wish we'd had a dad like that?' A lump formed in Sara's throat and she couldn't say anything. Hailey seemed oblivious and carried on. 'He's just gone back out to do some more work, he said. Make up for lost time. It's such a juggling act for him now you're out working.'

Sara pulled off her wet shoes while she tried to formulate a fitting response. Hailey was making it sound like Matt was doing everything, with no regard for her input and sacrifices. She could feel her temper rising and went to put her shoes in the hall while she calmed down.

'Hey,' she heard Hailey say to the girls when they walked into the lounge. 'Good session?'

Sara hurried into the room after them, determined to assert herself a bit more. She felt she was becoming invisible even to her sister. 'I'm so impressed, Hailey. You should have seen them.' She gave a wry smile. 'Obviously take after their father.'

'We're both in the first team, Auntie Hailey,' Sophia said, the excitement clear in her voice. 'The usual goalie dislocated a finger on Saturday, so I get to take her place.'

'And I'm going to be in defence,' Amelia said. 'Coach said my tackles were awesome tonight. Didn't he, Mum?'

'He did, and they were.' Sara looked at the girls, clapped her hands. 'Right, you two, go and get showers. Football kit in the washing machine, okay? I don't want it dumped in the bathroom.'

The girls wandered off and Sara sat down next to her sister. A shiver ran through her and she wrapped her arms round her chest. 'I'm bloody freezing.' She glanced at Hailey. 'In fact, I might just nip up and get a shower myself to warm up. If I'm not quick, they'll have used all the hot water. Why they couldn't have had a shower at the club like everyone else, I've no idea. But they were adamant they didn't want to.'

Hailey shrugged. 'They always have done when I've been there.'

'I think there must have been a falling-out or something. Maybe a bit of jealousy from some of the other girls that they're both in the team.'

Sara was about to go and get her shower when she remembered about the following Thursday. Her evening out with James and the clash with football practice.

'I don't suppose you'd be able to take the girls next week, would you? It's just… I have a meeting at work that I need to go to. It's… um, it's…' She looked away, her foot scuffing at a stain on the carpet. 'They're doing a training course. You know, with board members being volunteers it has to be done in the evening, as most of them have jobs. And it's a bit of a team-building thing, going for a drink after.' She glanced at Hailey, who was giving her a curious look. 'It's in Harrogate. I've got a lift back, but I might be late.'

Her sister stared at her for a moment, then nodded. 'Okay. Yes. I'm happy to take them, but Matt will have to keep an eye on Ezra, because you know Ez hates going to the football. And it depends what comes up at work, but it should be okay.'

Sara gave her a grateful smile. 'It's just a one-off.'

It's not, though, is it? she thought as she went upstairs and pulled off her damp clothes before getting in the shower. Lying to her sister felt horrible. *What's it going to be like lying to Matt?* She scrubbed at her skin, turned the water a little hotter, as if that would scald the thought from her mind.

She considered Matt's behaviour. He was being a bit secretive, shut away in his office. And she'd been sure she'd heard someone – a woman – leave late the night before. The idea that he was having an affair resurfaced and scratched at her skin as she dried herself, rubbing harder as if that would remove all trace of her doubts.

He wouldn't, she told herself. He wouldn't put his family life at risk. It was as sacred to him as it was to her, of that she was sure. But his comments that morning couldn't be ignored, and now she wondered if she was right. Basically, he was questioning whether he wanted to be in a relationship with her if she didn't play by his rules. Wasn't that what he'd said? And that felt harsh. Very harsh. It also made her wonder if he had an alternative future lined up for himself. *Is that what he's working on now?* And wasn't it strange that he went back out to his office the minute she got home? *Like he's avoiding me.*

With her thoughts completely scrambled, she got herself dressed and headed back downstairs, where she found Hailey in the kitchen making mugs of tea.

'Is everything okay?' she asked, pouring milk into the mugs. 'It's just you seem a little… fraught.'

Sara leant against the worktop and let out a big sigh, which said it all really, without the need for words. Hailey came and gave her a hug, murmuring into her hair, 'It's just a tricky patch, that's all. You've got to trust Matt to come through in the end. He will, Sara. He's determined. We had quite a chat tonight.'

Sara sank into the hug, laying her head on her sister's shoulder. 'I just feel like I'm losing everything. Even the kids don't seem to notice me any more. I'm out at work all day, then I've got to catch up with the housework at night and all the other stuff that goes with running a house and having three kids. I mean, the paperwork just for school is ridiculous. Then there's dentist's appointments and play dates and sleepovers and friends' birthdays and...' She took a deep breath, anxiety mounting, her voice rising with it, as she listed everything. 'Then on top of that I've got stuff to remember for work and I just don't think I'm doing well at any of it.'

Hailey rubbed her back. 'You're doing great, honestly you are. Maybe this evening out next week is just what you need. I know it's a training course, but enjoy the social after and don't worry what time you get back. Just be you, instead of a mum and wife and housekeeper and administrator.' She squeezed her a little tighter, gave her a kiss on the cheek then pulled away, one hand lingering on her shoulder as she looked her in the eye. 'I'll make sure I can take the girls. Honestly, don't you worry.'

Sara covered Hailey's hand with her own. 'Thanks, I needed that.' She studied her sister's face. 'I was wondering... Your conversation with Matt... did he mention anything...' She hesitated, then decided while Hailey was in a supportive mood, she could do with a bit more reassurance. 'It's just we had a row this morning, and I've had this feeling... Well, I heard a woman's voice in his office last night. I'm sure of it. Then he was late coming to bed and the window was open and I thought I heard her again. Outside. I heard the gate clang shut. I had a look but couldn't see anything.'

Hailey looked a little startled. 'What? You're not still worry-ing about that, are you? I can remember a similar conversation about him working late and you thinking he had someone else, but it turned out to be nothing. Do you remember, you had me following him from work?'

Sara nodded, heat creeping into her cheeks. *Perhaps I am imagining it.*

'You're just feeling a bit unsettled, which is natural with all the changes, but I don't think you've anything to worry about. He's a straight arrow, is Matt.' Hailey picked up her tea while she carried on talking. 'As far as I can tell, he's still upset that he lost his job. Feels he's let you all down, but he's determined to make this business a success.' She looked at Sara. 'Honestly, I've never seen him so fired up and passionate about anything. And he loves the fact he gets to spend time with his kids.'

Sara picked up her mug and took a sip, letting her sister's words settle in her mind. She was right. Maybe she *had* heard the woman in her dreams the previous night and thought she was real. That was very possible.

Her mind was being devious, deflecting attention from herself. If anything was going to tear the family apart, it was her own actions. She would be the one to blame.

SIXTEEN

The next day, James came into the office to drop off some figures he'd been working on for the new project.

'I wonder if you could ask Fiona to run her eye over these when she's in later.' He held out a file. 'Deadline's on Monday and she's getting twitchy. You know what she's like. Has to dot every i and cross every t herself. But I've got all the supporting documents together, so I think we're about there.'

Sara had work to do on the project herself and was reminded now that she needed to push it up her list of tasks. 'No problem,' she said, and took the file from him, slapping it on the desk on top of the other papers.

James cocked his head, looked at her. 'Things any better today? You still look a little peaky.'

She caught his eye and sighed. He sat down on the other side of the desk and she looked away, gathering up the invoices she'd been sorting out. 'Everything's okay for next Thursday, if that's what you're worried about.'

'I'm worried about you, actually.'

She glanced at him and saw genuine concern in his eyes. Those very blue eyes, which held her in their steady gaze as she tried to work out what she was feeling, what was pulling at her insides, making her want to reach out to him.

'Look, I never meant to cause trouble,' he said gently. 'I've only ever wanted to help you. That's all.' He gave her a quick grin. 'Tell you what. How about I take you out to lunch? I need to brief you for next Thursday anyway, and it'll do you good to get out of the office.'

Sara gave a brisk shake of her head. 'Sorry, I don't think I've got time.' She indicated the piles of paperwork on her desk. 'I've got all the project application forms to go through. Not to mention getting the monthly accounts ready for Julia. She's coming in with Fiona tonight. They're having a working supper, so I've got to organise food for them as well.' Her voice sounded as weary as she felt.

'I do believe I'm your boss,' he said firmly. 'And as I'm responsible for your health and welfare at work, I'm insisting you take a lunch break. Just an hour, that's all, then you'll feel energised and refreshed and you'll work twice as fast this afternoon.' He stood up, checked his watch. 'Come on. We're going. We'll get served quicker if we're there early.'

Sara looked at her desk – the mass of papers strewn across the surface – and a flare of panic burned through her chest. Her stomach gurgled. *I can't, though, can I?*

James turned at the door and beckoned to her, eyebrows raised when she didn't move.

She gave a tentative smile. Why not? she thought. I'm supposed to get a lunch hour and never take it. Maybe I *will* feel better afterwards. It was starting to sound like a good idea, and anyway, James wasn't going to take no for an answer.

She followed him outside, where his racing-green Audi TT was parked, gleaming in the sunshine. It was another warm May day, and the cherry trees that surrounded the car park were in full bloom, their pink petals coating the ground around them like confetti. He opened the door for her and waited for her to get settled in the seat before he closed it and went round to the driver's side.

An unexpected thrill of excitement fizzled through her. She'd never been in such a posh car before. Leather seats. No empty crisp packets or sweet wrappers or drinks cartons stuffed in the pockets of the doors or littering the floor. The whole interior was immaculate and smelt clean and fresh, a hint of sandalwood in the air. She buckled herself in, even the silky feel of the seat belt shouting quality. The engine thrummed to life, settling to a soft purr. He turned to her and grinned, his delight infectious, and she felt like she was doing something she shouldn't. Being a little bit bad.

He's my boss, she told herself. He insisted.

It was a rock-solid justification, and she sat back, telling herself she had no choice in the matter. *He'll be able to insist until the debt's repaid*, a little voice in her head reminded her. She shifted in her seat, not sure she was entirely comfortable with that thought.

James's arm draped over the back of her seat as he turned to reverse, and his proximity made something stir inside her. She tensed and inched away from him, looking out of the window as they drove along the high street until he spoke, pulling her attention back inside the car.

'I thought we could go to the pub up on the moors. It'll look fabulous today. How about it?

It was a popular place to eat and the food was always good, but there was a chance she'd see someone she knew, and that could make her life difficult. Sara squirmed.

'Could we go a bit further afield?' She cringed, feeling awkward about asking. 'It's just Matt has a bit of a jealous streak. He wouldn't understand about business lunches. He'd jump to the wrong conclusion and I honestly haven't the energy.'

She listened to her own words and realised it was exactly how she'd reacted to Matt and the mystery woman in his office. Perhaps it *was* a work thing? She turned her attention to the countryside again, wondering if she had a jealous streak too. *He denied there was anyone there, though. Why would he do that if it was all above board?*

'Okay, I hadn't thought about that,' James said, and turned towards Skipton instead.

They went to a country pub in a little village on the edge of the Yorkshire Dales, the drive taking fifteen minutes where it would have taken Sara half an hour. James was showing off, she thought, throwing the car round bends like a rally driver, and the machine stuck to the road on its big fat tyres. Surprisingly, she found it exhilarating, rather than scary, a hidden part of her thrilled at the excitement and danger of driving so fast. Her life had been so safe since she'd had the children, their limitations becoming her boundaries, and when she thought about it, she'd rarely done anything just for her since they'd come into her life. Now she was ready to broaden her horizons, do more to meet her own needs before she disappeared as a person completely.

The pub was quiet, and they sat in the garden at the back, where wicker seats with comfy cushions surrounded the tables. Large pots had been planted with colourful flowers and high walls sheltered the area from any breeze, making it a pleasant suntrap. Sara sat back in her chair while James went to place their order at the bar, enjoying the warmth of the sun on her skin. She tipped her head back and closed her eyes, letting out a contented sigh.

This wasn't such a bad way to repay a debt, was it? If that was in fact what she was doing. She had no idea, and that bothered her. Even if it didn't count – and this was just James being nice to her – it was good to have a bit of time outside the workplace to get to know him better, and maybe get a firmer grasp on the limitations of their deal. Is there a timescale? she wondered. And how will I know when the debt is paid in full?

It was all a bit vague for her liking, and she knew she'd feel more comfortable if she could tick off progress, like a loan repayment scheme, so she knew how much further she had to go. The longer it went on, the more chance there was of Matt finding out, and that would be a disaster. She shuddered at the very thought.

James came back with a couple of halves of beer and two glasses of sparkling water.

'I know you said water, but I thought a half wouldn't do any harm.' He put the glasses on the table. 'Your choice.' He smiled. 'I'll drink it if you don't want it.'

Sara looked at the beer, a sheen of condensation on the side of the glass, so cool and inviting. What the hell, she thought. Live a little. And before she could think about it any more, she'd picked up the glass and taken a sip. 'Nice,' she said, savouring the taste of hops as it rolled around her tongue. 'Thank you.'

'They said the food should only be fifteen minutes, so you don't have to worry about us being out for too long. And I can stay and help this afternoon for an hour to make up for lost time.' He took a sip of his own beer, eyes twinkling at her over the rim of his glass. 'Can't have my staff worrying.'

She laughed, and they slipped into easy conversation, discussing the community centre and how it worked. A bit of gossip about board members, which made her giggle.

'Fiona is a little scary, don't you think?' she said after she'd finished her beer, feeling tipsy. She didn't really drink these days, and on an empty stomach, her inhibitions had definitely been lifted. In fact, she was so relaxed she'd practically melted into her chair, and James looked equally chilled sitting opposite. He really was easy company outside the office. Quite charming, and full of anecdotes.

He laughed. 'I'm glad you said it, not me. I'd be way too frightened to voice an opinion like that.' He looked around, lowered his voice to a whisper. 'Walls have ears, you know. Better be careful. Do not diss the all-powerful one.'

'Don't get me wrong,' Sara whispered back, joining in the charade. 'I really admire her. I've no idea how she fits everything into her life and still seems so bloody relaxed. Just like Julia. The two of them are awesome.'

James nodded. 'Awesome they might be. Doesn't stop them being scary, though,' and something in his voice made her wonder if he was joking or being deadly serious.

A young man appeared with their food, and Sara hauled herself into a more suitable position for eating. The mood shifted and they were quiet for a little while as they started to eat. It took her a few minutes to pluck up the courage to ask the question that was buzzing at the back of her brain, like a bee trapped against a windowpane looking for a way out.

'James, I've got to ask you about our deal,' she blurted out. He glanced up, stopped chewing. 'I need to know... well, this is a bit stupid of me and I should have asked before I agreed, but how do I know when I've paid back my debt?'

He finished chewing and swallowed, took a sip of water. 'Well now, I haven't really thought about it myself, but I suppose we should set some parameters, shouldn't we?'

She smiled, relief melting the tension at the back of her neck, glad now that she'd finally made herself ask.

'Let me have a think. We'll see how things go next Thursday, shall we, and talk again after that? Then we can come to a definite agreement as to how much of your time it will take to pay back the nine thousand.'

Her jaw clenched. *Nine thousand pounds.* It was an awful lot of money to owe somebody.

James studied her face and gave her a warm smile. 'Don't look so worried. I promise I won't be asking you to do anything you're not comfortable with. It's just a meeting. Eating great food, chatting to interesting people. You never know, you might actually enjoy yourself.'

Her mind grasped hold of his words and folded them into a new way of looking at things. 'It's like another job, then?'

He gazed at her, a little smile playing on his lips. 'I suppose so, yes. If it helps, let's consider it like that.'

It does help, Sara thought. It helps a lot. Because if by any chance Matt should find out, she could tell him it was just work and she was doing her bit to bring in some extra money.

'It's not a big dinner,' he continued, 'just a networking thing that's been arranged by a sportswear supplier in Leeds. I haven't even met the guy who's organised it, but he's got some selected suppliers attending that we're interested in doing business with, to either increase our current range or expand into new areas. I've got to shake things up a bit to keep the business viable. That's what it's all about.'

'So why do you need me there?'

'Well, firstly it's going to be a mixed audience, so I want you to talk to the men while I talk to the women.' He held up a hand. 'I know it sounds sexist, but this is business and I'm afraid it's how it works. Think of it as market research. We need to find out what they're looking for in terms of a deal. Where their negotiation points are. Just slide little questions into the conversation, see what you can discover that will help when we come to start the sales process proper.'

It didn't sound like an honest way to do business to Sara, but what did she know? Her business studies degree had prepared her for theoretical situations only, and the real world was a very different beast. She supposed James knew the ways of the sportswear industry, and, however unsavoury it sounded, she figured if she did a good job, she'd get her debt paid off faster.

It's going to be okay, she told herself as they got up to leave, knowing that her priority was to do whatever it took to pay back what she owed and keep her secret safe.

SEVENTEEN

The day before the networking event, Sara's stomach griped and gurgled like there was an alien in there scratching to get out. Nerves always affected her this way and she knew it was the thought of her evening out with James that was to blame.

He'd been to the community centre more often over the last week, as they were approaching an unusually busy patch. He was in meetings with Fiona, and spent time handing over more jobs to Sara and getting prepared for the implementation of the new project, which he would be managing once the funding came through. Sara would then be formally appointed as deputy manager of the centre, on a permanent contract, with an appropriate pay rise. That was the plan, she'd been told, although nobody had sought her opinion on the matter, Fiona having assumed she'd be happy with this as a way forward.

The idea of a permanent contract made her feel queasy. *Is it really what I want?* She wasn't entirely sure, but until Matt's new client paid him, she had to carry on working to keep their finances on track, while every day she felt further away from her family.

James was taking her out to lunch again today. This would be the third time, and she'd found she'd begun to relax in his company. For once she could just be an adult – rather than a mother or wife – and their conversations ranged far and wide. The only time she'd dared to ask about his private life, though, he'd avoided her question and made no mention of his daughter.

'I'm a divorcee,' he'd said. 'I live alone with a crabby old cat called Monty.' Then he'd smiled and added, 'Really I'm a pretty boring old fart. Let's talk about you. What are your ambitions?'

He liked asking her big questions. The sort that only had answers in her dreams, because reality was never going to allow her to achieve them. But more importantly, he listened to her replies, seemed properly interested in her as a person, and it made her realise what a long time it had been since Matt had listened to her like that. These days, their conversations were little snippets, sound bites between dealing with children or going to work, coming back from work. She couldn't even remember the last time they'd been out together as a couple without the children. Her lunches with James made it very clear that her relationship with Matt was in the doldrums and needed some serious attention if things were going to improve. But there was no time, no space, no opportunity, and it added to the pile of worries that were collecting in her mind, a mental in-tray that was full to overflowing.

James took her to the same pub every time, as it was nice and quiet, and it was unlikely that anyone Sara knew would be there at that time of day.

'I need to ask you about tomorrow,' she said when he arrived back at their table with drinks.

'Yes, I was wanting to talk to you about that too.' He placed her half of beer in front of her before sitting opposite, raising his own glass in a silent toast and taking a sip.

Sara gave him a relieved smile.

'You first,' he said.

'Mainly... I was wondering what to wear. How fancy will it be?' Actually, she was panicking because she literally had nothing suitable for a business dinner. The best she could do was smart casual, as all her dresses had been bought before she'd had Ezra and acquired a few more inches round her middle and thighs.

She would have to go out and buy something, hopefully from a charity shop so it wouldn't break her meagre budget.

He laughed, amusement twinkling in his eyes. 'You know, I'm sure you're telepathic. I was thinking about this very thing only yesterday. I saw a fabulous dress in a shop window and I thought of you.' He looked away, put his beer down on a mat. 'Sorry if this is presumptuous in any way, but I bought it.'

Her heart skipped a beat and she wondered if she'd heard him properly. *He bought me a dress?*

'The colour will be just perfect with your skin and your hair.' He looked up at her, a sheepish smile on his face. 'And those lovely brown eyes.'

She blushed, mouth opening and closing, lost for words. No man had ever bought her clothes before. Not even Matt had done that. James didn't seem to notice her shock, and carried on talking.

'I was also thinking it would be better if I give you a lift. There's engineering works on the line at the moment and people have been telling me how unreliable the train service is. Can't have you stuck or arriving late, can we?'

Sara was about to answer – say she didn't think it was a good idea for them to travel together – when he started speaking again. 'I know you think it's risky, but I've checked and there's nobody in the centre tomorrow night. So why don't I pick you up from there? I can bring the dress over, you can get changed in the office, then you can change back into your work clothes on our way home. What do you think?'

Sara didn't know what to think, or where to start with an answer, her mind still stuck on the fact that he'd bought her a dress. She picked up her beer and took a couple of sips, her eyes firmly on the table.

'I can't let you buy me clothes,' she said eventually. 'That's hardly me paying off my debt, is it?'

'Too late, it's done, and it was in a sale so can't be returned.' He gave her that smile again, and her heart did a little flip. 'You'll light up the room. And that will make it all worthwhile.'

What could she say to that? The answer appeared to be nothing, and she found herself agreeing to his proposals in lieu of a better alternative. It'll be fine, she told herself as she left work that evening, but her stomach was telling her otherwise.

The following day, Sara's anxiety had notched up to another level completely. She found she couldn't face lunch, and kept making mistakes as her thoughts filled with everything that could go wrong with the arrangements for her evening out. How could she keep it secret from Matt?

It had been a struggle to tell the lie in the first place, the words hesitant, tasting sour in her mouth, her eyes flitting all over the place as she spoke. But she'd made sure she was busy unloading the dishwasher when she told him so he couldn't see the guilt on her face and she couldn't see the frustration in his eyes that his routine would be disturbed. He'd responded with a bang of the door as he stormed off into his office and he hadn't mentioned it since. His apparent acceptance of the arrangements didn't make sleep any easier though, her lie chattering inside her head, keeping her awake. She wondered if it would be better to just tell him everything, but each little deception made it harder to come clean and confess the truth.

I'm putting it all right, she told herself. No need for him to know. Just have to be patient.

Once Hailey had taken the girls to football and Matt was busy bathing Ezra, she started to get herself ready. After a quick shower, she did her hair and make-up, then put on a clean set of work clothes – navy trousers and a white blouse – so Matt would believe her story of it being a work event.

'You're looking all dolled up,' he said, coming into the bedroom as she was putting the final touches to her make-up. The mascara wand froze on its way to her lashes for a moment before she carried on with what she was doing, hoping she didn't look as flustered as she felt.

'I've decided I need to up my game. Fiona and Julia always look so impeccably turned out, I felt quite shabby at the last meeting.'

'So who else is going to be there?' he asked. He was trying to sound casual, but she knew it was a loaded question. 'And what exactly is this incredibly important event you're going to anyway?' There was an edge to his voice, and she knew he was put out that she'd taken his work time away from him that evening, delaying his progress.

He was watching her in the mirror, and she glanced down, busied herself packing away her make-up. She kept her voice light, as if this betrayal of trust she was about to embark upon was nothing of any consequence. The knots in her stomach pulled tighter. 'I told you. It's an event for board members and managers of voluntary-sector groups. A compliance update. There're so many new laws about data protection, risk assessment, health and safety, safeguarding...' She shrugged, gave him a little flicker of a smile. 'It's a job to keep up to date with them all. So that's what it's for and that's why it's important.'

She caught his expression in the mirror, his eyes narrowed, assessing. *He doesn't believe me.* Her stomach churned. She'd never been a good liar and she felt her cheeks redden. Just get out of the house, she told herself as she pushed her feet into her shoes and stood, ready to go. It's like having another job, she reminded herself. That's all. Nothing bad.

She could sense Matt's eyes on her, watching every move. 'What time are you going to be back?'

She halted, realising she had no idea. If they were going to Harrogate, the journey alone would take the best part of forty minutes, and James hadn't mentioned when he expected the dinner to finish. Perhaps they go on into the night, she thought, wishing she'd got more details. *Oh God, what do I say?* She pretended to wipe a mark off her shoe, unable to look her husband in the eye. 'Um, I'm not really sure. Not too late, I don't think.'

She straightened up, slung her bag over her shoulder and gave him a quick peck on the cheek. 'I'd better go,' she said, hurrying out of the bedroom and down the stairs, where she picked up her car keys and made a swift exit before she blurted out the truth. *He'd kill me if he knew I was going out with another man. Even if it is only work.*

But was it? Or was there a part of her that saw this blossoming relationship with James as something different? A little piece of her heart that was vulnerable to his attentiveness, his thoughtful actions, his interest in her as a person.

She pushed the thought away. Stupid, stupid woman, she chided as she started the car and pulled out of the drive, focusing instead on her family and wondering how the relationships she'd been trying to protect had fallen apart so quickly. The girls weren't talking to her because she was missing football practice. Matt was annoyed with her for going out when he wanted to get some work done, and even Hailey had been a bit snappy when she came to pick up the girls.

I'll do this event, just this one, she told herself, feeling a little sick. Then that's the end of it. I'll see if I can negotiate another way to repay the money.

She unlocked the community centre and went into the office, where she found a stunning aqua dress hanging behind the door. The fabric had a gorgeous sheen to it and the beautiful cut made it drape softly. Elegant and classy and undeniably expensive, she thought, as she checked the tag. Size 12. Perfect. She wondered how he knew. It was hardly the sort of thing that came up in conversation. There was a matching pair of shoes, and she tried one on, surprised to find that it fitted too. Higher heels than she was used to, but she could manage for one night. Quickly she got herself dressed, carefully folding her work clothes into the bag she'd brought, hiding it under the desk so it would be out of sight if, by some remote chance, someone came into the office.

She smoothed the fabric of the dress round her hips, delighting in its silky feel against her skin. Perhaps she was showing a bit more cleavage than she was happy with, but there was nothing she could do to cover herself up, and anyway, maybe that was the point. Thankfully it was a flattering cut, so she didn't need to feel embarrassed about the extra weight round her middle. She went into the loos and studied her reflection in the mirror, did a little twirl, delighted with what she saw. Amazing what a difference a fabulous dress could make to your confidence, she thought as she gazed at herself, sure that it had taken years off her.

She heard the front door open and close. Aware that it was probably time to go, she stepped out of the toilets.

'James, I—' She froze. Fiona stared back at her, looking as startled as Sara felt, her hand on her chest, eyes wide.

'Christ, you scared me,' she said, looking Sara up and down. 'I was driving past and saw the office light on and thought I must have forgotten to switch it off earlier.'

The door opened and James walked in, looking suave and sophisticated in a slate-grey suit, white shirt and a tie that was the same colour as her dress. A nice touch, Sara thought, as was the matching silk handkerchief in his breast pocket. There was no doubting the fact that they were going out together, no possibility of explaining this away as pure coincidence.

Fiona's eyes flicked from James to Sara.

'You said you were going to football practice tonight,' she said, the line between her eyebrows a deep furrow, an accusing tone to her voice. 'I asked you.'

Sara cringed, couldn't speak. She glanced at James, who winked at her before he turned to Fiona with an easy smile.

'Sara's kindly helping me with a business meeting. That's all this is.' And the way he said it made it all sound very natural, Sara thought, watching the scene as if she were an interested onlooker, disassociated from what was really happening.

Fiona turned to look at him, face pinched, clearly annoyed. 'Right, I see,' she said, her voice cutting the air like a pair of scissors, all snippy and sharp.

'I'm sorry about football,' Sara mumbled, her face burning. 'I didn't... I couldn't...' She ground to a halt, aware that there was no excuse for her bare-faced lie earlier in the day.

'I told Chelsea we could all go out afterwards. She was so excited.' Fiona's lips disappeared into a thin line. 'I was looking forward to a catch-up too. We only have time for business here, don't we? And I want to...' She gave James another hard look, and their eyes locked for a moment before James glanced at his watch, then at Sara.

'I'm sorry to rush things along, but we'd better be off.'

Sara's gaze fell to the floor, unable to deal with the stare that Fiona was giving her – a look so full of accusations and questions and disapproval that her body burned with shame. She hated letting people down, and that was all she'd managed to do tonight, Fiona being another one to add to the list. Although Fiona was technically her boss, she'd also been a good friend to Sara over the last few years, and she didn't want to think she might have done something to bruise their relationship.

She followed James out of the building, feeling the prickle of Fiona's glare on her back until James opened the car door for her and she got in. She won't say anything, she reassured herself as she fastened her seat belt. She might be cross with me but she's very discreet. Her heart raced; she wasn't completely convinced. *What if she says something to Hailey? Or the girls?* She clung on to the seat belt as James whipped the car round a corner, shushing the voice in her head. She couldn't listen, not now.

'That was like being caught out doing something naughty by the headmistress,' she said into the silence of the car as she watched the outskirts of the town fade away. She turned to James. 'If looks could kill, you'd be dead.'

He was quiet for a moment, then a wry smile twitched at his lips. 'Yeah, I think she'd quite like me to be dead.'

'I've noticed a bit of... a niggle between you two.' Sara watched his reaction, saw a frown appear.

He sighed. 'Okay, if I tell you this, it stays in the car.' He glanced at her.

'I'm not going to tell anyone anything. Who have I got to tell anyway?'

'Fiona, for one. It's better if she thinks you don't know.'

'I promise I won't utter a word. You've got me intrigued now.'

'Me and Fiona, well, we had a bit of a...' He pursed his lips. 'I'm not sure what you'd call it. A fling?'

Sara stared at him, eyes wide. That was the last thing she'd been expecting to hear. Fiona was such a pillar of the community, exuding virtue and involved in so many good causes, it seemed like a contradiction in terms. An affair? Fiona and James? She turned to look out of the window so he wouldn't catch the incredulity that was surely plastered all over her face.

She let his words roll round her mind. Fiona's husband was quite a bit older than her, and was away a lot, but when he was home, he doted on her, buying her expensive gifts, taking her on romantic weekends away. Sara had often thought Fiona had hit the jackpot, having plenty of free time to pursue her own interests and still being treated like royalty by an adoring spouse. In truth, she'd felt a little jealous of the way Fiona's husband so obviously cherished her, when she and Matt seemed to be drifting apart.

'Really?' The word burst out before she could stop it, struggling to believe it was true.

James laughed. 'Don't sound so surprised. Some women do find me attractive, you know.'

Sara looked out of the window. *I do know.* She could see his reflection in the glass, his profile, the amused curve of his lips, his straight nose, not too big, not too small. Everything in his face in proportion. There was no doubt that he was attractive, no doubt at all.

'It didn't last long. I felt there was... I don't know.' He pursed his lips, considering. 'Let's just say I wasn't comfortable and ended things before it got started really. But you know what Fiona's like. Has to have everything her own way, and she hasn't forgiven me.' She studied his reflection in the window, saw him glance at her. 'She employed you to get back at me, you know. Wanted to oust me from my post when Dad was ill and I couldn't put in the time. Thankfully, the other board members wouldn't agree. I've been managing the place for years. Since way before Fiona joined the board.' He sighed. 'Anyway, we are where we are. But if she starts being funny with you, well, you'll know why. She's got a bit of a jealous streak, has our Fiona.'

Sara closed her eyes, suddenly weary, wondering how her life had got so complicated. One lie on top of another. She thought about football practice, Fiona turning up to collect Chelsea. Quickly she got her phone out of her bag, tapped out a message.

So sorry about tonight. I owed James a favour so I said I'd help him with a business meeting. Didn't want Matt to find out. Please don't mention anything to Hailey or the girls. Can we have a chat and I'll explain?

A reply came back a few minutes later.

No problem. Just surprised. How about Monday?

She replied with *Perfect*, although she knew she'd be worrying about things all weekend, then switched off her phone, put it back in her bag and gave James a quick smile. 'Just had to remind Hailey about something.'

They drove in silence for a while, then James started chatting about the dinner and she tried to focus her mind on the rest of the evening. But a voice in her head kept on interrupting, asking questions she didn't want to answer. *What if Matt finds out? Have I ruined my friendship with Fiona? Will she tell Hailey that she saw me with James?*

EIGHTEEN

The hotel was outside Harrogate, a handsome new building designed to look like a stately home, with a gritstone facade and a sweeping driveway planted with an avenue of trees. It was set in landscaped grounds, the lawns dotted with mature trees that must have been there before the place was built. They arrived at a circular drop-off point in front of the entrance, punctuated with a bubbling fountain at the centre. Sara stared about her, bemused by the grandeur of the place.

'If you'd like to wait here, I'll go and park up.' James hopped out and came round to open her door for her. 'Won't be two ticks,' he said, before getting back in the car and driving round the side of the building, where the car park was hidden behind a screen of shrubs, keeping first impressions of the place picture perfect.

Nervously she waited for him in front of the imposing entrance, which featured a gritstone arch with a couple of gargoyles guarding the smoked-glass doors. She felt exposed in her evening dress, and wrapped her arms around her chest, turning her back on the building and anyone inside who might be watching her. Goose bumps prickled her arms, and she shivered in the evening breeze, wishing she'd thought to bring a pashmina or a jacket.

James was humming to himself as he walked towards her a few minutes later. He beamed and offered his arm, which she took gratefully, needing support to navigate the gravel in her high heels. 'You look stunning, by the way. Did I tell you that?'

A blush crept into her cheeks. She could feel his eyes on her as she concentrated on where she was putting her feet. 'Oh, I don't know about that,' she muttered, unsure what to do with such a compliment.

The inside of the building was just as impressive as the outside, although the decor was more modern and sleek than she was expecting. The walls were a dazzling white, the floor of the foyer polished limestone, a reception desk on the left, two lifts at the rear. To the right was a seating area, with three leather sofas surrounding a pool, water flowing out of the wall and splashing down a series of gritstone steps.

They walked over to reception, and while James found out where the event was being held, Sara picked up a glossy brochure and leafed through it. Her hands were clammy, leaving fingerprints on the cover, but she discovered that the hotel offered spa days and weekends as well as having exclusive entertainment suites, as the literature called them. She put the brochure back in its holder and surreptitiously wiped her hands on her dress, ready for the inevitable handshakes. It was that sort of place, that sort of do, and she'd never felt more out of her comfort zone in her life. The idea that she might have to do this more than once, made her feel queasy.

If I do well tonight, maybe we can call the deal off, she thought. Though if she did do well, perhaps James would want her to do it again. It was hard to know. Her heart was pounding, her stomach griping and her legs felt all shaky. She was on the verge of telling him she couldn't go through with it. You're here now, she told herself sternly. Only a couple of hours then you can go home. Or would it be longer? She wished she'd asked.

The lies, that was the problem, and the circle of people she was lying to was growing all the time. Now Fiona was involved, and that in itself felt like juggling with fire.

The irony was, she'd always prided herself on her honesty. After her upbringing – seeing how her mother's lies had backfired so spectacularly – she'd vowed never to tread the same road. *But look at me now, Mum. I didn't bloody learn, did I?* Her teeth ground together. One momentary lapse. One desperate lunge to keep her family on the right side of solvency and her marriage intact. She couldn't believe she'd ever thought that stealing money was the answer, however desperate she'd been. It was a loan, she reminded her inner critic. I was always going to put it back. Always.

James turned to her, his hand on the small of her back as he guided her towards the lifts. 'Second floor. I've been to this suite before.' There was a note of excitement in his voice. 'I think you'll be impressed.'

And she was. It was a far more intimate setting than she'd imagined. Two round tables set with eight places each, small groups of people already gathered in a seating area in front of the large bay window, which was swathed with heavy golden curtains. The lighting was subtle, the carpet deep and a delight to walk on, all soft and springy, muffling the sound. A pianist played a grand piano in the corner. Sara felt like she was in a London club in the 1930s. It was classy, very sophisticated, and she was glad of the dress and shoes.

A tall man with dark hair and an even darker beard strode towards them. 'James,' he said, holding out his hand, which James shook enthusiastically. 'Good to see you. And this must be the lovely Sara.' He bent towards her as he shook her hand, his clasp firm and lingering. 'I'm Lewis. As in Hamilton.' He gave a little laugh and led them over to the seating area, grabbing a couple of glasses from a tray as a waiter passed and handing one to Sara, the other to James.

Champagne? She took a sip, felt the bubbles fizz up her nose. Took another sip to steady her nerves as they joined the gathering and introductions were made.

'Just waiting for two more, then we're all set to go,' Lewis said, beaming at them, his teeth unnaturally white and even. 'Good journey?'

He was the sort of man who demanded all your attention, his eyes locking with hers in a way that made her feel it would be rude to look away. She was aware of James moving off, chatting to someone else. Then another man came and introduced himself – an importer of training shoes – and Lewis excused himself to greet the final two arrivals.

A waiter appeared to top up Sara's glass, and she hesitated, feeling a little tipsy already. 'Go on, be a devil,' the man she was talking to said, noting her hesitation. She felt unable to refuse, but decided she wouldn't drink any more until she'd at least had a starter.

Thankfully, a little while later, Lewis called everyone to their tables.

'Everything okay?' James asked as he took his place next to her. She smiled and nodded, glad that he was back by her side. She'd spoken to half the men in the room already and found them to be a little intense. She thought she'd done all right; had asked about their businesses and responded with appropriate feigned interest when they started telling her the details. Now she really needed a little catch-up with James to debrief on what she'd learned and find out exactly what he wanted her to do next.

He leant towards her, whispered in her ear, 'Keep up the good work. You're doing great.' His breath tickled her neck and she giggled, then told herself to grow up, because she sounded like a teenager on a first date. It was the champagne. It always made her silly.

Keep your distance, this is business, her sensible self whispered.

She leant away from him, unfolded her napkin and spread it on her lap while waiters served the first course.

Lewis was sitting opposite her, and as the person in charge of the event, his eyes roamed the room, making sure everything was okay. But several times his gaze caught hers and he gave her a little smile. She wasn't sure why it made her uncomfortable – maybe because she'd never been to such a formal event, with people she didn't know – but she wished she didn't have quite so much cleavage on show. It was coincidence, she told herself when she found him looking at her again, inevitable when you sat opposite someone. But still she felt hot and bothered, like a child forced to sit at a dinner table with distant relatives talking about them as if they weren't there, wanting to go home. It's just this once, she reminded herself as she took another mouthful of smoked salmon. Tough it out, keep your eyes on your food.

The night trudged on, the buzz of chatter and laughter getting increasingly loud as more champagne was consumed. After her first glass, Sara made a point of not drinking any more. There was no way she could roll home drunk without Matt having serious suspicions about where she'd been, and anyway, she had to drive herself back from the community centre. She checked her watch. Almost nine. The meal was being served at a snail's pace, all five courses of it, and there was still dessert to come, followed by a cheese board. She'd been hoping to be home by ten, but it was going to be much later. The muscles at the back of her neck pulled tighter, the tension almost unbearable now.

Her neighbour, a portly middle-aged man called Alan, was very attentive, leaning in towards her when he spoke so she could hear what he was saying. He was pleasant enough, told her about his ex-wife, his children. Then they got on to her family, to the point where she didn't want to tell him any more details and changed the subject back to business. Apparently he imported a range of women's yoga wear, and at last she was on familiar ground. Christ, this is hard work, she decided as he regaled her with the technicalities of weft and weave and Lycra versus cotton.

Her eyes wanted to close, the lids getting heavy. The air was thick and warm, Alan's garlicky breath pungent in her nostrils, the heat of him as he leant close to her, his arm brushing against hers making her skin crawl. She had a sneaking suspicion he was looking down her cleavage and finally decided she'd had enough.

She turned to get James's attention, wanting to ask him what time they were going to leave, but he was deep in conversation with the lady on the other side of him – a petite Chinese woman in a beautifully ornate dress, who was giggling at his jokes as though they were hilarious.

Her phone buzzed and she pulled it out of her bag, heart skipping a beat. It was a message from Matt.

Where are you? Ezra making a fuss because he's woken up and you're not here.

Grateful to have a genuine excuse to leave, she tapped James on the shoulder, and he turned, obviously surprised at being interrupted. 'I'm so sorry, but I've got to go. There's a problem at home. Ezra's not well and Matt doesn't know what to do.' She stood, her mind made up. 'It's all right, you stay. I'm going to get a cab.'

James made a grab for her arm, trying to stop her, but she pulled away.

'Thank you so much for a lovely evening,' she said to him before turning to Alan. 'So nice meeting you.'

Alan's eyes widened in surprise. 'You're not going, are you? You can't, not yet.'

'I'm afraid I have to. My little boy isn't well.'

James stood, following her as she started to make her way to the door, aware that she was being watched. Nobody else had left, and she hoped her departure wouldn't undermine his efforts to get some good deals. *Will it still count as payment off my debt? Oh God, I hope so; please don't let this be for nothing.* It had been a tortuous evening and she couldn't contemplate having to do it again.

'Let me make sure they call you a taxi,' he said, ever the gentleman.

Once they were outside the room, however, the smile slipped from his face, to be replaced by a scowl. 'You going home early was not part of the deal,' he murmured, clearly not wanting their conversation to be overheard, even though the door was shut.

'I'm sorry, but that man next to me was getting a bit creepy; honestly, if he'd touched me again, I would've hit him.'

James stared at her for a moment, his hand clasping her wrist so she couldn't walk away. 'So there isn't an emergency at home then?' His eyes sparked with annoyance.

'Oh well… yes, there really is a problem,' she stammered, her cheeks burning. Ezra not wanting to go to sleep was hardly a matter of life or death, but now she'd made up her mind, she was desperate to leave. 'Please, James. I've got to go. I didn't think we'd be out this late, and if Matt finds out where I've been, he'll kill me.'

James's eyebrows shot up his forehead. 'I'm sure it wouldn't be that drastic.' He huffed out an impatient breath. 'This really is not ideal. Alan is an important supplier and I can't piss him off.'

The walls closed in around her, and she suddenly felt vulnerable. She was a long way from home, with people she didn't know, in a situation she was far from comfortable with. As far as she was aware, given the conversations that she'd eavesdropped on, very little business had been discussed. Maybe that would come later, after dinner. The thought of having to stay any longer brought sudden tears to her eyes.

James softened then and let go of her wrist. 'Okay, I suppose I should have been clearer about times. My fault. At least he enjoyed talking to you, so maybe your job here is done.'

He led her to the lifts, went down to the foyer with her and waited until a taxi arrived, before saying goodbye with an unexpected kiss on the cheek. Sara blushed, very aware of the musky scent of his aftershave, his beard tickling her skin, the whisper of his breath on her face. It made her shiver, brought a surge of unwanted feelings fizzing through her.

'I've got some follow-up work to do, so I won't be in the office for a few days now,' he said. 'But we're pretty much up to date, aren't we?'

She nodded, desperate to get back to her own little world.

When she got home, having changed out of her dress at the community centre, the bedroom light was on and she found Ezra sitting in bed with Matt, reading his favourite storybook.

She stopped in the doorway, her heart filled with a rush of love. *This is where I belong.* A new resolve sparked inside her. *I've got to talk to James about our deal. I can't do this again.*

She went and sat on the bed, Matt's face breaking into a relieved smile.

'How was your night?' he asked as Ezra snuggled up to her, wrapping his arms round her neck. 'I saw Fiona at football, and she told me what was going on. She said it was her fault. Apologised for taking you away on a Thursday.'

Sara buried her face in Ezra's hair, aware that she owed Fiona yet another favour now. She'd have to thank her for covering up. Then Matt's words registered, and she looked over at him, puzzled. 'How come you were at football? Hailey took the girls tonight.'

He nodded. 'Yes, she did. But Ezra wouldn't settle, so I gave her a ring and she talked me into joining her for a bit.' He laughed. 'She told me I was a boring bastard working all the time and I needed to spend more time with the kids, so I caved in.' He leaned back against the pillows, hands behind his head, a smile playing on his lips as he stared at the ceiling. 'We actually had quite a laugh, and Ezra was up for it for a bit.' He ruffled his son's hair. 'Especially with the promise of milkshakes at the end. He did pretty well, to be honest. I even got him to have a little kick-about with me, so I've not lost hope.'

Sara felt a prickle of annoyance, a longing for something that she couldn't have. Time she'd missed, an occasion that all her family had enjoyed without her. *You've only yourself to blame*, said the voice in her head. And she was more determined than ever that it wasn't going to happen again.

NINETEEN

By the time it got to Monday, the events of the previous Thursday had started to dim in Sara's mind while she worried instead about her husband's blossoming friendship with her sister, and their ability to manage perfectly well without her. She told herself she was being stupid, but still, something niggled at her.

I put everything on the line for Matt, he gets all the fun and I've got a bloody debt to pay.

The debt. The very idea of it set off a chain reaction in her body, making her pulse race, sweat gathering under her arms, the muscles tensing at the back of her neck. She was meeting James for lunch and was determined to get clarification this time. You can't have a deal with no boundaries, she kept telling herself as she went about her work. That wasn't a deal at all. That was manipulation. It was bothering her, the not knowing, buzzing around her head like an angry wasp, and however much she tried to swat it away, it kept coming back.

The sound of the office door opening startled her from her thoughts, and Fiona walked in. 'I can't stay long,' she said, sitting on the opposite side of the desk, her bag on her lap and a grim expression on her face.

Sara blanched, the arrangement to meet having slipped her mind.

'Thank you so much,' she said before Fiona could get started. 'For covering for me last Thursday. Matt would have a fit if he knew I was out with James.'

Fiona gave her one of her laser stares, which seemed to pierce into her mind. 'I need to talk to you about James. He's not...' She scrunched up her nose, like she'd smelt something repulsive. 'He's not worth the hassle and he has some evil little ways once you get to know him. I don't want to see you throwing away all the good things you have with Matt for that piece of shit.'

Sara's eyes widened. She wasn't sure she'd ever heard Fiona use crude language before. Heat rushed through her body. 'No. No, you've got it wrong. I'm not having an affair with him or anything. It's not a relationship.' She stopped herself, backtracked, her words tripping over each other in her eagerness to refute Fiona's assumption. 'Well, only in the business sense.'

Fiona's eyes narrowed. 'What do you mean? I've seen you going off for lunch together. Or at least I assumed that's what you were doing. Looking very cosy.' Her stare was intense and Sara looked away, tidied the stack of invoices on the desk in front of her while she tried to find the right words to explain.

'I'm doing some extra work for him in connection with his sportswear business. Just to bring some more money into the house while Matt gets his new business going.' She gave a quick smile, gone before it had properly formed. 'Last night was a one-off.'

Fiona gave a dismissive snort. 'I'm happy to cover for you once. But I'm not going to make a habit of it.'

Sara cringed inside and knew she had some making-up to do. 'I'm so grateful. Really I am. It was very kind of you and I feel bad that you had to lie for me. It won't happen again, I promise.'

Fiona checked her watch and got up. 'Look, what you do with your life is your business, but my advice would be to steer well clear of that man on anything but a business level. He has a way of...' She stopped what she was saying, flapped a dismissive hand. 'I'm sure I don't have to spell it out for you.'

Sara watched her leave, not sure what to think. Was that jealousy talking? Her warning had certainly struck a chord. The idea of meeting up again with the group of people who were there on Thursday made her stomach churn. There had been something a bit off about that event, and although she couldn't work out exactly what it was, she knew she wanted no part of it.

James appeared on the dot of twelve, and she was still mulling over Fiona's words as they settled in their seats at their usual pub. Her nerves were on edge, making her fidget, her leg bouncing up and down under the table.

'What's wrong with you?' James said after they'd sat in silence for a few minutes. Normally the conversation flowed, but Sara's thoughts were locked on how to phrase her question.

It's now. Ask him. Go, on, do it!

She steadied her bouncing leg, took a deep breath and looked him in the eye. 'It's about our deal.' His eyebrows lifted, his eyes meeting hers while he waited for her to carry on. 'I need to know how long it will take me to pay off the debt and exactly what's involved. I don't like it being so vague. And Matt was suspicious about Thursday and I hated having to lie to everyone.' She shook her head. 'I don't want to do it.' Her voice sounded whiny, and she hated that she'd put herself at his mercy. *The same mistake as Mum. How stupid was that?*

He picked up his beer glass and took a long swig, wiped a hand across his mouth. 'I do see your point, and I think we said we'd review the situation after Thursday's event, didn't we?'

She nodded, hardly able to breathe while she waited for his pronouncement, like a criminal in court anticipating the verdict. I *am* a criminal, she reminded herself, and wondered if owning up might be the better way forward. Whether Fiona would take it to the police. She couldn't take the risk, though. Think about the kids, she told herself, memories of social workers escorting her to a new temporary home springing to mind. Echoes of the confusion and misery she'd felt filled her head. *That won't happen. They've got Matt.* Another voice added, *And Hailey.* She gritted her teeth. She was going to be the one looking after her family, nobody else.

'Are you listening?' James asked, an amused smile on his lips. 'You were miles away then.'

She took a big gulp of beer, the coolness of it a welcome relief. 'Sorry. I'm listening now. It's just there's a lot going on.'

'So, what I'd like to do is take you away for a treat. A spa weekend.'

She wasn't sure she'd heard him right. 'What? Why?'

'Because I've been under a lot of pressure and need a little break, and I don't want to go on my own.' He shrugged. 'Simple as that. It will be counted as part of your repayment.'

'How can it be if it's costing you money?' She fiddled with her beer mat, picking at the edges, separating out the layers. 'I don't understand any of it, to be honest, and I hate that feeling.' Her voice cracked and she took another gulp of beer while she collected herself.

He smiled at her over the rim of his beer glass. 'I promise I'll think about the repayment terms. Perhaps we can give it some proper consideration while we're relaxing at the spa, and I can assure you that by the time we get back, we'll have sorted something out. How about that?'

A weekend away? It was a tempting prospect, and she couldn't deny she enjoyed James's company. If, by the end of the weekend, she decided she didn't like whatever terms he came up with, then she'd try and devise a different way to pay him back. Matt kept telling her he was very close to finishing the contract. When he was paid, they could catch up with the mortgage, pay off their temporary overdraft extension, clear a couple of the credit cards. *Oh God, will there be anything left?* It seemed unlikely. Panic froze her thoughts. *I don't think I've got a choice.*

'When were you thinking?' she asked.

'This weekend. I've got it booked.'

She gasped, incredulous. 'But it's Monday now! I can't just drop everything.'

'Oh, I think you can.' His hand reached across the table and covered hers, his voice gentle. 'I love spending time with you, Sara. Just this once, please. Humour a lonely man and give me the pleasure of your company.' His eyes met hers, hypnotic, appealing.

The lure of a break, some time to regroup and re-energise, was tempting. It was exactly what she needed. Hadn't Hailey said as much just the other week? Despite her better judgement, she was almost persuaded. There was one major stumbling block, though. 'What will I tell Matt?'

James looked at the ceiling, then back at her. 'I think a friend from college has invited you to a hen party. Nothing raucous. A spa treatment for the girls, a weekend of relaxation and pampering. That won't be far from the truth, so it won't feel like a lie.' His thumb stroked the back of her hand.

She gazed at him, getting hotter by the minute, wondering if his intentions were what she thought they might be.

'I'm a married woman, James.' Her voice wavered and she cleared her throat before carrying on. 'I want to be clear. I'm not having sex with you.' It wasn't that she hadn't thought about it. He was an attractive man and she was undeniably drawn to him, to his easy company. The way he was so considerate and gentle with her. But she wasn't about to cheat on her husband. That was something she'd never do.

He snatched his hand away as if he'd been burned, looking thoroughly shocked. 'Oh my goodness, no. There's no hidden agenda here.' With a surge of embarrassment, she remembered they'd had a similar conversation when he'd first suggested the deal, and she felt mortified for even suggesting his intentions might not be honourable. 'I honestly think of us as friends. That's all.'

'I just don't see how you taking me to a spa is repayment for a debt when it's going to cost you quite a bit of money.'

The smile faded from his face and she could see a sadness in his eyes. 'The truth is, I'm lonely. I have no wife, no contact with my daughter, and my father is being very difficult.' He sighed. 'The handover of the business is stressful, and I need to switch off for a couple of days. I don't want to do that on my own.' He glanced up at her. 'It won't be too much of a chore for you, will it?'

She felt bad then for questioning his motives, and desperately started backtracking lest she cause more offence. 'No, no, not at all. It sounds like a lovely treat.' In fact, the idea of a spa weekend – no children to think about, no meals to cook, and a bit of pampering – sounded like bliss.

'I feel like we're pals now, and we work so well together. I'd really appreciate it if you'd just accept that your company has value to me.' He gave a rueful laugh. 'I suppose it's quite hard to understand when you're in the opposite situation, and every minute of your day is spent dealing with other people's needs.' He took another swig of his beer, put his glass down and held up his hands. 'There it is. Nothing complicated or untoward. I'd like the pleasure of your company and we'll knock some money off your debt.'

She considered the proposition for a moment. All that mattered was the fact that James considered this as part repayment.

Nine thousand pounds.

She wondered how much her time was worth. How many meetings, how much companionship James would need before he considered the debt repaid. It could take years. The thought landed with a thud in her belly. Years before she could put her crime behind her without fear of repercussions. She looked at the man across the table, and heard Fiona's warning to stay away, remembered the vitriol in her voice. What had he done to make her react like that?

TWENTY

It was the end of Thursday – football practice done and dusted, children settled – and Sara was finally getting ready to go up to bed when Matt bounced into the kitchen. He reached into the fridge for a beer. 'Finally,' he said, with emphasis, 'I'm getting there.'

She looked up, his words not really registering. Now's a good time, she decided, having been wondering all week how to break the news of her impending weekend away without causing friction. Time was running out. *Do it!*

Her mouth went into action before she could chicken out. 'I forgot to mention… I've been invited to a hen party with the uni girls this weekend. You remember Louise? I said no when she first asked because you're so busy, but someone dropped out and she's asked me again. It's years since I've seen them and… well, I'd really love to go.' She took a deep breath. 'I'll be going Friday night, coming back Sunday.'

I'm paying back the debt, she reminded herself. This is the only reason I'm doing it.

'You must remember her,' she said, when Matt's confusion seemed to have rendered him temporarily speechless. 'We lived next door to each other in halls.'

Matt scowled, banging his beer onto the worktop while he looked for the bottle opener. 'I didn't think you were in touch with any of your old uni mates. I thought you'd outgrown them.'

Her jaw clenched and it took a beat to dampen her annoyance. 'We chat on Facebook and I fancy meeting everyone again, so I already said I'd go.' Sara hated how defensive she sounded. *Why shouldn't I have some time with friends?* Even if they were imaginary, it was the principle of the thing.

He opened his beer, took a long swig, then leaned against the worktop, giving her a hard stare. 'And I'm looking after the kids, I suppose?' He sounded like she'd asked him to lick the toilet clean.

'They're your kids as much as mine.' She spat out the words, annoyed that he was making it sound like he was doing her a reluctant favour. He was being so awkward about her being away for two measly nights when he'd been off on all sorts of jaunts with his football mates over the years without a backward glance. In fact, now she thought about it, this would be the first time she'd been away from the family since the twins were born fourteen years ago.

Her resolve hardened, forming a lump in her throat. *I deserve a break.* The idea that she should be able to take some time for herself was rooted in her mind now, blossoming into full-on indignation.

'I'm going. It's all sorted. Nothing to pay because the girl who backed out is mortified she had to cry off at the last minute. She's happy for me to take her place.' The lies were coming easily now, fuelled by anger. 'I know you've nothing on. I've been working flat out and I need a couple of days off.'

There was a hard glint in his eyes. 'You really don't care about me and my work, do you?'

There was no answer to that, so she busied herself with sorting out the washing-up, rinsing the dirty dishes before stacking the dishwasher.

He scowled and guzzled his beer, almost half a bottle gone before he took it away from his mouth. She glanced at him, wondering if she actually knew her husband any more. Had he changed, or had she just not noticed the things about him that annoyed her now? *Maybe it's me who's changed. Different expectations.*

She thought of James, his gentleness and impeccable manners. How considerate he was. The dress he'd bought her, the lunches out, little treats with morning coffee if he was passing. He did everything for her that she'd like her husband to do, but she knew that sort of consideration really wasn't in Matt's make-up. He was a different kind of man altogether, and more of a stranger to her by the day.

A new thought hit her then, making her stop what she was doing. *Is James really making me repay the debt, or is it his way to spend time with me?*

She followed the logic, like tugging on a fishing line, waiting to see what was on the end of it, unsure where her thoughts would lead. *Is he in love with me?* The very idea made her blush. Certainly his behaviour was that of a would-be lover, a gentle courtship by a lonely man who was too shy to be up-front about it.

Fiona's words came back to her then, as she sorted dirty cutlery into the holder; the sharp blast of contempt in her voice when she'd given her the warning. Was it jealousy, or was there something about James that Sara didn't yet understand? So many questions and uncertainties. At least the weekend would give her a chance to get some clarification and assess the situation, then she could decide what to do for the best. *No action without information.* She'd learnt that on her degree course. *Do the research.* The weekend wasn't a blissful retreat with a lonely friend. It was business. She slammed the door of the dishwasher shut. That felt better.

Matt finished his beer, got another out of the fridge while Sara wiped the worktops. She was stunned by her reasoning, testing out whether it changed anything about the way she felt. James knew she was fundamentally honest, knew her theft had been for Matt and her family, a desperate act when she wasn't thinking straight. He'd acted out of kindness, wanting to help. Perhaps getting her to pay back the debt with nothing but her company was his way of making her feel better about his generosity.

Matt's voice made her jump out of her thoughts and back into the room.

'You're not listening, are you? Did you even hear what I said when I came in just now?'

She stared at him blankly, stopped wiping and put the cloth back on the sink. 'Sorry, I've got a lot on my mind.'

'I've had a breakthrough.' There was a smug expression on his face now, his earlier frustration apparently forgotten. He was on his third beer, she noticed, the two empties standing together on the worktop, which probably had something to do with the mellowing of his mood. His smile was a little bleary, his body swaying like a tree in the wind. He's drunk, she realised, remembering that he'd taken a six-pack of beer into his office earlier. He reached into the fridge, opened another bottle and held it out to her. 'Celebrate with me.'

She shook her head, still annoyed with him and confused by her thoughts about James. 'No thanks, I'm off to bed as soon as I've finished tidying up.' She cracked a brittle smile, waiting for him to explain what he was talking about.

He frowned, and tried to put the bottle back on the worktop, but got it wrong and banged it down hard, sending a spurt of beer over the floor. 'Oops.' He chuckled. 'I'll just have to drink it myself then. Reckon I deserve a celebration.' He leant back against the worktop, legs crossed at the ankles. 'I've just cracked the code,' he slurred. 'Nobody will be able to find it. Honestly, it's pretty devious, even if I do say so myself.'

'I've no idea what you're talking about,' she muttered as she picked up the cloth again, remembering that she hadn't wiped the table ready for the morning.

'I'm talking about a bloody genius bit of work. That's what. So all I need to do is run a few tests and it's all ready to load up the content.'

She looked at him then as the implications registered. 'You mean you'll get paid?'

He smiled and nodded. 'That's right. I know it's taken longer than expected, but hiding things on the internet is not as easy as it used to be.' He grinned. 'Nobody's going to find this one.'

'Hiding things?' She frowned. 'What things? What do you mean?'

The smile slipped off his face, and his eyes slid to the side. 'Nothing.' He downed the rest of his beer, wiped his mouth with the back of his hand. 'You don't need to know the technicalities.' He pointed the empty bottle at her. 'All you need to know is I've done a bloody good job and the client is going to be ecstatic. And I'll get paid.'

Sara's heart skipped with delight, relief coursing through her body, making her legs feel weak. She swiped the last of the crumbs off the table and into her hand and walked back over to the sink to rinse out the cloth, all her chores finished. 'Do you want me to do the invoicing for you? I know finance isn't your thing.'

'Nope. No need. They're gonna pay cash.'

'Cash?' She frowned at him, thinking she must have heard wrong. 'Thousands of pounds… in cash?'

He laughed. 'Brilliant, eh? The tax man doesn't need to know anything about it.'

'What?' she gasped. She'd had enough of deception; wanted the future to be thoroughly legal. 'That's no good. It's got to be done properly.'

He waved the bottle in the air, his eyes telling her he was on his way to being as drunk as she'd seen him in a long while. 'Oh, I don't think my client would approve of that. Anyway, it's not what we agreed. It's been a cash deal right from the start. No records.'

'So if the tax man asks, how are we going to explain thousands of pounds going into our account?' To Sara, hiding money was almost as bad as stealing money, and she couldn't countenance a second misdemeanour.

'It's not going into our account.' He looked delighted with himself. 'There'll be nothing to explain.'

'But you can't—'

His face screwed into an angry snarl. 'Don't you tell me what I can and can't do.' His mood had flipped in an instant, and when he started jabbing a finger at her, she knew better than to argue. 'I know what the deal is. And I know what I'm doing. I don't need Mrs I've-got-a-business-studies-degree to lecture me, thank you very much. It's my job and I'll do things my way.'

He reached out to pick up the remaining bottle of beer, but miscalculated, and it fell to the floor, smashing on the tiles. Sara jumped back, beer splashing her feet and legs, watching as splinters of glass skittered in all directions, glittering against the dark tiles like stars in the night sky.

She glowered at Matt, and he glared back. 'I didn't do it on purpose, did I?'

'Oh, just...' She pressed her lips together, let her curses rattle round inside her head instead of speaking them out loud. 'Why don't you go to bed. I'll sort this out.'

'Yeah, well done, Matt, for bringing a shitload of money into the house.' His voice mocked hers. 'Thank you for providing for your family.'

'It's brilliant, love. Brilliant. I'm really pleased,' she said in a voice that sounded as excited as if he'd just announced he'd bought a loaf of bread. She grabbed the cloth and started to wipe up the mess of glass and beer.

'Christ, I don't know what's got into you recently.' Sara looked up, realising it was a mistake as soon as she saw the accusation in his eyes. 'You're seeing someone else, aren't you?'

'I'm bloody not. I'm working my arse off to keep money coming in after you lost your job.' She concentrated on clearing up the glass, not wanting to catch his eye in case he could see what was happening in her heart. How it was wavering, being treacherous, developing feelings that she knew were wrong.

'It's that James, isn't it? That's who you're having it off with.'

'I'm not. I work with him and that's it. Don't go accusing me of—'

'Yeah, like you're gonna be honest with me.' He pointed at her, his finger swaying in the air. 'I'm watching you.' He stumbled backwards towards the hallway. 'Eyes all over the place, and if I find out you're cheating on me, then you're gone. You hear? You're out of this house with nothing.'

She carried on cleaning the floor, her body shaking. She'd never seen him like this before. Couldn't believe the change in him. He was drinking more, got angry so quickly. She'd put it down to stress. Thought it was because he was trying so hard to make up for losing his job. But maybe that wasn't it. Maybe she'd been making assumptions that were just plain wrong.

Perhaps there was a side to him that had lain dormant all these years.

His threat bounced round her head and she had to take it seriously. This weekend with James had to be the last, then she had to put more distance between them, because she could feel that her heart was betraying her, pulling her towards James and away from her husband. And her family. She couldn't let that happen. Keeping the family together was paramount, and she'd go to hell and back to make sure her children had the security she'd always yearned for when she was growing up.

Her mind scratched away at the problem while she searched the floor for stray pieces of glass.

Her deal with James had to end. But how?

The only way was to own up to Matt. Tell him what she'd done and use some of the cash from his contract to repay her debt. She nodded to herself. That was exactly what she'd do. She'd tell James she had the money. Then she'd confess to Matt and…

She sat back against the kitchen cupboard, knees to her chest, and hung her head, exhausted and confused, appalled at how her life had spiralled out of control. *How do I get back to where we were before?* She didn't have the answers, knew it was impossible. Things had fundamentally changed, and like tectonic plates shifting on the surface of the earth, her world and Matt's no longer fitted together. They were sliding in different directions and she had no idea how to pull them back together. A tear ran down her cheek, then another. She brushed them away, determined not to give in to despair. After the troubles of her childhood, surely she could work this problem out.

As she sat in the quiet of the kitchen, nothing to hear but the clock ticking on the wall, her thoughts calmed until there were no more ripples on the surface of her mind. And then, like a fish breaking the surface of the water, a new question jumped into her head.

Is Matt's work even legal?

TWENTY-ONE

Sara's hands shook with nerves as she packed her weekend bag, Matt scrutinising every little thing she put in there. They'd hardly spoken since their row the night before. Ezra had gone to stay with Hailey for the weekend, something he enjoyed doing as there was a family living next door with a little girl his age and they'd struck up an unexpected friendship. The girls were having a sleepover with Chelsea, Fiona's daughter, so Matt had the house to himself and could focus on his work. Sara thought he'd be happy with the plan, but he'd discovered a way to find fault.

'So you think I'm not capable of looking after my family now? Is that it?' His arms were folded across his chest as he leant against the wall.

'No, it's just you were annoyed that I was going away when you had work to do, so I made arrangements to give you space to get on with things and not have to think about kids and getting meals ready.' She walked into the bathroom to pack her toiletries, not wanting to argue about it. Whatever she did wouldn't be right; he was in that sort of mood.

When she came back out again, he'd gone, and she heaved a sigh of relief. She wondered if he'd seen the guilt on her face, if he could sense the fluttering of her heart. *Eyes all over the place.* That was what he'd said, and now she was worried. Had she been seen with James when they'd been out for lunch? Lunches she'd never mentioned to her husband because she knew what he was like about her being friendly with men. It was non-negotiable, something she'd understood not long after they were married, when he'd started a massive row at a bar when he thought a man was chatting her up. Imagine if he knew she was going away with James for a weekend, even if it was just for companionship. Would she come back to find her possessions littering the front lawn, her key no longer working?

She zipped up her bag and took it downstairs, pulse racing. She hated the deceit, of course she did, but part of her couldn't wait to be out of the house for a couple of days. Away from the tension that crackled between them, an argument never far away. Thank goodness the kids would be having a fun weekend as well. At least that made her feel better about leaving them.

Matt wasn't around to see her off, and she called goodbye through his office door, not surprised when he didn't respond. 'Stupid bad-tempered bloody idiot of a man,' she muttered under her breath as she marched to her car.

Sara had suggested she and James should arrive separately, given her worries about Matt finding out where she was going and with whom. They were staying at the same country-house hotel near Harrogate where the networking event had been held a couple of weeks earlier; a special offer, James had said, for network members. That was why it had to be this weekend.

As she drove through the undulating Yorkshire countryside, at its finest in its May clothes – with frothy hawthorn blossom adorning the hedgerows, the grass lush and green in the evening light – her mind had some space to work at her knotted thoughts.

I'm going to have a lovely restful time, she told herself, hands gripping the wheel tightly as the radio sang to her in the background. She'd never been on a spa weekend, although Fiona raved about them and regularly treated herself to a break away to recharge, as she put it.

She pondered then about Fiona and James. An unlikely couple, she thought. Fiona was way too forceful for a gentle soul like him.

She'd trample all over him, leave him wondering which way was up. Fiona's warning echoed in her mind. Jealous. That's definitely it, she decided. She'd have hated to be dumped. Sara let herself imagine how the conversation might have gone, the look on Fiona's face when James told her the relationship was over. She had such an expressive face at times – able to control her daughter with a mere stare – and she would have been horrified that he'd dared do that to her. Sara laughed, then admonished herself. *That's no way to think about a friend.*

As the music played and her thoughts settled, the tension in her shoulders started to ease. A massage would be heaven, she thought, and two full nights of proper sleep without a small child worming his way into the bed, keeping her awake with his wriggling. Despite all her reservations – and with Matt's suspicions put firmly to the back of her mind – she allowed herself to imagine that she could actually enjoy her weekend.

When she arrived, James was waiting for her in the reception area, sitting on one of the leather sofas next to the water feature, reading a book. He tucked it under his arm as he stood to give her a quick hug and a peck on the cheek. Her heart flipped as his lips brushed her skin, and she wondered again about his agenda. Nervously she followed him into the lift, a sudden heat flushing through her. *What if we're sharing a room?* She closed her eyes for a moment, tried to compose herself.

'Feeling tired?' James asked.

She blinked, watched the doors of the lift swish open. 'It's been a tricky week,' she said, flinching at the touch of his hand on the small of her back as he guided her along the corridor. He stopped outside a door, reached into his pocket and pulled out a key card, which he inserted into the lock. A rush of adrenaline coursed through her and she chewed her lip, wondered if she should say something. Turn round and go home.

*

'This is your room,' he said as he opened the door, indicating that she should go in first. 'I'm across the hall if you need me.' Her body sagged and she had to make a conscious effort to keep her relief hidden, make it seem like she'd assumed all along they'd be having separate rooms.

She glanced around the spacious bedroom, beautifully decorated in cream and gold and bronze, with a comfy seat by the large window. She put her bag down and walked over to study the view of landscaped gardens scattered with seating areas, trees and flower borders creating private nooks for relaxation. It looked wonderful and she was itching to get out there, stretch her legs and have a wander in the fresh air.

'Do you fancy a stroll?' he asked as he came to stand next to her, seeming to read her mind. 'Then we can have dinner. I've booked us in for eight, so we've got an hour or so to settle in.'

She turned and smiled at him. 'Oh yes, I'd love to explore the gardens. They look beautiful, don't they?' It would give her a chance to assert herself a little, she decided, make sure he knew she'd be able to pay back the money very shortly and then their deal could come to an end.

'We can pick a spot to sit outside tomorrow. The forecast is good, so we might as well enjoy it.' He sounded so happy, so evidently looking forward to their weekend, she was reluctant to spoil the mood. Relax, she told herself. There's plenty of time to talk. Her hand rested on her chest, her heart still beating far too fast. She needed to calm down first.

James was in a chatty mood, and she found herself laughing at his dry observations as they wandered round the paths, testing out each seating area until they'd chosen one they would try to claim the following day. They were just heading back inside to get changed for dinner when her phone pinged. A message from Matt. Her heart stuttered and she stopped to read it.

How are your hen girls? Send pics.

She chewed her lip, sent back a quick message.

Not arrived yet. Will send pics later.   -

James raised an eyebrow. 'Problem?'

'Um… just Matt checking I got here okay.' She sighed and rubbed at an ache in her neck where the muscles pulled tight. 'He wants pictures of the girls I'm supposed to be here with.'

James gave a slow shake of the head. 'Got you on a tight leash, hasn't he?'

Sara studied her feet, drew a pattern with her toe in the gravel. 'We had a terrible row when I said I was coming away, and he accused me of having an affair. Said he has eyes everywhere and if he finds out I'm seeing someone else, that's it. End of our marriage and he'll throw me out.' Just repeating Matt's threat made her break out in a cold sweat.

She watched James's feet as he moved his weight from one to the other, hands in his pockets. 'Well, we'll just have to make sure he doesn't find out then, won't we?' She nodded, but didn't dare look up, as then he'd see that tears weren't far away.

Silently she carried on towards the entrance, James following, her phone still clasped in her hand. A new thought crept into her head. *He'll know where I am.* Her phone would have told him her location, if he'd cared to look. Thank goodness we're actually in a spa hotel, she thought. That was a good idea of James's, to keep her lie close to the truth, but then he must have had practice with Fiona, given that she was a married woman. *Has he been here with her?* It seemed quite likely, and she wondered if she was just one of a succession of women; if James was the type who wouldn't commit, or who got a kick out of being with other men's wives.

She shook the thought away. We're not having an affair, she told herself, more forcefully than should have been necessary. Work colleagues, that's what we are. Her body tensed. *What if Matt comes here to check up on me?* The idea brought her out in another cold sweat. It was no good, she had to be straight with James about how she felt.

She turned to him as they waited for the lift to arrive. 'I really don't like this, you know. I hate all the lies.'

He didn't answer for a moment, his eyes meeting hers. 'It's not too much of a lie when you think about it. The problem is your husband not liking you having friends of the opposite sex. I could be gay for all he knows.' He gave a snort. 'What would he think about it then?'

'It's not that,' Sara protested, while the little voice in her head told her that it just might be.

James guided her into the lift. 'I'm sure there are plenty of women here who would be happy to have their picture taken with you if you asked nicely.'

She frowned. 'But I won't know them.'

He gave her a quick smile. 'And neither will Matt.'

Sara chewed her lip. He had a point. Unless Matt decided to look on Facebook and found out that none of the faces in the picture matched that of Louise Moss. Sweat prickled her skin, a headache pounding at the base of her skull.

James gave her a sideways glance. 'It might be an idea if you got rid of your phone, you know. Maybe stash it in your car. People can put all sorts of spyware on phones these days. Listen in to your conversations.'

Sara gulped, horrified at the idea. Matt was certainly capable of doing something like that. She looked at the phone still clasped in her hand, her heart racing as if she had hold of an unexploded bomb. She wondered if it was already too late. If Matt had heard their discussion about faking a photo.

'I can't leave it in the car,' she whispered, holding the phone behind her back, pressed against her clothing in the hope that it might muffle any sound. 'What if there's a problem with the girls, or Ezra? I need to be reachable.'

He thought for a moment. 'Well… just text the phone number here to anyone who needs to know. Then they can contact reception.' He shrugged. 'Say it's a no-phones weekend.'

Sara was impressed and appalled at his ability to construct believable lies without a second thought. A shiver of unease ran through her.

The lift doors opened, and she scurried to her room, wanting a bit of space to think.

'Have a look in the wardrobe,' he called to her before she closed the door, promising to be ready in half an hour.

Relieved to be alone, she stripped off and went to take a shower, welcoming the luxurious splash of hot water, the aromatic body wash filling her nostrils with a combination of essential oils designed to calm and relax. Still her heart was pounding, her mind so full of conflicting thoughts it felt like there was a wrestling match going on in her head.

She was desperate to tell someone, get advice on what to do for the best, but she was starting to wonder who she could trust. Fiona had definitely cooled towards her and could cause trouble if she wanted to by telling Matt she'd been out with James. Even Hailey was being a bit awkward with her, although it seemed she would do anything to oblige Matt. *Is everyone playing their own little games with me?* Suddenly her life was balanced on a knife edge, and she knew that one wrong move could tip her into disaster.

TWENTY-TWO

When she came out of the shower and opened the wardrobe, she found another beautiful dress, black this time, along with matching shoes. Tied to the hanger was a little evening bag. She looked inside and found a box containing a matching necklace and earrings. Costume jewellery, she told herself as she studied the sparkling stones, the colour of sapphires, set in a gold-coloured metal. The dress fitted, flattering her curves rather than making her feel chubby. James has quite an eye for clothes, she thought, but then she remembered he'd studied fashion design at university, and worked for a number of clothing manufacturers before he'd tired of the industry and decided he wanted to do something in the community that would also use his business skills.

She slipped her feet into the sparkly high heels and studied herself in the mirror, turning this way and that, amazed at the transformation a nice outfit could make. Aware that her half-hour must nearly be up, she dried her hair and applied a bit of make-up, just enough to add a touch of glamour to her face and hide the shadows beneath her eyes.

James knocked on the door as she was adding the last flicks of mascara to her lashes. 'Nearly ready,' she called, before slipping the evening bag over her shoulder and opening the door.

His eyes scanned her body, up and down and up again. He gave a low whistle. 'Looking gorgeous, Sara.' He grinned at her. 'I knew that dress was just right for you the minute I saw it. Perfect. And

I know I've put you in a difficult situation, asking you to come here with me, but does the dress help make up for it?'

A rush of emotion glued her lips together, the genuine look of appreciation on his face unexpected. She wasn't used to compliments. Not any more. She'd been with Matt so long now she didn't think he even noticed what she was wearing, let alone whether she looked good or not.

James gave a little bow and offered her his arm, and she took it, welcoming the extra support as she struggled to get the hang of walking in the high heels. But she felt good. She really did. And it was wonderful to be appreciated. Am I that shallow? she wondered as she stepped into the lift. When the doors closed, she was aware of the proximity of him, the delicious smell of his aftershave, the warmth of his body next to hers. She inched away, reminding herself that there were boundaries that must not be crossed, because that would surely undermine everything she had built. This was business. And somehow she had to move the conversation round to their deal, tell him that things had changed.

Her phone pinged as they were making their way to the dining room. James glanced at her, raised an eyebrow. They both knew who it would be without her even looking. He put a finger to his lips, and she remembered what he'd said about people being able to hear conversations.

It was indeed Matt, repeating his request for pictures of the girls, and she knew she couldn't stall again. Her eyes scanned the dining room, which stretched down one side of the building, looking out over the gardens. High ceilings and bay windows made it feel light and airy, while screens and large potted plants had been used to break it up into more private areas. She spotted a group of four women, perhaps a bit older than her, but not much. If she used the right filter, he wouldn't know. Maybe do a silly one with bunny ears or something. She made her way over to their table, James following.

'Excuse me, ladies,' she said in her best professional voice, with her brightest smile. 'We're doing an article about the hotel – trying to push the spa weekends – and I just wondered if you'd mind posing for a quick picture. We want to make it look natural.' She held up her phone.

The women looked at each other and – with a few giggles – nodded their assent. Sara passed the phone to James, who rattled off some shots, then he handed it back and she took a couple of group selfies, the women laughing and playing along. Once she'd thanked them, she followed James to their table.

'Look, I think you're right about my phone.' She glanced at the entrance, then back at James. 'I'm just going to send these pictures and then I'll leave my phone in the car. I'll be ten minutes, okay?'

'No problem.' He gave her a reassuring smile. 'Take as long as you need, then we can relax properly.'

She made her way back to the foyer, where she perched on one of the sofas while she chose a couple of pictures, applied filters and sent them. Then she followed James's advice and tapped out messages to Matt, Fiona and Hailey, telling them it was a phone-free weekend and if they needed her to ring reception. Once that was done, she dashed out to her car and stashed her phone in the glove box, throwing it in there like it was about to spontaneously combust.

With her heart thumping, and feeling more than a little flustered, she made her way back inside, hoping that she had allayed Matt's fears.

'All done?' James asked as she sat at their table.

She flashed him a smile and nodded, feeling the opposite of relaxed.

'I hope you don't mind – I ordered champagne to calm the nerves.' The glass was fizzing gently in front of her, condensation beaded on the sides. No drink had ever looked more inviting. She took a grateful sip, then another, relishing the bubbles in her mouth, the sudden whoosh of well-being that swept her fears away. James beamed at her and topped her up.

'Here's to some time out,' he said, a twinkle in his eyes as they chinked glasses.

'Rest and relaxation,' she replied, drinking the second glass as quickly as the first.

She started to enjoy the evening, her mind fuzzy with champagne, which hushed her worries until they were indistinct murmurings that were easy to ignore. James entertained her with anecdotes, and the food was delicious, but as the evening wore on, she felt increasingly tired, fighting to keep her eyes open.

'I think it might be time to retire to bed.' He laughed. 'I've been talking you to sleep, I think.' He stood, held out his arm. 'Come on, let me help you.'

She forced herself to move, and took off her shoes to make it less of a struggle, giggling at the state she was in after a couple of drinks.

'Sorry, I'm such a lightweight with alcohol,' she slurred as they walked to the lift. 'And it's been a hell of a week.'

'No problem,' James assured her, patting her hand. 'It's been a lovely evening and I'm quite tired myself.'

When they arrived at her room, he took her bag, retrieved her key card and opened the door for her, helping her inside before saying goodnight. She staggered over to the bed, flopped down and closed her eyes, her head spinning.

She woke up slowly, eyelids stuck together, feeling groggy and sluggish. After a moment's panic, thinking she needed to get up and deal with Ezra, she remembered she wasn't at home, and allowed herself to enjoy the dreamy moments of not quite being awake for a little while longer. When her eyes finally decided they had the will to open properly, she realised she desperately needed the loo.

Hauling herself out of bed, she noticed her dress and underwear hung neatly over the back of a chair, her shoes tucked underneath. *Amazing what you manage to do when you're drunk.* She didn't even remember getting undressed.

To be honest, she felt better than she'd thought she would. Her head didn't hurt, just felt a bit woolly, her mouth dry as dust. Nothing that some orange juice and a good cup of coffee wouldn't resolve. It was only when she'd finished dressing and was putting on her watch that she realised what time it was. Eleven o'clock! No wonder she felt muzzy-headed, with all that sleep. Quickly, she left her room, crossed the corridor and knocked on James's door, but there was no answer. Not surprising, given the time, she thought as she walked towards the lifts. He'd probably had his breakfast and was enjoying the sunshine in the gardens somewhere.

She was thankful they'd decided to keep the morning free, booking some treatments in for the afternoon. James had insisted, even though she'd resisted initially, telling him that a weekend away was relaxing enough. A massage would be lovely, she thought. And a facial. Then she was getting her nails done. And at some point, when the time felt right, she'd have that conversation with James.

I should probably check in with Matt and Hailey. Real life took charge of her thoughts again as soon as she exited the lift into the foyer, all the worries scurrying out of their hidey-holes, so many things she hadn't allowed herself to think about. Like Matt's business and whether he was doing something illegal. Something that could get them into trouble. *Like you did,* a voice in her head reminded her. *But I'm putting that right.* Her fingers flexed. *I am.*

James was still in the dining room, reading his book, and he smiled at her when she arrived at the table.

'Sleep well?'

'Like a proverbial log.' She sat down and poured a glass of orange juice from the jug on the table, gulped it down. 'I don't know when I last slept this late. Before I had kids, I suppose.'

James poured her a cup of coffee from the cafetière that had miraculously arrived on the table. 'Well, you must have needed the rest. And there's nothing to do today except relax.'

Relax? Fat chance of that happening. She stopped the ticking-off she was about to give herself and decided there would never be a right time to have the conversation with James. Now would have to do.

'James, I need to talk to you properly about...'

He turned his back on her and signalled for the waiter to come over. She tutted, annoyed that he wasn't listening, then hesitated and decided to wait. Can't do anything on an empty stomach, she told herself, her thinking still a little foggy.

James turned to her. 'Sorry, what were you saying?'

She gave him a quick smile, shook her head. 'Nothing. Just... It'll keep.'

He started chatting about his book – the latest Andy McNab thriller – and she sipped her coffee, no longer listening as she wondered how best to phrase her question, how to put herself in a position to negotiate. It was a tricky one, because as she saw it, if this was a game of poker they were playing, he had all the best cards.

'I've got a couple of things to sort out,' he said when her breakfast arrived. He held up his phone, as if that explained everything. 'I'll see you outside, shall I? In that seating area we picked out yesterday. I'll be half an hour at the most.'

In one way, it was a relief that he'd gone, but it was frustrating too, as she'd just got herself psyched up for talking about the terms of their deal. Had he sensed that? By the time she had some food inside her, and another cup of coffee, her brain had started to function properly again, and a slow smile crept across her lips as a new idea formed.

By covering up her crime, James was an accessory. *That's right! He's done something wrong too.* And Fiona would use that in an instant to sack him. Which left them with stalemate. But that wasn't a bad place to be, she decided as she mulled it over. Better that they were both in debt to each other, then she could repay him the money, nullify their deal and everything could get back to normal. How she longed for that.

Although James was the perfect gentleman, and she had enjoyed his company, there was something a little odd about him. His precision, the desire to buy her clothes, have her dress the way he wanted. Fiona's warning rang in her mind again. Maybe it wasn't jealousy that had made her speak out. Maybe she'd been talking to her as a friend. The more Sara thought about it, the greater her sense of unease, stirring the contents of her stomach, making her feel a little sick.

I don't want to be here.

She wanted to be at home with her children and her husband, doing the things they always did on a Saturday. This was an alien environment. *What was I thinking, imagining I'd been missing treats like this from my life?* It was an empty pleasure compared to spending time with Ezra and the girls. And spending time with Matt? Well, that was something she needed to do more of too.

An urgent need to speak to her family swelled inside her, filling her chest until she couldn't bear it, and she dashed outside to her car to retrieve her phone. It took her a moment to realise the battery was flat. With a silent scream, she slammed the car door and locked it before taking the phone up to her room to recharge.

Feeling more resolute now she had her bargaining position worked out, she plugged in the phone and waited for it to buzz to life. No messages. A twinge of hurt squeezed at her heart. You told them it was a no-phones weekend, she reminded herself. Still, it would have been nice to feel needed, or to know they were missing her.

Out of the corner of her eye, she saw the dress draped over the chair. It suddenly felt like a symbol of James's control. Was this what Fiona meant? she wondered, thinking of the way James had gradually been taking more of her time, slowly separating her from her husband and family. She gave a little shiver, and hung the dress up in the wardrobe, out of sight, along with the bag and the jewellery. He could have it all back. She didn't want him to decide what clothes she would wear.

The more she thought about it, the odder it felt.

I'm going home, she decided. I'm going to have that chat, get this sorted, then I'm going.

She rang Matt. No answer.

She rang Hailey. No answer.

Where are they?

A knock on the door made her jump. She answered it to find James standing there.

'I was waiting for you,' he said, a note of impatience in his voice.

'I'm going home.' Sara opened the door wider to let him into the room. 'I'm sorry, but I don't want to be here. I can't relax.' She caught the panic in his eyes, made herself go on. 'I just feel too guilty. I should be with my family.'

'But what about our deal?'

She stepped away from him, not so confident now. 'You covered up a criminal act by lending me that money, so the way I see it, if the truth comes out, you're in as much trouble as me.' At last she'd stood her ground, and she straightened her back, pulled herself up to her full height.

He looked startled, just for a second, then regained his composure and gave her a warm smile.

'Look, why don't you come into the garden? Let's get a coffee and have a proper chat about this.'

She knew she'd feel happier talking about everything outside, where there were other people around, rather than in the confined space of her bedroom, so she followed him down the corridor. They made their way to the gardens, ordering coffee at reception on the way.

Sara perched on the edge of her chair, determined to get their discussion over with.

'Don't look so worried,' James said, settling back in his seat. He smiled at her, eyes searching hers. 'I'm just trying to treat you in the way you deserve, that's all. I know it may seem strange, but it gives me pleasure to see you having a good time.' He raised an eyebrow. 'And we did have a good time last night, didn't we?'

She thought about their dinner, the easy chat, the laughter, and nodded. 'Yes, we did. But the thing is… I'm homesick. I know that sounds daft, but I've never been away from the kids before, and although I might have yearned for this type of weekend, the reality is different. You know Matt's being really awkward and suspicious, and now I've started thinking about it, I can't relax. I need to go home. Be with my family.'

James pressed his lips together, thoughtful. He picked up his coffee and took a sip before putting the cup carefully back on the saucer. 'I don't want to bully you into spending time with me.' He looked a little sad, and she realised she'd been insensitive, perhaps hurt his feelings. 'But a deal's a deal.'

'I can pay you back.' This was her trump card, and she saw the surprise in his eyes, felt a moment of triumph, like she had the upper hand for once. 'Matt's finished his contract, so he'll get paid soon. I can pay you some of the money, if not all of it.'

He stared at her, an intensity in his blue eyes that she hadn't seen before, and she looked away, hands fidgeting in her lap. It was all she could do to stop herself from getting up and making a run for it back to her room.

'Well, I'm pleased for you.' The curtness in his voice suggested the opposite. 'But until that money is in my account, our deal has to stand, doesn't it?' He sighed. 'I think you've got me all wrong, though, Sara. I'm not trying to make life hard for you. I'm just a friend, someone who wants to look after you. And now you're going to run back to that yob of a husband.' He held up a hand. 'Sorry. No offence, but I can…' He took a deep breath, his voice gentle, pleading. 'Why don't we stick with plan A? Just for this weekend. I've booked the treatments for this afternoon. Then we can have a lovely dinner tonight. You get another good night's sleep and we'll leave before lunch tomorrow instead of staying the whole day. How about that? Just allow yourself to relax and be treated for once in your life.'

She thought about the massage, how nice that would be, how much she needed her muscles untangling, all the stress smoothed away. She glanced at him and he gave her a hopeful smile. 'Nobody's expecting you home until tomorrow. Your family will have made their own plans, and to be honest, it's good to let them try and manage without you. Then they'll understand what you do for them and they might treat you a bit better.'

She bit her lip as she wavered.

He carried on. 'I know I can trust you, Sara. I know you're an honourable woman. I know taking the money was a moment of madness, a mistake. And I know you'll pay me back one day. But...' he shrugged, 'humour me, however strange it may seem. I like making people happy; it has value to me. So our deal stands, but just until the money is in my account, okay?'

She let his words sink in, still torn, part of her wanting to run home, another part yearning for time to herself so she could work out what had happened to her life and who she could really trust. She studied his face, his eyes imploring her to stay. He looked like a dog waiting for its owner to decide if it was time to go for a walk, scrutinising her every move. She thought about the time they'd spent together. Although he'd been attentive, he'd never made a move to seduce her, even when she'd been a bit drunk the night before. He'd only ever been kind to her.

'This has to be the last time. The last favour,' she said.

He smiled and finished his coffee. 'Is wanting to look after a friend such a bad thing?'

She had to admit that it wasn't. And so she stayed.

TWENTY-THREE

The rest of the day passed in a pleasant blur of treatments, and by the evening, the stress had been kneaded from her muscles, her skin was silken, her nails perfect and her face glowed. Never had she felt so pampered. But it was tiring work, this relaxation, and by the end of their evening meal, her limbs were so heavy it was a job to lift a spoon to eat her dessert.

After her conversation with James, she understood this was about him being lonely and needing somebody to lavish attention on, and she felt more comfortable about the situation. It was sad that he'd got to the age of forty-five and was alone, nobody to share his life with, but that wasn't her problem. He knew their deal was nearing its end, which meant this was the last time they'd be having dinner together and despite everything, that made her a little despondent. Once she'd got over her initial nerves, it had been nice to get out of the house on her own, nice to experience the company of a different type of man to her husband. And if she was being honest, she'd miss James's attentiveness.

A pleasant and slightly strange interlude, she told herself. She'd still see him at work; Matt couldn't argue with that. They could still do lunch, if they were careful. *Friends*. It was a thought that warmed her heart, because James had added a new dimension to her life that she rather enjoyed. Innocent bordering on the illicit.

When she nearly fell asleep in her dessert for the second time, she remembered the therapist's warning that she might feel weary after the massage, something to do with expelling toxins. 'I'm sorry, James. That was a lovely meal and I hate to cut the evening short, but I'm dead on my feet here. I'm going to have to have an early night.'

He dabbed at his mouth with his napkin, finished his wine and gave her an indulgent smile. 'No problem. Here, let me make sure you get back to your room. Can't have you falling asleep in the lift.' He stood and offered her his arm for support as they made their way to the foyer. 'I bumped into a friend, actually, while you were having your massage, so I'll probably go and have a drink with him. He's on his own, I think he said.'

Sara was relieved that at least James would have some company for the rest of the evening, her focus now on getting to bed. She stumbled out of the lift and down the corridor to her room, glad of James's support.

Once he'd opened the door for her and made sure she was okay, he left, and she wondered again if he might be gay, or maybe bisexual; whether this man he'd bumped into was more than a friend. Was that why he hadn't made a move on her?

It was an odd situation, she thought, to want to dress a woman up, get her preened to perfection and then not try and sleep with her. It really didn't make any sense. Friends, she reminded herself, too tired to think, to even get undressed. She climbed under the covers and instantly fell asleep.

Sara woke on Sunday morning feeling stiff and sore, muscles aching, her skin tacky after a sweaty night. Her clothes lay in a tangled pile by the bed, where she must have thrown them off in the night. She wondered if she was coming down with something, or perhaps it was just the after-effects of the treatments, working the toxins out of her body.

She got herself washed and dressed, then packed all her clothes, except the things James had bought for her. She couldn't take those home, because every time she wore them, she'd think about this weekend, and that wouldn't feel right if she was with Matt. She put them in a neat pile on the bed, ready to return.

James was already eating breakfast in the dining room when she joined him. He was very chirpy and seemed in the best of moods, even though she'd cut their weekend short. She, on the other hand, was feeling grumpy and thick-headed. She wondered if his good mood had something to do with the mystery friend he'd gone to meet last night, and the thought made her smile.

'That's better. You've got a beautiful smile,' he said, observing her as usual. She blushed and focused on her food, gobbling down the organic granola as quickly as she could so this whole peculiar episode could end. It was time to go home.

Sara went to pick up Ezra from Hailey's first. He was sitting on the windowsill in the lounge, waiting for her. She waved when she saw him there, her heart warmed by the instant delight on his face. He disappeared from view, and the minute Hailey opened the door, he threw himself at Sara's legs. She swung him into her arms, her heart bursting with love for her child, and as she hugged him to her, she had a moment of clarity, an understanding that she'd got her priorities all wrong. Being with her family was all that mattered; everything else was a distraction, taking her away from the people she loved most in the world. Tears sprang to her eyes and she buried her face in Ezra's neck, filling her nostrils with the scent of him.

Hailey gave her an appraising look as she held open the door. 'Have a good weekend with… Louise?' The way she said it, one eyebrow raised, made it very clear she didn't believe Sara's story about the hen weekend. 'Back early, aren't you?'

Sara smiled and kissed Ezra's head, avoiding her sister's gaze. 'You can have too much of a good thing. Anyway I missed everyone.'

Ezra hugged her tighter. 'I missed you too, Mummy. You won't go away again, will you?'

'No,' Sara said with certainty. 'No, I won't.'

'We had a good time, though, didn't we, Ez?' Hailey ruffled his hair. 'And we have a surprise, don't we?'

Ezra wriggled out of Sara's grasp, sliding down her body until his feet reached the floor. 'We made cakes. I made you a special one.' He grabbed her hand, and led her to the kitchen, Hailey following. On the table, centre stage, was a plate full of cupcakes, and sitting on its own was the one he'd made for her, decorated with skittles and sprinkles and lots of icing. Her heart squeezed with love. Her shoulders tensed with guilt.

'That's just wonderful,' she said, choking on the ball of emotion that blocked her throat. 'Wonderful.'

Hailey packed the cakes into a Tupperware container, and after a brief chat, Sara headed home. Fiona had said she'd drop the girls off, as they were going on a shopping trip to Leeds, which they had been beyond excited about. It was something Sara could rarely bring herself to do these days; it wasn't just the cost of such an excursion, but Ezra was a reluctant shopper and the girls liked to take their time, which created way too much stress for the day to be enjoyed by any of them. The girls both had some birthday money to spend, so Sara was sure they'd come back laden with bags, and she was excited to see what they'd bought.

Matt was in the lounge, watching TV, when she finally got home. He looked up when she came in, and she smiled at him, a little wary of his response, given the way he'd been acting before she went away. But he surprised her by smiling back before turning his attention to their son, who'd jumped on his lap and was telling him what he'd been doing.

Half an hour later, the girls arrived, faces flushed with excitement, and Sara was swept up in the bustle of getting a meal ready and looking at her daughters' purchases, which they paraded for her like a fashion show. It was a busy, chatty afternoon and she couldn't help feeling that they'd all benefited from a little time away from each other. Matt seemed especially cheerful, and that evening, when the children had gone to bed, she found out why.

She'd just returned to the living room with tea for both of them, the room feeling empty, the atmosphere charged with a sudden tension now they were alone. This is it. My chance to come clean, she decided as she carefully put the mugs on the coffee table, her hands shaking so much she was in danger of spilling scalding tea all over the place. But before she could say anything, Matt spoke.

'I got paid yesterday.' There was a triumphant gleam in his eye as he waited for her response.

She blinked, wrong-footed, all the words she was about to say disappearing like a wisp of smoke from a lighted match. 'Fantastic,' she said after a beat too long, hoping he hadn't noticed her hesitation. She sat next to him on the sofa, made herself look him in the eye and fixed an enthusiastic smile to her face. 'Come on then, tell me all about it. It's been a bit of a mystery, this contract of yours.'

'They want me to do more.'

He looked so pleased with himself, she wavered about her confession. Maybe it can wait, she thought, her hands fidgeting, pulling at the hem of her T-shirt.

She smiled harder. 'Well, that's good, isn't it?'

He grinned, picked up his tea and blew on the surface before taking a sip. 'This is just the start. Just you wait. Things are going to be so much better for us.'

'So…' Sara tried to remember what he'd said about payment before she went away. 'They paid you cash?'

'That's right.'

'How much exactly?'

'Enough to pay off at least one of the credit cards and catch up with the mortgage.'

She bit her lip; his answer was too vague to work out the exact amount. 'It would be good to save some, wouldn't it?' She averted her eyes, brushed imaginary fluff off her jeans. 'Just in case the next contract takes longer than you think.'

Silence.

There was an edge to his voice when he eventually spoke. 'You know, it would be really good if you had a bit of confidence in me.'

Oh God, I've upset him now. She put out a hand, rubbed his leg. 'I do. Of course I do. It's just—'

'Just what?' he snapped, making her jump, his good mood in danger of turning nasty.

She smoothed the fabric of the settee, picking at a blob of chocolate as she searched for an answer, still unable to look at him. 'It feels like we're still quite vulnerable. Financially, I mean. My full-time contract is only until September. Then they're reviewing the whole staffing of the community centre to see if they can find cost savings. That's what I read in the minutes of Fiona's meeting with the new treasurer.' She glanced at Matt, grimaced. 'Might be good to have a nest egg to fall back on.'

If only she could persuade him to put some of his cash in the savings account, she'd be able to pay off a bit of her debt to James. And that would make her feel a whole lot better. *What if I can't pay any back?* The idea sent a flutter of panic through her chest. Would James reinstate their deal? Ask her to attend more events with him, maybe more weekends away? If that happened, Matt was bound to find out, and then… Her mind galloped along the line of logic to the worst possible conclusion. Her life as she knew it was hanging in the balance and she had no idea how to tip things in the right direction.

Matt scowled. 'Since when have you been in charge of how I spend my earnings?' She bit her lip a little harder, didn't reply that she was the one who ran the household finances, sorted out the bills. His hands were flying in the air. Annoyance scrunched his forehead into deep furrows. 'I'm perfectly capable of working out priorities. And anyway, it's my job to provide for my family, so I'll do what I see fit without you lording it over me.' He stared at her. 'Thing is, I have to invest in the business as well. There's some new kit I need, so I've ordered that. And I've thought about savings. I'm not stupid. That's why I got half the payment in bitcoin.'

Bitcoin? She had no idea what that was, apart from an inkling that it was a computerised currency. 'But how will…' She stopped, the look on his face telling her that now was not a good time to be pushing anything that contradicted his view of things. Persuading Matt to do anything against his will was a skilled operation and something she'd had little success with over the years.

He picked up his tea and took a few gulps before standing. 'Look, I'm sorry to get a bit uptight.' He sighed and ran a hand through his hair, eyes on the ground for a moment before he caught her gaze. 'It's just… Well, it's my job to look after you all, and I think I've done all right up to now.' His eyes challenged her. 'Haven't I?'

'You've been brilliant,' she said, all enthusiastic because she could sense trouble in his tone.

'Well, you'll just have to trust me, then.' He crouched in front of her, hands on her knees, and leant forward to give her a tender kiss, taking her by surprise. 'I'm doing this for us, so we don't have to worry about the future. Honestly, Sara. This could be big. Really big.'

'I'd just like to know…' She tried to stop herself, but the question was too enormous to keep inside any longer. 'Is it legal?'

He stared at her for a moment, clearly thrown. 'I just write code,' he said at last. 'What people do with that is nothing to do with me.'

He got up and walked into the kitchen. She heard the back door open, then close, leaving her with nothing but a chattering disquiet. Instead of the money she stole getting them out of trouble, it seemed his activities might land them in it. *We could both end up in prison.* She shuddered. The idea that her children would be on their own, facing the uncertainties that had marred her own childhood, made her squeeze her eyes shut and pinch the bridge of her nose to stop herself from descending into sobs of self-pity.

In doing what she'd thought was for the best, she now found herself in the worst possible situation. Caught in a marriage that made her feel helpless, with a man who was building their future on something that was probably criminal, indebted to another man who had an agenda she didn't understand, while she herself was guilty of a crime that could separate her from her family if she was found out.

It can't get any worse than this, she told herself.

But it did.

TWENTY-FOUR

Later that evening, Sara was making herself a sandwich when Matt flung open the back door and charged into the kitchen, the door bouncing against the wall as he waved his phone in the air.

'What the hell do you call this?' His face was scrunched in an angry snarl, a vein popping out on his forehead.

She stopped buttering bread, clutched the knife a little more tightly in her hand as she tried to guess what he was talking about. Had someone spotted her and James together? Had she been seen having cosy chats over coffee, candlelit dinners with champagne, giggling her way back to her room, leaning on James for support? Her pulse sped up as the possibilities scrolled through her mind, every image incriminating if taken out of context.

He thrust his phone in front of her face, and it took a minute for her eyes to adjust and her brain to register what she was seeing. A video clip. One that made her recoil in disgust. A naked man and woman on a bed. The man stroking a hand up and down the woman's leg before it started creeping higher, towards her breast.

She pushed the phone away. 'What do I want to see that for?' she snapped.

He looked at her as if she'd gone mad. 'It's you.' He pointed at the figure, slowly enunciating every word. 'That is you.'

She frowned, confused. 'What are you talking about?'

'Look at the tattoo on her thigh.' His fingers snatched at the screen, making the image bigger.

Her eyes grew round, a terrible sinking feeling in her chest. Her legs weakened and she leant against the worktop for support. He was right. Her tattoo was very distinctive: the names of her three children entwined with roses. She made herself watch the video for a moment, disgust churning the contents of her stomach as the man's hands roamed over her body. She seemed to be responding with little grunts and movements – although she had no recollection of any of it happening.

James. That was her first thought. Then she noticed a signet ring on the little finger of the man's hand. A red stone set in gold. It wasn't James. The skin on her scalp pulled tight with the horror of what she was seeing, her heart skipping and flipping in her chest. *Who the hell is it?*

'I knew it!' Matt shouted, stomping up and down the kitchen, hands waving in the air. 'I knew you were having an affair. You can't deny it now, can you?'

Her mouth opened, her head full of denial, but shock made the words stick in her throat, still no clue as to who the man was or how it had happened.

Finally she found her voice. 'Who sent you that? How did—'

'Doesn't matter, does it?' he snapped.

She looked at the screen again, noticing that the clip went on for almost an hour. An hour! *Oh my God. What's he doing to me?* She watched in appalled silence as the man's fingers trailed ever so slowly from her ankle to her knee, before inching higher. She couldn't bear to see any more, didn't want to know what else had happened in the hour of filming. This had to be something to do with James. Fury flared in her chest as she sent the file to herself, determined to confront him with the evidence.

Matt snatched the phone off her, his face red now, as furious as she'd ever seen him. 'I told you what would happen if I ever found out you were cheating, didn't I?' He pointed the phone at her, his eyes almost popping out of his head.

'Matt, no,' she pleaded, tears of desperation in her voice. 'You don't understand. I'm not! I don't know how that happened. I don't. I have no idea who that man is.'

'You expect me to believe that?' he snarled.

'But it's true, it—' She ducked as he swiped at her with his hand, adrenaline coursing through her veins, then watched in horror as he started throwing things while she cowered on the floor unable to say or do anything to stop him, the butter knife still firmly clutched in her hand.

Mugs went flying, then the plates she'd stacked ready to put away. He swiped the fruit bowl off the worktop, sending apples bouncing in all directions, the wooden bowl sliding across the tiles. She hoped the children hadn't woken up, frightened by the racket, glad that the kitchen door was closed and their bedrooms were at the front of the house. For a moment, there was silence, and she thought maybe his anger had abated. She daren't look, her arms clasped over her head, knees to her chest. Suddenly he grabbed her wrist, the knife was wrenched from her hand and he started dragging her across the floor. 'No, no, no,' she sobbed. 'You've got to listen to me. There's something weird—'

'I'm not listening to any more of your lies,' he snapped, uncurling her fingers from the table leg where she'd tried to anchor herself. Chairs toppled as she kicked out, desperately seeking something to grasp on to. But he was a man possessed – his strength reinforced by fury – and he shoved her out of the back door, leaving her shocked and shivering in the cool of the night. She heard the lock turn, knew he was beyond the point of reasoning.

A few minutes later, the door opened and her handbag flew out, followed shortly after by her car keys, thrown with such force, they smacked against her face, leaving a throbbing pain that matched the ache in her heart.

'Matt. Please listen to me, please.' She scrambled to her feet, desperate to explain. To tell him she had no idea who the man was or how the video had been taken.

'You slag! How could you?' He stood in the doorway, sobbing with rage, chest heaving, face contorted and wet with tears. She lunged forward, trying to get back inside, but the door slammed in her face. The lock turned again and she heard the bolt slide home.

She slapped at the door in disbelief, body shaking with shock. Only a few hours ago, she'd come home believing this to be her sanctuary, her safe place, happy to be back at the heart of the family, full of laughter and smiles. And now this. Expelled.

A cool breeze brought goose bumps to her skin. Wearing only a T-shirt and jeans, her feet bare, she started to shiver, and rubbed her arms to try and get warm as she stared at the house. There was no point knocking. No point begging. Not until he'd calmed down. She trudged down the driveway to her car and got in. There was only one place she could go: Hailey's.

She reversed out of the drive, the pedals cold against her feet, reminding her of the time she'd had to leave home in nothing but her nightclothes, Hailey tugging her along, urging her to go faster when she was still half asleep.

'Come on,' her sister had pleaded. 'He'll start belting you too if we're not quick.'

Sara had dug her heels in, staring back over her shoulder towards the little terraced house they'd moved into only a few months before. 'We can't leave Mum,' she'd whimpered, but Hailey's hand pulled harder and she wasn't strong enough to resist.

'We've got to go and get help. Come on,' Hailey had urged, leading her to the end house of the row, where she'd started banging on the door, all the time glancing back the way they had come, frightened they'd been followed.

Luckily, Mrs Greenwood had been in that night. It had all worked out, after a fashion, although it had been weeks before their mother was out of hospital, and months before Sara saw her again.

She shook the thoughts away, concentrated on the road ahead of her.

Hailey might be able to talk to him, she thought as she drove. The two of them seemed to be getting on better these days. It hadn't always been the case, but Matt appeared to have become more palatable to Hailey once he'd lost his job and she'd seen the vulnerable side to him. Hailey liked vulnerable. She hated cocky men, alpha males, and Matt generally fitted in that category. She'd told Sara a few times over the years that she thought he was too dominant, but Sara hadn't wanted to listen. She knew marriage was a compromise, knew Matt had a soft side and his need to be in control came from childhood insecurities, but she couldn't explain it all to Hailey. It was Matt's business and it had taken long enough for him to talk to Sara, his wife, about it, so she wasn't going to gossip to her sister.

Compromise was not a word Hailey was very familiar with in her own relationships with men. She was not going to be dominated by anyone and was probably oversensitive to any signs of control. It was the reason why her marriage had fallen apart after nine years, and why she'd been on her own ever since. Given their past, it wasn't surprising.

Being four years older than Sara, Hailey could remember more about their chaotic home life, her mother's ragtag boyfriends and their associates. Rare conversations about their childhood – usually after they'd drunk too much wine and Hailey had dropped her guard – had also revealed a dark side to one of her foster placements. A man with wandering hands. Hailey hadn't gone into detail, and Sara could only guess at what might have happened. They certainly avoided the subject these days; now their mother was dead, it was like that part of their past had died with her.

When she pulled up outside Hailey's house, she was glad to see the lights still on. It wasn't late, just before ten, but Hailey went to bed early and got up early; an off-for-a-run-before-breakfast sort of person. She was slow to answer the door, opening it a crack, the security chain on as she peered out, suspicion written all over her face. She frowned when she saw it was Sara, clearly puzzled.

'What are you doing here?'

'Matt's thrown me out,' Sara said, before the words made it real and the tears started to fall. 'Can I come in?'

She could hear Hailey muttering as she undid the security chain, scanning the street as if she was expecting trouble, before closing the door and locking it again as soon as Sara was inside. Bolts top and bottom, as well as the chain and the lock. A bit over-the-top, Sara had always thought, but Hailey's work had repercussions at times, and a few years ago she'd been attacked in her home by a disgruntled father who'd decided it was her fault that his son had pressed charges for assault. It was that sort of clientele she was dealing with. Damaged and vulnerable children from dysfunctional families. She was passionate about it – above and beyond what was expected – and Sara always felt it was more her sister's vocation than her job.

Sara followed her into the kitchen, where Hailey flicked on the kettle and grabbed a couple of mugs from the drainer; tea being her answer to every problem. Sara sank into a chair at the kitchen table, her head in her hands, body shaking from head to toe. *How has it come to this?* She still couldn't comprehend what she'd seen in the video. After a minute, she pulled her phone from her pocket, hesitating before she tapped in her PIN to bring it to life, not sure if she could bring herself to look again.

Hailey came over with the tea. 'Come on then. Tell me what's going on.'

Sara let out a heavy sigh that seemed to come all the way from her toes. I'm going to have to tell her, she thought, holding her phone a little tighter.

'I'm in a mess,' she said to the table, shame burning her cheeks. 'I thought I was helping. It seemed like the right thing to do at the time. But everything I've done has been flipped on its head, and now…' She looked up at her sister, her voice hardly more than a whisper. 'Matt thinks I'm having an affair.'

Hailey's eyes widened and she froze on the spot, hands on the back of the chair she'd pulled out to sit on. 'And are you?'

Sara's mouth dropped open, appalled that Hailey would think her capable of such a thing. 'No! Of course I'm not. I wouldn't do that. You know I wouldn't do anything to break up my family.'

Hailey frowned as she sat down, her eyes on Sara's face. 'Why does Matt think you are, then?'

'Someone sent him a video. Of me and a man.' Hailey's eyebrows shot up and she froze, her mug of tea halfway to her mouth. 'And I've no idea where it's come from or how it can even exist.' Desperation filled Sara's voice; she knew how improbable it sounded. 'I haven't been with another man. Not ever. I've only been with Matt.'

Hailey put her mug back on the table, clearly shocked. 'You'll have to stop right there, back up a bit, because I'm not following this at all.'

Sara took a deep breath and started from the beginning, frowning as she tried to make sense of it herself, her finger tracing a pattern on the wooden table. 'Everything was fine when I got home. Then we started talking about money and this contract he's just finished.' She sighed. 'But that's another story altogether. Anyway, he got annoyed with me – all defensive, you know what he's like – and went out to his office. A bit later on, he came storming into the kitchen with this video on his phone. Me and a man I don't even know.' She closed her eyes, hands rubbing at her forehead as if to erase the images. 'All hell broke loose. I have never seen him so mad. Honestly, Hailey, I was so scared. He just went wild, accused me of having an affair, started smashing things, then dragged me outside and locked me out.'

Hailey remained silent. Sara gulped. *I'll have to show her.*

Heart racing, she swiped through her phone to find the video she'd sent to herself. She pressed play, but couldn't look, her face on fire as she passed the phone across. Her hands fidgeted, twisting her wedding ring round and round her finger as she waited for her sister's response.

Hailey was quiet for a while before she finally spoke. 'Bloody hell, Sara. Who is this guy?'

'I told you, I've no idea. It's cleverly filmed, isn't it? You don't get to see his face, just what… what he's doing to me.' She buried her hands in her hair, revolted at the thought of a stranger molesting her.

Hailey grimaced and put the phone face down on the table. 'Have you watched it all?'

Sara shook her head. 'There's fifty-five minutes of it.' She swallowed a sob. 'I don't even know…' She covered her face with her hands.

'Did you have sex with him?' Hailey's question hung in the air.

'I don't know,' Sara muttered into her palms, unable to look at her sister. That was the worst thing about the whole episode. *Was I raped?*

'You don't remember?' Hailey sounded incredulous, and Sara would have to admit it sounded improbable. But it was true. She lowered her hands and looked at her sister as tears trickled down her face.

'As far as I'm aware, I haven't had sex with anyone except Matt.' She caught Hailey's expression, saw the way her eyes had narrowed, assessing. 'You've got to believe me,' she insisted, hands pressed together.

'And you don't know where Matt got the video from?'

Sara shook her head, swiping the tears from her cheeks.

Hailey glanced at the phone, still face down on the table. 'Well, you can't blame him for the way he reacted, can you? I mean, what does it look like to you?'

Sara was startled by her sister's tone. She'd expected sympathy but instead she felt an element of judgement. Their eyes locked.

'What?' Hailey snapped. 'There's a video of you with a man sucking your nipples. What's your husband supposed to think's happening?'

Something clicked in Sara's mind, a detail that had been niggling away. She picked up the phone, studied the image carefully, ignoring the naked figures but checking the surroundings. Yes, there it was. Her dress draped over the back of a chair.

'Oh my God,' she gasped. 'It was this weekend. See that dress? James bought—' She clamped her mouth shut. *I've said too much.*

Hailey's eyes widened, her mouth gaping. 'You were with James this weekend? So you weren't at a hen party?' Her expression hardened. 'You know, I sort of had a feeling that something was off.' Her finger jabbed the air. 'You lied to me!'

'It's not what you think,' Sara gasped. 'It isn't.'

'Bloody hell! What am I supposed to think?' Hailey glared at her, a look full of questions and doubt and anger. 'I'm not even sure I want you here. You know I can't stand liars and cheats.' She forced her words through gritted teeth. 'After everything we went through together, the promises we made each other, and you just…' She stood and grabbed hold of Sara's arm, pulling her to her feet. 'I'm too angry to listen,' she said as she marched her to the door. 'You had everything you could possibly want, and you've thrown it all away. For what? A bit of casual sex?' Her fingers dug into Sara's flesh as she tried to undo the bolt at the top of the door.

Christ, she's going to throw me out too! I've got to make her listen.

Sara squirmed out of her sister's grasp and ran up the stairs. The bathroom was straight ahead and she dashed inside, locking the door behind her.

With her heart pounding, she leant against the door, listening to the footsteps thundering up the stairs. If Hailey wouldn't let her stay, she had nowhere else to go. Her chest heaved. *What am I going to do?*

TWENTY-FIVE

Sara's entire body rattled as Hailey pounded on the door.

'Come out of there, Sara! I don't want you in my house. I thought you were better than this.'

'You need to listen to me!' Sara had to shout to make herself heard over the thudding of Hailey's fists. 'Just let me tell you the whole story and then you can judge me.'

'You can't stay in the bathroom. Why don't you come out, then I can hear you?'

Sara huffed. 'I'm staying here.' She slid to the floor, adrenaline pumping round her body, the sound of her pulse whooshing in her ears. 'But you've got to let me speak.'

Silence.

'Okay,' Hailey said eventually, a weariness in her voice. 'Don't you go lying to me, though. I want the truth.'

Sara took a deep breath and told her sister everything. About losing her inheritance, stealing the money to help Matt start his business, being found out, feeling cornered into accepting James's offer, her debt and everything that had happened since.

When she'd finished, she felt spent, her stupidity, her bad choices so apparent now she'd laid it all out. It was a while before Hailey finally spoke.

'Well, you need to talk to James, don't you? He's obviously the one behind everything. He took you to that place.'

'But that's not him in the picture. That's the part that doesn't make sense.'

'Doesn't mean he didn't set it up. Do you think he drugged you?'

Sara thought about their evenings together, how quickly she'd seemed to get drunk, how fast she'd fallen asleep, the way her clothes were so neatly tidied away that first night with no recollection of taking them off. A cold chill of realisation brought goose bumps to her skin.

'I think maybe he did.' Sudden tears caught in her throat, sobs heaving in her chest. 'Oh Hailey, what have I done?'

'It's not your fault you were drugged and bloody molested.' Hailey sounded indignant now, finally understanding that Sara was telling the truth. 'Look, open the door. Then we can talk properly.'

Sara reached up and turned the lock, then hauled herself to her feet. When she opened the door, Hailey held out her arms for a hug and Sara clung to her as she cried, Hailey rubbing her back until the tears finally stopped. She let go of her sister, accepting the toilet roll Hailey grabbed for her to blow her nose and wipe her face, feeling completely spent.

'You can have the spare room,' Hailey said as she led Sara down the landing. 'I haven't changed the bed since Ezra was in here.'

Sara picked up a pillow and breathed in the scent of her son as she sank onto the bed. The prospect of being separated from her children hit her then, a pain so raw it ripped through her heart.

'You've got to help me, Hailey. Matt won't let me back home. I know he won't. He's so black-and-white about everything and you can't argue with that video on the face of it. He won't let me explain. And if he knows about James, well… he's not going to believe our relationship is innocent, is he?'

Hailey sat next to her on the bed. 'Maybe James *isn't* innocent, though. You haven't watched the whole video, have you?'

Sara clutched the pillow to her chest, eyes wide at the thought. 'You think there might have been more than one man?'

Hailey put an arm round her shoulder, dipped her head so she could look Sara in the eye. 'We're going to have to watch the whole thing, so we know exactly what happened to you. Then tomorrow we go to the police.'

Sara pulled away, horrified at the thought. 'I can't do that! Don't you understand? If the police are involved, everything will come out about me stealing the money. I'll end up in prison.'

Hailey grimaced. 'Oh God, I hadn't thought of that. What a bloody mess!'

'And there's more.'

Hailey looked worried. 'What more can there possibly be?'

Sara squeezed the pillow harder. 'I think this contract of Matt's involves something illegal. He says it's to do with writing code, and what his client does with that isn't his business.'

Hailey puffed out her cheeks. 'I suppose he could be right there. Technically. If he says he doesn't know what they want it for.'

'But you understand I can't have the police sniffing round our business for any number of reasons. I've got to sort this out myself.'

Hailey nodded, thoughtful. 'Okay, I see your point, but I'm not sure I agree. You know there *are* mitigating circumstances. The money you took hasn't technically gone anywhere, so the community centre hasn't lost out.' She shrugged. 'Has a crime been committed?' She was quiet for a moment, thinking. 'I'm not sure how they would view it, to be honest. But filming people without their consent is definitely a crime. Drugging and molesting women is definitely a crime. And who knows what else happened to you?'

Sara thought back to her weekend, her body trembling at the thought of someone having sex with her while she was unconscious. Her stomach lurched, bile shooting up her throat, acrid on the back of her tongue. She closed her eyes, pushed the images away. 'I don't... I don't think I was raped.' She turned to her sister. 'You'd know, wouldn't you?' She sounded uncertain, her voice wavering as she thought about how grubby she'd felt when she woke up. Sweaty and sticky and... She shuddered and wrapped her arms round her chest, hugging herself tight.

Hailey nodded. 'I suppose you would.' But she didn't sound sure.

They sat in silence, absorbing the implications. Sara was determined she wasn't going to discuss it any further because... what if... She started speaking to rid her mind of the horrible pictures, the appalling possibilities. 'I want to go home. I can't be separated from my kids. I can't.'

Hailey gave her arm a reassuring rub. 'How about I try and talk to Matt for you? See if I can smooth things over.'

Sara considered her suggestion. 'Why not? He seems to have warmed to you recently.'

Hailey made no response, ignoring the implied question in her comment. Instead she pulled Sara into a sudden hug. 'You really know how to sabotage yourself, don't you, sis? Honestly, you had it all. But it wasn't enough, was it?' She sighed. 'That's you all over, always wanting the next thing. You were like that as a kid. Never wanted the toys you had, always wanted the thing you couldn't afford.' She pulled back, a hand on Sara's shoulder, and gave her a determined smile. 'We'll get it sorted, don't you worry.'

But Sara was worried. Because the only way to sort this out was to watch the video. She couldn't challenge James until she knew what had actually happened. That was the reality. Her skin crawled. She clasped Hailey's hand, grateful that she had at least one person she could rely on.

Hailey went downstairs and got Sara's phone, brought it up to the bedroom. They held hands as they sat next to each other and Sara pressed play. Two different men, neither of them James. Just less than half an hour each. The only good thing about it was there was no evidence of rape. Fondling, caressing and everything else you might like to do to someone. One man spent a good fifteen minutes sucking her toes and licking her feet.

'It could have been worse,' Sara said when the video finished and she switched the phone off, trying to diminish the effect it'd had on her. Not wanting to allow these men to have taken anything from her, to have broken her. But her skin itched to be washed, crawling with the ghostly touch of their fingers.

'Two of them. Bloody hell,' Hailey whispered, sounding as stunned as Sara felt.

'Neither of them was James, which makes me wonder if he was filming it.' Nausea stirred the contents of Sara's stomach, and she ran down the landing into the bathroom, hugging the toilet bowl as she spewed up her last meal. Strangers taking advantage of her when she was unconscious. Filming and sharing it. Once again, bile burned the back of her throat as she heaved and heaved until there was nothing left.

She ran the shower, washing every inch of her body, then doing it all over again, the water as hot as she could stand it. Finally, when the water ran cold, she dried herself and went into the bedroom, finding an oversized T-shirt and dressing gown that Hailey had put out for her. On shaky legs she made her way downstairs, feeling distanced from herself somehow, the reality of what had happened almost impossible to comprehend.

Hailey was in the kitchen making tea. 'I've put extra sugar in yours for the shock,' she said, handing Sara a mug before they both sat at the table. 'Don't you worry, we'll get the bastards who did this.'

Sara wasn't sure they would. *How can we even start to find out who's behind it?* She was shrivelling up inside, disgust and shame stamping on any self-worth that might have been in there. She thought about James, how lovely he'd been to her, so kind and caring she'd actually thought he might be a little in love with her. But there was another puzzle to solve.

'What I don't get,' she said, as she slumped into her seat, 'is who sent the video to Matt. And why.'

Hailey stared at her, gave a derisive snort. 'Are you blind?'

'What do you mean?'

'Well, it has to be James. He wants you for himself.' She pursed her lips, getting her argument in order before she spoke. 'Look at his behaviour, the way he's been grooming you. You told him how jealous Matt is. You told him if Matt found out you'd been going out with another man, he'd blow a fuse.' She pointed at the phone, which Sara had brought down with her. 'Looks like he just threw a stick of dynamite into your marriage. And I suppose he'll be around to pick up the pieces.' She took a sip of tea and gave a dismissive huff. 'Oh yes, I've met his sort.'

Sara scrunched up her nose. 'I'm not sure that makes sense. Wouldn't he know I'd work out it was him?'

Hailey took another sip of tea, frowned. 'Hmm. I see your point.'

'And I see yours. Maybe neither of us is quite right.' Sara ran her hands through her wet hair, teasing out the knots. 'Whatever game he's playing, I haven't a clue what outcome he's looking for. Does he want to make me helpless?'

They sat in silence for a moment, thinking.

'Well, we can theorise as much as we like,' Hailey said with a sigh. 'Only James knows the truth. You're going to have to ask him.' She must have noticed her sister's appalled expression and reached across the table, grasped Sara's hand. 'I can come with you, if you like.'

Sara was tempted, but shook her head. 'I think he's more likely to tell the truth if it's just me. Perhaps this is how I'm supposed to repay my debt, but he couldn't tell me because I'd never agree.' She chewed her lip. 'You see, that's what doesn't make sense. I had no idea any of this had happened. He could have just carried on organising little getaways, making me think it was a treat for me and companionship for him. But now I know… well, I'll never go anywhere with him ever again.'

'What if he says you have to, or he'll tell Fiona and the police about you stealing the money?'

'I'm not sure he would, though, because surely he covered up a crime by paying what I owed?' Her head was aching, and she rubbed at her temples, trying to ease the pain. 'The deal is off, I've already told him that. But I need to know if there's any more video footage.' She felt the blood drain from her face, hands covering her mouth the moment she'd spoken the words. 'I was there for two nights.'

What else did they do to me?

A shiver of revulsion ran through her. 'I've got to go to bed. Honestly, I can't think about this any more.' Her jaw clenched. 'But tomorrow, I'm going to get to the truth.'

Hailey nodded. 'And I'll have a chat with Matt. See if I can get him to reconsider.'

'It's a deal.' Sara flashed a quick smile at her sister before making her way upstairs.

As she lay in bed, her head on the pillow that smelt of Ezra, she ached for her children, for the life that she'd had. The life that she appeared to have lost.

Unless I can work out a way to get it back.

With that thought in her head, and determination in her heart, she finally fell asleep.

TWENTY-SIX

Sara woke suddenly, a loud bang making her sit up, wondering where she was for a moment. Then she remembered she was at Hailey's house. A child's clock sat on the bedside table, with big numbers and a picture of SpongeBob SquarePants on the dial. It was seven o'clock, and Sara knew that Hailey went out jogging every morning, whatever the weather. Had that been the door banging?

She covered her head with the duvet, not ready to face the day, but memories of the previous evening crowded into her mind, jabbering at her, filling her head with shouting and images she didn't want to see. Today was going to be a make-or-break sort of a day. A day to find out exactly what was going on with James and persuade Matt that she was the victim of a crime rather than a cheating wife.

Take control, she told herself as she threw back the duvet and went for a shower. You can't let the bastards win.

With her pep talk in mind, she dressed in yesterday's clothes and went down to the kitchen to get the coffee on, thinking that she'd have to borrow an outfit off Hailey for work, including a pair of shoes. They were a similar height, and although Hailey was slimmer, she favoured stretchy sports clothes, which made her feel more approachable to the youngsters she worked with. Sara was sure there'd be something she could squeeze into.

*

'You're looking a little casual today,' Fiona said when Sara reached the office and found her sitting behind the desk looking at something on the computer. She didn't usually appear this early, and never on a Monday, due to other work commitments, and it caught Sara by surprise. She blushed as Fiona looked her up and down, the expression on her face an indication that she didn't approve.

'Long story,' she said, adjusting the oversized T-shirt that Hailey used as a nightshirt. It was the only top she had that was big enough and Sara was wearing it over black leggings, with trainers that were a size too big. From a distance, it didn't look too bad, and was the sort of ensemble a lot of the young mums wore. Not to work, though.

She was hoping to go home at lunchtime, when Matt wouldn't be expecting her, and see if she could have a sensible conversation with him. She'd decided that she would have to make a complete confession if he was going to believe she wasn't having an affair and allow her back home. It would be a relief, she thought, to tell him about her failed investment and her debt to James. Once everything was out in the open, maybe it would encourage him to be more honest about his own business dealings.

'Did Louise enjoy herself?' Fiona said as she finished what she was doing and stood, hitching her bag on her shoulder.

Sara frowned, wondering for a moment who Louise was.

'Have I got her name wrong?' Fiona gave a little laugh. 'I'm so bad at names. Anyway, did you have a good weekend?'

Sara moved towards the spare desk, where she had been sorting out some files for archiving, not wanting to catch Fiona's eye. 'Lovely, thanks. And my girls had a wonderful time with Chelsea. All that shopping, they think they've been to heaven.' She flushed, embarrassed that she hadn't rung Fiona the previous evening to thank her. 'I should have been in touch. You must think I'm awful, it's just…'

Fiona was standing next to her now. She put a hand on Sara's shoulder and peered at her face, looking concerned. 'You're a little peaky. Is everything okay?'

Sara glanced at her friend and sank into her chair, all the strength seeping from her limbs, as if she was slowly dissolving. It took so much energy to keep up a pretence, and she wondered if she really needed to with Fiona.

'No,' she mumbled, with a weary sigh. 'Everything isn't okay.'

Fiona put her bag down and pulled up a chair. She rubbed Sara's shoulder. 'Come on, then. Tell me all about it,' she said, gently. 'Maybe I can help. And it always feels better to talk about problems, doesn't it?' She frowned then. 'It's not James, is it?'

Sara closed her eyes. *I can't tell her about that, can I?* She cringed at the very idea. Fiona was a bit of a prude really and the thought of telling her about the hotel and the video was unthinkable – it would shock her to the core. Better to keep that to herself.

She glanced at Fiona. 'Matt's thrown me out.'

Fiona's mouth dropped open. 'Oh no! When? Last night?'

Sara nodded. 'He's got this idea I'm having an affair.'

'With James?' The distaste was evident in Fiona's voice.

Sara shook her head, laced her fingers together. 'No. He got this… He's made all sorts of assumptions that are just plain wrong, and he wouldn't let me tell him the truth.' She blew out a long breath. 'Honestly, Fiona, I've never seen him so worked up.'

'Well, you'd probably get worked up if it was the other way round, wouldn't you?'

Sara tensed. Fiona always did like to present both sides of an argument, which made it difficult to work out whose side she was on.

'I know, I understand, but someone sent him…' She stopped herself, aware that once she started explaining the details, the whole truth was in danger of coming out. And she couldn't let that happen. Fiona could never know the truth. Because then she'd tell the police, and Sara would be no better than her mother. Stealing was never a solution. Funny how life had a way of slapping you round the face with things you said you'd never do.

'Sent him what?' Fiona coaxed, obviously curious.

Sara swallowed her temptation to confess, took a deep breath and redirected her thoughts. She looked at Fiona, whose face did sympathy very well. Not telling the whole truth is not a lie, she told herself before she answered. 'He misunderstood. That's what happened. Then he overreacted and threw me out of the house. Wouldn't let me back in. So I had to go and stay with Hailey.' She pulled at her T-shirt. 'These were the only clothes we could find to fit me.'

'Oh Sara, I'm so sorry to hear that. And Matt's just getting on his feet again, isn't he? Such a blow getting made redundant, especially in the IT industry. You don't expect it, do you?' She gave a little shake of the head, lips pressed together. 'The girls were telling me all about it over the weekend. They said... Well, they did say there'd been a bit of tension in the house, you know. That you two had been arguing.'

Sara focused her gaze on the wall in front of her, unable to deal with Fiona's sympathy any longer. Fiona with her perfect house and perfect husband and perfect daughter and loads of money and everything she could possibly want. How could she even begin to understand?

'They're so proud of their father for setting up his own business,' Fiona continued. 'Maybe he's just feeling a bit stressed and will have calmed down today. Have you spoken to him?'

She shook her head. 'I thought I'd give him some space, go and see him later.'

'Is there anything I can do? Would it help to have some time off, do you think?'

Sara lined up the papers on the desk as she thought, but before she could answer, Fiona carried on.

'Look, the truth is, I came in early because I wanted to speak to you anyway. I had a meeting with Julia, and she's concerned that we don't have enough in reserves and thinks we need to cut our costs a little. To be honest, it's becoming obvious that our last treasurer really wasn't up to speed on everything and hasn't been giving the board the best advice.' She sighed. 'The upshot is, Julia has recommended we get more of the volunteers involved around the place. So that would make the manager's job a smaller role. And when we looked at it like that, we think we might actually only need part-time hours.'

Sara's heart gave a stutter, her eyes studying Fiona's face. 'You're reducing my hours?'

Fiona gave a little grimace. 'Actually… I'm afraid Julia thinks we should let you go.'

'What do you mean, let me go?' Fiona had Sara's full attention now, because she knew exactly what she meant, she just didn't want to believe it.

'This isn't me. This is the treasurer and the board.' Fiona's eyes glistened, her voice full of regret. 'I know this job's important to you, but my hands are absolutely tied, I'm afraid.' She looked at the floor for a moment, gathering her thoughts. 'To be honest, though, I do feel there's a bit of a conflict of interest with you and James being so close these days.' She pulled a face, like she'd eaten something sour. 'Look, I really don't want to be covering for you. I hated having to lie to Matt when you were out with James. Poor man is such a brilliant dad, so dedicated to his kids. I despised myself, I really did.' She ran her tongue over her bottom lip, clearly uncomfortable. Sara tensed, waiting for the punchline. 'The thing is, James has a permanent contract and has already negotiated a reduction in hours. Yours is temporary and I know we said we'd extend it until September, but we never formalised that, did we?' She gave Sara an apologetic smile. 'Julia has insisted, and given her expertise, we can't ignore her advice. I've rung round the rest of the board and I'm afraid they all agree.'

'You're sacking me?' Sara's voice rose an octave, her disbelief squeezing her vocal cords. She put a hand to her throat.

'No,' Fiona said with forced patience. 'We're not renewing your temporary contract.'

'Oh my God! You said you were happy with my work. Didn't we talk about a permanent position?'

Fiona nodded, a pained expression on her face. 'Yes, I know, I know. But that was before I'd spoken to Julia. I'm sorry.' She blinked. 'I shouldn't have made promises I wasn't in a position to keep, but Sara, given everything that's happening at home, I'm not sure your mind's going to be on your work anyway.' She squeezed Sara's arm. 'I think your family need you more. I know it's been hard on the children with you working full-time. Sophia and Milly couldn't help letting slip that you don't seem to have time for them any more. Perhaps Matt feels that way too. Put your energy into your marriage. That would be best, don't you think?'

Sara bit back her anger. Shouting at Fiona wouldn't help, however much she wanted to; if the worst-case scenario happened, and she and Matt separated, then she would need her own income, and even if she wasn't working at the community centre, she'd need a reference.

'Okay. Well, I can't pretend I'm not disappointed.' Her voice was sharp as a knife, cutting through the air between them.

'Of course you are. And I'm so sorry to have to give you the news when you're going through a bit of a rough patch.' Fiona gave her arm a quick rub. 'I'm happy to have the girls any time if that helps. Chelsea loves having them over, and they're no trouble. They're a credit to you and Matt, they really are.' She stood and picked up her bag. 'Well, I've got to go. Just wanted to catch you and let you know our decision. It seemed only fair. Shall we say

you'll work till the end of the week? Then you can tidy up any
loose ends and we can sort out who will be taking over what jobs.'

Sara nodded, jaw clamped shut, too angry to speak. It was only
when Fiona was out of the building and she could see her getting
in her car that she allowed herself to scream.

She was still seething an hour later when James arrived.

'I was hoping to see you today,' she said when he came into the
office, her voice chilly as an Arctic wind. The sight of him repelled
her now, and she wondered what she'd been thinking in her little
daydreams where they were more than friends. Her finger stabbed
the air. 'You've got some explaining to do.'

'Nice to see you too,' he said as he closed the door, clearly
confused. 'What's the problem?'

'The problem is someone sent Matt a video. It was filmed at the
hotel this weekend.' She spat out the words like bullets, hoping
she'd find her mark and see guilt in his face.

He looked genuinely surprised. 'Someone saw us together? A
friend of your husband?'

'No.' She glared at him. 'Friends of yours, I believe. Friends
who drugged me and abused me while I was unconscious.' He
reeled back at the accusation, his jaw dropping, clearly lost for
words. 'How could you, James? How could you do that to me?'
Her voice cracked and she fought to keep her composure, holding
back her furious tears. 'I trusted you, and I thought…' Her hands
closed into fists, frustration and rage and shame balling together
as she beat them against her thighs with such force it made him
jump. 'And then you do that!' She wanted to hit out, make him
understand her pain, but first she needed the truth.

He looked stunned, completely taken aback. 'I've no idea what
you're talking about. Why don't you just take a deep breath and
start again. Somebody saw us at the hotel and told Matt, is that it?'

She stared at him. *Has he really just ignored what I said?* Then she understood. He was trying to make her believe it didn't happen. Her fury ratcheted up a notch.

'No, that's not bloody it. Weren't you listening?' She picked up her phone and swiped through, looking for the video. 'I'll show you...' She frowned and searched some more, but she couldn't find the clip anywhere. A flush of heat raced through her body and her mind froze as she realised the truth.

It's gone.

Someone had deleted it.

TWENTY-SEVEN

She stared at her phone, and frantically went through the process again from the beginning, making sure she hadn't missed it, but no, the video wasn't there any more, vanished as though it had never existed. Her shoulders tensed as James stood behind her, looking over her shoulder.

'Show me,' he said, so close she could feel his breath on the back of her neck.

She stepped away from him, panic freezing her brain, making her unable to do anything but repeat the process she'd already been through three times. 'It's not... I don't understand. It's not there.' James put a hand on her shoulder, and she shrugged it off, spun round to face him. 'You keep your filthy hands off me,' she spat. 'I know what I saw.'

He stared at her, and she could see the confusion and hurt in his eyes. 'Look, I'm really sorry if I've done something to offend you, but I'm still no wiser as to what you're talking about.'

She glared at him. 'You and your creepy friends.' She jabbed her phone at him as if it was a lethal weapon. He flinched. She carried on with her rant. 'I don't know exactly what's going on, but someone sent a video of me and two different men to my husband.' She registered his shock, and nodded. 'That's right, two men, strangers, and they were... they were molesting me, and Matt's thrown me out.' Her chest was heaving, her head bursting with rage as tears started to fall, thickening her voice. 'And the only person who could have anything to do with it is you.'

James blew out his cheeks, tugged at his beard, clearly lost for words. 'That's… Oh my God, that's terrible.' He looked properly concerned. 'If you need somewhere to stay while you sort everything out, you're always welcome at my house, you know.'

Did he just say that?

'You're not listening,' she snapped. 'I know this is you, I know it. You and your shady bloody deal.'

He put up a hand as if to defend himself, eyes wide. 'Now just hold on a minute. You can't think I'd do anything to harm you, Sara. I…' He stopped himself, looked at the ground. 'You know I'm very fond of you.' He sounded genuine, and a ripple of doubt ran through her mind. His eyes met hers. 'Look, without seeing the video, I still don't know what you're talking about. I'm not sure I heard you right. You said two men? You were filmed with two men?' There was a look of pure disbelief on his face. 'And you're sure it was you?'

'Yes, it was me. I have a tattoo on my thigh. There's no mistaking it.'

He started pacing the floor, clearly agitated, his hands opening and closing. 'Christ, Sara, I don't know what to say. Honestly, you'd think a hotel like that would be safe, wouldn't you? I heard a similar incident on the news, but that was London. You'd think in the Yorkshire countryside…' He stopped and turned to her. 'Did you recognise either of them? Could they be members of staff?' He stopped pacing. 'Shouldn't we go to the police?'

There was nothing in his demeanour to suggest guilt, only shock and anger, and she started to wonder if she'd been jumping to conclusions. But *he's the common denominator*, she reassured herself. *He took me to that hotel.* *Ah, but that doesn't mean he was involved*, said a voice in her mind.

She remembered the news story James was referring to, a woman who'd been drugged and raped in a hotel and it turned out to be one of the housekeeping staff. *Isn't that a possibility?* Her resolve wavered. Had she wrongly accused James when he'd been nothing but lovely to her?

She clasped her forehead, unsure what to do next, feeling like she was standing on quicksand, being sucked under, and there was nothing she could do about it.

'I can't go to the police with no evidence, can I?' In reality, getting the police involved wasn't an option, given her theft from the community centre.

He looked thoughtful, his fingers pinching his lips, and it was a moment before he spoke.

'Do you think Matt still has a copy of this video?'

She sighed. 'He won't speak to me.'

'And he didn't say where he'd got it from?'

'No. He just said someone sent it to him and he was mad as hell. I really didn't have a chance to ask him any questions – he'd already made up his mind about what was going on. I don't even know if he watched it all.' Her voice cracked again, her guard crumbling. 'I don't understand it. Any of it. But I know what I saw, and it makes me feel sick and humiliated and… filthy.'

She started to cry, covering her face with her hands as her body shuddered.

He grabbed the box of tissues from the desk and handed them to her. 'Sit down, Sara. Come on. Let me get you a cup of tea. I can see it's all been a horrible shock.' He pulled out her chair and gently pushed her into it. 'I'll be back in a tick.'

True to his word, he returned with mugs of tea and a packet of chocolate biscuits.

He gave her a tentative smile. 'Let's talk this through and see if we can sort out what's been going on and what we're going to do about it.'

She gazed at him then, scrutinised his face for clues, little tells that he was being dishonest, but there was nothing untoward, nothing suspicious at all. *He said 'we'.* And she felt a tremor of relief. James wasn't the enemy. He'd never been the enemy. She remembered Hailey's comment, how she thought he had romantic feelings towards her. *I'm very fond of you*, that was what he'd just said. And if he was fond of her, he wouldn't have let other men grope her. She sipped at her tea, the hot sweetness scalding her tongue.

She felt quite useless. Her life as she knew it was like a mirage that was growing hazier by the hour. Trust was a fragile thing, she'd learned that as a child, and she knew that even if she could prove her innocence to Matt, there would still be an element of suspicion in his mind. Because she'd lied to him, hadn't she? She'd lied about the money, her deal with James, and who she was with at the weekend. Lie upon lie. And even though everything had been innocent and above board with James, Matt wouldn't believe her. Not now he'd seen the video. And then, in the future, he'd question everything she said.

My marriage is over. The realisation thumped her in the chest, taking her breath away. *And it's my own fault.* One stupid decision had caused her life to fall apart, and she had no idea how to repair it.

There was no going back. She could only go forward, but where she was headed was shrouded in darkness and she was stumbling like a drunkard. It's not about who trusts me, she told herself. The future depends on who I choose to trust. She glanced at James, on the surface a benevolent presence in her life. But can I be sure what's really going on?

He caught her eye. 'Let me ask you this, Sara. What do *you* want to happen now?'

She clasped her mug a little tighter. *I want my life to go back to the way it was before I got this stupid job.* Everything had been fine then. More or less. She pulled at that thought, unravelled it a little to find the truth. It hadn't been completely fine, though, had it? Otherwise she wouldn't have been yearning for a job, needing to scratch that itch to get out of the house, do something different, use her brain. She'd lost her focus, let it drift away from the most important people in her life – her family. Her needs could wait. There'd be time for her when the kids left home. *Why didn't I see that?* This situation was a result of her impatience, her dissatisfaction with her lot, always wanting what others had, like Hailey had said. In that moment, she hated herself with a passion.

'Sara?'

She'd forgotten James had asked her a question, but now she was very clear about her answer.

'I want to know who those men were,' she said between gritted teeth. 'And I want whoever was responsible brought to justice. Stuff like that can't be allowed to happen.' She slammed her empty mug onto the desk. 'I can't ignore it, and Matt needs to know I haven't been unfaithful. How do you get over something like this? I've seen the video even if the evidence has gone. I know what happened. And I feel so disgusting I want to rip my skin off.'

'It was that bad?'

The sympathy in James's voice threatened to undo her. She could hear her teeth grinding. This wasn't the time to fall apart. It was the time to fight. She looked up when he spoke again.

'Look, I'm sorry, but I've got to dash.' He grimaced. 'Meeting with the bank. I only dropped in because Fiona rang me earlier and told me about your contract being terminated.' His eyes met hers. 'That's what I really came to talk to you about. Because I've had an idea, you see. As part of our deal, I'd like you to come and work for me, in Dad's sportswear business.'

His suggestion came out of nowhere, and it was a moment before Sara could comprehend what he was saying. 'But why employ me when you could work full-time in your family business and then I could have the position here? Why do you need two jobs? That's just ridiculous.'

He gave her a quick smile. 'Family politics, Sara. Can't have the old man thinking I'm shoving him out the door before he's ready. He doesn't pay me anywhere like the going rate in the family firm. But I think he'd like you as his assistant. You'd be doing me a favour. And we could take two hundred pounds a month out of your wages as debt repayment, if that would make you feel more comfortable. No more repayment in kind. We've already agreed that, haven't we?'

Sara shook her head, completely confused. 'I'm sorry, that makes no sense.'

'It might not make sense to you. But it makes perfect sense to me.' He stood and walked to the door, threw a final comment over his shoulder. 'Anyway, have a think about it. If your husband's kicked you out, you're going to need a job, aren't you?'

She stared after him as the door clicked shut. *Do I have a choice?*

She had no other way of repaying him the money she owed. And what he was offering her was something she needed – a job.

TWENTY-EIGHT

Sara sat and thought for a long time, unable to come up with a single positive thing to help her situation. Maybe Hailey had news. She gave her a call.

'Have you had a chance to speak to Matt yet?' she asked when her sister answered.

'I'm sorry, Sara, he wouldn't really talk about it. I said I'd go over later and help with Ezra. He's playing up, apparently. But that's no surprise, is it?' Hailey sounded weary, an edge of annoyance in her voice. 'Honestly, I can't believe what a mess you've made of everything. I'm so bloody angry with you.' The static of her breath crackled down the phone. 'I know you didn't deserve what happened to you at that hotel, but if you hadn't stolen that money and done that stupid deal…' She gave a grunt of frustration. 'So much of this you brought on yourself.'

Sara ignored her sister's telling-off, the words skimming in one ear and out of the other, her mind fixed on Ezra, her heart breaking at how confused and upset he would be without her. He was a sensitive little boy, and Matt didn't have the patience with him that he had with the girls. 'I can have Ezra. He can come and stay with us.'

'You're not listening!' Hailey snapped, her words rushing out in an angry hurry, the volume cranked up so Sara would take notice. 'Look, I'm not sure I even want you in my house. You've hurt all the people I love most in the world. The girls are fuming, and have told Cassie, so she's upset and mad with you as well. And someone has told Matt you were with James at the weekend, so that's added fuel to the fire.'

Sara gasped, horrified. Who would have done that? 'Someone? Which someone specifically? Did *you* tell him, Hailey?' She must have done, because nobody else knew.

'No, I bloody didn't! But I guess it's a small world, isn't it? People see things.'

'What people? Who?'

'I don't know. I didn't ask.' Hailey was beyond impatient now. 'Look, I've got to go. I'm working. I'll talk to you later.'

Sara stared at her phone, shocked by her sister's attitude. She'd been so supportive yesterday, but now she'd spoken to Matt, she'd become just short of hostile. She checked the community centre schedule for the day and was relieved to find that she'd done everything she needed to for the groups who were using the facilities. There were plenty of volunteers around who knew where everything was, and she didn't think she'd be missed if she took an early lunch. She grabbed her bag and left.

Poor Ezra. She knew how impatient Matt could get with his fussy little ways, the clothes he would and wouldn't wear, the cuddly animals that had to keep him company at the table or he wouldn't eat. She hurried to the car, pulse racing as she thought about Matt's rage the night before, hoping he'd calmed down.

Hailey's words echoed in her mind, and she wondered what Matt had told the girls. It was half-term this week, so the girls would be at home, and she bit her lip as she drove, terrified of what she was about to face.

By the time she pulled up outside the house, she was sweating. *How do I have a conversation with Matt without upsetting the kids?* Would he even let her see them? The severity of her predicament started to hit home, the possibility that she could be separated from her family. Her very worst fear. She'd vowed that it would never happen to her, that she wouldn't repeat her mother's mistakes. She would be different, her life would be different – and it had been, up to a point. But there were also similarities she'd chosen to ignore.

She pushed the thoughts from her head and hurried to the front door, put her key in the lock, but the door wouldn't budge. The bolt was on. She went round to the side door, frightened that she was locked out of her own house. Tentatively she tried the handle, letting out the breath she was holding when it opened.

Sophia and Amelia were in the kitchen, making toasties, and looked up when Sara walked in, their expressions quickly changing from surprise to anger.

'Does Dad know you're here?' Sophia demanded, looking over her shoulder towards the lounge.

'I've come to talk to him,' Sara said, unsure how to play this, feeling so vulnerable not knowing what the girls did and didn't know.

'Well, he doesn't want to talk to you.' Sophia's hands were on her hips, her body blocking the way through.

'In fact,' Amelia snapped, eyes flashing, 'none of us want to talk to you.'

Sara stopped, startled by the venom in their voices, desperate to hold her daughters, hug them to her and explain what had happened. But she couldn't, and it broke her heart.

'Cheater,' Sophia said, pointing at her. 'You've ruined everything.'

'Dad!' Amelia shouted. 'Mum's here.'

Suddenly Matt appeared from the hallway, and before she could react, he was bundling her out of the back door, which he shut behind him, standing in front of it like a bouncer, arms folded across his chest.

'You're not welcome here.' There was a stony look on his face, and as her hopes went into free fall, her mouth went into overdrive, gabbling her excuses before he could go back inside.

'Matt, please let me explain. I was drugged. Unconscious. I can show you, but the video has disappeared off my phone. You must have a copy, though.'

She clung to his arm, eyes pleading with him, hoping that she'd put some doubt in his mind, made his case against her crack just a little bit.

He peeled her fingers off. 'I can't believe a word you say. You're as bad as your mother, aren't you?' He sneered at her. 'I deleted that filth.'

She ignored his jibe, concentrated on practicalities, not wanting to believe he'd destroyed the evidence. 'You can't have deleted it from my phone.'

'I did.'

'But how?'

He gave a derisive snort. 'You wouldn't understand if I told you.'

She closed her eyes, tried to calm herself down. She knew she had to stay rational, not fight back; that was the best way with Matt. Taking a deep breath she looked him in the eye, her voice low and urgent. 'I'm so sorry I haven't been completely honest with you, but I got myself in a situation I couldn't get out of. Please let me explain.'

He glared at her, the stony expression back on his face, but at least he was still there. This was her chance.

She began to speak, and at last she was able to tell him everything. Matt's face didn't change, his eyes ice cold.

'Finished?' he asked when she finally stopped talking.

She nodded.

He pointed at her. 'You need to learn to listen. That's your problem. Always thinking you know best.' He gave an angry snort. 'You think you can distract me with this story about stealing money for me, don't you? Think I'll somehow overlook the fact that you went away for a weekend with your lover and ended up having some sort of kinky sex with these other guys, and one of them filmed it.'

She gasped, couldn't believe he could think like that. 'No, Matt. No. That's not what—'

He stepped back a pace, his hand on the door handle, hatred in his eyes. 'I'm not listening to any more of your lies. Goodbye, Sara.'

'But what about—' He went inside before she could finish, slamming the door behind him. She heard the lock turn, the bolt ram home.

The strength drained out of her legs, along with any hope that she could persuade Matt of her innocence. She leant against the wall, sliding slowly to the ground, too shocked to cry or scream, her mind an empty vessel with the final goodbye echoing inside it.

That's it, we're over. Eighteen years they'd been together, and look how quickly they'd been torn apart, her family ripped from her before she could understand what risks she was taking, what danger she was in.

By trying to make good on a bad decision, she'd ruined everything.

Just like Mum, she thought. Matt wasn't far wrong with that. He'd thrown it at her as an insult, the worst insult he could think of. He'd never had a good opinion of Sara's mother. But Sara understood now what had happened in her mum's life. It hadn't been wilful neglect; it was a struggle for survival.

She dragged herself to her feet. *I have to get through this. I have to be there for my kids.*

Hailey will know what to do, she thought as she trudged back to her car. She turned for a last look at the house, and there was Ezra, his face at the lounge window. He was crying, banging on the glass, wanting to be with her. She couldn't bear it, and turned back, desperate to comfort him, but although she rang and rang at the doorbell, hammered on the door, nobody answered, and when she looked again at the window, Ezra had gone and the curtains were closed.

There was no choice but to leave. Her presence was causing too much upset for her children, and it wasn't doing anyone any good. She'd made enough of a scene, a couple of the neighbours opening their doors to see what all the noise was about. Head bowed, she slunk back to her car and sat in the driver's seat, looking at the house. All the curtains at the front were closed now, blocking her out. *Banished from my own home.*

She started the car and drove up to the moors, stopping in the car park, which only had a couple of other cars in it. She should have gone back to work, but she was in no fit state, her mind numb with the completeness of her family's rejection of her. Except Ezra. He'd wanted her, and that thought broke her heart even more.

There was so much that she didn't understand, forces at work that had done this to her. Somebody was behind it all. Somebody had organised for her to be drugged, for those men to have access to her unconscious body. *Did they pay for the pleasure?* It was possible, and the more she thought about it, the more it made sense. And still she couldn't escape the idea that the only person who might have been able to arrange everything was James.

She closed her eyes and forced herself to visualise the scene in the video. No shots gave any clue to the men's identities – it was too cleverly filmed to reveal them in such an obvious way. But one man had worn a signet ring on his little finger, and now that she thought about it, she was sure she'd seen it before somewhere. But where? The man who'd been messing with her feet was older, she felt; something to do with his posture, the slackness of the skin on his body, even though he had dark hair. Probably dyed.

Her eyes sprang open and she grabbed her handbag, found a little notebook she kept in there and started making a list, capturing any memories that might help identify the men. The older man, a big mole on his forearm, quite distinctive, about halfway up. The other one, really hairy hands. He was slender, long-limbed, with olive skin. No distinguishing marks, just the ring.

She made herself focus, ask the questions that would lead her to whoever had done this to her.

Who had been filming?

She frowned as she tried to work out the logistics. Had the two men filmed each other, or was there a third party in the room? Providing the video as a keepsake, a way of reliving the experience they had just bought? Or was it more opportunistic – two of the hotel staff who had worked out how to gain pleasure at their guests' expense without them even being aware they'd been violated? Maybe that was where the thrill came from. She shivered, not wanting to keep the images in her mind a moment longer.

Instead, she switched her thoughts to the next puzzle. Somebody had sent that video to Matt. The first question was who. But even more puzzling was why.

TWENTY-NINE

Thoroughly confused, she decided to go for a walk to see if that would help her think straight. The steep hill pulled at her leg muscles, making her chest heave, her heart pound. She didn't stop until she'd climbed to the top of the quarry, the valley laid out below her in the milky sunshine of the day.

Such a beautiful view, but there was danger down there underneath the loveliness, and the more she thought about it, the more certain she was that she'd been targeted. It wasn't a coincidence, her being at the hotel, the men able to access her room. It was planned. And however much James protested his innocence, he had to be involved, didn't he?

Fiona's warning made sense now. Had something similar happened to her when she and James had been seeing each other? She pondered on that for a moment, and decided it was possible, because Fiona wouldn't have got the police involved, not at the risk of her marriage. Was James someone who manipulated people with kindness, got them cornered, then took advantage? A wolf in sheep's clothing.

The ringing of her phone startled her from her thoughts. It was Hailey.

'Where are you, Sara? I just went to the community centre looking for you.' She was whispering, her words hissing into Sara's ear. 'We need to talk.'

'I'm on the moors. Top of the quarry.'

'Bloody hell, what are you doing up there?' She sounded panicky now. 'Don't do anything stupid, okay?'

Bit late for that, Sara thought, glad that at least her sister sounded more sympathetic than the last time she'd spoken to her. 'I'm fine, no need to get your knickers in a twist. I just needed some space to think.'

'I'll come and get you. I've found something out, and… Well, it's better I tell you face to face.' Sara's heart stuttered. *Sounds ominous.* 'And I have a little something for you as well.'

Before Sara could respond, Hailey had gone, leaving her wondering what she'd been up to. And why was she whispering?

Ten minutes later, from her perch on a large boulder, she watched Hailey's car drive up the road and pull into the car park. She saw her get out of the driver's side then open the back door and reach inside. A small figure hopped out. *Ezra!* Sara slid off the boulder and ran down the path to meet them, her feet pounding on the uneven ground, her breath catching in her throat as she forced herself to go faster. Running had never been her thing, but her body took over, the need to be with her son driving her onwards.

'Mummy! Mummy!' Ezra shouted, dashing to meet her, his cuddly Pikachu in one hand, bouncing against his leg.

Too breathless to speak, Sara scooped him into her arms and buried her face in his hair, breathing in the scent of him, relishing the warmth of his body, the softness of his skin against hers. She clamped her jaw tight, fighting back tears. Now was not the time to cry. She had to be strong. Ezra clung to her like a koala, arms wrapped round her neck, legs round her waist, and her body responded with an innate recognition that a missing part of her had been returned. They moulded together, mother and son, and for a few moments, nothing else mattered.

Hailey cleared her throat. 'Don't mind me,' she said, but there was a smile in her voice.

'Oh Hailey. Thank you! I can't... I don't know how...' Sara swallowed, her throat too clogged with emotion to speak.

Hailey rubbed her shoulder. 'I haven't been fair on you, sis.' She pressed her lips together, chin quivering, and Sara could see a sheen of tears in her eyes. She gave her a wobbly smile, then laughed. 'We're as bad as each other, aren't we?'

Ezra's hands clasped Sara's cheeks and he planted a sloppy kiss on her nose. 'I love you, Mummy.'

'And I love you too, little smudge.' She kissed him back. He wriggled to get down and she gave him another squeeze before finally releasing him.

'Come on, let's go and see the cow and the calf,' he shouted as he ran up the path, swinging Pikachu by the ear.

Sara turned to her sister. 'I don't know what to say.'

Hailey linked arms with her as they followed Ezra up the path, her voice low and urgent as she talked. 'Quick update. I went to see Matt, to try and talk to him like I promised. Must have arrived just after you'd been there, because Ezra was beside himself, and Matt hadn't a clue what to do with him. He was just yelling at him to shut up. So I said I'd take him out to the playground and Matt seemed happy just to get him out of the house, because he really was screaming the place down. God knows what your neighbours think is going on.'

She took a deep breath and carried on, the words racing out of her. 'I put Ezra in the car with my tablet to play with and told him we were going to see Mummy, so he was happy enough, but then I realised I'd left my bag in the house. Milly let me in. Matt was in his office in the garage by that time, and once I'd found my bag, I went to have a quick word with him – see if I could persuade him to listen to your side of the story. The door wasn't quite closed – I think he'd just popped in to get something – so I took my chance and went in, thinking it was good to catch him on his own like that.' Hailey's hand tightened round Sara's arm as she relived her experience. 'Well, he went bloody ballistic when he saw me, bundled me right back outside again, pinned me against the wall. Said I'd no right barging in to his private workspace.' She stopped walking, pulled Sara to a halt. 'I saw what was on his computer screen, though. A video was playing. It wasn't the same one, but it reminded me of that video of you.'

Sara gasped, shocked at her sister's revelation. 'You mean… you think he's been looking at more of that stuff?'

Hailey looked grim. 'I only got a glimpse, so I can't be sure. But we need to find a way to have a proper look.' Her eyes locked with Sara's. 'It made me wonder what this work he's doing is all about. Could these videos relate to this website he's been designing?'

'What website? He just told me he was doing coding for something.'

'When I was chatting to him at football practice, that's what he said he was doing. Designing a website.'

Sara's head spun with the idea that Matt might be involved. Was it possible? He'd never really explained exactly what the contract was for; always said he couldn't divulge details because the content was highly confidential. She was used to him working on government contracts and understood he couldn't tell her everything so hadn't pressed for more information.

Ezra ran back to them then and grabbed Sara's hand. 'Come on, Mummy, why are you being so slow?' He tugged harder and she followed, Hailey speeding up to walk beside her.

'We'll have to talk later.' Hailey nodded towards Ezra, the implication clear. Whatever they had to discuss, neither of them wanted him to hear. He bent to look at a ladybird on a bilberry bush, and the sisters moved on a little, out of earshot.

'Ezra can stay with us, can't he?' Sara asked. 'At your house.' The thought of being separated from him again was something she couldn't contemplate.

'God, yeah.' Hailey's mouth twisted. 'I hadn't realised...' She watched him as he tried to get the insect to crawl onto his finger. 'I'd always thought of Matt as a great dad, but just now... Well, it's clear he doesn't know how to deal with Ezra when he's playing up. He completely lost it with the poor lad, and it reminded me of Doug. You remember him? One of Mum's...' Her gaze returned to Sara, the shadows of past experiences clouding her eyes.

'I do. He really didn't like me, did he?' Sara had tried to forget about the man who'd shared their home for a short while, probably no more than six months, a man who'd swung from charmer to devil in a matter of seconds and whose mood was always hard to gauge. His erratic behaviour had the two sisters hiding in the room they shared for most of the time he lived with them. 'Matt's not as bad as Doug, I don't think. But I know what you mean. He thinks shouting's the answer.'

'Verbal abuse can be just as harmful as physical abuse.' Hailey pursed her lips, anger burning in her eyes. 'I see it all the time in the kids I work with. Not a finger laid on them but made to feel so bad about themselves that they...' She tailed off, and Sara was glad that she'd stopped short of giving distressing details.

Matt's parenting style with Ezra was something she'd tried to remedy, but his beliefs were ingrained in him, following his father's lead. She was definitely talking to herself when she tried to point out to him that his upbringing had been harsh. And it was okay for boys to cry and like cuddly toys and dressing-up. He couldn't be convinced, and Sara had to be on constant alert to make sure Ezra was being boyish enough in his father's eyes. Now she had to wonder if she'd been doing right by her son, or whether she should have been brave enough to step in and tell Matt it wasn't acceptable from the start.

'What about the girls, though?' Her thoughts turned to her daughters, hating to think of the family being split up. Even though they were close to their father, they needed a mother's support through their tricky teenage years. She knew there was something going on with them, even if they hadn't been ready to tell her, and now they were in the care of a man who might be involved in activities that exploited women. She shuddered. *Oh my God, what a mess.* A headache pulsed at the base of her skull, panic fluttering against her breastbone as she tried to work out what to do.

'They're very loyal to their dad, aren't they?' Hailey sighed. 'And he's turned them against you.'

'It's always been that way. Real daddy's girls, with the football and everything. And you're right, they hate me at the moment. I don't know exactly what he's said to them, but they turned on me earlier when I went to talk to him. Called me out for cheating on him.' She kicked at a stone, her voice steeped in sadness. 'I don't think they want to be with me at the moment.'

'Hmm. I don't suppose we have much option but to leave them there for now. Just for a little while, until we can get this whole thing sorted.' Hailey looked worn out, her cares pulling at the corners of her mouth, creating a deep furrow between her eyebrows. Sara wondered what else she'd found out; whether she'd told her everything. 'The girls have a football match tonight, over in Otley,' she continued, 'so I was thinking I could go. I know Matt won't want me to take them, not now I've sneaked Ezra out and won't be taking him back. But maybe I can find a way to chat with them, see if I can get them to at least talk to you and hear your side of the story.'

Sara glanced at her sister, grateful to have her support. 'That would be brilliant.' She frowned then, remembering the girls' behaviour the time she'd been to football practice with them, like there was a secret they were keeping. 'I have a feeling there's something going on at football, you know. They were a bit on edge afterwards when I took them, wanting to rush off.' She hesitated, reluctant for a moment to ask yet another favour of her sister. 'I don't suppose you could try and find out what's bothering them, could you?'

Hailey was about to speak when Ezra came running up with the ladybird on his finger, a look of delight on his face.

'Mummy, look! Look what I got. I catched it.'

Sara studied the little insect for a moment as Ezra glowed with pride. 'We'll let it fly away home, shall we?' She helped him put the ladybird back on a bilberry bush, and he skipped off again, on the hunt for more unsuspecting wildlife.

'Let's put it all to one side for now,' Hailey said, putting an arm round Sara's shoulders and hugging her close before letting her arm drop. 'Let's enjoy the afternoon, and maybe our brains will work something out.'

'Sounds good,' Sara said, liking the idea of tidying her worries to the back of her mind and enjoying some time out with Ezra. But her brain had other ideas and refused to switch off, her troubles going round on a continual loop in her head. Her daughters hated her and had problems of their own they were keeping secret. Matt thought she'd cheated on him and had thrown her out, splitting the family in two. As far as she could see, their relationship was over. On top of that, he was involved in a business that looked decidedly shady and might even have a connection to the abuse she'd suffered. She had no job, and still hadn't decided what to do about her debt to James and the constant threat that he would tell Fiona and the police what she'd done. It was quite a list, and the more she studied it, the faster the thoughts went round until she felt like a child on a fairground ride, feeling sick and willing the experience to end.

They walked to the Cow and Calf in silence, Ezra running ahead of them, and it was clear that despite her words about enjoying the afternoon, Hailey was struggling with the situation too.

She had brought a bag full of picnic food – sandwiches, crisps and drinks – and they sat in the sun to eat, Ezra chattering away, his upset forgotten as he snuggled next to Sara. She tried to block out everything except her son, this lovely moment; wanted to believe they could still do normal family things, but she knew that her life had fractured, the cracks getting ever wider, and normal was a thing of the past.

Although she was desperate to discuss everything with Hailey, it would have to wait. Once Ezra was in bed this evening and Hailey was back from the football match, they could look at all the information they'd gathered and plan a way forward that wouldn't involve the police. They both knew that the truth didn't always lead to justice; that victims could be made to look like perpetrators. They'd seen it happen as children, when their mother was used as a scapegoat.

After their father's death, their childhood had been punctuated by police visits. Often in the small hours of the morning, uniformed men bursting into whichever house they'd lived in with their mum at the time. The adults usually got dragged away, while Hailey and Sara were processed by friendly policewomen and social workers before being sent off to foster homes, often separated. Their mother had spent several short stints in prison for possession of drugs and shoplifting. When she was released, she'd get settled in a house and the children were allowed home. Until it happened again.

Sara was determined that her own children would never experience that sort of horror. But that meant she had to make sure nobody ever knew about her theft. And that in turn meant she had to pay James back, or their deal still stood. It was all such a risk. The more she thought about it, the greater the risk seemed to become.

James is playing a game with me. Cat and mouse. He has all the power and he's loving it.

Her hands balled into fists. Rage at what he'd allowed to be done to her burned in her belly, firing up her resolve. *He's not going to win. I won't let him.*

The only way to get out of the deal was to find evidence of the game he was playing with her. But how on earth was she going to do that?

THIRTY

Ezra was worn out after all the upset and his afternoon playing on the moors. They'd been out for hours after Hailey had left them to go back to work. Sara realised how much she'd missed time with her son while she'd been working – time she'd never get back – and the thought of going to prison, being separated from her children for goodness knew how long, weighed heavy on her mind as she bathed him and put him to bed.

Matt had called several times; she hadn't answered, and he'd left increasingly angry messages asking when Ezra was coming home. Eventually she'd sent him a long message explaining why it was better that Ezra stayed with her. So far, she'd had no reply, but she didn't expect him to come charging over to Skipton to demand his son's return, because realistically, he wouldn't get any work done over the next week with Ezra at home. The girls would entertain themselves, but Ezra definitely wouldn't. Sara thought he'd leave things as they were now until after half-term, but she couldn't help listening for the sound of a car pulling up, the door banging shut, angry footsteps slapping up the path.

She went downstairs and poured herself a glass of wine, and as she sipped at her drink, she started to separate the threads of her problems, trying to work out how to untangle everything and move forward. She pictured James, the expression on his face when she'd told him about the video; his confusion, which had seemed completely genuine. She remembered the gentleness of her previous interactions with him, his generosity. He'd lent her the money to help her out of a sticky situation. He'd given her a meaningless way of paying it back, making her believe that her company had some currency for him. Then the job offer, which made no sense at all because he'd be paying her. It really didn't add up.

She'd always prided herself on being a good judge of character, her natural instinct being to mistrust after the tribulations of her childhood, with its empty promises and deceptions. She could see now, though, that she'd been kidding herself. Look at Matt. Had he changed, or had he always had that short-tempered side to him and she'd chosen to ignore it? Or maybe she'd always done what he wanted up to now, and it was the fact that she was pushing against his will that had brought out his anger?

Was James just a lonely man with a crush on her, using the debt to buy her company? Was it manipulation, or was he genuinely trying to help? He'd seemed to enjoy giving her lovely things, wanting to treat her and make her feel like a princess. She gave a derisive laugh. *A princess!* Whichever way she turned things over in her mind, she couldn't help thinking he must be involved in her abuse in some way; it was too much of a coincidence for him not to be.

She drained her glass, poured herself another, teeth grinding with frustration. Everything had been going round in her head all day and she wasn't getting any further forward. What she needed was facts, not assumptions. She got out her notebook and jotted down other snippets that she remembered from the hotel that might be useful. Other guests she'd noticed staring at her, the staff members she'd been in contact with. Any of them could be involved.

She thought back to the previous occasion she'd been at the hotel – the networking event – and recalled how the atmosphere had changed over the course of the night. She'd definitely felt uncomfortable and had been glad to leave. Was there a connection? In her mind, her eyes travelled round the table she'd shared with four men and three other women. The guy next to her, Alan. He was definitely a slimeball, his arm creeping round the back of her chair as he leant in to talk to her, his leg brushing against hers. She'd remembered thinking that middle-aged men really shouldn't dye their hair because it made their faces look older—

Her glass clattered onto the table, the remnants of her wine dripping to the floor.

Oh my God! The man messing with my feet in the video. It was Alan!

Her hand went to her chest, heart racing as she reran her memory of the event in her mind, like watching a replay. As the evening had worn on and the room had become warmer, he'd taken off his jacket, rolled up his sleeves, and she distinctly remembered the mole on his arm, like a splodge of ink had been spilled. She closed her eyes and tried to visualise every little detail about the evening, because there was something else, a blurred memory that she couldn't quite catch hold of before it slipped away from her into darkness.

The sound of the door banging shut startled her awake, her cheek pressed against the kitchen table where she'd slumped forward, her hand wet with spilt wine, her glass tumbled on its side. Hailey walked into the kitchen, and flicked on the light, making Sara blink in the brightness. She wiped her hand on her joggers, rubbing the sleep out of her eyes, while Hailey reached for the wine bottle and poured herself a glass. She picked up Sara's fallen glass and filled that too before sinking into a chair.

'Oh my God, what a day.' Her face looked drawn, eyes bloodshot and tired.

'Are the girls all right?' Sara leant across the table, put a hand on her sister's arm. 'Tell me they're okay.'

Hailey took her hand. 'Now I don't want you to worry, but I think I've found out what's been bothering them. I managed to nab them when they arrived at football. Matt dropped them off, but he didn't stay. The girls said he had a meeting. Anyway, I left as soon as he turned up later, and I don't think he saw me.' She took a big glug of her drink.

Dread pooled in Sara's belly. 'What's going on?'

'Milly broke down and told me everything. Poor kid's been keeping it all bottled up.' Hailey puffed out her cheeks, gave Sara's hand a squeeze and downed the rest of her drink. 'There was a video posted online. Milly in the showers at the football club. She was singing and doing a little dance while she washed her hair, and a whole stream of trolls made fun of her.' She grimaced. 'Everyone at school has seen it. Poor kid is mortified.'

Sara knew immediately when it had happened.

'That was about three weeks ago, wasn't it? I caught them looking at something on the laptop, and Milly was crying, but they denied anything was wrong.' Her heart ached for her child, tears springing to her eyes. 'Oh Hailey.' Her chin wobbled, no words to describe how she felt.

'I know, poor kid. And the thing is… Well, the only way to stop it happening again is to report it.' Hailey's lips pressed together, her face grim. 'I had to notify the unit because we've got kids we're responsible for in and out of that football club all the time. Who knows how long the cameras have been there or how many kids have been affected? Anyway, it's all going through the proper channels now. Police are involved and there's going to be an official investigation.'

'Of course it has to be investigated.' Sara was clasping the stem of her wine glass so hard it was in danger of snapping. How dare someone do this to innocent kids? It was evil. Pure evil.

'Yeah, well it might not be quite so good for Milly. She'll be asked to give evidence, and to be honest, it's going to be a bit of an ordeal.'

Sara leant her elbows on the table, head in her hands, finding it hard to take it in. Amelia going through all this anguish without her mum there to support her. The timing couldn't have been worse.

'Who would do such a thing?'

Hailey shook her head sadly, her voice despondent when she spoke. 'So many people use the club, from kids right up to seniors. And cameras can be so tiny these days, you wouldn't see them. Honestly, it's going to be tough tracking down whoever did this.'

They sat in silence, a heavy stillness in the air, both of them lost in their thoughts, until something shifted in Sara's mind. Two things clicking together.

She sat up, turned to Hailey. 'Seems quite a coincidence that both Milly and I have been through similar experiences, don't you think? Covert filming for someone else's pleasure.' Her eyes widened. 'What if there's a connection?'

Hailey considered for a moment, puffed out her cheeks. 'I think they're different things. This could just be kids with a vendetta. They're pretty tech-savvy these days, aren't they? And these cameras are cheap and easy to buy online. Wireless transmitters.' She shrugged, poured the last of the wine into her glass. Sara's remained untouched.

The silence spread between them, neither looking at the other, Sara's anger burning in her chest. She thought back to her own teenage years, and knew exactly what Milly was going through. Knew exactly why she'd kept her problems to herself. It wasn't easy talking about incidents that made you feel ashamed, because somehow you carried a guilt with you; a feeling that in some way you were to blame.

The ringing of her phone broke into her thoughts. It was Fiona, the last person she wanted to speak to. She debated whether to answer or not, wondering if she was going to get a telling-off for leaving work at lunchtime and not going back.

'Hello,' she said, deciding it was better to get it over with. At least it gave her the opportunity to tell Fiona that she'd taken her advice and was going to focus on her family. Fiona would like that, and Sara needed to keep her onside.

'Sara, I'm glad I've caught you. I did wonder if you'd be at the match tonight, but I was late picking up the girls and missed everyone.'

'No, Matt took them. I've got Ezra with me, so I couldn't go.'

'You're still with your sister, then?'

'Yes, for the time being.' Sara took a deep breath. 'I'm sorry I left work early today. I don't know if anyone mentioned it. But I've had a think about what you said and I'm going to take your advice and focus on the children until Matt and I have got everything sorted out.'

'Oh, thank goodness. You've no idea how hard it was for me to give you the news about your contract being terminated. I really am sorry about that.' Fiona's relief seeped down the line. 'Anyway, I hope a bit of time out will help smooth things over. I'm sure James and the volunteers can cover for now, so it's not a problem... But that's not actually what I was ringing about.'

'Oh, okay.' Sara's hand tightened round her phone, hardly daring to think why else she'd call. 'So... is there a problem?'

'No, no, well, not for you. The thing is, we've booked a lodge at Center Parcs in the Lake District for a few days, and Chelsea is making a terrible fuss about it because she says it'll be boring on her own. I was wondering if the girls would like to come? What do you think? I thought it might give you and Matt a bit of space to talk things through. Win-win for everyone. What do you say?'

Sara didn't have to think twice about her answer. It was a perfect end to the holidays for the twins and would give them a treat, away from all the family troubles. 'I'm sure they'd love to. And you're right. It might help resolve things one way or the other.'

'Thing is, we're going tomorrow afternoon. Last-minute booking, you see. I thought it would be a nice surprise for Chelsea, and then she had a complete meltdown about it. Is that too soon?'

'No, that's fine. I'll just give them a call, then ring you back, okay?'

They said their goodbyes and Sara looked at Hailey. 'Fiona wants to take the girls to Center Parcs for a few days to keep Chelsea company. I think that'll be good for them, don't you? Give us a chance to corner Matt.'

Hailey stared into space, thoughtful. 'Perfect. And if we can organise a play date for Ezra with Holly next door…'

Sara understood exactly where her sister's thinking was heading, and their eyes met across the table. 'Surely we can work out how to get into that office and see what Matt's up to? I think he's the key to this. Because someone sent him that video of me and he must know where it came from.' She sat bolt upright, her brain rebooted now there was something constructive she could do. 'What if this site he's been setting up is for people who do that sort of thing – you know, covert filming? People with that sort of fetish.' She frowned, an idea starting to form in her mind, but not yet clear enough to see. 'There's something weird behind all this. And I think Matt has the answer.'

Hailey pursed her lips, pensive for a moment. 'There's another thing I have to tell you about tonight.' She hesitated. 'I saw Matt with a woman.'

Sara's heart leapt into her throat. 'I bloody knew it! He tried to make me think I was imagining things.'

'I didn't see her face. I nipped off to get a coffee at half-time and saw her getting out of his car. She had a baseball hat on, and running gear, and she jogged off before I could follow her.'

'Bloody hypocrite!' Sara seethed.

Hailey reached across the table and grabbed her hand. 'Look, we're going to get this sorted. You and me. We've been through worse and come out the other side.'

Sara's jaw hardened, and she knew she was up for whatever trouble lay ahead. One way or another, they would get to the truth.

THIRTY-ONE

The girls wouldn't talk to Sara, so Hailey spoke to them and explained about the holiday, while Sara listened on speakerphone.

'Four days at Center Parcs, who doesn't want to do that?' Hailey asked, incredulous when they didn't seem keen. She glanced at Sara and pulled a face, obviously puzzled.

'It's short notice,' Sophia said.

'Fiona and your mum thought it would be a nice surprise. You deserve a treat and it'll give you some time away while we sort out what's been going on at the football club.'

'Milly doesn't want to go.' It seemed that Sophia was spokeswoman as usual, dressing her own feelings up as her sister's.

Hailey sighed. 'Look, guys. It's not always about what you two want. You'd be doing your dad a favour. He's got an important bit of work to get on with. Think about it – Fiona won't be skimping on the treats. You'll have a brilliant time. You always do when you stay with her, don't you?'

'Not always,' Amelia mumbled in the background, making Sara wonder if there had been a falling-out since the weekend. Then she remembered what her daughter was going through and thought she understood her reticence: she felt humiliated, just as Sara did. Perhaps Chelsea had teased her about the video.

Hailey gave Sara an exasperated look, obviously struggling to know what else to say to persuade them.

'Hey, girls,' Sara said.

'We're not talking to you,' Sophia snapped, and Sara's breath caught in her throat before she forced herself to speak.

'No, no, please listen. I don't know what your dad's told you, but it's not true. The problem is… well, it's a misunderstanding, and we need to sort it out. If you go on holiday for a few days, it'll give us a chance to talk things through.' She tried to insert a note of reassurance, put a smile in her voice. 'Hopefully everything will be back to normal when you come home.'

There was silence, then a whispered conversation. Hailey and Sara looked at each other, waited.

'Okay,' Sophia said. 'I hope you're telling the truth, Mum.'

Sara bit her lip. What were the chances of normality, of her and Matt staying together, after all this? Slim, was the answer. But she needed to buy this time, needed the girls out of the house, then Matt would think he was on his own and might not be quite so security-conscious. There was a chance he might leave his office door unlocked when he went into the house for a break.

'I'm doing my best for our family,' she said with conviction, because whatever happened, that was the truth. 'I love you girls. You kids are my world and I've hated not being there with you, and I hate it even more that you're angry and upset with me.'

'Love you, Mum,' Amelia said, voice thick with tears.

'Me too,' Sophia echoed, before they said their goodbyes.

The words worked their way into Sara's heart, soothing the wounds of the last few days. *I'm going to make this right for them. I've got to.*

Later, with arrangements made, Sara and Hailey settled down to lay out everything they knew and make plans for the following day.

'Fiona's picking them up just before lunch, so we'll have all afternoon to try and get into Matt's office and find evidence of what he's up to.' Sara was looking at her notebook, scanning through all the things she'd jotted down, which now amounted to a few pages. 'That's got to be a priority, hasn't it? When he was telling me about his contract, he said he just did the nuts-and-bolts work, but I suppose he has to check that the website's working, and verify users and all that stuff?' She scrunched up her nose. 'What do you think, Hailey? Are we jumping to conclusions, or do you think the video of me was posted on whatever site he's been building?'

Hailey was deep in thought, tracing the pattern of knots in the wood of the kitchen table with a finger. When she didn't respond, Sara carried on with her train of logic, arriving at the question she couldn't answer. 'Why else would someone send it to him?'

Hailey looked up and leant across the table.

'Like I said before, what if it's someone who wants to break up your marriage? Someone like James. As I see it, he's using this debt to slowly take control of your life.' Their eyes met, Hailey's words articulating thoughts that had already been gathering in Sara's mind, like storm clouds massing in the distance. 'The video has separated you from your husband and broken up your family. Then there's this new job offer, which is just another way of getting closer to you, manipulating you, because as a single mum you'll be dependent on him for your income.' Hailey gave her a hard stare. 'And he still hasn't told you the terms of the deal, has he?' Sara shook her head. 'It's not a deal at all. He's bought you. I think that's how he sees it. He's playing a game, getting his kicks from knowing what's going on, while you're clueless.'

Sara sighed, certain her sister was right. 'He said I could stay with him as well, if I was stuck.'

Hailey snorted. 'Yeah, like that's going to happen. No way are you going to do that.' She stared at Sara, eyes narrowing. 'Tell me you didn't actually consider it.'

Sara blushed, flapped a hand, dismissing the suggestion. 'God, no. But the point is, he was really shocked about the video. Honestly, he was. I'm convinced nobody could act his response.

And I just felt… he was properly worried about me.' She stared at the wall as she re-enacted the scene in her mind. 'He wanted to go to the police about it. If he had sent the video to Matt, why would he suggest that?' She rubbed her temples with her fingers. 'God, my head's going to burst with all this. I'm so confused. I don't know what to believe.'

'Look, we can theorise as much as we like, but what we need is evidence.' Hailey had a determined glint in her eye. 'We need to confront both of them – Matt and James – goad them into telling us more than they should, or even confessing, and make sure we've recorded the conversations. Even if it's just a snippet when they're off guard, hopefully that'll be enough to go to the police and get this thing properly sorted.'

Sara blanched. 'I can't go to the police, can I? Not when I stole that money. I can't risk it. We've got to sort this out without the authorities getting involved.'

Hailey's jaw clenched, eyes closing for a moment. 'I keep forgetting about that.'

'Well, I don't, because that's what started this whole thing off. If I hadn't been in debt to James, I wouldn't have gone to that networking event and met that creep and then…' She slapped her hands to her cheeks as a crystal-clear memory flew into her mind. The one that had been lurking on the edge, blurry and indistinct, avoiding being seen. Now it was so obvious, she wondered why she hadn't seen it earlier. 'The man with the ring! I do know who it was. Lewis. It was definitely bloody Lewis.'

Hailey looked confused. 'Who's Lewis?'

'He was the organiser of the sales event. Sat opposite me on our table, kept staring at me.'

Her mind scurried around, gathering up all the little bits and pieces of memories and putting them together into a full picture. And when she looked at it afresh, she was drawn to a horrible conclusion.

'What if the whole networking event was a sham, a front for something else? Bear with me if this sounds a bit off-the-wall, but it's in my head now, so I've got to say it.' She hesitated, hoping Hailey wouldn't think she was being melodramatic.

'Come on then, spit it out.' Hailey frowned, impatient.

'What if it was a showcase, for men to choose the women they wanted? Then arrangements were made to give them access, either on the night itself or at a future time?' Her thoughts raced ahead. 'James said the weekend away was a special offer to network members, that's why there was no flexibility with dates.' She met Hailey's puzzled gaze. 'It makes some sort of sense, doesn't it?'

Hailey's jaw dropped, her hand covering her mouth. 'Oh my God, that would be horrendous if it's true. But we can't discount it, can we? We've got to leave it as a possibility.' She thought for a moment. 'Perhaps you could confront James with it. See how he reacts. And video any conversations you have with him, if you can. Then we'll have facial expressions as well as his voice for evidence.'

Evidence? Sara shook her head, adamant. 'No police,' she said. 'I already told you that.'

Hailey gave an exasperated sigh. 'Look, I know it's not ideal, but if you really want to get this sorted out once and for all, you're going to need the police.' Her expression softened. 'I just don't think it's as big a deal as you imagine. We could go and talk to Fiona together if you like. Explain everything and beg for clemency. She's your friend, isn't she? I'm sure she'd understand.'

Would she? Sara wondered, her heart racing now as the implications of Hailey's plan sank in. From her experience of working with Fiona, she'd proved to be quite strict as far as rules were concerned, and she took her responsibilities as board chairperson very seriously. 'No, I can't take the risk.'

Hailey stared at her for a moment, then her shoulders slumped in defeat. 'Okay, well it's your shout. We won't think about getting the police involved just yet. We can speak to James and Matt, record the conversations should we need them as evidence in the future, then decide what happens next. Do it in stages.'

It seemed like the best approach, certainly more palatable than the alternative. 'Speaking to James is pretty straightforward,' Sara said. 'I can do it at the community centre. Get him to come into the office, I'll set up my phone to record our conversation and he won't suspect a thing.'

'Perfect. Sounds like a plan. The question is, who do we tackle first?'

Sara thought for a moment. 'Let's talk to Matt. We know exactly where he is, and we can do it together. I know this sounds pathetic, but after last time, I can't face talking to him on my own.'

Her phone pinged and she had a quick look, thinking it was going to be a message from the girls, or even Matt, objecting to their last-minute holiday plans, but it wasn't.

She frowned, glanced up at Hailey. 'It's James. He wants to meet me. Now. Says it's urgent.' Adrenaline fired through her veins, her heart racing. 'He's got information about the video.'

She checked the time. Ten o'clock.

'It's a bit late to be meeting, isn't it?' Hailey voiced Sara's own thoughts.

'Yeah, you're right.' She chewed at her lip, deliberating. 'But what if he's found out the truth? What if he knows who's behind it all?'

Hailey stood and yawned, clearly exhausted after a difficult day. 'Your decision. I'm way past being able to decide anything.' She went to the fridge and pulled out another bottle of wine, unscrewed the cap and poured some into a glass. 'I'll stay with Ezra if you really want to go.'

Sara swallowed, nervous about the idea of meeting James, given all their theories. Her hands twisted together as she dithered. 'Oh God, I don't know. Is it a good idea?'

'Where does he want to meet?'

'In the car park on the moors. Says nobody will see us talking there.'

Hailey's mouth dropped open in horror. 'What? No, don't be ridiculous! You can't go up there on your own at this time of night. No way are you doing that.'

Sara tapped out a message on her phone, telling him no, glad that her sister had persuaded her against it. Stupid idea, she reassured herself, though a part of her still wanted to know what he'd found out. She stopped typing, looked at Hailey.

'What if I call you when I get there and leave the line open, then you'll be able to hear what's going on and can get help if there's a problem?'

Hailey looked at her like she'd grown a couple of horns and turned into a fantastical beast.

'Sara, no. Think about it. There's plenty of places you can meet where nobody will see you. And anyway, why does it have to be so secret? I really don't understand that. Surely it would be safer to meet where people *can* see you?'

Sara got up and pulled on Hailey's jacket, which had been draped over the back of a chair. She wasn't sure if this was the most stupid thing she'd ever done in her life, but the desire to know what James had discovered was stronger than the desire to stay.

It was a cloudy night, pitch black in the car park when she pulled up, hands clammy and slippery on the steering wheel. James's car wasn't there, and as she waited for him to arrive, eyes nervously scanning the entrance to the parking area, she began to hope he'd changed his mind. Her phone pinged. Another message lit her screen.

I'm at the quarry.

She hesitated a moment, the hairs standing up on the back of her neck. This didn't feel right, not good at all. How was she going to find her way up there in the dark? And why the quarry?

She wound down the window, a damp mist now billowing around outside, making visibility almost zero. Sod this for a game of soldiers, she said to herself as she glanced around the car park. Even with the torch from her phone, all she could see was a wall of white as the mist enveloped the car.

Muffled shouts in the distance made her heart jump up her throat. *What was that?* She held her breath, body rigid, listening. Another shout.

This is a stupid idea. She wondered if the messages were some sort of practical joke. Or something more sinister? A shiver ran through her body. She wound up the window and rang James, determined to do things on her terms, not his. We can talk in my car, she decided. I'm not going out there.

His phone rang and rang, but there was no answer. She sent a message and waited, but nothing came back. After ten minutes, she started the car and drove to Hailey's house, confused and angry that he'd dragged her out on a wild goose chase.

'I've no idea what that was all about,' she said to Hailey when she got back, teeth chattering with cold. 'There was nobody there. The mist was down, couldn't see a bloody thing. I thought I heard something, but sound travels up there when it's still, doesn't it? Really misleading. It could just as easily have been people at the pub.'

'Well, I'm glad you're back,' Hailey said, giving her a hug before releasing her and going into big-sister mode. 'You shouldn't have gone off like that on your own. We said we'd do this together, didn't we?'

Sara gave an apologetic smile and tried to ring James again. Still no answer. What on earth was he playing at?

THIRTY-TWO

Hailey woke her the next morning, gently shaking her shoulder.

'You're going to want to see this,' she whispered.

Sara slid out of bed, trying not to disturb Ezra, wondering what had happened.

'It's not the girls, is it?'

Hailey shook her head and beckoned for her to follow her out into the hall. She was still in her pyjamas, hair mussed up. She showed Sara her phone, a news report: *Local man found unconscious in Ilkley Quarry.*

Sara's gut wrenched as she read the article. It was James. She blinked a few times, trying to clear the sleep from her eyes, wondering if she'd read it right, and scanned the brief report again. Found by dog walkers. He had head injuries and had been kept in hospital for observation. Police were keeping an open mind and were asking for witnesses.

Her hands covered her mouth as she looked at Hailey. 'Oh my God! I heard a shout when I was there last night. I wonder if that was him.'

'Problem is, it messes up our plan to get things sorted out while the girls are away.' Hailey tapped her chin with her phone, lost in thought. 'Mind you, if he's in hospital...' She gave Sara a slow smile. 'Well, they encourage visitors. Nobody will think it odd if you go and see him, will they?'

Sara thought for a moment. 'I suppose his dad might be there, but he's only just out of hospital himself, and he's still not well, so I doubt he'll be visiting. Anyway, he's got the business to run. It'll all be on him again if James is in hospital.'

'I'll wait outside while you go in,' Hailey said. She gave a satisfied smile. 'There'll be no running away, and if he's in a weakened state, we might just have a chance of getting something close to the truth.'

A little hand landed on Sara's leg, making her jump, and she turned to see Ezra, sleepy-eyed, behind her. She glanced at Hailey, who understood they should save the rest of the conversation for later, when Ezra was on his play date with the girl next door and they could talk openly.

Hailey had taken the day off, and once Ezra was happily playing with Holly, the sisters got ready for their first mission of the day – talk to Matt. Visiting hours at the hospital weren't until after twelve, so James would have to wait. Sara had rung the hospital and found out which ward he was in. Apparently he had concussion and a broken wrist but was comfortable and could have visitors.

She was still bothered about his accident, unsure why he would have chosen to meet up at the quarry when he hadn't been worried about them being seen together previously. And he'd had something to tell her. She had a horrible feeling that maybe it hadn't been an accident at all. She'd heard shouting, hadn't she? Had someone attacked him? She told herself not to get carried away. She'd find out this afternoon, and in the meantime, she needed to focus on Matt.

Hailey was being slow to get ready and Sara was desperate to see her girls, even if only from a distance, so she told her sister she'd go on ahead and wait for her at the house.

Their home was on a hill, and she pulled up behind a car at the top of the road, where there was a slight curve. In this position, she could see down the pavement to the house, but her vehicle was more or less hidden. Fiona would be coming from the other direction to collect the girls, so there was no danger of Sara being spotted. She sat for a moment looking at the street of gritstone terraces, with their neat gardens and tidy hedges, sadness infusing her very bones. There were two blocks of five houses on each side of the road, a gap between each block giving access to the backs of the houses where the garages were. It all looked so normal, so benign. Who could tell that at number 5, there was a family being torn in two?

Ten minutes later, Fiona drew up in her huge black 4x4 and jumped out of the driver's seat, dressed in skinny jeans and a T-shirt, her blonde hair gleaming in the sun. Sara grabbed the kids' binoculars that Ezra used for wildlife watching up on the moors, wanting to get a better look.

Fiona rang the doorbell, and a few moments later, Matt answered and ushered her inside. *That's my house*, Sara thought. *I should be there with my children, not out here watching.* Anger burned in her heart as she watched her daughters come out and hug their father goodbye before getting in the car, Fiona fussing about with bags, making sure they were all neatly stowed in the boot.

Once the girls were settled, Fiona ran back to the house and went inside, the door closing behind her. Sara frowned. What was she doing? Had they forgotten something? Five minutes later, she came back out again, Matt behind her. He stood on the doorstep leaning against the frame, hands in his pockets, watching Fiona walk back to the car.

Does she look a little flustered? Flushed. Sara changed her focus to Matt, studying his familiar face. A face she'd woken up to almost every day for the last eighteen years. A face that… *Is that a smudge of lipstick?* Her heart skipped a beat and she dropped the binoculars as her mind came to the obvious conclusion. *Fiona and Matt?* By the time she'd picked the binoculars up off the floor to have another look, Fiona was pulling away from the kerb, doing a neat three-point turn while Matt gave the girls a cheery wave. He watched the car until it turned right at the end of the road, then disappeared inside the house. The front door shut.

Fired with an indignant rage – her thinking blurred by hurt – Sara got out of the car and ran down the road. She stopped at the front door and took a moment to calm herself down. It would be better if she was stealthy, if she had the advantage of surprise. As quietly as she could, she slid her key into the lock, but it wouldn't go all the way in. She stared at it, tried again, then realisation dawned. *He's changed the locks.*

Her neighbour came out of her front door, glanced over. 'Morning, Sara,' she called. 'Another lovely day.'

Sara gave her a tight smile and walked away, pretending she'd been coming out of the house rather than trying to get in. She stalked back up the road to her car, got in and drove away, her mind a haze of racing thoughts. The changing of the locks felt like a big thing. A permanent thing. A statement that she was no longer welcome, that she'd been evicted and wasn't going to be allowed back.

Whatever ideas she'd had that she and Matt might be able to repair their relationship, given time and patience, had well and truly been stomped into the dirt. It all made sense now: Fiona's friendliness, getting to know the girls, creating situations where she and Matt could be together, like at the football. And giving Sara the job at the community centre, which made sure she was out of the house. *Christ, I am so stupid. So very, very stupid.* Her hands tightened round the steering wheel as if they were wrapped round Fiona's throat.

She heard her mother's voice in her thoughts: *It takes two to tango…* Matt was as much to blame as Fiona. *Bloody two-timing hypocrite, accusing me of being unfaithful when he and Fiona were…* She slammed on the brakes as a bike swerved in front of her, and took a deep breath. She didn't even know where she was going;

remembered that she was supposed to be meeting Hailey back at the house and pulled over. She called her sister.

'Where are you?' Hailey asked when she answered.

'Slight change of plan. Meet me at the coffee shop. You know, the one by the station. I just need to calm down and get my head straight. I'll tell you when you get here.'

'Oh, okay.' Hailey sounded puzzled. 'I'll be there in ten.'

Sara took a few deep breaths, hand on her chest as if that would be enough to steady the thundering beat of her heart, and set off on the short drive to the coffee shop. She was glad to park up and get out of the car. This new information changed everything. And there was something flickering in her mind, an elusive thought she was trying to grab hold of, but it was slippery as an eel and she couldn't quite keep it in her grasp.

Caffeine. I need caffeine, she thought as she pushed open the door. Maybe then her mind would make the creative connection she needed.

When Hailey arrived a few minutes later, she found Sara sitting at the back of the coffee shop, where they could talk without being overheard.

'Fiona and Matt?' She almost spurted coffee all over the table when Sara told her. 'That's not something I would ever have imagined.' Sara would have to agree that they weren't two people you would naturally put together; two dominant characters who were more likely to fight than agree.

'I know.' She took a sip of her coffee, wondering whether she was jumping to conclusions. 'She had an affair with James, though, so it's not like she thinks her marriage is sacred.'

'Her husband's a lot older than her, isn't he?' Hailey said, blowing on her drink before taking another sip. 'You know, when I've seen pictures of the two of them at charity dos, I always thought of her as a sort of trophy wife. She's so glamorous and intelligent, isn't she? Just the sort of woman a successful businessman would want on his arm.'

'Hmm. I think she likes the money and status and living in that amazing house of theirs. But I get the feeling she's happier when he's away on business trips than when he's home.'

'You never know what goes on in other people's marriages,' Hailey said, with feeling, and Sara knew she was referring to her own experiences with a husband who was a serial cheater. 'I mean, Matt's a good-looking man. Maybe she decided to make a play for him. They see each other often enough at football, don't they?'

Sara put her cup down, a new thought coming to mind. 'The woman you saw getting out of Matt's car the other night. Could that have been Fiona?'

Hailey narrowed her eyes as she thought, then nodded slowly. 'You know, I think it might have been.'

THIRTY-THREE

Having convinced herself that Fiona and Matt were having an affair, Sara was more determined than ever to find out what Matt was doing with his business. She had told him all of her secrets. Now she needed to know his.

Fortified with coffee and cake, they parked round the corner from the house and crept up the footpath that ran down the back of the properties. There was a gate into the garden, which was bolted on the inside and too high for them to climb over. But the footpath ran down the side of the garage to the road at the front of the house, and they snuck around the corner, careful to be quiet.

Matt had arranged for a small glass window to be put in the side wall, to give some natural light in his office. It was frosted security glass, with wire inside, and although they couldn't see through, they could make out the glow from the lights, a shadow moving. Matt was in there.

Their plan was already decided. Sara would stay out of sight while Hailey knocked on his office door, pretending she was a delivery driver with a package that needed to be signed for. When he opened the door, they'd rush him and get inside. Then he wouldn't have time to turn things off and hide what he was doing.

Sara's pulse raced as she had a quick look up and down the street to make sure the neighbours weren't around, then she pressed herself to the side of the garage while Hailey knocked on the door.

'Got a package for you here,' she called in a gruff voice.

No answer. She knocked again. Called louder.

'Got a delivery that needs to be signed for.'

The key turned in the lock, and as soon as the door started to open, Hailey pushed forwards, Sara behind her, their joint momentum making Matt stagger back. His arms windmilled as he lost his balance, and Hailey was on him in a flash, grabbing his arm and pulling it up his back. He screamed, and she gave a satisfied smile, while Sara looked on in alarm, wondering when her sister had learnt to be a ninja.

'Don't hurt him, Hailey.'

'I'm not,' she said, between clenched teeth, giving his hand a twist and making him wince. 'I'm just securing him. It's a restraining technique we use at work. Quite safe.'

Matt's eyes slid to the two large screens set up side by side on his desk, both of them blank.

'You can't do this. You can't barge in here,' he said, all stern and authoritative, as if that would be enough to stop them. 'This is confidential. I have an obligation to my client—'

'Oh shut up, will you?' Hailey snarled. Her eyes had a steely glint and Sara didn't think she'd ever seen her look quite so ferocious. 'Start searching. Let's see what we can find, shall we?' She tugged Matt backwards to give Sara access to the desk.

'No, Sara, no, don't you dare.' Matt tried to move to stop her, but Hailey held him tight. Was that fear in his eyes? Sara thought it might be.

'Or what? What you going to do to me?'

'It's not what *I'll* do, it's what they'll do.'

'And who is this mysterious "they"?' Sara scoffed.

He shook his head, eyes wild. 'I don't know. It's all done electronically.'

She clicked the mouse and the screen in front of her came to life. Not a video as she'd expected, but something that looked more like a spreadsheet. She scanned it, scrolled down, then went back to the top of the page, trying to make sense of what she was seeing. The headings across the top read: *Client, Location, Date, Fee* – but the clients had numbers instead of names, so that wasn't too helpful. However, the location was very familiar – it was the hotel she'd stayed at with James.

Her jaw dropped, appalled at what she was seeing; her worst fears, that Matt was involved, now confirmed. She slipped her phone out of her pocket and took screen shots before turning her attention to the second computer. Tentatively she clicked the mouse, and a page appeared with two headings: *Sleeping Princesses* and *Voyeurs*.

When she clicked on *Sleeping Princesses*, a list of options came up: *Meet a Princess; Book a Princess; Buy a Video; Chat Room.*

She turned to Matt, still not completely clear what she was looking at. 'What exactly is a Sleeping Princess? What does that even mean?'

His Adam's apple bobbed up and down, but he didn't respond until Hailey gave his arm another twist. 'Answer the question. We're intrigued, aren't we, Sara?'

His face contorted with pain. 'Only if you ease off,' he gasped. 'You're going to break my bloody arm.'

Hailey gave his wrist another tweak, making him scream again, before she relaxed her grip a little. 'There you go. Come on, enlighten us.'

He ran his tongue round his lips, eyes on the floor when he started to speak. 'As far as I'm aware, it's women who get a kick out of seeing themselves being… well… fondled while they're unconscious. Bit like a rape fantasy sort of thing.' Sara saw him wince.

She snorted. 'Don't be ridiculous! It must be the other way round. Men getting a kick out of molesting unconscious women.' Her eyes scoured his face for evidence he was lying. 'I was unconscious when those men abused me. I didn't give them permission.' She jabbed a finger at him to make her point. 'I didn't even know it had happened until you showed me that video.'

He wouldn't look at her. 'It's… it's just a fetish site. For people who want to act out their fantasies. It's all between consenting adults, and although it may seem weird, they're not doing any harm.'

Sara was so incensed she couldn't speak.

Fortunately, Hailey didn't have the same problem. 'Oh come on! You don't believe that, do you?' The scorn in her voice would have stripped paint. 'That makes it all sound okay, doesn't it? Instead of your wife being sexually abused for money – a business transaction that you were involved in facilitating – you're saying she made herself unconscious after inviting two strange men to molest her?' Her voice finished an octave higher and a few decibels louder than when she'd started.

As usual, Hailey had gone straight to the heart of the matter, and hearing it summarised so clearly turned it from a theory into reality. But it was a hollow victory. Hurt and shame and disbelief surged through Sara in quick succession, an almost overwhelming blast of emotions that exploded in a fury like she'd never known before.

'You make me sick!' she yelled, hands flying in the air. 'How the hell did you get involved in this? And how can you not see what's really going on here? Talk about deluded!'

Hailey put more pressure on Matt's arm, and he squealed. 'Answer her,' she said, teeth gritted, 'because I'd really like to know too.'

There were tears in his eyes now, but Sara didn't care how much Hailey was hurting him. It was nothing compared to the damage he'd allowed to be done to her, his own wife.

'Okay, okay, I'll tell you everything I know. Just… let's calm down.' He whimpered until Hailey loosened her grip a little, then began to speak. 'It was just after I'd lost my job. I got an email asking if I'd like to help design a secret erotic website for a closed group of friends.' He swallowed, eyes on the floor. 'It sounded okay – maybe a little dodgy – but they assured me it wasn't illegal, just a fetish they shared that they wanted to keep private. They were all in high-calibre jobs, and if it went public, their reputations and careers would suffer. I honestly took it at face value. I didn't need to know what they were going to put on the site, and they assured me it was only between consenting adults. Like a dating site for people with matching fetishes.' He ran his tongue round his lips again, a nervous habit Sara knew well. 'I thought it was, you know, a bit weird, but whatever floats your boat. Who am I to judge? I'm just the tech guy, the architect. And I needed the work, didn't I? To keep our family going. So I agreed.'

He shook his head, his eyes meeting Sara's for the first time. She glared at him until he looked away. 'I honestly thought everything was consensual. You've got to believe me. When I saw the video of you, I thought you must be into the fetish as well. It was only when they wanted to develop the site that I got a bit twitchy.'

Sara gasped. 'You are kidding me? We've been together eighteen years; don't you think you would have known by now if I was into stuff like that?'

He hung his head. 'Looks like I jumped to the wrong conclusion,' he mumbled. He looked up then, eyes brimming with tears. 'I'm sorry. I shouldn't have gone off on one like that. I know it was jealousy speaking and I know I didn't listen to you.'

An apology from Matt was a rare thing, and she gazed at him, at the tears, but made herself stand her ground, hands clenched by her sides. His emotion might not be real. *I can't trust him.* There was more, she knew there was, and this could be a ploy to get her sympathy, prevent him having to tell her everything. She folded her arms across her chest, a hard edge to her voice. 'Carry on, you were saying?'

'When they asked for the Voyeurs section to be added, I wanted to stop.' His eyes pleaded with her. 'I said I couldn't be involved any more, but they wouldn't let me out of the contract. They put... they put that video of Milly in the shower all over social media and said if I didn't carry on working for them they had other videos I wouldn't want to be made public.' His eyes glistened, pain in his voice. 'Can't you see? I had no choice.'

'You bastard,' Hailey hissed. 'Exposing your own family to these filthy animals, not to mention all the other victims. I bet most of them don't even know they've been filmed, do they?'

He didn't answer, but he didn't need to. The truth was obvious as soon as his eyes dropped to the floor and stayed there.

'Who are they, Matt? Who's behind all this?' Sara stood in front of him and grabbed his chin, made him look at her.

'I don't know, honestly I don't.' His voice sounded convincing but his eyes told another story. Sara fought the urge to lash out. Instead, she backed away, needing time to think.

'So what happens now?' Matt asked, grimacing as Hailey gave his arm another twist.

'I want any videos of me destroyed. And any of the girls. Take the site down, get rid of the content.' Sara glowered at him. 'That's the least you can do.'

Hailey's eyes widened. 'But what about evidence for the police? We can't just wipe it all. These people have to be stopped, brought to justice. Otherwise it'll just keep happening.'

Sara sank into the chair by the desk and pointed at Matt. 'You think he'll cooperate? He'll probably just hide everything or start a new site or something. These things don't go away, do they? Once they're online, they've got a life of their own.'

Matt's eyes widened. 'I won't. Honestly, Sara, I want this to stop as much as you do. Just tell her to let me go and I'll do whatever you want.'

Sara glared at him, incredulous. 'You think I trust you after everything you've done? You're a two-faced liar.' She caught her sister's eye. 'You're right, Hailey. Let's get him somewhere safe, where he can't mess up the site, then we can call the police.'

'I think it's the right call,' Hailey said, her face a little red with the effort of keeping Matt under control. She glanced at the door.

'Look, shall we take him into the house? We can lock up the office so it's secure. Then we can make that phone call.'

'Good idea.' Sara got up from her seat and led the way. A shout made her turn just as she reached the door. A fist caught the side of her head, sending her sprawling to the ground, smacking her hip on the concrete as she landed. Winded and helpless, she watched Matt lock the office door, trapping Hailey inside. Then, without a backward glance, he ran down the garden path and out of the back gate.

THIRTY-FOUR

Sara watched Matt disappear, her head spinning from the force of the punch, her eyes unable to focus properly. *He hit me.* That was the only thought she could fit in her head. It was so shocking, so unexpected, it pushed everything else from her mind.

It took a few minutes for the dizziness to fade enough for her to get to her knees and lever herself to her feet. But as soon as she was upright, the ground started to sway, nausea struck and she spewed her breakfast into the flower bed, leaning on the wall for support, her legs so weak and wobbly she felt like a sailor in a storm at sea.

She heard a faint sound from the other side of the office door, a low moan. *Oh my God, has he hurt her?* She rattled the door handle, to no avail. 'Hailey! Are you okay?'

No response.

Her eyes darted around, looking for some way in, but she knew it was hopeless. Security had been high on Matt's agenda when he'd set up the office, and with the door locked, there was no way to get access. *My phone's inside.* She groaned, leaning her head against the door. *What am I going to do?*

Then she heard a muffled grunt and pressed her ear to the door. 'Hailey, are you okay?'

She could hear movement, then her sister's voice. 'I'm all right, I think. I was just winded for a minute.'

Relief flooded through Sara's body. 'What happened? You seemed to be well in control, and then...'

'I got cramp in my hand. He must have sensed the pressure come off, elbowed me in the face, punched me in the stomach. Next thing I knew, I was on the floor and he was bloody gone.'

'He's locked the door, I can't get in,' Sara said, rattling the handle again. 'He punched me so hard he knocked me off my feet and then he scarpered out the back gate.'

Hailey groaned. 'Goddammit. What do we do now?'

'I honestly don't know. I've no idea where he's gone.' Sara winced, her fingers finding the place on her cheek where Matt had hit her. 'My God, I never thought he'd punch me. Vicious with words sometimes, but never with his fists.'

They were quiet for a moment, until Hailey spoke, back to her usual businesslike self. 'Look, I'll ring a locksmith, then once I'm out of here we can sort out what to do next.'

'What if he comes back, though? We can't have him destroying evidence.'

Sara closed her eyes and slid down to the floor, her back against the door.

'Even if it means I have to come clean about everything, I can't let this website carry on. I can't. My conscience won't let me. Goodness knows how many women have already been abused. It won't just be me. There's lots of dates on that spreadsheet. What if there are more spreadsheets, more venues? I didn't look that carefully. Christ, it could be massive.'

'That's the dilemma.' Hailey sounded as weary as Sara felt, the burden of this decision weighing heavy on her. 'Do you look out for yourself or do what's right for the greater good?'

Sara's brain was humming, her face throbbing.

'Perhaps we should try to talk to James before we go to the police. He said he had some information for me.' She thought about it for a moment, the mysterious request to meet on the moors. His accident. 'He must know who's behind all this.' She checked her watch. 'It's visiting time at the hospital. How about

I go and see if I can talk to him while you wait for the locksmith to come? You can tell him Matt accidentally locked you in or something.'

'Okay, if you think it'll help. And if Matt comes back, I'll be ready for him. I won't let him just come in and press a few buttons and delete everything, all right?'

Sara's jaw tightened. 'Sounds like a plan.'

James was in the Airedale General Hospital, situated in the next valley. After a quick conversation with the help desk, Sara followed the directions she'd been given through the maze of corridors. Eventually she arrived in the right place and was shown to a side ward with four beds, all of them occupied. Two of the other patients had visitors and it felt a little cramped – no privacy at all with the curtains drawn back. She hovered in the doorway, heart sinking as she realised there was going to be little opportunity for a confidential conversation. Still, she was here now, and even a snippet of information would be progress.

James was dozing, his head bandaged, left arm in a plaster cast, lying on top of the covers. She spoke softly as she sat by the bed.

'James, are you awake?'

His eyes flicked open and he blinked a few times as if unable to believe she was real. He glanced around, clearly unsettled. 'You can't be here,' he whispered.

Sara frowned. 'I asked at the desk and they said—'

'No. No, I can't speak to you.' He looked… frightened.

Sara glanced over her shoulder, but there was nobody there and the other people in the ward were more interested in their own conversations.

She leant towards him, her voice a low murmur. 'I'll go in a minute. But I need to know what you were going to tell me last night.'

He stared at her but didn't speak, so she carried on.

'I found out what Matt's been up to and I think I understand what happened to me at the hotel. But I need to find out who's behind it all.' She studied his face. 'You know, don't you?'

There was a wild look in his eyes, sweat beading his brow. 'I can't tell you anything. I can't.' He pressed his lips shut, clutched the blanket that covered him closer to his chest.

'I think you're involved,' she hissed at him. 'I think you took me to those men. It was all prearranged, wasn't it? What was in it for you, eh? Was it money?' Her anger was building, and she had to clasp her hands together to stop herself from slapping him.

James leaned his head away from her, his voice an agitated stammer. 'No, no, no... you're wrong. I had no idea what was going on at the hotel. Honestly I didn't.' His face flushed red. 'I was given the weekend tickets as a sweetener, from the network, and I wasn't... I wasn't going to go. But they said I'd be doing them a favour if I did and took you with me.'

People were glancing at them, frowning, James's body language giving out clear signals that he felt under threat.

'You've got to go, and don't come back,' he said, his voice suddenly much louder.

Sara's cheeks burned. 'I just want to know—'

'Leave me alone!' he shouted, and she sprang to her feet, aware that she was probably about to be thrown out.

'I'm going,' she said to the nurse who hurried to the bottom of his bed. 'I didn't mean to upset him.' The nurse gave her an annoyed frown and stood to one side, following her to the main door of the ward and watching as she left.

She drove back to her house hoping that Hailey had been freed from the office by now, her thoughts on James and his reaction. He'd been asked to take her to the hotel – it wasn't him who was behind this. He was a pawn in the whole thing, an enabler. *Had he known what was going to happen to me, and still agreed to it? Or was he telling the truth when he said he knew nothing about the arrangement?*

Still struggling to work out what she knew and what she believed to be true, she parked outside the house, behind the locksmith's van. It was only when she got out of the car that she saw the smoke pouring out of Matt's office.

THIRTY-FIVE

Sara ran up the drive to where Hailey was leaning against the wall of the house, staring at the office. 'What's going on?' She put a hand over her mouth and nose in an attempt to stop herself from breathing in the acrid smoke that was pouring out of the office door.

'I think it's an electrical fault or... I don't know.' Hailey looked dazed and definitely puzzled. 'Is it possible Matt had it wired up to destroy the hard drive if the lock was forced?'

She coughed, and Sara pulled her away to the back garden, the breeze taking the smoke in the other direction.

'The locksmith took the old lock out and put a new one in, and we were chatting on the road by his van while I sorted out payment when I noticed the smoke. Well, it wasn't just smoke – by that time the carpet had gone up in flames. Luckily the locksmith carries a fire extinguisher, and he charged back in there.'

As she finished speaking, a stocky middle-aged man with a shaven head came out of the office door and walked over to them. He pulled off his sooty face mask, leaving a clean triangle on the bottom half of his face. 'It's all out now, but there's a bit of damage. Better get the insurance people over to have a look. All the computer equipment is ruined, and the desks and chairs.' He gave an apologetic shrug. 'I'm sorry, I did what I could, but those acrylic carpets without fire retardant are lethal.' He held out a blackened phone: Sara's. 'I don't suppose this is going to work now, either.'

Sara took it off him, the case still hot to the touch, and tried to switch it on, but the shattered screen remained blank. 'Thank you so much,' she said, thinking that a dead phone was the least of her worries. 'Thank goodness you were here, or it could have been much worse.'

The man looked embarrassed and wiped a hand across his sweaty forehead, leaving a black smear above his eyebrows. 'Happy to help.' He looked back towards the house. 'Home offices can be death traps if the electrics aren't set up properly. Overloaded sockets, all sorts of problems.'

Sara gave a tight smile, wondering if Hailey's theory was right. 'Well, I really appreciate your help, and thanks for getting my sister out of there. Do we owe you anything else? Let me compensate you for—'

'Nah.' He shook his head. 'All part of the service. Anyway, I'm going to get off and get myself cleaned up.'

Sara looked at the house – her home – and a new determination gripped her. She smiled at the man. 'Before you go, I wonder if you could put new locks on the house for me as well? I've lost my keys, you see.' She gave him a hopeful smile. 'Only if you've got time. Otherwise I'll have to break a window or something.' She grimaced, tucked her hands in the pockets of her joggers and looked longingly at the house. 'My husband's away, so I'm a bit stuck.'

He looked at her for a moment, checked his watch. 'I'll just have to give my next client a call, tell them I've been delayed. And I'll need proof this is actually your address.' His eyes didn't leave hers. 'Don't want to be aiding and abetting any wrongdoings, do I?'

Sara gave a strangled laugh. 'No, you wouldn't want to be doing that.' She pointed to the road. 'My bag's in the car, I'll just go and get it, see if there's anything in there.'

She hurried away, coming back a few minutes later with a reminder for a smear test, the only document she could find in her handbag with her address on it. He glanced at it, handed it back, his eyes not meeting hers.

'Sorry, but I had to ask,' he said. 'Okay, I'll crack on, shouldn't take too long. I suppose you want high-security standard?'

Sara nodded. 'Absolutely.'

They watched him walk back to his van, and Hailey gave Sara's shoulder a gentle punch. 'Nice work, sis. I don't know why I hadn't thought of that.'

Sara could hear her teeth grinding and stretched her jaw, massaging the aching muscles. 'It's as much my house as Matt's, and now I know what he's been doing, I don't see why he should assume possession. I need to be here for the children. This is their home, and this is where we're going to be.' She took a deep breath, emotion swelling in her chest, threatening to choke her words. 'He's not coming back into my family. Not after this.'

She looked at the office, wisps of smoke still wafting out of the door.

'I suppose all the evidence has been destroyed?'

Hailey puffed out her cheeks as she followed Sara's gaze. 'I don't know. Sometimes they can get information off damaged computers. Just depends how bad it is.' Her expression wasn't hopeful, though, and Sara wondered if they really were getting anywhere, or whether they had already lost the battle.

They went to assess the damage, standing in the doorway as they scanned the room. The edge of one computer screen had melted, making it look like something out of a Salvador Dali painting; the desk it was sitting on was blackened, and the hard drive standing underneath had become a deformed skeleton, a mere remnant of its former self.

'I wish I understood how these things worked from a technical point of view,' Sara said, glancing at Hailey. 'If the hard drive is ruined, does that mean all the information stored on there has gone, or does it still exist on the internet?'

Hailey's fingers tapped at her lips as she thought. 'Don't you think he'll have a backup?'

'Oh God, you're right.' Sara could hear his voice in her head, telling her about it. 'I'm pretty sure he mentioned the Cloud.' She looked again at the ruined office. 'He's just made sure there's no physical evidence, hasn't he? Nothing that can link him directly with the site. But it's still there somewhere.' She sighed, despondent. 'When he was employed, he worked on a government project to track down criminal sites on the dark web, so he knows all their software tools and how to avoid them. We've got to find him and make him destroy it, because I'm not sure anyone else is going to be able to. Not quickly, anyway.'

'Yeah, and how are we going to do that?' Hailey threw up her hands, frustrated. 'We don't know where he's gone, or if he's planning on coming back. And even if he said he'd destroyed it, I wouldn't believe him.'

Sara wiped her hands over her face, wincing when she touched the tender spot where Matt had punched her. 'Bloody hell, Hailey. I can't believe he's the same man I married.' She leant against the wall as an unwelcome thought popped into her head, another blow to her battered self-respect.

'I'm just wondering about the Matt and Fiona situation.' She looked up at the fluffy clouds drifting across the sky before focusing on her sister again. 'I know we're sort of friends, but she keeps her cards close to her chest. Doesn't give out much information about what she's up to, while she just hoovers up all the details of what's going on in everyone else's life. In fact, she makes it her business to know. And she does love it when you owe her a favour. It's like...' She stopped talking, a sudden moment of clarity illuminating her thoughts like a searchlight. 'Oh my God, that's it.'

Hailey scowled at her. 'What's it? What are you talking about?'

'Something James said earlier. I haven't told you, have I? He was so scared when he saw me, basically had me chased out of the ward, but not before he'd let slip that the person behind this scheme persuaded him to take me with him on the weekend

because it would be doing them a favour.' She nodded, sure she'd
got it right. 'He was scared to be seen talking to me. Which makes
me think he was warned off. Whatever happened to him in the
quarry, I don't think it was an accident.'

'Christ, Sara.' Hailey ran a hand through her hair, frowning.
'What have we got ourselves into?'

Sara chewed on her lip as little pieces of information gathered
together, starting to make a clearer picture in her mind. 'I told you
James and Fiona had an affair, didn't I? She told me to be careful of
him. Said he had "evil little ways". But James said he was the one
who dumped her, so that doesn't make sense. I wonder… What
if she's the one with the evil little ways and he wasn't interested
in playing?'

Hailey's mouth opened and closed. Her face crumpled into a
mask of disbelief. 'You think Fiona's behind all this?'

'It's possible, isn't it?' Really, it was the only theory they had to
go on, if they'd discounted James from being involved. And the
more she thought about it, the more it made sense.

'Well, it's pretty twisted if she is. Especially with the video of
Milly in the shower being spread around.' Hailey pulled a disgusted
face. 'That's just sick.'

They stood in silence for a moment, working through the
implications.

'Do you think he might have gone to her?' Sara said. 'To
Center Parcs?'

Hailey rubbed her lips with her fingers as she thought. 'Well,
it's a good place to hide. And he could just say he'd decided to
surprise the girls.'

'Or he might be watching us now. Waiting for us to go so he
can come home.' Sara gave a harsh laugh. 'Not that he'll be able
to get in.'

'He's not going to stay around here now we know what he's been doing, is he? He'll expect the police to be after him at the very least.'

Sara's thoughts clashed together like a rousing finale of cymbals as her conscience was pulled in different directions. 'I can't deal with this. I can't live with myself if I think all this awful stuff is out there and it's still going on. I just need to go to the police. Take my chances.' She caught Hailey's eye, unsure what her sister was thinking. 'The whole thing about me stealing the money might not even come out. I don't think James will say anything. He's clearly scared to death at the moment.'

Hailey stared at her for a moment, her voice measured when she spoke. 'Well, if he's worried what they might do to him if he talks, don't you think you should start to focus on what might happen to *you*?'

Sara stared at her sister, fear gripping her throat as her words sank in.

Am I in danger too? And what about my family?

THIRTY-SIX

It took a moment for Sara to find her voice, panic whipping her words away, making her heart race.

'I've got to get the kids. Now. I've got to go and get them.' She started towards her car, but Hailey put a hand on her shoulder, hauled her back.

'Hey, calm down. Let's think this through.'

Sara tried to tug her arm from her sister's grasp. 'We'll get Ezra first. Come on. Let's go.'

Hailey's grip stayed firm. 'Better if I drive,' she said. 'You're in no fit state.'

Sara stopped struggling, realising the truth in her sister's words. She took a deep breath – an attempt to calm herself down – while Hailey continued. 'Let's wait until the locksmith has finished, get the place secured, then we'll pick Ezra up.' She checked her watch. 'Say you're right and Matt is heading to Center Parcs in the Lakes. How long do you reckon it'll take?'

'No idea. Why don't you google it?'

'Whinfell Forest, is that the one?' Hailey asked, swiping at her phone. Sara nodded, thinking about her girls, so far away from her. *Have I put them at risk?* She'd never forgive herself if something happened to them because of her stupidity. 'Says here it takes two hours; let's call it three.' Hailey sounded reassuringly calm. 'Google's always a bit over-optimistic with these things.'

Sara picked up her line of thought. 'It must be a good hour and a half since Matt left. He won't be there yet, if that's where he's going.'

The locksmith appeared then, breaking up their conversation with a cheery 'All done.' He handed Sara an invoice for an eye-watering amount and she forced a smile onto her face. *Small price to pay to get my house back,* she decided. He handed her two sets of keys, and her smile broadened as she took back control of her family's domain. 'Thank you so much. I'll do a bank transfer if that's okay?'

'No problem. That'll do nicely.' He hitched up his trousers. 'I'll be off now. Got customers waiting.' And with that, he hurried back to his van, while Sara and Hailey went into the house.

'I need a couple of painkillers,' Sara said. 'My head's throbbing so much I can't think straight.'

The messy familiarity pulled at her heart as she filled a glass with water and popped a couple of tablets from the packet she kept in the cupboard, the detritus of family life reminding her of what she'd lost. It would never be the same again. *But do I want it to be?* The thought hit her out of nowhere, and now it had appeared, she understood that although this was the death of one phase in her life, it was the birth of another; one that might have room for her needs as well as those of her family.

She walked over to the table, where Hailey was sitting, her phone to her ear. 'Hi, Marian. I just wanted to make sure Ezra's okay with you for another half-hour or so.' Her eyes widened. 'What do you mean? When?' She ended the call, stared at Sara. 'Matt picked him up. He's got Ezra.'

Sara gasped, and the glass she was holding fell to the floor, smashing on the tiles, pieces skittering in all directions. 'Oh my God, no.' She clung to the back of a chair. 'That's it. We've got to call the police. This has gone too far. I've got to put the safety of the kids first.'

Hailey blew out a long breath, clearly shocked. 'How did he know where Ezra was, though?'

To Sara, it was obvious. 'If we're here together, then someone must be looking after him, and your next-door neighbour is the only person he'll stay with, isn't she?'

'Yeah, you're right. Wouldn't take a genius to work that one out.' Hailey swiped at her phone, put it to her ear, her face pale but determined. 'Let's just check in with the girls, shall we? See what they're up to. Then we can give the police the full picture. Matt might get cross with Ezra, but he's not going to hurt him. He's safe enough.'

Sara paced the floor, too agitated to sit down, her hands buried in her hair. 'What if he's going to get the girls and make a run for it? What if he and Fiona have got a contingency plan worked out?'

Hailey tutted, looked at her phone. 'No reply. I'll message Soph.' She gave Sara a hard look before she started tapping away at her screen. 'You've been watching way too many TV dramas. You know your daughters. Nobody's going to make those girls do anything they don't want to do.' She pressed send and gave Sara her full attention. 'The only reason Matt would take Ezra is as a bargaining chip. That's what it's all about. He's desperate and thinks if he's got Ezra, he can control you.'

They busied themselves with clearing up the mess on the floor while they waited for a response from Sophia. When they'd still heard nothing, Hailey made mugs of tea, while Sara stood gazing into the back garden, paralysed by fear.

'Come and sit down. Panicking isn't going to get us anywhere, is it? Let's have a proper think about this.'

Sara slid onto a chair, her hands cupped round the hot mug, her body shaking. Just when she'd thought she was in charge of her life again, Matt had been one step ahead.

Hailey's phone pinged and she frowned as she read the message out loud: 'Chelsea is being a bitch. Fiona is being weird. Can we come home?'

Sara stood up. 'That's it. We're going to get them.'

Hailey followed her. They were almost at her car when she stopped. 'I just had a thought. Fiona set off not long before Matt did a runner, didn't she?'

'That's right.'

'They might not even be at Center Parcs yet.' Her fingers flew over the screen of her phone. 'Let's find out where they are. We don't know if Fiona was going straight there. She might have stopped on the way somewhere. We don't want to go bombing up there if we can pick them up closer to home.' She pressed send.

They waited, Hailey checking her screen every few seconds for a reply, but nothing came. After a couple of minutes, they looked at each other, and Sara knew from the expression in Hailey's eyes that she was worried.

'They might just be in a blank zone.'

'What if Fiona's taken Sophia's phone off her?' Amelia had stopped using her mobile in recent weeks, something Sara now realised was probably due to the shower incident. 'Or the battery has gone flat?'

'Maybe wait a few more minutes.'

'We can wait at the police station. Honestly, Hailey. It's the right thing to do.' Sara's stomach clenched at the thought, but the prospect that her children might be in danger was far more important than anything else.

THIRTY-SEVEN

They had only been travelling a couple of minutes and were at a T-junction heading into the middle of town when a familiar car went past, the driver a woman with short blonde hair, wearing large sunglasses.

Sara did a double-take. 'Bloody hell, Hailey.' She pointed at the black 4x4 heading down the road. 'It's her. It's Fiona. What the hell's she doing in Ilkley?' *And where are the girls?* Her heart skipped as Hailey sped away from the junction after Fiona's car, which started winding up towards the moors. She was confused now. 'Where on earth is she going?' Fiona lived on the other side of town, so she wasn't going home.

'We'll just have to follow and find out.'

They were directly behind her, Hailey keeping a bit of distance so she wouldn't be too obvious. But a few moments later, Fiona sped up, zooming well ahead of them.

'Crap. I think she's seen us.' Hailey sat forward, hunched over the steering wheel as if she was pushing the car up the hill. 'Come on, car, please go faster.' But Fiona was pulling away, heading up to the top of the moors.

Sara pointed. 'Look, she's going into the car park.' They watched her swing the 4x4 into a parking spot, jump out and run off up the track towards the quarry. Moments later, Hailey screeched to a halt and they clambered out and started running after her.

Fiona had a head start, and she darted nimble-footed across the moors. Sara was no match for her speed, stumbling over stones and losing her footing in gaps between the heather, air ripping into her lungs as she pushed herself forward as fast as she dared go. Hailey was way ahead of her, fitter and used to running, while Sara thought her lungs might explode. She had to watch where she was treading, unable to keep her eyes on her target as Fiona sped towards the jumble of gritstone boulders.

After a few minutes, Hailey stopped, gazing around, and Sara caught up with her, pulling to a halt, puffing and panting so hard she couldn't speak.

'What the hell is she playing at?' Hailey frowned, scanning the moors, but there was no sign of Fiona anywhere.

'Oh no, don't say we've lost her.' Sara turned in a full circle. 'There,' she said, her heart flip-flopping as she pointing to a figure on a narrow path that eventually led back down to the car park. 'She's doubled back.' They set off at a jog, Hailey pulling ahead again while Sara concentrated on where she was putting her feet, her legs shaky and weak after the unaccustomed exercise.

A sharp scream made her stop and scan the moors ahead of her. Fiona had disappeared. Sara stood looking around at the boulder-strewn landscape, the ground cloaked in heather and bilberry bushes. There were endless hiding places; all Fiona had to do was duck down when they weren't looking and she'd be hidden from sight. Hailey had stopped too, and glanced back, throwing up her hands. 'Where the hell did she go?'

With her heart pounding in her chest, Sara methodically scoured the hillside for movement. 'Over there!' she called, as she spotted a hand flapping in the air. Relief surged through her. *Looks like she's tripped and fallen over.* She started running before she had time to even think about it, and dashed down the path after her sister, determined to reach Fiona before she could get up and make her escape.

She arrived just after Hailey, both of them panting hard, dragging in air as they bent over the crumpled figure. Fiona was lying on a bed of bilberry bushes at the side of the narrow path, wedged between a couple of boulders.

'Help me,' she said, her leg folded beneath her at an unnatural angle, her hand cradling her elbow, face screwed up in agony.

Sara stared at her, hands on hips as she tried to speak between rasping breaths. 'What the hell are you doing? Where are the girls? You're supposed to be in the Lake District.'

'They're still at my house,' Fiona gasped. 'I had to come back to attend to... some urgent business.'

Urgent business? Had she met up with Matt? Because if she had, it meant he and Ezra were still close by. *They're safe.* Her children were safe, and Fiona wasn't going anywhere. Sara's heart gave a lurch of relief and she turned her attention to the figure on the ground.

'My leg,' Fiona wailed, her face contorted with pain. 'And my arm. Call an ambulance, Sara. Can't you see I need urgent medical attention here?'

Hailey watched, impassive, clearly in no hurry to ring for help, and Sara knew why. This was their chance to get some proper answers and she decided to try a bluff, see how Fiona would respond. The truth was, she had very little evidence of anything. But she could try and trick Fiona into incriminating herself. It was the only strategy she could think of.

'I can't help you there, I'm afraid. I don't have my phone with me. But I'm sure Hailey will call the emergency services once we've had a little chat.' She gave Fiona a tight smile and sat on the ground next to her, where she could watch her face, work out what was truth and what was lies.

'No answers, no help. That's the deal,' Hailey said as she settled herself on a boulder by the side of the path, her phone grasped in her hand. She glanced at Sara. 'We'd better check the car, don't you think? She was obviously running away from us, so maybe she's got something in there she doesn't want us to see.' She held out her hand. 'Car keys, Fiona.'

Fiona glared at her, a look that said she wanted Hailey to shrivel up and die.

'I don't think she's going to cooperate,' Hailey said. 'Remember, no emergency services, no pain relief until we have some answers.'

'Jacket pocket,' Fiona gasped. 'Right-hand side.'

Hailey bent and rummaged in Fiona's pocket – not being as gentle as she could have been – while Fiona whimpered with every movement. Hailey held up the keys like she'd won a trophy and grinned at Sara. 'Okay, back in a tick.'

Sara watched as her sister sauntered down the path to the car park, obviously in no hurry. Then she turned her attention back to Fiona, giving her a bright smile. Fiona closed her eyes, her face deathly pale.

'Look, Fiona, it's your choice how fast you get medical attention. You can pretend you weren't running away from us. You can even pretend that your urgent business is not connected to the fact we surprised Matt and got him to tell us what he's been working on. But it seems like one hell of a coincidence, and I'm not buying it.'

She was silent for a moment, letting her words sink in. There really was no hurry now she knew where the girls were, and she'd put bets on Matt and Ezra being there as well. 'The sooner you tell me the truth, the sooner you get to hospital.' She shrugged with feigned nonchalance. 'Your call.'

Fiona's teeth were clamped on her lower lip as she fought against the pain. Sara glanced down the hillside, watched Hailey reach the 4x4 and start searching inside.

'I know all about Matt's business,' she said, as her mind finally put the pieces together. She couldn't see Matt and Fiona as lovers. Hailey had been right when she said Matt wouldn't do that, not with his upbringing and the beliefs his father had instilled in him. It was far more likely this was a business arrangement. 'I'm guessing you might be his client.'

Fiona's eyes flicked open, and Sara saw the panic, an admission of guilt.

'This is your venture, isn't it?' Rage roared in her ears as she understood the truth. 'Why, Fiona? Why would you do that to me and Milly? Why humiliate us like that? And your disgusting website.' She smacked the boulder she was sitting on to stop herself from slapping the woman at her feet. 'How could you?'

Fiona whimpered again, clearly in a lot of pain. It looked like her leg and elbow might both be broken. 'Okay, let me tell you,' she said, her words forced out from between clenched teeth. 'None of your stupid guessing. You're making a big fuss about nothing. If you hadn't seen the video, you would never have known anything about it. So what harm would it have done? If Matt hadn't decided to look at the videos to make sure they were loading properly, you'd have been none the wiser.' Defiance shone in her eyes. 'I gave you a job, Sara. Gave you a way of earning money when your family was in a mess. Created a business idea for Matt. That was me being a friend and supporting your family. Looking after you.'

Sara's mouth dropped open and she was speechless for a moment, unable to comprehend that Fiona could possibly imagine her actions had been benevolent. *Deluded doesn't come close. It's all about money.* That was the real truth. She stared out over the moors as her thoughts gathered to a logical conclusion. She'd seen the figures on the spreadsheet, seen the bookings and how much men were prepared to pay to play out their Sleeping Princess fantasy.

'And you owed me a favour,' Fiona continued, pressing her point. 'Several favours. Let's be honest, I've done a lot for you, and what have you done for me? Nothing. That's the answer. You owed me. I chose the repayment method.'

Sara shook her head in disbelief. Was that it? Had her debt really been to Fiona?

'It's a pity Matt couldn't see he was on to a good thing with me. The stupid man's besotted with you; he just brushed me away.'

She tried to seduce him, and he resisted? Sara didn't feel any less betrayed by the people she'd trusted. Her body was rigid with fury.

Fiona moaned as she moved in an effort to make herself more comfortable. 'I think we're quits now.' She attempted a smile, which turned into a grimace. 'So let's not say anything about it. And I won't tell anyone you stole from the community centre.'

Sara's breath hitched in her throat and her heart gave a weird little skip. 'You know?'

'Of course I know.' Fiona grunted, adjusting the position of her arm so the weight of it was supported on her chest. 'Julia did a thorough audit of the accounts when she started, something our previous treasurer never bothered to do. She spotted it straight away. I told her I'd investigate, spoke to James, and we came to... an understanding. It has been documented as an admin error, but of course I can do further investigations and discover that James wasn't being truthful with me, can't I?' She raised an eyebrow. 'Then we'll have to get the police involved and, well, we don't want to go there, do we? So if you say nothing about the website, I'll say nothing about the theft.'

Sara shuffled her feet, nudging Fiona's leg. She squealed in pain.

'Oh God, I'm so sorry,' Sara said, as if she meant it, while anger flared in her chest. *Does she really think I'm going to let this go?* She sat in silence, seething as she considered Fiona's ultimatum.

'Do we have a deal?' Fiona asked, a tear trickling down her face. 'Look, I need an ambulance. Please, Sara, Let's just agree on this.'

Sara glared at her, too angry to speak. When she did, there was a steely edge to her voice.

'Think of all those women who were exploited. It's not just me, is it? I know you tried to tell Matt that it was all consensual, and you might have convinced him, but I know it isn't. You're facilitating paid abuse.' Sara's feet itched to kick her again, harder this time, but she resisted. It was more important to understand why she'd been the target of Fiona's scheme.

Fiona closed her eyes. 'Okay, some of it was wrong. I'll admit that. I saw a business opportunity, didn't think it through in terms of consequences.' She grimaced, another tear rolling down her cheek. 'It's all over, anyway. Matt's put an end to it. He said he's destroyed everything.'

Sara stared at her, willing her to open her eyes so she could see if this was the truth. The hardware was ruined, but what about the backup in the Cloud; what about the copies that were already out there, being shared by God knows who?

The sound of footsteps made her look up, and she got to her feet, caught Hailey's arm and led her away so Fiona couldn't hear.

'I had a good look in her car,' Hailey whispered. 'There's something that could be a backup drive in the boot, all wrapped up in plastic. I didn't touch it, didn't want to leave fingerprints.'

'A remote backup? God, I never thought of that. Do you think she was coming up here to hide it till all the fuss died down?'

Hailey nodded. 'That makes sense.'

'Did you call the police?'

Hailey looked at her. 'You sure you want me to?'

Sara swallowed her fears of what might lie ahead for her. 'Do it,' she said. It was the only way she'd be able to live with her conscience. How could she act to save herself when all those other women were being robbed of their dignity, molested without even being aware of what was happening? 'Who knows what Matt can do in terms of starting it all up again? And I don't trust Fiona as far as I can throw her, not with that much money at stake. It's got to be stopped. Properly finished.'

'I'm proud of you,' Hailey said, her eyes gleaming. She walked a little way down the hill to make the call, while Sara chewed at her lip, thinking about what would happen next. She wasn't ready to deal with the police. *The kids. I need to make sure they're okay.*

She waited for Hailey to finish.

'Can I borrow your phone? I need to ring Matt. I've no idea what state he's in, or where he is, and he's got Ezra.' Her voice sped along, propelled by the overwhelming desire to be with her children. 'And then I need to check on the girls, tell them—'

'Hey, calm down.' Hailey held out her phone. 'You take this. I've got my work phone in the car, so you can contact me on that.' She gave Sara's arm a reassuring squeeze. 'Go and get the girls, ring Matt, do whatever you've got to do to make sure those kids are safe. I'll stay with Fiona, make sure the police know what's been going on.'

Sara took the phone, gave Hailey a grateful hug and hurried down the hill. It was only a twenty-minute walk back to her house, where she'd left the car, and as she walked, a plan formed in her mind. She'd go and get the girls and then phone Matt. If he wouldn't talk to her, she'd get Sophia to speak to him. Between them they could sort this out and get Ezra back home. As a last resort, she told herself, the police would be able to find him.

But as she hurried down the road towards the house, she realised none of that would be necessary. Matt's car was parked outside.

THIRTY-EIGHT

She started to run, adrenaline pumping through her veins, unsure what Matt was going to be like with her, but desperate to hold her son. *He'll be furious I changed the locks and he can't get in.* She slowed as she neared the car, expecting Matt to jump out and start shouting at her, but the vehicle was empty. With her heart racing, she checked the back garden, but there was no sign of Matt or Ezra.

Bloody hell! Where are you?

She pulled Hailey's phone from her pocket and dialled his number. It rang and rang, but no answer. She tried again. And again. Eventually, she left a voicemail.

'Matt, look, this has all got out of hand. We need to talk. Hailey called the police. Fiona's been arrested and I promised her I wouldn't tell the police anything in return for her silence about the money from the community centre. We've got to get our story straight. For the sake of the kids.'

It was a dangerous game she was playing – the lies mounting up – but she hoped he couldn't tell that her message was the opposite of the truth. She had a clear goal in sight: to put right the wrongs that had been done and get life back to normal without anyone she cared about getting hurt. Hailey would look after the children if Sara ended up in prison. Yes, it would bring humiliation to the family, but that was a price she was willing to pay. It would pass. Things would be forgotten. She could move to Skipton; not far away but another world in terms of the reach of local gossip. Her mind whirred through the consequences, none of them great, but it was a matter of damage limitation.

When she turned towards the house after leaving her message, she noticed broken glass, the kitchen window propped open. *Matt. Is he still here?* Quickly she unlocked the back door and ran inside.

Ezra was screaming upstairs. She crept through the hall until she could hear Matt's raised voice. 'We're just going on a little holiday. You do not need every single bloody cuddly toy.'

He's taking him away! She clung to the banister as she listened.

Ezra's screams got louder, and she knew Matt was fighting a losing battle. There was no rational conversation to be had, no reasoning with him once he'd worked himself up into this sort of paddy.

Quickly she crept outside, where she wouldn't be heard, and rang Hailey to tell her what was happening.

'What a relief you found them. Don't worry, the police are here. I'll tell them Matt's at your house and threatening to run off with Ezra. That should get them round pronto. I've already given them a run-down of what's been happening, but they want a full witness statement, so I'll be here a little while longer.'

Sara finished the call, then picked up a piece of the broken glass and crept out to Matt's car, stabbing the two back tyres. Satisfied that he wouldn't be going anywhere, she went back into the house, bumping straight into Matt as he carried a screaming, thrashing Ezra into the kitchen.

'Mummy!' Ezra shrieked, battering his father with his fists, his face red and tear-stained. Matt stared at her, a look of horror in his eyes. The shock of seeing her must have made him loosen his grip, allowing Ezra to wriggle free and run to Sara, who scooped him up, her heart skittering with relief as he wrapped his arms and legs round her body.

A sheen of tears blurred her vision and she blinked them away, glaring at Matt, who was standing open-mouthed, obviously unsure what to do next. His eyes slid to the back door.

'Locked,' she said.

His mouth twitched.

'Look, love,' he said, as if it was a normal day and she'd just come back from work, 'let's have a chat, shall we?' He walked through into the lounge, turned on the TV and flicked through until he found the CBeebies channel. 'Hey, Ezra,' he called. 'Look what's on telly.'

At the sound of the familiar theme tune, Ezra's eyes lit up and he gave Sara a kiss on the cheek before scrambling down and going to sit on the sofa to watch *Teletubbies*, his thumb in his mouth.

Satisfied that his son was occupied, Matt came back into the kitchen and leant against the worktop, just a few feet away from her. It felt too close, but they needed to be able to speak without disturbing Ezra.

'You punched me,' Sara said in an urgent whisper, before he had a chance to speak. His mouth opened and closed. She gave a derisive snort. 'Yeah, there's no excuse for that, is there?' She pointed towards the lounge. 'And what's the plan with taking Ezra?'

Matt stuffed his hands in his pockets, mouth twisting from side to side before he answered, his eyes on the wall above her left shoulder. 'I was just going away for a few days until everything settled down. Fiona said to go to Center Parcs as the booking had already been made.'

'Don't you think that's a bit of an obvious place?' Sara scoffed. 'She's played you good and proper, hasn't she?'

Nerves tugged at her stomach and her hand found Hailey's phone, felt the reassuring coolness of the metal casing. She sneaked a quick look at the screen as he studied the floor, then slipped it back in her pocket.

'I've spoken to Fiona,' she said, and noticed another twitch of his lips. 'I know she was your client, the one who runs the website business. I know it was her idea... but Matt, you didn't have to do it. You could have said no at any time, when you knew what it was all about. Can't you see how something like that can ruin people's lives? Innocent women being exploited to feed men's fetishes. Can't you see it's wrong?'

He stared at her for a long moment before he finally spoke, scuffing at the tiles with the toe of one of his trainers.

'I needed the money to keep our family solvent.' His voice was low and even, as though he was having to patiently explain something obvious to someone who was being a bit thick. 'She assured me the women had given their consent. She said they were willing participants. No harm done. And it would earn us a shedload of money.'

Sara's anger burst into flame, her finger the only weapon to hand as she stabbed the air. 'But you know that's a load of rubbish, don't you? Look at what happened to me. In no way did I consent.' She realised she was shouting, and glanced into the lounge, worried that Ezra would hear, but thankfully, he'd fallen asleep.

When her gaze came back to Matt, his expression told her she'd caught his lie.

'I got it wrong, love.' He ran a hand through his hair, searching the wall for an excuse. 'She mesmerised me, enticed me with talk of all the money we would make, how it would give the family stability, how you weren't coping and needed me to step up.' He gave a slow shake of his head. 'She said she was doing us a favour, helping us out.' His voice cracked. 'I can't understand how she did it, but she made me believe it was the right thing, the only thing I could do.'

'Oh Matt.' Sara wasn't having any of it, suddenly immune to his wheedling ways. 'You're not that gullible. She's not a bloody snake-charmer, is she?'

Matt huffed. 'Well she charmed you well enough. Look how she took over the girls. Always offering to take them on trips with Chelsea, feeding them all sorts of ideas. Separating them from us. Did you see that?'

His words made Sara pause and think for a moment. Her anger flickered. *He's right*. Her head *had* been turned by Fiona. She *had* been flattered by her desire to be friends. *Am I to blame for this too?* A shiver of doubt ran through her and her hands found each other, twisting together.

'You've ruined everything.' His voice was getting louder, and she glanced towards the lounge, hoping he wouldn't wake Ezra. 'We were doing great until you brought her into our lives.'

'Me?' Sara's voice was incredulous. '*I* ruined everything? How is this my fault?'

'Shh,' Matt said, motioning with his eyes towards the lounge. 'Keep your voice down.' He took a step towards her and put a hand on her arm, tried to draw her to him. 'I'm sorry, love. I'm just really stressed about everything.'

She shook his hand away and stepped back, determined not to let him break her resolve. 'You need to give yourself up. Tell the police everything you know and let's get the whole thing stopped. That's the only way forward.'

He pursed his lips and shook his head. 'Nope. I can't do that.'

'Why not?'

'Because... I'm not going to prison.' He shuddered. 'I couldn't...' He bit his lip, looked away.

'I've had to face up to my mistakes. I know it's not going to be great for a while, but we'll get through the bad patch and then rebuild.'

He glanced at her, his voice hopeful. 'You mean we'd still be together?'

She heard a knock at the door and looked her husband straight in the eye.

'No, Matt.' Her voice was hard, her meaning clear. 'After what you've done, we can never be together.'

She ran to the door and let the two uniformed officers into the house, handing them the phone from her pocket that had recorded the conversation. Then she watched as they cuffed Matt and led him away, his head bowed.

This is the end, she told herself. But in truth, it wasn't quite.

THIRTY-NINE

The police were very polite and listened to Sara's story, but then they listened to Fiona too. Her account put a very different spin on everything, turning Sara and Hailey's version upside down.

Fiona said she'd gone for a run on the moors as she regularly did and had tripped and hurt herself. Sara and Hailey had found her. Nothing more sinister than that. She denied having anything to do with a Sleeping Princess or voyeurism website, appalled that anyone could think such a thing. She pointed out that she was Sara's boss and had simply been trying to help her through a sticky patch. Matt was clearly lying to save his marriage.

Sara knew this was what had been said, because the police reflected everything back to her, suggesting alternative interpretations of what had happened through their questions. She became quite flustered, wishing she'd thought to record the conversation with Fiona on the moors. Fiona had told the police that Sara was under a lot of stress because her home life was rocky. She'd been worried about Sara and told her to take time off work. That was true, of course, but it implied a certain amount of emotional instability that made Sara a less than credible witness. Without the incriminating video evidence, all Hailey knew of the alleged crimes was what she'd heard second-hand from Sara. Even the pictures she'd seen on the screen in Matt's office could be quite innocent; just a man looking at a bit of porn.

Fiona could be so convincing, and she was a person of authority, an influential character in the area. As the questioning wore on, it became clear that the police believed her version of events. The item wrapped in plastic in her car was indeed the sort of external drive used for backups, but Fiona claimed to know nothing about it. Her car had been in for a valet the day before – maybe someone had put it in there? The data was all encrypted, so the police technicians were having a struggle to find out exactly what was on it, and Sara doubted they ever would.

Without any concrete evidence, Fiona and Matt had been free to go – though the allegations were still being investigated – and all Sara could see was trouble coming back to her door. Matt was denying everything; said the conversation Sara had recorded had been taken out of context, and had explanations lined up to justify his comments. Sara had been under a lot of stress working full-time, he'd said. She could be a little fanciful at times. He'd been taking Ezra and the girls away for a few days to give her a break and had no idea why she was saying she didn't know anything about it.

She was well aware she was losing the battle. Matt and Fiona would be free to carry on with their venture and she was being painted as a neurotic woman who was having a bit of a breakdown.

After a restless night, she woke with a new determination. If the police weren't going to help her get to the truth, she would have to sort things out herself. And the first thing she was going to do was visit Fiona. *Surely I can appeal to her as a mother?*

It was Monday, the first day back at school after half-term, and once she'd dropped Ezra at nursery, she drew up to Fiona's house and rang the bell. Fiona's husband, Maurice, answered the door, impeccably dressed in a Pringle jumper and golfing slacks, his silver hair slicked back from his forehead. He had the bearing of a man who had lived most of his life as the boss, the man in charge.

'Hello, Sara. This is a surprise,' he said with a worried frown. 'I don't think Fiona's expecting you, is she?'

Sara held up the bouquet of flowers she'd bought on the way.

'I wanted to apologise. If she'll see me.' She looked at the ground. 'Of course, I'll understand if she doesn't want to.'

'Well, if you'd like me to take the flowers, I'll just go and ask her.' Sara handed him the bouquet and Maurice started to close the door. 'If you'd like to wait there a minute.'

She rocked back on her heels as the door shut in her face. She'd never been left standing on the doorstep before, and she stuffed her hands in her pockets as she waited. Finally she heard movement, and Maurice opened the door, waved her through into the hall.

'She says to come in.' He closed the door behind Sara, waited while she wiped her feet on the doormat before walking ahead of her. 'She's in the orangery.'

Sara followed him through the living room to the large glass-panelled room that stretched across the back of the house, giving a magnificent view over the roofs of the town and across the Wharfe Valley. Fiona was sitting like a queen on her throne with her leg up on a padded footstool, her arm resting on a cushion. She looked pale, and Sara hoped she was in a great deal of pain. She gave a sheepish smile, ready to play the part of sinner coming to beg forgiveness.

'We need a little time alone,' Fiona told Maurice with a dismissive wave, waiting for him to leave before she addressed Sara. 'Well, I have to say I admire your nerve.'

'I'm so sorry, Fiona. That was Hailey getting the police involved. I tried to persuade her not to, but you know she's always been so protective of me, and… well, when she gets something in her head, there's nothing I can do to stop her.' She gave a heavy sigh, looked up at Fiona from under her lashes. 'I'm assuming it's all okay, though? No harm done?'

Fiona huffed. 'No thanks to your bloody sister. They gave me a bit of a grilling, but as we went on, they could see my point and I managed to persuade them you were a bit doolally.' She made a spiralling motion with her finger, gave a satisfied smile. 'They came round to my point of view in the end.'

Sara's heart fluttered. Just as she'd thought. Fiona was one of those people who could persuade the Eskimos to buy ice, and it was no surprise she'd persuaded the police that her version was the truth. But in reality, without concrete evidence, what were the police supposed to do? It was Sara's word against Fiona's.

'Can I assume our secret is still safe?' she asked, tentatively.

Fiona gave her a cold stare. 'Oh no. I'm sorry. No second chances. I've done enough for you and that's it. A line has been drawn as far as I'm concerned. You've used up all your favours. I had to tell them about your theft. It was only right.' She gave a little snort. 'I have to admit, it came in handy as a diversionary tactic.'

Sara's jaw clenched. 'So we're quits? All debts repaid?'

'I think so. And it's better if you don't come here again.' Fiona looked towards the doorway. 'Maurice! Maurice!' she called, and a few moments later, her husband strode into the room. 'You can show Sara out now.'

Sara followed Maurice to the door, her heart heavy with disappointment. She hadn't even had the chance to talk to Fiona about her business venture with Matt; hadn't come close to saying everything she needed to say.

She was expecting to be shown out and the door closed firmly behind her, but Maurice came outside with her, gently pulling her to the side of the house, out of sight. 'Look, Sara, I couldn't say anything before, but...' His hands were in his pockets, jingling the small change he had in there, his worried eyes studying her face. 'I've heard your accusations. The police questioned me as well, and I defended Fiona, because I believed everything she said.'

Sara braced herself for more bad news. *Is he going to take legal action against me?* Or perhaps he'd do something to tarnish her reputation more publicly. She looked at her car, desperate to get in and drive away.

'Since she's had her accident, I've been running around after her, getting this and that, and I found a phone hidden at the back of a drawer.' He had Sara's attention now. She watched him cringe, obviously uncomfortable with what he was about to tell her. 'I know this doesn't sound good, but I checked through it. Fiona always uses Chelsea's birthday for PIN numbers, so it was easy to get in, and...' He sighed and his whole body seemed to deflate. 'I was shocked. There are conversations with James on there, a lot of them quite cryptic, but in one of them, she tells him that if he doesn't do the favour she's been asking of him, then she'll make some pictures public that would suggest he was raping her while she was unconscious. It's clear she was blackmailing him.' His discomfort was palpable. 'I know they had a short affair and she obviously kept some video evidence so she had a hold over him when he ended it. James wouldn't stand a chance against Fiona. She can be very vindictive and he must have known to just do what she asked without necessarily understanding why.'

He pulled a face, his distaste very clear. 'My wife has some very strange... let's call them predilections.' He sounded lost, defeated. 'Anyway, I just wanted you to know I'm going to hand it over to the police. There are also messages to your husband on there. She seems pretty keen on him, but from his responses, I get the idea the sentiment wasn't returned. It was a business arrangement. He said that more than once.' He looked at her, sadness in his eyes. 'Fiona and Matt both knew what they were doing, Sara. It's clear from their conversations. Careless of them really to communicate like that, but Fiona has an arrogant streak. It wouldn't have entered her head that she might get caught.'

Tears pricked at Sara's eyes as the betrayal by her husband and her friend was spelled out for her. 'Why me? Why would she pick me to be one of these Sleeping Princesses? And why humiliate Milly?'

'Fiona is a strange and jealous woman. I suspect she thought you had the perfect family, the perfect marriage, whereas… well, our marriage was over a long time ago. We've stayed together for Chelsea, but this is the final straw. The police will have their evidence and I'm filing for divorce.'

FORTY

Ten days later

Once Matt had realised he was trapped, his solicitor had advised him that being helpful would reduce his sentence, and he had cooperated fully with the police. By the end of the week, Sara had been fully updated on the situation and was starting to feel more in control of her life.

James had been cleared of all wrongdoing, the evidence showing that he'd been manipulated by Fiona to think he was doing Sara a favour by taking her away for the weekend, when in fact his role had been delivery boy, serving her up like a delicacy for others to feast on, without him knowing anything about it. Fiona liked it that way. She liked to be the puppet master, pulling the strings and watching everyone dance along to her tune. A tune that only she could hear. James had suspected he was being played by Fiona, but had simply thought he was getting Sara out of the way so Fiona could spend time with Matt.

The accusation of theft against Sara had been dropped after she had called Julia and been open and honest about the situation. Julia – who'd quickly stepped into the role of chairperson at the community centre – had assured the police that no money had been stolen. Yes, there had been an admin error, but it had been put right straight away and no harm had been done. The accusation was just Fiona being malicious, she'd said. James had backed her up and had also reiterated his job offer to Sara, but she had declined. Her debt to him was well and truly paid, and she wanted to put a bit of distance between them so she could start to forget what had happened.

With the whole terrible experience at an end, Sara vowed to make sure nobody could ever manipulate her like that again. She understood the value of information and had made it her mission to find out as much as she could about Fiona. Maurice had been very forthcoming.

It seemed Fiona had a chequered past. When Maurice had met her, she was homeless, having just been declared bankrupt and evicted from her property, narrowly escaping a conviction for fraud. With his help, she'd reinvented herself and become queen bee in the small Yorkshire world she inhabited.

Now that she'd been charged, she was not allowed to contact Sara or her family, but if she ever became a threat to them in the future, Sara would ensure the secrets of her past were spread far and wide.

But she knew that Fiona wasn't the real worry. The person she really needed to protect herself and her family from was Matt.

She couldn't forget the way he'd lied to protect himself, nor the physical violence he had shown to her and Hailey and the verbal abuse he'd inflicted on Ezra. Not to mention his disregard for all the women who would suffer, often unknowingly, because of the website he'd designed, the business venture he'd entered into.

But most of all, she could never forgive him for causing the video of Milly in the shower to be distributed. Who knew how that experience would affect her daughter going forwards? He wasn't the man she'd thought she knew; he was someone else entirely. And he'd shown himself to be a danger both physically and mentally. But it was a difficult situation, and a decision as to the way forward didn't come easily. Her priority was protecting her kids from any harm and creating a safe and happy home for them. That was the touchstone she kept coming back to.

The girls were old enough to know a bit about the case, and with social media being what it was, there was no way she could protect them from the news reports and local gossip. However, she had managed to keep secret from them Matt's involvement in circulating the video of Milly. That was something they could never know.

Once charged, Matt had been allowed out on bail, and was staying with a friend in Otley, only a few miles away down the valley. It felt uncomfortably close. Sara didn't want him near her family, but he was the children's father and they missed him. It broke her heart to see their upset and confusion, and she was more than a little confused herself. How much to tell them? That was the real conundrum. And how much access to allow Matt?

After managing to fob off both the children and Matt with excuses as to why they couldn't see each other, she knew she was running out of time. It was important for everyone to be clear about contact arrangements and what part he was going to play in their lives. Face to face was the only way she would be able to get her message across. So she arranged a meeting, something Matt readily agreed to.

It was Saturday, and Hailey had offered to take the kids out for the day. They were going to visit Cassie in Lancaster, where she was studying, and the children were all excited about seeing their cousin and having a look round the university and the city. It was not too much of a drive, but far enough away to be an interesting day out, and it had done the job of distracting them from everything that had been happening at home.

Sara had insisted that the meeting with Matt should be some-where public, where he wouldn't be tempted to shout at her or bully her into anything. This was going to be on her terms and hers alone. They'd finally agreed on a coffee shop in Otley.

She arrived first and got herself a coffee. She was nervous about anyone ordering for her these days, a hangover from her experience. You never knew, did you? It was a habit she thought she'd probably keep and pass on to the girls. Better safe than sorry, she'd decided, even if she did come across as overprotective and fussy.

She gazed out of the window, across the square, watching people coming and going.

'Hi there,' Matt said, his familiar voice making her jump. She hadn't seen him come in, and he was standing behind her, smiling. She took in his appearance, the chinos and summer shirt, short-sleeved and brightly patterned, and wondered how he could look so normal. How what he'd done wasn't etched on his face. But there was no apology in his eyes, no indication of regret. Her resolve hardened, setting like concrete in her heart. He didn't understand – would never understand – what he'd done to her. How his actions had torn her to shreds.

She watched him sit on the other side of the table, saw how he frowned when he noticed she'd already ordered. He stood. 'I'll get myself a drink then, shall I?'

Still she couldn't speak; just let him go off to the counter while her mind organised her thoughts, picking the words she needed to say.

He came back with a coffee and two slices of cake.

'I got you chocolate fudge cake. I know it's your favourite.' He took the plate off the tray and slid it in front of her. She didn't even glance at it, keeping her eyes on his face as she finished her drink.

'I'll keep this short,' she said, putting her cup back on its saucer. 'You have to stay away from the children.' His eyebrows shot up to his hairline, but she didn't wait for his response, didn't want to hear his protests. 'Obviously the girls know some of the details of the case, and I've encouraged them to talk to me about it. Just so they're clear about what's true and what's gossip.'

'What happened to innocent until proved guilty?' Matt said, all the bonhomie evaporating, to be replaced by a scowl. 'It's not been to court yet and my lawyer is pressing for psychological assessment.

You know I acted under duress. You know I was stressed out with work.' His eyes pleaded with her. 'I wasn't myself. It was totally out of character.'

'Whatever,' she scoffed. 'I know you'll try and wriggle out of it. But I know that you punched both me and Hailey, and I can't let a man who is capable of that violence near my kids.' She wiped her mouth with her napkin, screwed it into a ball in her fist. 'We both know you're guilty, whatever the legal system decides and however clever your lawyer is. You were happy to see women being abused. You didn't care. You were even willing to let a video of your daughter be posted on the internet! What sort of father does that?'

'Hold on a minute. I didn't know that video had been posted. If I had, I wouldn't have—'

She held up a hand to stop him from speaking. 'I'm going now. But this is the deal.' She ran her tongue round her lips, took a deep breath. 'Milly doesn't know your business relates in any way to the video of her being posted online. It would kill her to realise the father she adores had any involvement in that. And it would hurt Sophia just as much. You know how those two feel each other's pain. I'm not going to tell them, and there's no reason to suspect they will find out the truth from any other source. I'm willing to keep that secret, but in return, you don't get to be with them. You don't go anywhere near them or Ezra.'

His face paled. His mouth hung open.

'When they're eighteen, it will be up to them to decide what sort of relationship they want with you, but until then, any contact will be at their request and supervised by me. I think we can do FaceTime once a week. Just so they know you haven't deserted them because of anything they have done.' She tapped the table with a finger to emphasise her point. 'But you start blaming me for anything, anything at all, then contact will stop completely, and I will tell the girls every little detail of what you did. You hear me? And then you will lose them forever.'

Matt reached over the table and grabbed her hand. 'No, love, no. Don't be hasty. Don't go yet.' He gave her a plaintive look, the one that always used to make her feel guilty. 'Let's just discuss this, shall we?'

She shook his hand off as if it was a leech about to suck her blood, then stood and pushed her chair under the table, holding onto the back of it so he wouldn't see her hands shaking. 'Those are my terms. There's no negotiation. And if the children don't want to speak to you, then you have to respect their decision.'

'But they're my kids as much as yours.'

Anger was rising in his voice, and she could feel the distress flowing off him in waves. She wondered for a moment if she was being too harsh. Memories of how they used to be filled her mind. Happy days out. Laughter, all the little in-jokes that only they understood. Family cuddles on the sofa. All that had gone. Her voice cracked. 'You did this to yourself, Matt.' A sob hitched in her throat. 'Why didn't you think of the consequences for your family before you agreed to that contract? We could have worked something else out. I know I made mistakes, but ultimately they only put *me* in danger. Never our children. Never anyone innocent.'

His eyes gleamed, his bottom lip wobbled.

'Okay. Here's something to think about. If you tell them everything you've done – no lies, no spurious justifications – and they still want contact with you, then I'll reconsider.'

His face paled even more and she could see his mouth working, grasping for words.

She nodded. 'That's right. I think my first suggestion is going to be easier on all of us, don't you?'

With as much dignity as she could muster, she turned and walked away, sure in her heart that she'd done the right thing. Keeping that information from her children had been a hard decision, but she couldn't cause them any more hurt. It would make Matt keep his distance and ensure he never took whatever contact she allowed for granted.

She thought of their new living arrangement with Hailey, who'd moved in with them, the easy way they'd all come together as a different sort of family, and knew there was no going back. She had her happy home now – even if it wasn't the one she'd expected – and she would do whatever it took to protect it. To keep her children safe, she had to be the one in control.

Information is power, she thought as she walked away. And everyone needs an insurance policy, don't they?

FORTY-ONE

Seven months later

Sara walked out of the courtroom, blinking in the bright sunlight. It was an imposing building, but she supposed that was the point. You weren't meant to feel at ease in these places. You were meant to feel small, at the mercy of bigger powers.

After months of waiting, it had been a challenging week, listening to evidence, seeing the videos, but the end result had undoubtedly been the right one. Fiona and Matt had both been convicted of facilitating sexual assault, voyeurism and hiding revenue. They would be sentenced in a few days' time, but Sara's solicitor estimated that Matt would probably serve five years with parole, and Fiona a little more. It didn't seem long enough for the emotional damage and shame they'd caused, all for the sake of money.

After months of counselling for herself and the family, Sara was managing to find ways to come to terms with what had happened to her. That episode in her life had been compartmentalised in her mind, and even though she knew the pictures of her would be circulating forever, she was finding ways to address the anxiety, shame and guilt that were her constant companions. Trust would always be an issue, she knew, but at least she had her sister's support and the family were closer now than ever before.

Julia had approached her just before the trial had started to see if she'd like to take on a new role at the community centre now that James had left to run the family business full-time. Sara had arrived feeling nervous, and had perched on the edge of her chair, hoping the meeting would be brief. The community centre no longer felt benign, the shadows of the past lurking in every corner.

'Thank you so much for coming in,' Julia had said, swinging gently from side to side in the office chair behind the desk. 'I have a little proposition for you and thought it would be better to do it in person.' She smiled. 'I do hate the way everything is done by message these days. So much room for misunderstandings, don't you think?'

Sara's body tensed, echoes of previous conversations held in this very office reverberating in her mind. Julia carried on speaking, but Sara could only sit and stare, her hands clutching the edge of the seat as she waited to propel herself into an upright position and walk out of the door the moment the opportunity arose.

'You'd be doing me an enormous favour,' Julia said with a wink once she'd outlined her proposal.

Sara's heart fluttered, and she wondered if she'd got herself trapped all over again, because if it wasn't for Julia, she'd certainly be facing charges of theft. Julia laughed when she saw her horrified expression.

'Sorry, it was a joke. Fiona did like her favours, didn't she?' She gave a satisfied smile. 'I have to admit you've done *us* the biggest favour – by getting Fiona out of the way. She was getting far too big for her boots, lording it over everyone.' She tutted. 'I can't see her coming back here, can you? Not since her arrest was splashed all over the news. I hear Maurice is selling the house. He told me Chelsea won't have anything to do with her mother, and I do think a fresh start in London will be the best thing for the child. Goodness knows what the future holds for Fiona, but I think we can assume a prison sentence will feature in there.'

Sara understood now why Julia had been so helpful. With Fiona out of the way, there were empty shoes to be filled, and Julia was all about raising her profile. She was ambitious, had her eye on becoming the local MP. Yes, it had all worked out perfectly as far as she was concerned.

'I'm done with favours,' Sara said. Julia's sense of humour certainly took a bit of getting used to. Had it really been a joke?

'Sure I can't tempt you? Maybe a pay rise? Obviously, the role no longer involves the finances. That's been contracted out, so you don't have to worry on that score. But we could do with your enthusiasm and your fund-raising ideas.'

Sara shook her head. 'No, I'm sorry, I can't come back here. We're moving to Skipton anyway. My house has been sold and I'm buying a place with my sister; that way we can afford something with enough room for all of us and share the costs. It'll be easier with childcare. Better all round really, especially as the girls didn't want to go back to school in Ilkley after what happened.' She managed a smile. 'It'll be a fresh start.'

'Oh, well that's a shame,' Julia said. 'But if you're looking for a new job, I can put a word in for you at a few places.'

Sara shook her head. She hoped she didn't seem ungrateful, but she was determined never to be indebted to anyone ever again. 'That's a very kind offer, but I've already got myself a job; just part-time as a home carer. It'll keep the money coming in while I retrain.'

Julia raised an eyebrow.

'I'm doing a community development course with the Open University,' she added, somehow feeling the need to justify her plans. 'And I have to get the kids settled before I think about my career. They've got to be my priority.'

Julia gazed at her. 'Well, you've got my number if you change your mind.'

Sara nodded and made a mental note to delete the number as soon as she left the office. Although Julia had been extremely supportive, she wasn't sure she trusted her. She was part of Fiona's network after all, and Sara shuddered at the thought of being pulled back into that web of deceit.

She was free now. All debts paid, all favours returned. And that was how it was going to stay.

A LETTER FROM RONA

I want to say a huge thank you for choosing to read *One Mistake*. If you enjoyed it, and want to keep up to date with all my latest releases, just sign up at the following link. Your email address will never be shared, and you can unsubscribe at any time.

www.bookouture.com/rona-halsall

The inspiration for this story came from three different strands; news stories that I found equally shocking and which, when combined together, made a perfect storm.

The first strand is, sadly, a recurring theme in the news – innocent people being drugged and abused by a wide variety of perpetrators. There have been several such cases and it feels like a frighteningly common occurrence; one that tumbles an innocent life into a nightmare scenario.

The second strand was an article about mothers on benefits selling sex in lieu of rent, or to earn money to buy food, and it made me think about debt and how prevalent it is in our society today. How people who are struggling to survive have to consider the unthinkable just to get by.

The third element of the story, which really hit home to me after doing research, was the amount of abusive videos available online. We are talking millions. And these don't go away, even if the perpetrators are caught and punished; the videos have a life of their own once they have been circulated. This means that people are re-victimised every time a video is shared. It makes you wonder if the internet is a blessing or a curse, doesn't it?

My heart goes out to anyone who has been in any of these situations and I sincerely hope they find the strength to seek the help they need to come to terms with what has happened to them and move forward with their lives.

I hope you loved *One Mistake*; if you did, I would be very grateful if you could write a review. I'd love to hear what you think, and it makes such a difference helping new readers to discover one of my books for the first time.

I love hearing from my readers – you can get in touch on my Facebook page, and through Twitter, Instagram or Goodreads.

Many thanks,
Rona Halsall

         @RonaHalsallAuthor

         @RonaHalsallAuth

         18051355.Rona_Halsall

         ronahalsall

ACKNOWLEDGEMENTS

Writing is a collaborative process. Yes, the initial idea is mine, but so many people help to shape it during the process of turning that initial nugget of an idea into the 95,000 words of a book!

As always, I'd like to thank my agent, Hayley Steed of Madeleine Milburn TV, Film and Literary Agency, for her enthusiastic support and wise words. I am so proud to be part of team MM!

My publishers do a fantastic job of turning a rough idea into a finished book, and I have to thank my editor, Isobel Akenhead, for her creative input from the ideas stage right through to final draft. Getting the story right is definitely a team effort. Big thanks to managing editor Alex Holmes for doing a fantastic job of organising copyeditors, proofreaders and the audio production. And then there's Kim Nash and Noelle Holten in the publicity team, who shout about my books and get them noticed. Supported by Alex Crow and the marketing team, who produce the best graphics and do all sorts of magic with adverts behind the scene! There are many other people, I know, within Bookouture who will have had an input at some stage, so I thank you all for your dedication and hard work in making my book the best it can be.

My little team of early readers braved a rough second draft to point out the mistakes and make the book better, so big thanks to Kerry-Ann Mitchell, Gill Mitchell, Sandra Henderson, Wendy Clarke and Sarah Hardy – your feedback was very much appreciated. Also thanks to Hailey Mitchell for letting me use her name and job!

I would also like to thank members of the admin team at the Fiction Café Book Club (a great place for book lovers to hang out) for letting me use their children's names for characters in this book. Thank you Wendy Clarke for Sophia, Chloe Jordan for Amelia and Michaela Balfour for Ezra.

As always, thanks to my book club for lively discussions and enthusiastic support.

Last but not least, thanks to my kids, John, Amy and Oscar, for their interest, enthusiasm and moral support, and my husband, David, for picking me up when I'm down, reassuring me that I really can do it and making lots of cups of tea.